Beneath the Heavens

a novel

LINDSEY BARLOW

For my amazing mom
who taught me Christ-like love through her example.
Thank you for always being there for me.

Prologue

New Hampshire 1891

Esther looked down at the letter for what must have been the hundredth time. The etched lines of folding rested deep in the tear-stained paper. She read the words again, though they were practically memorized by now. The letter was imploring, kind and genuine. She could not remember when she had last encountered such sincere words.

Had she ever had any sincere kindness in her life?

A gentle gurgle pulled Esther from her reverie. She walked over to the small bed. Nested between two pillows was her son. It would soon be time to nurse him. It was a moment that she treasured, to feel his tiny warm body against hers as his chubby legs curled against her stomach. She leaned down and kissed his rose petal skin. Her pregnancy and delivery had been… well, terrifying. For nine months she had slowly travelled away from her home in Boston. For nine months she had lived off cabbage and potatoes. Then when her time came, she had been forced to find a cheap, inexperienced midwife whom Esther had to guide throughout the entire labor, an experience she would wish on no one. Esther had never been more grateful for the school of nursing she had attended in Boston.

The baby stretched and then fell back into a peaceful sleep. Esther gave him one last kiss before walking over to an old chipped vanity and looking in the mirror. Gone were the curves and the soft, rosy face. Stress and an inadequate diet had brought out her cheekbones, emphasizing her slender neck and making her eyes appear larger. She hardly recognized herself from the young pregnant girl who had fled her parents, her mansion, and her nightmare.

She looked at the letter again. Her parents must have written to Uncle Tim and Aunt Lily, informing them of her situation. They themselves did not try to find her, and why should they? After what happened she would now be considered tainted, and by association, they would be as well. No, they would never want to bring her back home, not after what happened. Rather than reconcile, they, out of some twisted sense of duty, sent a monthly payment. Enough for a small, cold flat and meager food, but nothing more.

Uncle Tim, however, offered a new life, a new start. Tall Pine, Colorado, was a small valley nestled at the base of the Rocky Mountains. Not too far from Denver and a growing town itself. His clinic was busy and the work drove him and Aunt Lily ragged. A midwife who could make home visits would be most welcome. Uncle Tim pointed out that she could bring her son on her visits and not have to leave him with some stranger, as she would have to do if she were to stay back East.

Perhaps, Uncle Tim had written, *this is God's plan for you to come to Tall Pine. Enclosed is payment for a ticket. We hope to see you and your child very soon.*

God.

The word made Esther inadvertently glance at her small Bible, placed by her bed so she could purposely ignore it, as she had God, for these long months. Why should she give Him room in her heart after He had allowed such a horrible thing to happen to her? Why would she think of Him? Pray to Him? He had abandoned her, and so she had abandoned Him.

Esther tried to pull her eyes away from the Bible, but she couldn't. It seemed another force moved her feet as she walked over and picked up the book. She skimmed through the dusty pages, once such a comfort to her. Her father had disliked religion. It was the only thing she had ever rebelled against until her untimely pregnancy. She had kept a Bible under her bed, and it had given her some silent freedom in the cage she had once called home. Her father had told her that religion was delusion, but to her, it was conclusion. The answer to all her problems, until it wasn't.

The pages fell with a hush to Psalms... her favorite book. A crushed wild flower covered a marked scripture. Esther gently removed the bookmark of her childhood and read the scripture.

Weeping endureth the night but joy cometh in the morning

Tears stung Esther's eyes. It had been night for so long. So much weeping, so much anger that gnawed at her soul. She looked over at her son Michael who surprised her every day with the love she felt for him. He was her morning and her joy. The greatest gift that could be given; something as perfect as he could only have come from God. God had given her Michael; out of a dark event, He had blessed her with an antidote to her pain.

Esther walked over to her baby and picked up the bundle wrapped in a soft cotton blanket. She kissed the warm round cheeks, inhaling that new baby smell. She couldn't live her life weeping and feeling sorry for herself. It was no longer about her anymore. It was about Michael. He needed a happy mother, a mother who could provide him a safe and loving home, a mother who could show him goodness and hope... and faith.

A sudden warmth began to spread through Esther. The heavy weight that had been strapped to her shoulders for so long seemed to lift. This was right. Colorado was right. Being a mother was right. She could do this. She could move forward. If God gave her Michael, then maybe He still loved her. Perhaps, even if He had allowed terrible things to happen to her, He would help her heal.

Michael cooed and Esther laughed audibly as a new strength sprouted within her. Michael would have a good life; she would make sure of that. A sudden flame sparked in her eyes. She would also protect Michael—she must protect him from the mockery that would come should people know of her past. She would tell no one, not even her own son. Most of all, she would keep out the one thing that had hurt her most throughout her life: men.

One

Colorado, 1897

Abigail Silver sat on her suitcase and squirmed. She longed for someone to answer her questions, but she also dreaded speaking to the strangers around her. From what she could see, Denver was, well, rough. She'd known there'd been an economic downfall when the price of silver dropped. Considering Colorado was the kingdom of silver mines, the change affected the state badly. Now all she saw were beggars and overly-rouged women stalking the few remaining wealthy businessmen.

She glanced down at her lace gloves, stroking the silver locket she had kept clenched in her hand throughout her journey from Texas to Colorado. It was not a fancy locket, no etchings nor engravings. The silver had been polished, kept clean, but one could tell that the locket had seen better days. Abigail's bottom lip began to tremble. She bit it quickly before anyone noticed. Crying had always been her habitual defense. When she had stepped on the train and taken one last look at her parents' faces, she promised herself that she would no longer cry in front of others. She was tired of being the weak one, the silly and frivolous girl who was always described as simply pretty, never useful, never smart, or kind, just pretty. She often felt like a piece of art whose sole purpose was to hang on a wall and adorn her surroundings.

The locket in her hand was warm now from her continuous stroking. Her mother, Hannah, had given it to her for luck. Although Abigail wondered if it was more of a reminder as to why Abigail's beloved parents, who had spoiled her, pampered her, and given her an abundance of love, were now sending her away.

"I don't understand," Abigail had cried. Sinking to her bed, she looked up at her mother's beautiful face that looked concerned and sad, but also determined. "I've been sending out inquiries to teach in Texas… around here." Abigail wrung her hands. In truth, she had not planned on teaching at all. There were many suitors, many men of notable professions who courted her on a regular basis. She expected a proposal soon from one wealthy lawyer in particular. She would marry, live in a fine large house and hopefully, God willing, children would not come too soon so that she and her husband could travel and enjoy some pleasures before settling down.

All that had crumpled when her mother came to tell her that she now had a position in Colorado—a cold rough country she had no desire to see.

"Abby," her mother had said gently while lowering herself to sit beside her distraught daughter. "I really feel you need this. You know I pray for you every day, asking the good Lord to guide me that I might raise you in love and wisdom. I want the best for you, and I feel the Lord wants this." She took Abby's hand. "My darling, you know this breaks my heart to send you away. I would not do it unless I felt it was the right thing."

Abigail pulled her hand away. "You are showing your love by sending me away? I don't understand. Why do I need to go? What have I done wrong besides be a good daughter, a good person? Do you want me to be gone like Joseph? Always gone so you and father can have peace and quiet without your troublesome children in the way?" she had said bitterly.

Her mother, Hannah, sighed and shook her head. "You know

that's not true Abby, and you're not troublesome, nor have you done anything wrong. The problem is that you just haven't done anything." Her mother threw her hands in the air. "Once you became—" she waved at Abby's body and face, "beautiful, your life was suddenly centered on parties, fashion, men, and being a popular socialite. Gone was my sweet girl with a firm faith in God and who she was."

"You're saying I've lost my faith?" Abby frowned. Despite her anger, Abby did know her mother loved her, and she also knew her mother was a wise woman. What she said struck Abby... had she really become so shallow?

"No, I don't think you've lost it, but it has been shoved back into the far cupboards of your heart while silly, unimportant things have taken higher priority." Hannah touched the silver locket she always kept around her neck. "You know when I met your father, I was a rough-handed cook for a hundred cowboys herding cattle. Your father wasn't the well-to-do rancher he is now. He had just settled his own ranch with a few skinny cows and no business connections. Marrying a poor widowed cook with a son only added more to his plate." Her eyes softened remembering the old times. "But he worked, and me and your brother worked, and worked, and it was wonderful. I promise that the greatest happiness comes from knowing hardship. It's the only time we are forced to go to God."

Once again she reached for Abby's hand. "You, my dear, have not had enough challenges, and I love you too much to let you become a shallow, silly woman." She looked down at the locket. "This was my only piece of jewelry for many years as I struggled to feed your brother Joseph, put up with my by then drunken husband, and eventually earn my way as a widow. Your father has offered many times to buy me a new one, but I keep this to remind me of the blessings the Lord has given me, and I'm not talking about having a prosperous ranch. I am talking about the insight, the love, and the happiness He has given me by allowing me to struggle."

Abby now unclasped the locket and placed it around her neck. It looked especially old against her fancy frock and large hat; a part of her wanted to take it off, embarrassed at its antiquity. When the thought settled in, Abby shook her head and scolded herself.

Goodness Abby, you have become a high and mighty snob, she thought shaking her head.

Maybe Colorado was what she needed. Still, it had been hard to go, hard to leave her beautiful home with the rich grassy fields and the smell of roses outside her window. She had hoped to see Joseph, her older brother and best friend, but as always, he had been too busy.

She sighed and looked around. She had captured several stares. Women glared disapprovingly at her dress and five cases. Men nodded, some winked and tipped their hats. Abby felt her face go red.

Men. Generally she loved men. Loved the attention and presents they gave her. That was, until her father told her that several men had asked for his permission to marry his only daughter, and when Jefferson Silver explained that his daughter would not be receiving a significant inheritance, or a part of the ranch, their proposals had been suddenly withdrawn.

"Of course when your mother and I are passed away, you will receive an inheritance," he had explained to her. "But most of these men sniffing around here are after my land, not you. I don't want to rob you of true love for some gold digging hound.

The revelation had shocked Abby and then had broken her heart. Here she had believed her beauty and charm had won the men's hearts. Now she knew it had been her father's fat cattle that had enticed the roses and chocolates. Right now she was angry. Truth be told, she did not care if she never saw another man again.

"Miss Abigail Silver?" a deep voice asked. Abby looked up from her self-pitying trance. Her rosebud lips parted and her large gray eyes blinked once... twice... three times.

In front of her stood a young man in his mid-twenties—a little older than her, a little younger than Joseph. His jaw was square, masculine, and free of facial hair, which he made up for by the deep mahogany locks that hung a good solid two inches below his ears. What took Abby aback was his size. The tallest, most muscular man she had ever seen had always been Joseph. This man was nearly as tall and strong looking as her brother—nearly.

Abby gulped as she met his intensely blue eyes, the patched trousers and working boots contradicted his jaw-dropping beauty.

"Uh, yes, I am Abigail Silver. You can call me Abby," she tried to laugh gaily, but it came out more like a throaty cough. She blushed crimson as the man raised an amused eyebrow.

"Abby, huh?" he nodded. "I'm Pastor Will, from Tall Pine. I've come to, uh–" his eyes widened slightly at her multiple, large cases, "to collect you, I guess." He glanced again at the cases, and Abby cursed herself for bringing too many. Now she felt even more like a silly girl. She was a schoolteacher for crying out loud, not a princess on holiday. She did not need to bring every dress and blouse and buckle, but she had and she couldn't change that now.

"These all yours?" Will asked with a sigh.

Abby nodded. "Most are just school supplies. You know, should the school house not be able to provide much." She lied in desperation, so as to not appear so foolish.

The pastor's lips twitched playfully. Pastors weren't supposed to look like him were they? Wasn't there a law that said pastors needed squinty eyes and a large belly? Maybe Abby had sworn off men a little too quickly.

Will scanned Abby's fancy lace dress. "School supplies?" he questioned with a grin, obviously seeing right through her lie.

Abby looked away, feeling flustered. What a horrible way for an introduction. A much-too-fancy dress, too much luggage, and a transparent lie. "I thought a coach would be taking me to Tall Pine," she said, straightening her shoulders.

Will shrugged. "Lots of the transportation was cut down in Denver with the fall of silver. You wouldn't be able to get a coach for a couple days, and with the crime rate in Denver—" he glanced at a group of men drooling over Abby and looking at her cases. "I didn't feel right about leaving a school teacher alone in a hotel for several days."

Abby smiled gratefully. "Thank you; that would have been a bit unnerving."

Will gave a half nod and stopped one of the station's employees to ask for a dolly of some sort to carry the cases to his wagon. "You don't have any more of these, um, school supplies do you?" he asked with a smile.

Abby laughed and shook her head. "No I don't, but I could always send for more if you think I should," she teased.

Will chuckled. "I think five is ample." He was silent for a few minutes as he stacked the cases onto the dolly without breaking a sweat. Abby noticed that periodically his gaze would dart over to her and linger no more than a blink's worth. She straightened her hat. He was being polite in a cheeky sort of way, but he was not acting as men usually did with her… he was not attentive. Suddenly anger flared within Abby. Why should he pay any attention to her? He wasn't aware of her father's good standing amongst the ranchers, or of his acres, or of her fine house. Why should he give her attention since, apparently, all she had to offer was what her parents had earned?

"Miss Abby?" Will asked, looking amused. Abby jumped. Had she been staring off again? She often did that when deep in thought. How embarrassing.

"Oh sorry, I was… thinking," she stammered and cleared her throat.

Will pressed his lips together, obviously trying to refrain from smiling. "I figured as such." He nodded towards the left, "Come on, the wagon is outside the station and Tall Pine is a long ways off."

Abby was grateful to get out of Denver. Supposedly they would pass another town where Will would water the horses, and then Tall Pine was not too far after that. Abby could not help the quick beat in her heart. What would Tall Pine be like?

Will must have read her thoughts because after a few moments of silence he began to talk. "You know, Denver took a hard hit with the reduction of silver value," he explained. "Lots of city folk invested in silver, lots of businesses, too. Then when they crashed, the poor miners all flocked to the city hoping for work, but none was to be found." He frowned, shaking his head. "A few years back they had a big festival trying to raise people's spirits. Things are getting better, but it still has a way to go."

Abby nodded. "Tall Pine, did it get hit hard, too?"

Will shook his head with a smile. "No, Tall Pine is a farming valley, some ranches, too. Our currency did take a hit but not like the city. The town is small, with family businesses. Some of the miners tried finding work in Tall Pine, rather than going into the city. A few managed, but there's not enough work to go around. People give the jobs to family or friends first." He sighed. "Miners tend to have it hard."

Abby nodded, feeling a little better. She wanted to hear more, but once again Will grew silent. For a few hours he said nothing. His jaw was set tightly with a slight tick that flexed every few minutes. Abby straightened herself. Why was she paying so much attention to him? She had always been the one being chased, not the other way around.

Will suddenly grinned arrogantly. "You like my face, Teacher?" he asked with a chuckle, "Cause you keep looking at it."

Abby's mouth dropped. Of all the conceited things to say. Who cared if it were true or not? How dare he speak to her in such baseness? "I... I," she was speechless. Why could she not come up with something to say? "What else is there to look at?" she asked, knowing it was a dumb thing to say.

Will raised an eyebrow. "You kidding? Look around you. Colorado has the best scenery in the country, if you ask me. In fact, doctors send people to Colorado for their health, saying it has the best air."

Abby looked around her. Despite it being late summer, it was still chilly. She shivered; her coat and thin lace dress were not enough to keep her warm. Most schools were closed during late summer and through the fall, so the children could help with the harvest. Tall Pine, however, was an exception due to the snow and blizzards. So Tall Pine's school stayed open through the autumn. The Mayor had written that Tall Pine was at its most beautiful during the harvest season. Abby found it hard to admire the beauty when she couldn't feel her toes. Still, she could admit the mountains were majestic. She'd never seen anything like them in Texas, which had its own kind of beauty in the open, flat landscape.

"Here you go," Will said suddenly, handing her a thick wool blanket. "It's only going to get colder, Miss. You better learn to dress appropriate."

Abby took the blanket and wrapped it around her shoulders. The thick wool felt heavy around her—and comforting. Soon her teeth stopped chattering and her toes began to move. Why had she brought so many of her fancy dresses instead of following her mother's advice and buying some wool and flannel ones? The blanket warmed her but not completely, and soon her stomach began to twist in hunger. She tightened her arms around her hoping to smother the growling sound. She slid a glance at Will; his gaze was set forward in concentration. He must have gone back to his thoughts. Abby bit her lip. She was never one who did well in silence. She loved a good conversation. So did Joseph. A small smile danced across her lips: she missed Joseph. She and her parents had spent the past few years trying to convince her brother to leave the Rangers. With several gunshot wounds and knife scars, it would not be long before Joseph ended up like his own father… dead. The thought made Abby sick; she loved her big brother— she needed him. He always gave such good advice and helped her laugh at herself.

"You ought to join the Rangers, Abby," he would tease her. "You could talk any outlaw to death and never waste a bullet."

"At least I have interesting things to say, unlike you who only talks

of guns and Indians. Why I thought you were gonna frighten Miss Rose to death talking about cannibal Indians."

"Karankawa Indians," he corrected. "And, if a woman can't handle a little story about cannibal Indians, then she isn't a real woman."

"What?" Abby shook her head. "That is nonsense. I am just saying it is vulgar."

Joseph grinned like a cat with a helpless bird. "Vulgar, huh? Should I tell mother about the books you have hidden beneath your clothes? Pirates, Abby? That is the best you can do? Pirates and—" his grin broadened into a crooked smile that her friends often called his 'heart breaking smile', "gunfighters who steal away princesses and ladies?" He produced from behind him one of her forbidden books.

"You went through my bloomers?"

"No, I paid Manuel. He's the cook's son, right?"

Abby snatched away the book. Her mother usually preferred to do the cooking herself; she had only hired Rosa because she had a weakness for a widowed mother with a son. Now Abby wished that her mother's frugality had overcome her compassion.

"I will have a word with Rosa," she said, knowing she would not.

"Oh, don't worry about it little sister. I like you better knowing that you dream about other men besides soft-handed attorneys." He winked, and just like that, Abby's anger dissipated. Joseph's winks had a way of doing that.

A slight sprinkle of rain tickled Abby on the nose. She brushed the wet stuff away and a giant yawn overtook her. Will glanced over with no expression before giving a slight jerk to the reigns, speeding up the horses. Another yawn made Abby's eyes water. She ought to close them. Not fall asleep, not with Will next to her— that was far too intimate—but closing her eyes, resting them for a minute would not hurt.

Joseph stood still, hands folded respectfully in front of him as the judge announced the verdict.

Joseph Silver, Texas Ranger and servant of the law had shot Bill

Cuss in self-defense, and by doing so had fulfilled his duty to stop outlaws and prevent crime. Standing beside him were two other Texas Rangers standing as still as he was: steady heartbeats, cool skin; they were used to these types of trials. The killing of Bill Cuss, a murdering, thieving, woman-beating type of man, had been done by Joseph's bullet. Joseph wished that he felt some remorse. Perhaps he would have had he not come across so many of Bill Cuss' victims.

"All arise," the judge announced in a voice heavy from the thick Texas heat. Joseph waited, as did the other two Rangers beside him. Each was a witness, and each one had a bandage, one on the arm, the other on the shoulder.

"Ain't fair, you're the one who shot him, and yet you ended up with not even a scratch," one of them whispered to Joseph, who grinned despite himself. Jesse was a seasoned Ranger who had lived longer than most and had lived in the days when being a Ranger meant battling Indians.

"Just means I'm quicker," Joseph whispered back.

"Silence, please, gentlemen, "The judge glared down at them like an angry hawk.

The Rangers bowed their heads in apology.

"Now then," the judge continued. "I hereby rule that Joseph Silver shot Bill Cuss as was his duty to protect Texas citizens and his fellow Rangers, and in self-defense while protecting the hostage Alice Greene." He cracked the pulpit with his hammer, the sound echoing through the large courthouse. "This case is dismissed. Thank you, gentlemen."

The youngest Ranger, new on the job, winced as Jesse brushed by his wounded arm. "Is it normal to get shot on your first shoot out?"

Jesse scrunched his face. "That wasn't even a shoot out boy."

"That was a shoot out. He shot, and we shot back," Sabine, the young Ranger, argued.

"No. You got excited, shot a bush twenty yards away from the actual target; oh, and that was after we instructed you to hold your fire. Bill Cuss returned fire, and were it not for Joseph, who had the brains to climb the slope and get behind Bill, then you and I would both be dead."

Joseph remained silent; his eyes were on the twenty-year-old Alice Greene who had been called as a witness. She now clung to her parents, who gently led her out of the courthouse after casting a grateful nod to Joseph. It was times like this that he remembered why he was a Ranger. It was not just because his father was a true-blooded Texas Ranger who had died on the job when Joseph was ten, but there was a satisfaction that came from bringing justice to the world. Alice Greene was a bit slow, yet her parents adored her. When she'd been taken hostage by Bill Cuss as he fled to the border, Mrs. Greene had clawed at Joseph's shirt begging him to bring back her little girl. Joseph had. He wasn't a trigger crazy Ranger, although he was the best shot among them, and most of the time taking a life left him with a sick pit in his stomach. But when he remembered scared Alice with her tear-stained face and the threats Bill shouted, he didn't feel so sick this time.

"Joe, who's that man looking at you?" Sabine asked, narrowing his eyes at a tall tanned figure. Joseph glanced across the courthouse to see Jefferson, his stepfather, nod with his customary grin. Joseph lifted his chin in acknowledgment. What was Jefferson doing here? Joseph hadn't made it back home for a while and he knew his mother and little sister Abby were upset about that. Had Jeff come to drag him back home? Joseph suddenly frowned. Even if he were to return home, Abby would not be there. She was up in Colorado or halfway there. A beautiful state, from what he had heard, but one he had no desire to visit.

"Why, that's Jefferson Silver," Jesse answered for Joseph. "A respected man in the ranching business, owns the third largest ranch in Texas, mostly Angus cows." He looked at Joseph for correction. "Has a pretty big influence in the Cattle Raisers Association, don't he?"

Joseph nodded. "Jeff's honest and doesn't do any shady business with the slaughterhouses back East, and he's pulled through several droughts," Joseph said proudly. He and his stepfather never had a talkative nor open type of relationship, but it had developed, at least on Joseph's side, to a respected friendship. Jeff had started from nothing and had worked until his calloused hands were scarred and weathered. He'd taken in Hannah, Joseph's mother, and had been a good husband to her. Joseph hated to admit it, but Jefferson had been a better husband and father than Joe's old man, no drinking, no beating or cursing. Still, Joe's old man gave him life, and he'd been a Ranger, a hard and noble work. No matter what logic told him, Joseph felt that bonding with another father figure would be betraying his own.

"Well fellas, this is where I leave you." He gave Jesse, his old friend, a pat on the back.

"You ain't gonna head to the saloon with us?" Sabine asked.

Joseph laughed at the puppy-like eagerness of the young man who just discovered the legendary romance that came with being a Texas Ranger. Joseph saw no romance in the job. A Texas Ranger could not, or at least should not, marry. Early death, always away from home, and especially the stress of the job didn't induce good qualities for a family man. He knew all this firsthand.

"I don't drink kid, and besides those saloon girls aren't my type." He tossed Jesse a knowing wink.

The grizzled man laughed and tugged Sabine with him. "You want saloon girls? Come, I will give you saloon girls. Though I got to mention the ones around these parts ain't got no teeth."

Joseph chuckled, not hearing Sabine's groan. He preferred to avoid saloons altogether. Drinking could do ugly things to a man.

Jefferson watched Joseph walk over to him. The young man towered over most of the courthouse crowd, and his silver-and-turquoise-studded belt buckle shone as the sun peaked through the small windows, reflecting on the silver. He was all in all an impressive looking man.

"You finally following the Ranger fashion, I see." Jefferson laughed, motioning at his own lip to indicate Joseph's mustache.

Joseph chuckled and pulled his stepfather into a tight embrace.

It was good to see family. "What are you doing in these parts?"

Jeff smiled and gripped Joseph by the shoulders looking into his handsome face, noticing the small lines etched with worry across his forehead.

"Well, I heard about the trial. Heard about your shot. Didn't know you could aim from that far a distance."

Joseph gave a low whistle. "Never been so scared in my life. Sabine had gotten excited and fired, and then Jesse had to distract Cuss by running around while I climbed a slope. I was too far, but when I saw Cuss aiming at Jesse who was hiding behind some small brush, I had to fire or watch my good friend die."

Jeff nodded approvingly. Although he hoped Joseph would give up the Ranger life, he could not help the swell of pride he felt knowing his stepson had never lost a man while he served as Captain. Those who went with him always returned—even if it meant Joseph coming back bloody and bruised. One of the proudest days of Jefferson Silver's life had been the day when Joseph took the name of Silver as his own.

"I have to ask," Jeff folded his arms, "Colt or Winchester?"

Joseph laughed and shook his head. "Winchester. I love the Colt, but those boys are for shoot outs, not for a perfect aim." Joseph instinctively placed his hands on the strapped-on pistols. Sturdy, revolving Colts, they had practically become a symbol for a Ranger.

The Winchester though, a long elegant rifle that smelled of heated wood and steel, that was Joseph's woman and child, all in one. The Winchester had been his father's rifle. Joseph had watched his father clean the gun, polish it, talk to it. He took better care of that rifle than he did his own family. Joseph often teased that his father had polished his very soul into the Winchester, as such, when it came to a lucky shot, the Winchester won over the Colt every time.

"You hungry?" Joseph suddenly asked. He did not like thinking about his father. It took him to a dark place.

Jeff nodded. "Saw a promising restaurant not far from here. Let's get us some dinner and I'll explain my mysterious appearance."

"There's a reason?" Joseph mocked a disappointed expression. "I was hoping you just wanted to see my handsome face."

Jeff rolled his eyes. "Your mother was about to flatten that handsome face with her fists when you didn't show up this summer." He raised his hands in protest before Joseph could speak. "But, she understood when she realized you were stalking down Bill Cuss. Texas will sleep better now that he is gone."

Joseph smiled. "When the law calls not even blood or love can hold me, right?" he laughed. That had become the unofficial motto of Rangers, a weak explanation that young Rangers gave to weeping sweethearts. Joseph suddenly frowned. It was the same words that his father had always recited to him.

A large plate of grits, biscuits, and a thick-cut steak was placed in front of Joseph, and he grinned. He loved good food. He really, really loved good food.

"So what's the secret? Why *did* you travel all the way out here?" he asked before taking a large bite of his grits.

Jeff sighed and held his fork a little tighter. "It's about, well, it's about your future."

Joseph raised his eyebrows. "*My* future? I was sure it was about you and Mom shipping Abby to Colorado."

Jeff gave a helpless shrug. "You received a letter from her?"

Joseph laughed and nodded, then smothered his biscuit with butter. "I'm not a religious type to know the Scriptures and such, but the one about wailing and gnashing of teeth came to mind when I read her letter."

Jeff chuckled. "Abby does have a dramatic flair, doesn't she?"

Joseph nodded. "Mom sent a letter as well explaining your decision."

"You agree?" Jeff asked with a creased forehead.

Joseph took another bite before giving an amused nod. "I absolutely agree. Abby is my favorite person in the world, but she's become quite the—" he grinned, "lady."

Jeff chuckled. "That is about what your mother feels. Abby has become the socialite of Texas, and not in a good way."

"Has Abby ever seen snow?"

Jeff shook his head. "Nope. The school year actually starts earlier there. I guess the town she is going to has no attendance in December and part of January due to the snow."

"You worried about her?" Joseph asked, noting the slight catch in Jeff's voice. It was a redundant question. Of course Jeff was worried. He was a good father and a good man, and Abby was the baby of the family.

"Of course I'm worried about my little princess," Jeff said, vocalizing Joseph's thoughts. "But that's the problem. She is a princess who attracts soft-handed, money-sniffing boys."

"Not like Mom, huh?" Joseph took another large bite.

"No, not like your Mom," Jeff agreed, his expression softening. "Your mother was a woman, a real queen who carried a skillet that she used to smack any cowboy who said a vulgar remark to her. I fell in love with an equal, a woman, who I was proud to have by my side. I want the same for Abby. I want a man who sees her as the prize, not the accessory to the prize, meaning my ranch."

Joseph nodded. "Well, then you're doing the right thing."

Jeff looked up, his eyebrows knitting together. He said nothing for a moment and Joseph grew uncomfortable. He wasn't used to having a man stare at him if it wasn't over the barrel of a gun.

Finally Jeff cleared his throat, clasped his hands and leaned his forearms on the table. "And are you doing the right thing, Joseph?"

Joseph frowned. "What are you talking about, Jeff?"

Jeff broke eye contact for a second before reaffirming his gaze. "Joseph, your mother and I, well, we are reaching that age where handling such a large ranch is tiresome. I would like to have the time to take her to New Orleans or New York, have more nights with us reading quietly together, knowing that we don't need to be up at the crack of dawn." He paused, turning slightly red. "We would like some holidays with... with grandchildren."

Joseph raised his eyebrows. "Well, then maybe sending Abby to Colorado wasn't the wisest choice—"

"I'm talking about you Joseph," Jeff said suddenly. "I'm worried about you, about your future. If you even have a future. You're a good Ranger, a fantastic Ranger even—"

"But?" Joseph asked warily.

Jeff opened his mouth and hesitated for a breath. "But, I don't think, I don't feel," he growled in frustration unable to find the words he wished to express. "Maybe what I feel is that although you are a fantastic Ranger and helping this world, maybe you would be an even better rancher, husband, and father." Jeff let out a weary sigh.

"You are telling me I should quit the Rangers and have *your* life?" Joseph asked with no sarcasm, but a slight dryness in his voice. Being a Ranger was who he was, his love was his work, and his life was fighting injustice. There was no room for romance, no room for family. He had the opportunities, beautiful women sighing as he passed by and fathers of marriageable daughters offering jobs when he had helped them in a matter. Being a Texas Ranger though was his soul. It was what his father had wanted him to be, and it was the only thing that made Joseph feel he still had, or ever had, any bond with his father.

"I know this sounds controlling or even arrogant on my part, but Joseph I want you to be happy, and there is no greater happiness for a man than having a woman to love and a family to work for. You feel a satisfaction every time you drag a criminal into court, or save a man's family and livelihood, don't you?"

Joseph nodded.

"Well son, I feel that every minute. I feel it when I look at your good mother and see Abby's bravery. 'Cause no matter how scared that girl is, she is in Colorado right now." He glanced at his hands. "And, when I see the man you have become, my heart swells with pride. Every ounce of sweat I ever dropped, every sleepless night when I went over cattle numbers, was an honor." His eyes locked on Joseph. "I want you to have that same satisfaction Joseph, that same pride and," he swallowed. "I want you to have half my ranch and eventually all of it."

Joseph choked on a piece of steak. He pounded his chest. "What? No, Jeff." He shook his head. "That honor belongs to Abby."

Jeff waved a hand in the air. "Right, I give Abby the ranch, or even half a ranch and it falls into the hands of some gold digger or one of those dreamers who swear there is oil in this state and tears apart the ranch, diggin'." He shook his head in disgust. "Abby will get part of the ranch, maybe, but a good number of years after she's married so I can see the true intentions of her husband."

Joseph gave a half smile. "Listen Jeff, I am honored, truly, by your offer, but I'm not the type to settle down. And I'm certainly not the type to chase after a woman, marry her, and then have a family." He touched the star pinned to his chest. "Ranger at heart, always have been, always will be." He lowered his hand, suddenly remembering his mother saying that only God could change a man's heart, but Joseph didn't need God. He never did. "Besides, the ranch should go to your real child. It should be Abby's. She is your daughter, your only child; I couldn't take that from her."

Jeff's face fell, and his eyes clouded over. Joseph caught that he had said something hurtful, although he wasn't exactly sure what it was.

Jeff shook his head. "Oh, Joseph," he sighed. "When will you understand?"

Two

A sudden bump in the road jolted Abby forward. She awoke with a small yelp and shook her dizzy head. Had she fallen asleep? She looked over at the pastor. The smug look on his face and the wide boyish grin confirmed that not only had she been asleep, but she had fallen asleep on his...

Abby glanced at the pastor's shoulder. Abby never slept with her mouth closed; hence, she was always battling chapped lips. And, sometimes she even—

"You snored," Will blurted out with a strange mix of a laugh and snort.

"I... I," Abby was at a loss. She had fallen asleep, on his shoulder, and snored. She snored in front of a handsome man who she was pretty sure already thought her ridiculous. "I did?" she asked with a trembling voice. Maybe he was just joking.

"It was a cute little snore. Like a kitten," he said and looked over and gave a sort of half smile, "but, a snore none-the-less."

They were pulling into a desolate and grim looking town. Abby's heart plummeted. Was this Tall Pine?

"This is a mining town, mostly abandoned, but they got a watering well for the horses. So I'm going to give them a break before we make the final ride to Tall Pine," he explained as he pulled the horses to a stop.

Abby nodded. If she had been cold, she was not any more; her entire body was blushing with the knowledge that she had snored, and fallen asleep, on a *pastor* for crying out loud.

Will pulled the horses to a stop and then sat for a moment looking around him at the depressing place. He sighed and then jumped off the wagon in a fluid move.

Abby looked around. It was dirty here, and the mountains looked frightening. A sudden homesickness overtook her. It had been a long journey, a hard one, and she had barely begun.

What am I doing?

How could she—a silly Texan who read too many fashion periodicals and obsessed over facial creams—how could she teach in a small valley school where the educational laws and regulations were fifty years behind the current times?

As if to increase her sour mood, Abby's stomach suddenly growled. She was hungry, and the cold was now returning, seeping through her lightweight clothing. Colorado so far was cold, and certainly not amiable. She'd been so preoccupied trying not to fall off the bumpy wagon and trying not to sleep, that, besides the light sprinkling of rain and the large mountains, she had hardly noticed the scenery. In her welcoming letter from the Mayor of Tall Pine, he'd spoken of the beauty that Colorado had to offer. So far, all Abby had noticed was a depressed city, overcast skies, and a pastor to whom she was doing a fine job of presenting herself as a fool. All in all, it wasn't the glowing sunset and welcoming adventure she had optimistically hoped for.

It's only been a week of travel, not even that. Abby reminded herself brightly, and the good thing about a bad start is that it could only get better.

The smell of cooked meat sent Abby into a dizzy spell as her stomach growled. A small bar that had several men cooking fatty pork out in front caught her eye. She needed food, badly. Opening her small purse she almost cried in disappointment to see that she had finished all her little sweets and the stale roll from the train. The smell reached her nose again, this time sending her stomach into spasms. Coins! She had some coins left. Surely she had time to go buy something to fill her stomach.

Abby counted out just a few cents. She didn't want to spend too much just in case there were some things she needed for her school. There was no way she would ask her parents for money. She'd sworn an oath to herself not to do so, especially since she'd been teased that she wouldn't make it without "Daddy's money." She looked down at her palm and put back three pennies. She'd eat only a little something.

Abby stood up steadily to lower herself from the wagon, but was stopped as a hand braced her elbow. It was Will, looking up at her with his striking blue eyes.

"Miss?"

A man this handsome should not be calling her "Miss." "Please call me Abby."

Did his mouth twitch?

"Miss Abby, what are you doing?" He nodded to the coins.

"I, uh," there she went stuttering again. "Do I have time to go get something to eat?" she asked, trying to hide the slight catch in her voice. By golly, why did she always cry when upset? Her mother was right. She needed to grow up.

"Don't really have time, Miss. We are already gonna have to quicken our pace to get you there before nightfall," he explained, looking around him uncomfortably. Clearly he did not like this town.

Abby's stomach suddenly growled like a thunderstorm as she sat back down. She was sure the wagon shook from it. Will's eyebrows lifted just about to the top of his forehead and Abby felt her cheeks heat up as hot as a rock in the sun. Goodness, could anything more embarrassing happen?

"You didn't bring anything to eat?" he asked in disbelief.

"I brought some sweet jellies, but I already finished those."

"Jellies?" he asked, scrunching up his face in confusion.

"Yes, jellies," Abby answered shamefully. She wanted to disappear, or have someone throw a giant quilt over her head to escape his scrutinizing eye.

"You brought jellies on an all-day wagon ride but no other food?" he asked again.

Abby frowned feeling anger rise up in her. Why did he have to make her sound so stupid? She felt foolish enough as it was.

"Yes, Pastor Will, for a treacherous journey into the frontier, I brought sweet little jellies in different colors because they were yummy and pretty," she said, stubbornly folding her hands on her lap and straightening her back.

Will pressed his lips together in a crooked line for a second and then burst into laughter. Not just laughter but a loud, bubbling laughter that seemed to echo through the small town. Abby felt her own lips twitch. His laugh was contagious and wonderful to hear. She bowed her head and let out a giggle, which seemed to amuse Will even more, because more laughter erupted from him. Before she even realized it, Abby was laughing along with him 'til tears filled her eyes and her sides hurt.

"Well, I don't have no sweet and pretty jellies." Will gave one last chuckle and rubbed the back of his neck. "However," he left her, holding up a finger to signal he'd be back. Walking towards the rear of the wagon Abby could hear him shifting through the gear and her luggage. She took the opportunity to stretch out her aching limbs and massage her neck. She must look terrible right now, and was rather surprised that the thought didn't unnerve her.

"Here you go, Miss." Will suddenly appeared handing her a basket.

"What's this?" she asked, wanting to know what was in it before opening it.

"It ain't jellies, if that's what you want." He gave a half smile and climbed in beside her.

Curious, Abby opened the basket and let out an exclamation of joy. Slices of ham nestled between thick bread, delicious smelling cheese and fat pickles crammed the basket. There were even a few apples. It was like manna from heaven.

"My temper isn't the best when I get hungry, so I make sure to pack a lot of food when I do this trip." He nodded for her to scoot over and she did. He climbed up smelling of pine trees and rain; he took the reins and gave a soft click with his tongue, sending the horses off. Abby imagined what they must look like the way they sat up front together sharing a meal. The thought made her flush. Not that Will wasn't handsome; in fact, if she were honest with herself, he was by far the most handsome young man she had ever met. Yet despite his good looks, this pastor had the uncanny ability to make her feel even more silly than usual. It was just that he was so different from the usual men she chose to fraternize with. She glanced up at him—different, yes. Worse? Definitely not... not with those eyes.

"So, I was thinking," Will muttered, "I am glad that we don't have any passengers riding in the back."

Abby frowned. "And why is that?"

"Because I wouldn't want them to witness a woman sleeping on me. I have a reputation to uphold," he said sternly.

Abby's mouth dropped. Was he really scolding her by saying that she would slight his reputation?

"Pastor Will, I swear that was an accident. I would never—"

She stopped when Will's face brightened with a smile that melted into a chuckle.

Abby laughed nervously. "Oh, you are—teasing?"

Will laughed louder. "Of course I am." He shook his head, pleased with his wit. "I suppose I ought not to tease, but it's a long ride."

"Teasing keeps you occupied?" Abby asked with a slight arch in her brow.

Will shrugged. "More or less."

Abby shrugged to herself. It was a good enough explanation. "So tell me about the scary town we were just in. You seemed unsettled."

Will shifted uncomfortably. "I used to live there. My father was a miner."

Abby's ears perked up in interest, ready for a good story. When

Will said nothing more she leaned forward. "And?" she asked.

Will frowned. "And, that is all."

At her disappointed look, Will laughed. "What's that look for?"

"Well, that you used to live there, which implies that you no longer live there. How come?"

Will had a puzzled expression on his face when he glanced at Abby. "Well… you really want to know?"

Abby nodded. "Of course I do. Why else would I ask? What brought you from growing up as a miner's son to being a pastor in Tall Pine?"

Will nodded. "Alright, uh, well, my father was a silver miner. No wife. Three children. Me, and two younger sisters."

"No wife?"

"Yeah, she died of influenza. I stayed at home and raised my sisters." His jaw tightened and Abby noticed he held the reins a bit tighter.

"Do they live in Tall Pine as well? Your sisters, I mean."

Will laughed wryly, bitterly. "No, they left Colorado as soon as they could. The eldest, Emily, couldn't wait to leave. She wanted cities and excitement." His expression saddened. "The youngest, Rosie, left to watch out for Emily. She was a good girl, smart, too." He swallowed and shook his shoulders. "I don't hear from them as much as I'd like."

Abby studied Will's face for a moment. It was steady, too steady to belong to the hurt in his voice.

"And your father?"

Will looked away from her. "Oh, I don't want to bore you…tell me about Texas."

"Texas is hot. Tell me about your father," she insisted.

Again the puzzled expression.

"Do you really want to know?"

Abby nodded. "Of course I do. Most pastors are pastors because it's a family occupation. The fact that your father is a miner and you raised two sisters is intriguing and admirable."

Will smiled thinly. "Was a miner," he corrected. "My father *was* a miner."

Abby tilted her head. "You mean, he changed his line of work, or—"

"He passed away. Cholera… it took a good part of the town, you know. Besides, I think when my sisters left, well, he gave up."

"I'm sorry," she murmured.

Will shrugged. "Sorry for telling a depressing story."

Abby frowned. "It's not depressing, just sad. Depressing would be if you became a drunken misfit who wandered around lost and hopeless, but you are a handsome, semi-amiable pastor, yes?" Abby said brightly.

Will's lips twitched and he looked mischievously over at her. "Did you say handsome?"

Abby's eyes went wide. "No," she lied. She had said it. This is why her mother was always trying to get her to control her tongue. She was so used to saying her thoughts that she rarely censured them.

"You did. You said I was handsome." He grinned broadly. "You, Teacher, not only slept on my shoulder, but you think I am handsome."

Abby stammered. "What… what I meant was that you are not… not handsome." She tried to remedy without success. "I mean, your looks aren't bad to look at, well, I mean, I'm sure there are others more handsome. Not that you are not, but…" Oh why did she keep talking? *Abby shut your mouth.* Abby snapped her lips together and looked forward, praying that she would disappear.

Will didn't say anything for a good minute, but then broke the silence with another chuckle. "Teacher thinks I am handsome."

Abby looked down at her lace gloves. Why had she acted like such a silly girl around him? With most men, she was the confident and witty Abigail Silver who was never flustered and always knew what to say. Right now, she felt like a little duckling trying to swim but instead managing only to flop around in circles. She leaned back to close her eyes. She just needed a bit more sleep, and no matter what, she would not fall onto Will's shoulder again.

It must have been at least two hours later when Abby sat up with a jolt. It was near evening time and Will had slowed the wagon to a stop.

Abby yawned and followed his gaze to what looked like a little farm with a white and yellow painted house, settled back behind a garden. A pinto was tied to the fence with a brightly-colored cart next to it.

"Are we… are we in Tall Pine?" she asked sleepily.

Will nodded. "Yeah, that's Miss Esther's horse and cart. I didn't think Melissa was due for another month."

"Who is Miss Esther?" Abby asked, noting the gentle attentiveness in Will's voice.

"Esther is the—"

His words were interrupted by an ear-shattering howl that echoed from the house.

Abby gasped. It was a cry of pure pain.

To her surprise Will smiled. "Esther is the midwife.

Esther placed some ice, wrapped in a towel, on Melissa Todd's back as the contraction started. This was back labor, one of the hardest kind in terms of pain and length. Melissa was a slight woman whose body could barely handle a plow let alone a hard labor.

"I can't do this no more," Melissa wailed as she dropped her weight into Esther's arms.

"You are doing so well Melissa. Let's count through this contraction, alright?" Esther encouraged, ignoring the stiffness in her neck. The labor had been going on for ten hours. Melissa's first three children had been delivered after long labors as well, but with them, the contractions had been low in front, normal. The back labor was taking a powerful toll on Melissa.

"I am going to die Esther…the baby is going to die," she cried as the contraction finished.

"The baby is going to come out healthy and fine." Esther stroked Melissa's damp hair away from her face. Melissa tried to sit down, but Esther stopped her. "We need to keep you on your feet Melissa, to speed up the labor."

Melissa nodded and bravely held onto Esther's forearms as she walked slowly around the room. A small knock on the door followed by a little blond curly head peeking through the door, made Melissa hiccup a small cry.

"You need to leave," she told her eldest daughter.

"We're hungry Momma, and Daddy isn't cooking anything," she whimpered.

"Luv you need to—" Melissa groaned and the door shut as her daughter scampered away.

"Alright Melissa," Esther braced her. "They're very close now, just a minute apart. The baby is almost here."

"My back!" Melissa cried.

Esther grabbed the ice and placed it on Melissa's lower back. She needed to relieve the pressure, for with every contraction, Melissa tensed, slowing the process of labor.

"Melissa," she said soothingly, as the contraction eased. I need you to get on your hands and knees."

"What?" Melissa asked with a choke. "But my other ones I was just walking or lying down."

"Melissa, we need to relieve the pressure on your back. Trust me, alright?" Esther said as she led her to the bed. Taking most of Melissa's weight she positioned the frail momma on her hands and knees.

"That's… that's better," Melissa grimaced. "Oh lordy, Esther, another one is coming… oh it hurts."

Esther grabbed the ice and pressed on Melissa's lower back, pressing harder to move the baby away from the spine. "One, two, three, breathe Melissa, try not to tense." Esther began to massage Melissa's back, but before her hands could even move, another contraction started.

"Oh, I know I really am going to die, Esther."

Esther smiled. A baby was coming.

"I don't understand why we are stopping?" Abby said as Will tied off the horses next to the Pinto.

Will jerked his head towards the porch. A tall man paced back and forth and two children were crying. "It looks like they could use some help," he said.

Abby sighed. She was nervous, meeting her first people from Tall Pine. How should a teacher act? What should she say?

A boy suddenly came out of nowhere, running towards them. Abby noticed locks of golden brown hair in wild curls.

"Pastor Will!" he shouted, waving his hand.

"Michael." Will raised his hand in greeting and trotted forward meeting the boy several yards in front of the house. Abby was surprised either of them could run on the muddy ground still showing puddles from the earlier rain. She walked slowly, afraid to fall.

"Your momma here?" Will asked.

Michael nodded. "We've been here for a long, long time," Michael sighed, slumping his shoulders. "James and Lucy are crying because they're hungry. Mr. Todd gave us some jerky, but Pastor, that's not enough," Michael said matter-of-factly. His light blue eyes fell on Abby. She smiled and gave a little wave with her fingers.

"Alright, Michael," Will patted the boy's shoulders. "We've come to help out." He looked back at Abby. "You may need to fix the kids some supper."

"Who's that?" Michael pointed at Abby with a big smile. Two dimples denting deep in his cheeks made Abby fall for him instantly.

"That's the new teacher Michael," Will explained, hurrying forward.

Abby continued to walk slowly behind. Make supper? She didn't know the first thing about cooking. Her mother had always cooked, and then later on she had hired a cook. The only thing Abby knew how to do was boil water, if even that.

Michael skipped up to her. "Hi, Teacher," he greeted brightly. "Why are you walking so slowly?" he asked.

Abby gave a small laugh. "I'm afraid of falling; these shoes are not meant for rain or mud."

Michael blinked. "You talk different. Where are you from?"

"Texas."

Did she sound funny?

Michael's eyes widened. "Texas? My dad is gonna be from Texas!" he exclaimed. Somehow this must have bonded him to Abby because he took her hand, making her feel more confident to walk faster.

"He's going to be from Texas? Is your momma engaged?"

Michael shook his head with a disappointed frown. "No, she hasn't met him yet."

Abby opened her mouth to inquire more, but she was interrupted by Will shouting for her.

"Miss Silver, we need you to hurry."

"The crying is getting worse." Mark Todd rubbed his hands across his tired face. "And I can't go in cause I am sore afraid of seeing her die," he shuddered.

Will nodded. "The teacher will go in and check on things, alright Mark?" he assured him.

Abby's eyes widened as she stepped onto the porch. "Wait, what?"

Will looked at her sternly, like a commanding father. "Miss Silver, you need to go check on Melissa Todd and make sure everything is alright." He was trying to tell her something with a commanding look, but Abby, once again, stared dumbly.

"But I… I've never been, or seen a labor, and I don't know—"

"Mr. Todd has been anxious all day, Miss Silver. He needs to know his wife is alright."

Abby's eyes went from the tired Mark Todd to the tear-stained faces of two blonde children then to Will's communicative look and Michael's bright smile. "I suppose I could peek my head in," she said weakly.

"I'll show you the way." Michael tugged on her arm and took her inside. Will followed closely and gently brought her to a halt when the front door closed behind them.

"I am awfully sorry Miss Silver," he said, his voice softening. "I don't act my best when nervous, but this family needs to know what is going on with their mother." A small smile flickered across his mouth. "And everyone knows not to interrupt Esther's midwifery. She's the best there ever was."

Abby nodded and gave a small shrug. "It will be a new experience," she said and then jumped as another wail shook the house.

Michael smiled. He must be used to this. "Come on, Teacher."

Esther leaned under the wailing Melissa to check the baby's progress. She could feel the head, and yes, see it, but Melissa still felt no need to push. Thankfully the baby had moved off the back and was in perfect position.

The door suddenly opened and a pretty young woman with large gray eyes stared timidly through. "Uh, hello. I am the new teacher, Abigail Silver. Mr. Todd wants to know how everything is… if it is alright."

Melissa cried out. "Oh I can't take it, Esther. Why ain't I feeling the need to push?"

"It will be soon, Melissa. Everything is just opening up," she explained. Sometimes midwives forced patients to push before they were ready. The result was lots of tearing and lots of bleeding. Esther had her fair share of hard births, but one thing she had learned was that the baby and the body knew what to do. It was just helping the mother through it.

"Tell Mark that everything is going as it should," she smiled with a twinkle in her eyes.

Abby stared at the beautiful elegant woman. This was Esther? No wonder Will was so impressed. What man would not be interested in this gracious woman? Her hair was coming undone, and her cheeks were flushed with sweat beading on her forehead; dark circles under her eyes showed her fatigue. She was gorgeous. Abby had never thought a woman could look so beautiful, especially in the severely awkward position she was in. Abby liked her instantly.

"Oh, Esther, it's coming! I need to push."

Esther looked up at Abby. "Shut the door Miss Silver, and please come in. I could use your help."

To her own surprise, Abby hurried over. She would like to impress this Esther, and the woman seemed so capable, so calm and happy in the situation that it automatically relaxed Abby.

"Alright, Melissa, we are going to turn you on your side." Esther began to shift the woman, showing experienced strength in her skilled movements.

"My side?" Melissa groaned.

"Your back will be all bruised and we can't have you lying on it." Esther smiled and hiked up Melissa's gown above her waist. Abby wondered if she should look away. She'd never seen a woman, or anyone, naked or so exposed. Esther did not seem to mind.

"Miss Silver, take hold of her arms so she can brace herself against you during the pushes. She is weak and will need the support." Esther took one of Melissa's legs and placed it on her shoulder and then placed her elbow on the outside of the other leg so she could see the baby. "Melissa, on the next contraction push... that's a girl, good, good."

Esther waited for the baby's head to peak out. Melissa's small narrow hips made it hard for the babies to get through; they tended to suck themselves back in over and over. She hoped after all the standing and long labor, this one would come quickly.

"Alright Melissa, pant, and wait... wait." Esther rubbed oil along the opening. The baby would have blond curls like its siblings. "Alright, small push. Good girl, now a big push... good,

good, keep pushing. The head is almost out. Keep pushing."

Melissa cried out in agony and clutched Abby's arms as she pushed. Abby gulped not knowing whether to be afraid of the pain Melissa was exhibiting or to be excited with the sheer joy that Esther had on her face as the head came out.

"We have the head, Melissa!" Esther exclaimed. "Wonderful, now don't push," she said, her smile turning to concentration.

"But I got to!" Melissa cried.

One more second and Esther nodded. "Alright, pretty girl, push slowly," she instructed. Melissa began a low groan. Abby looked over to see Esther twisting the baby's shoulders as it slid out. "Slow, slow…good, keep going and—"

A wet, pink baby followed by a bluish chord slid out of Melissa and into Esther's arms.

"It's a boy, Melissa! A beautiful, healthy boy!" She smiled as she quickly cut the cord and then stood up to wrap the baby in a blue blanket, flannel on one side, and calico on the other.

Melissa's strained face relaxed into teary eyes and a trembling smile. "A boy?" she choked with a laugh. "A boy!" She held out her arms and Esther gently placed the small crying bundle into them.

Abby watched as the mother's world closed in, consisting only of herself and her new baby. It was as if all the pain she had just experienced had never happened when only a moment ago, she had been crying out in suffering. Now, she lay peacefully with the most exquisite thing Abby had ever seen, a wrinkly pink baby that was nuzzling into his mother's breast. Abby glanced at Esther who was now between Melissa's legs again. Abby tilted her head curiously; she was surprised that the whole thing had not nauseated her. Usually the sight of blood or any kind of gore sent her into a dizzy spell, and yet she had just participated in birth. The mere thought of delivering a baby had always frightened Abby. The pain, the risk of death, so many horror stories had been told to her. Yet, this experience had seemed exhilarating… joyous. Perhaps it was the calm way that the midwife had handled it.

Abby studied Esther's face, composed, serene, with a perpetual soft smile on her lips. "What are you doing?" Abby whispered, not wanting to break Melissa's bubble of contentment.

Esther looked up. "There's one more step," she answered as she pressed softly on the mother's stomach.

Esther smiled and pulled out some supplies from a large basket.

"I'm gonna clean you up Melissa, alright?" she said gently before making eye contact with Abby. "Would you be so kind as to inform the father that he has a healthy baby boy?"

Abby nodded, aware that she was being politely dismissed so Esther could clean up Melissa privately. She scurried out and into the kitchen where three children sat pale faced and anxious. The husband, Mark, paced back and forth while Will seemed to be lighting the stove to warm up the place. All faces turned to her as she walked in. The mixture of fear and excitement was tangible.

"It's a boy!" A small giggle escaped her lips. "And the midwife said everything is fine."

Mark sat down in relief, his eyes misting up as he placed his head in his hands.

"Thank the Lord," he wept amidst the cheering children.

Will had stood up from lighting the stove. He patted Mark's shoulders. "See? I told you it would be fine. Miss Esther always knows what to do."

Again Abby noticed the softening in Will's eyes and face. After seeing Esther, she understood why. How could any man not be entranced by the woman? Heavens, she herself was entranced.

"Is it alright for me to go in?" Mark asked. Abby shrugged, but Mark paid her no mind. He was out of the room before she had time to take another breath. Will stopped the children who wanted to scurry in to see their new brother.

"Hold on, all of you; let your father and mother have some time." He glanced up at Abby. "I told Mark that I would see to his evening work, feeding the animals and such. Perhaps you could make these younglings some dinner?"

It was an order and not a request. Abby's eyes widened as Will left the house, shutting the door firmly behind him. She breathed out a weak laugh as she looked at the children. Mathematics, science, philosophy, history, Abby knew every educational subject there was. She loved learning, loved knowledge, but cooking...why had she never bothered to learn that? Abby tucked a loose strand of hair behind her ear.

"Are you the new teacher?" the eldest girl asked.

Abby nodded. Perhaps if she kept them talking and asking questions they would forget that they were hungry. She did not want Will knowing she could not cook. Not that she cared for his opinion, or needed it, but Abby did have her pride.

"I am the new teacher," Abby said with a little more gusto. "What are your names?"

The eldest pointed at herself. "I'm Beth." She nodded towards her brother and little sister. "That's my brother James and my sister Lucy." Beth studied Abby with a scrutiny much too astute for a little girl. "You're smaller than the last teacher," she noted.

Abby tried to smile. She'd never been an overly curvy thing, nor very tall. This tended to make her look young, which she was, but when trying to be an independent schoolteacher one would hope to appear older.

"What are you going to cook for us?" James asked with an exhausted sigh. "I'm starving."

So much for keeping them distracted.

"Well, let me look at what you have," Abby replied, faking confidence. She began busying herself by opening all the cupboards, investigating the contents. There were cans and jars, fresh bread, vegetables and some ham, eggs, and milk. Plenty of food, but Abby had no idea what to do.

Dear Lord, please help me, she silently prayed. Abby pulled out what looked like tea. She could make tea.

"I don't like that," Beth announced, grimacing at the tea.

Abby put it back. What in heaven's name was she going to do?

"Beth, James, Lucy," a rich voice spoke softly.

Abby looked up to see Esther walking in. "Your mother says that you can come see your new baby brother." The three children bounded off, pushing each other to get to the room first.

Esther lifted her eyebrows in an amused expression. "Nothing is as exciting as a new baby."

Abby nodded with a thin smile. "Will suggested I make dinner and I—" *am a qualified teacher with an impressive secondary education. Yet, I have no knowledge on how to cook or do anything useful it seems.* "I don't know what the children like," she gulped.

Esther nodded and crossed over to her. "You look tired; go ahead and sit down while I make you some tea, and I will do dinner," Esther smiled encouragingly. Abby could have kissed her. She was tired, but she could tell from the dark eye circles that Esther was also tired, possibly more than Abby, and yet her back was straight and her movements steady. Fatigue must be a habitual companion for her.

"Where are you from?" Esther asked, while pumping water into a pan.

"Texas," Abby answered quickly. "This is the first time that I have ventured away from home. It is an adventure that I'm sure has been overdue."

Esther looked up, catching the slight quake in the young teacher's voice. "And what brought you to Colorado?"

"Well, it was my parents' choice. They thought it would be beneficial for me to be more… independent."

Esther nodded. "Independence is a valuable thing for a woman."

"Do you think so?" Abby asked, placing her chin on her hand. She wanted to be more independent, but had never put much thought into it.

"Don't you think it is?" Esther asked, heating up some oil and then tossing in sliced onions. The crackle of raw vegetables in hot oil made Abby relax. Kitchens were always comforting.

"I believe so. Truth is, I never thought much about it."

Esther glanced over at her. Abby waited for the look. It was the look that said, *What a pretty little thing, so silly, so innocent.* Abby hated that look. Usually the lips would press together in an amused smug smile, the head would tilt and the eyes scrunch up in pretend compassion. Everyone gave her that look, even Will.

Not that I care what he thinks.

Esther's face looked interested, but not amused. Curious, but sincere. "Well I am glad you've come to Colorado," she said with a firm nod. "You did fantastic in the labor, behaving gently. No doubt you will handle teaching beautifully," Esther said with confidence.

Abby felt a spark of pride pop inside her. It was a sincere compliment, not one meant to make her feel better, but an observant opinion that was flattering. She had handled the labor, even after an all-day wagon ride. The thought gave Abby a new strength. She would go to school tomorrow and handle what was thrown at her in a mature, serene way.

Esther asked a few more questions about Abby, her home, family, likes and dislikes. Abby felt herself relaxing as she chatted about herself while sipping a cup of tea. A homey feeling overtook her as she watched Esther methodically cut, chop, stir, and fry a masterpiece of ham with some type of savory sauce, toasted bread with honey and a mixture of vegetables with thick slices of cheese thrown in. If Abby hadn't wanted to cook before, she very much wanted to now as rich aromas overtook the house.

"So Michael is your son?" Abby asked after realizing that Esther had made all the inquiries in the conversation.

"He is," Esther smiled proudly. "The best son a woman could ask for."

"And what does your husband do for a living?"

"No husband," Esther replied unruffled.

"Oh, I'm sorry. Did he pass away?"

Esther stopped stirring a biscuit batter briefly before answering. "No," she said simply.

Abby waited for a further explanation, but she received none. Instead, Esther asked a few more questions of Abby, dismissing the subject of a husband.

The door burst open just as Esther was laying out food on the table. Michael skipped in bringing the smell of a cool summer evening. Abby watched as Esther's whole face brightened. She held out her arms for the boy and then covered his head with her hand, kissing his curls.

"Were you out causing trouble, handsome?" she grinned, tapping his chin as he pulled away.

"I was talking to Pastor Will. He says the eggs need to be collected," Michael chattered without taking a breath.

"They do indeed, especially since I just used most of them."

"I'll collect them," Michael volunteered. It was a job he obviously enjoyed

Esther messed his curls. "What would I do without you?" she asked, handing him a basket that was hanging on one of the walls.

"Suffer and die of a broken heart," Michael answered with an air of words that were memorized.

"Exactly," Esther winked.

Michael beamed and began to skip out. He stopped in front of Abby. "You want to help?" he asked brightly. "You need two people to make it a game."

Eager for something to do, Abby agreed and followed Michael out the door.

❧

Esther watched as Michael and Abby headed out to the hen house. For a brief moment it was quiet, just her and the sound of simmering water for dishwashing. She liked the little schoolteacher; she seemed innocent, untried, but had a strength that was evident in her. Esther sighed, remembering leaving home, leaving Boston and the East for good. Colorado had been good to her... hard at first... very hard. A single woman showing up with a baby is enough to start all sorts of rumors and unwelcome looks, but like everything she did, Esther took it a day at a time. Prayer, hard work, and Michael were what got her through it all, and now—

A small cry broke from the back room and a splatter of giggles followed it.

Esther smiled, wiping her hands on a cloth. She had found

contentment, even a bit of peace. She and Michael were happy and well off, and nothing was going to change that.

Abby yelped as a giant rooster chased her out of the hen house. She dropped her empty basket, tripped over her dress, and would have fallen flat on her face were it not for Will, who caught her by the upper arm.

Abby was about to thank him until she saw that he was laughing hysterically. She narrowed her eyes at him. Was it fate that she must appear ridiculous every time in front of this pastor? She was really beginning to not like him.

"You should—" more laughter, "you should have seen—" snorts of laughter. "You should have seen your face!" Tears were gathering at the corners of his eyes. "White-faced and wide-eyed like a grizzly was chasing you."

Abby smoothed her dress and stood proudly. "Well, it may not be a grizzly, but that—" she pointed to the ruffled rooster. "That isn't exactly a docile bunny, either."

Will shook his head. "I must say, seeing you run out of there made the whole trip to Denver worth it."

Abby opened her mouth for a retort but was interrupted by Michael running up to her.

"Teacher, you don't lift the tail feathers of a rooster. Roosters don't lay eggs." Michael's face was knit with concern. "I was afraid he was going to peck your eyes out."

Abby smiled, touched by Michael's worry. "Well, I learned something new today," Abby said optimistically. She wasn't one to stay ashamed for long. "I just hope the poor rooster can forgive me for accosting him."

Will erupted into more laughter and Michael looked confused. "Well, I'm gonna fetch some more eggs," he announced. "When my dad comes, we'll be fetching eggs every day for Momma," he informed Abby happily, before skipping off. "You comin' Teacher?" he called back over his shoulder.

Abby tilted her head in puzzlement. "Pastor Will," she lowered her voice. "Miss Esther said she has no husband, and just now Michael said something about a dad… is she engaged?" She asked hopefully, and quickly wondered why she was hoping Esther was engaged.

Will glanced at Michael briefly. "No, she's not engaged." His face clouded over. "I don't think she ever will be. Miss Esther…" he paused, looking towards the house wistfully. Abby followed his gaze.

"Miss Esther keeps to herself, you see. She serves others, is kind and—" he sighed, "beautiful, but she isn't interested in men, and does just a fine job supporting herself and that boy of hers."

Abby watched the graceful outline of Esther's frame through the window. The excited chatter of hungry children scurrying towards the table could be heard yards away. So she was single and supported herself and a child. Abby was impressed. "Michael seems like a sweet boy," she suddenly said, realizing the silence was becoming awkward.

Will nodded. "Sweet as they come and the jewel of his mother's eye. We got a saying in Tall Pine that if you hurt Michael Callen, then you might as well strap yourself in front of a pack of hungry wolves, because they'll be easier on you than Miss Esther."

Abby's lips twitched. She consented that she might resent Esther's beauty, grace and attractive independence, as any single young girl would, but she knew one thing, and that was that she liked the midwife, and she aimed to become friends with her.

Melissa Todd was a rosy-cheeked redhead who had never considered herself of much worth. When Mark had asked for her hand in marriage, after the death of his first wife, Melissa had scarcely believed it. The thought of a man with some land, who was also hard working, godly, and kind, seemed like a dream. People gossiped that he had only married her for her beauty and youth, but when Esther saw the beaming married couple as they stared at their new miracle, she knew that the gossip was the outcome of boredom and nothing more.

"I was so scared," Mark sighed, kissing Melissa on the head. She nuzzled into him, stroking her little boy's chin.

"I was sure I was gonna die," she giggled like it was a joke.

Esther knocked politely on the open door.

"Melissa, I got some food for you. Mark, I can bring a plate for you too," she offered, coming in at Melissa's beckoning wave.

"Nah, Esther, it's alright. Mark was just saying he was gonna go eat with the little ones before you came," Melissa said.

Mark gave one last kiss to his son's soft cheek and another to Melissa. "I'll go make sure they're not overwhelming the new school teacher." He grinned at Esther on his way out. She smiled in return, then went and placed the steaming plate, as well as a large glass of milk next to Melissa.

"I wish there was a way I could eat and keep holding him at the same time," Melissa lifted her baby to her lips. "I was so sure I was gonna lose this one that I feel if I let him go he will be gone," Melissa's voice cracked, her bottom lip trembling slightly. The after birth emotions were so fragile.

Esther sat on the foot of the bed, reaching her arms out for the baby.

"I will stay right here so you can see him while you eat. I know there's no greater fear than the thought of losing a child."

Melissa nodded and gently handed the baby over to Esther.

"What are you going to name him?" Esther asked, gazing at the perfect little face. A wave of sadness washed over her. How she would love another child. To kiss the rose petal skin every day, play with the little toes and nuzzle their velvet earlobes.

"I was thinking of Clark," Melissa answered, sighing in delight at her first bite.

"Clark? I love it, very manly," Esther exclaimed. She smelled the baby; the newborn smell, in her opinion, was the best there was. "He took to nursing well, a sign of a strong man, right?"

Melissa smiled and took a bite of ham. "I did what you told me with my last one, cupping the breast and such… worked liked a charm. I remember the first time I nursed; I cried it hurt so badly. I sure wish you'd been my midwife then." She laughed softly. "Honestly, now, there is not a whole lot of pain besides labor that can make me cry."

"It's amazing how motherhood tends to toughen up a woman in more ways than one," Esther remarked.

"That is as true as true can be." Melissa glanced at her baby, the light in her eyes dimming slightly as a thought came to her. "Have you seen Mary yet?" she asked, lowering her voice and glancing at the doorway.

"Mary Higgins?" Esther asked.

Melissa nodded. "She's been pregnant for a while now."

Esther rocked the baby, feeling uncomfortable with the topic. "Once I knew she was pregnant I tried to see her, but so far she has refused. I can't force her."

"It's probably because of Toby. Such a horrible man. Do you know what he made her do to settle and smooth over some gambling debts? Who knows if the baby is even his."

Esther nodded curtly; she didn't want to hear the story again. Mary had chosen to marry Toby, a handsome and charismatic devil, despite everyone's warnings. Mary felt so fortunate that handsome Toby had wanted her, she was willing to do anything for him, no matter how shameless.

"Sometimes parenthood changes men for the better. Maybe this will help both Mary and Toby," Esther said hopefully, handing Clark back to Melissa. She would eventually visit Mary, even if it meant dealing with Toby who was indeed a monster.

Aren't all men?

Esther's eyes clouded over as the dark thought brought back the even darker memories.

When everything was washed, clean, and Melissa asleep with baby Clark snuggled to her breast, Esther went to untie her horse and prepare for the ride home.

Will told Abby he would drop her off at her new home and

then show her the old school house, which was literally right next to it. The schoolteacher looked scared, complaining that she didn't have enough time to prepare for school the next day. Esther had to quickly turn a chuckle into a cough when Will, with all the masculine sensitivity he could muster said, "Well, given that you didn't know the difference between a rooster and hen, maybe you can start out with them teaching you." He was clearly exhausted with this poor girl.

Michael pitched in defending Abby. "She's from Texas, Pastor; maybe they don't have roosters in Texas," he explained logically.

"Thanks, Michael." Abby patted his shoulder and glared at Will. Esther walked over after hitching the horse to her wagon.

"Michael, handsome, you ready to go? I'm afraid it is too late to go to town tonight. We'll have to go another time for supplies," she smiled at him.

"School supplies." Michael dramatically put his hand on his forehead. "I knew I was forgetting something."

"Miss Esther, do you want us to escort you home? It wouldn't be too much out of the way," Will offered politely. Esther saw Will's nervousness as he fingered his hat. Another wave of guilt washed over her. Will, kind and innocent Will who was trying so hard to be a good pastor despite his youth. In truth, he was not exactly a boy. He was Esther's age and yet she felt ages older than him. Life had given Will trials; it had given Esther hell. Will had tried to court her. She refused him as gently as she could, but no matter how gently she refused men, it always left them hurt.

"Thank you, Will, but it is only about three miles away. Besides, Miss Abby is right. She will need as much time as she can to prepare for tomorrow." Esther winked at Abby.

"You'll be there tomorrow won't you? I mean to drop off and pick up Michael?" Abby asked, earnestly wringing her dainty hands.

"Of course I will, and I should warn you that every parent will be there, as well as others without children, just to see the newcomer."

Abby gave a nervous laugh. "Thank you for the warning."

Esther nodded for Michael to come over. She helped him into the wagon and then climbed quickly up herself, before Will could help her.

"I'll see you both tomorrow." She waved, and then gave the reins a slight jerk before riding off.

Michael's head bounced softly against Esther as they rode together in the wagon, gently steered by her pinto Lancelot, a strong but gentle animal. He walked slowly over a slightly damp path shaking his head every now and then when a pesky fly would bother his nose. Michael stirred slightly. He had fallen asleep against her as he often did when they returned from a long day.

"We almost home, Momma?" he asked sleepily. Esther kissed the top of his head.

"One more mile to go, honey. You were such a good boy," she told him, giving him a little squeeze. Michael smiled and straightened up a bit, his sleepy eyes scanning the beauty around him.

"Dad will like it here, won't he?" Michael asked. Esther looked around her. A soft meadow decorated with multicolored wildflowers that melted into wild, untamed trees. Beyond that were endless mountains that seemed constantly tipped in snow reminding her of frosting on a cake.

"I think your dad will love it," she answered. She loved it now, too. When she'd first come to Colorado, it had seemed so rough with its cold long nights, the wolves and grizzlies and the tough mountain people. Years had smoothed over the rough edges. Esther had since come to believe that Colorado, with its mysterious forests, beautiful wildlife, and good-hearted people was probably the finest place on earth.

"Tell me more about Dad," Michael yawned.

"I will later," Esther agreed. "First we need to bathe you, feed the animals, and then I will tell you about your dad, alright?" This time it was Esther who stifled a yawn. Why were those things so darn contagious?

"Can you tell me where he will be from?"

Esther chewed her lip. This was a dangerous game. One she should not play, but it made her son so happy. "Texas," she said. Why not? She liked how the little schoolteacher spoke and liked her sun-kissed freckles. Texas seemed like a good place for Michael's fictional father to be from.

"Texas." Michael pronounced it slowly. "And he is friends with Indians, right?"

"Yes."

"And very brave?"

"The bravest." Esther smiled.

"And he will have brown hair like me?" Michael asked eagerly with memorized detail.

"Absolutely." Esther hugged Michael tight. She would tell him one day, tell him that she would never marry, that she had no intention of marrying. She hoped that when the time came, Michael would be old enough to realize that they were better off alone, and he would be over the youthful desire for a father.

Esther closed her eyes as a cool breeze kissed her skin. Tall Pine was home. All the single men had tried to win her at one time or another... there were none left who were interested. Rumors had stilled, friends had been made, and a way of life was set. Another Colorado breeze swept over her again, chilly for summer. It would be an early autumn. Esther's mind began to settle with thoughtless ease when a feeling stirred within her.

Again the wind blew, and again, Esther shifted. This had been happening more and more lately. Each time she reaffirmed that she had made a home, that she had survived the hard years of being a single mother and had finally reined in the trials and tribulations victoriously, the feeling arose. It was a feeling of hunger, of emptiness, as if something was missing from her life. It ate at her, and she didn't know why. She had everything she could hope for.

The Lord had given her so much, and she loved what she had,

but sometimes she could not help but feel that the Lord wanted something else from her, other than being a midwife and a mother to Michael. She looked down at her son. Surely there was nothing more; nothing that could bring greater happiness than Michael.

Esther decided that fatigue was speaking. She had so much more than most, and thoughts like these could only bring about discontentment. Shaking her head, she labeled her thoughts and tucked them away, far back into the corners of her mind. She would pull them out again when she was rested and had the time.

A small light showed through Esther's French-paned windows. A spark of alarm lasted only a second, until Esther saw the white buggy resting beside her home. Uncle Tim and Aunt Lily had stopped by. They often did, and always made themselves at home, even when Esther was not there. Still, she was glad they had, considering they had just returned from a medical lecture in Chicago with some of the world's leading doctors and scientists. She pulled Lancelot to a halt and scanned her home. It was a pretty house, with hardwood floors and blue and white paint that contrasted nicely with the rose bushes and potted geraniums. She was proud of it, proud of the work she had put into the rusty abandoned house it had been when she first moved to Tall Pine. Uncle Tim and Aunt Lily helped with what they could, but truth be told, they were so busy that it was not much. Still, she was grateful for even that, because she could honestly say that everything she had was hers.

"Esther! Michael!" Aunt Lily exclaimed, opening the door and hurrying out to the porch.

"Aunt Lily!" Michael called out. "You're back from Chicago!"

"Back safe and sound," Aunt Lily held out her arms for Michael who ran into them eagerly. "Sorry to stop by so late, but we brought presents and were eager to tell you about the lecture."

Esther smiled and helped Michael down from the wagon. "I am glad you did; I was planning on stopping by your clinic tomorrow to hear about it, but this is even better." Esther gave a quick shake of her head. She was tired, but she was often tired. It had become the normal feeling of her daily life. There were so many people to help, so many things to do that sleep often seemed to be a nuisance.

"Go ahead and go on in while I put Lancelot away... you hungry?" she asked, knowing full well what the answer would be. Aunt Lily was a highly intelligent woman, respected by several doctors for her nursing skills, but cooking was not her strong suit. Esther understood that many of Uncle Tim's visits were simply so he could have a good home-cooked meal.

"Oh, I don't want to trouble you—" Aunt Lily began weakly.

"It's no trouble," Esther reassured her, smothering a small smile.

"Very well then, but hurry, I can't wait to give you your gift."

Uncle Tim had exciting news, a new kind of baby bottle known as the "Allenbury" had been created. It was a design in which the baby could be fed unattended. Baby bottles had come far. Esther still remembered when the double-ended feeder by Allen and Hanbury was created some years back. The design made the flow of milk more constant and it was so much easier to clean than the black Indian rubber teats that had been used prior.

"This will enable mothers to keep more fat on their babies when they start to drift away from nursing," Uncle Tim said excitedly, his hollowed cheeks glowing with excitement.

"And help those who can't produce milk," Esther added. It was a nightmare for some new mothers having a hungry baby and not being able to feed it. "Did they talk about the sadness that sometimes occurs after a woman has a baby?" Esther asked eagerly. She had run into such cases quite a few times.

This time Aunt Lily made a scoffing sound. "Some still think of it as a mental breakdown, but others are of my opinion, that it has something to do with a woman's physical makeup. The same way she can get moody during her cycle, a woman can get depressed, horrifically sad, after having a baby. It is not her fault and it is not just uncontrolled emotions."

Uncle Tim smiled. "Your aunt had a few things to say to some of those old doctors."

"All of whom need to retire," Aunt Lily shook her head. "The instruments some still insist on using are prehistoric." Aunt Lily threw her hands in the air, but then brightened when Esther brought in a steaming bowl of chicken and dumplings with buttery biscuits on the side along with vanilla tea. "Before we eat, I do have some gifts."

Michael's eyes widened. "Did you get me something?" he asked eagerly.

"Of course we did, my boy," Uncle Tim answered. "We always bring you something." Uncle Tim handed him a ribbon-wrapped book of illustrated animals. Michael threw his arms around his uncle and aunt in thanks, and then hopped over to Esther to show her the illustrations.

"Goodness, this is beautiful!" Esther exclaimed, tracing a finger over a polar bear.

"We know he has a liking towards animals and that book has all sorts of interesting facts." Aunt Lily beamed, pleased with Michael's reaction. "There was an exquisite bookstore in Chicago we just had to see." She pulled out a wrapped package and handed it to Esther. "I thought you could make something with this for the Harvest Festival."

Esther's head tilted with curiosity. She carefully unwrapped the package and gasped as the paper fell away to reveal the most beautiful hue of poppy-red fabric she had ever seen. Her fingers gently pulled out the soft, silky material that glowed against her skin.

"Aunt Lily, I... I have never seen such gorgeous fabric. My goodness, it is amazing," she said in an almost reverent tone.

"Tall Pine has a very nice little fabric and trimmings shop," Aunt Lily said with a shrug, "but nothing compares to what these big cities have to offer."

Esther pulled out the entire fabric, laying it over her lap. There was plenty enough for a dress, and she had been wanting to make a new one lately... but red?

"I thought red would look so lovely on you and," Aunt Lily's eyes twinkled. "I imagine it will draw attention," she added with a wink.

Esther looked away. "Aunt Lily, you know my feelings on that. I am happy how I am, with… with my work. Nothing needs to change," she said, but more to herself than Aunt Lily.

"I know." Aunt Lily leaned back and took a sip of her tea. "Just promise me you will wear the fabric to the Harvest Festival—if only to appease your meddling aunt?"

Esther smiled. "I promise that I will wear that fabric. I will even make the neck a little wider if you want," she teased.

Aunt Lily nodded approvingly. "Wider and—" she winked. "Maybe a bit lower. Church worthy still, but a bit lower."

Three

Abby's head throbbed. The haunting sound of wolves had impaired her sleep, even though logic told her she was safe within the walls of her new home. As a mockery to her distress, her little abode had been freezing and lighting a fire had ended in discouraged failure. At first crack of dawn she had walked drearily over to the schoolhouse. She may look like a fatigued mess, but her schoolhouse would be in tip-top shape. She would make sure of it. The chirping of birds translated to shrieks to Abby's ears while she tidied up the schoolhouse. Any other time Abby might have enjoyed their morning praises, but this morning she felt like throwing a book at them. To make matters worse, the pastor would be coming to witness her first day teaching. Apparently the first day could be rough, and he thought he should be there just in case some of the boys acted out. This should have made Abby less apprehensive, but instead it just made her more nervous. She could tell Will thought her flighty and funny. Not witty, but silly. The last thing she wanted was for him to compare her to other teachers and see her stumble and fall over her lessons as she figured out how to teach.

Pastor Will had also explained that the church in town had burned down during early summer and Tall Pine was currently using the schoolhouse for their Sunday services, so she needed to make sure everything was all tidy Saturday night before the church service the next day.

"Will, Will, Will," Abby chanted angrily. "That cheeky pastor is taking over my life." She stomped her foot the way she had as a child, and still did, when she thought no one was looking. And at this moment standing in an empty, cold classroom she didn't care if the whole world was looking. She would still stomp her foot because things seemed to be getting worse and worse. She wanted to pick flowers, but she had no vase. She wrote her lessons, but there were no pictures to put up. Finally, a small stove stood in the corner, but Abby had no idea how to work it.

"Summer?" she scoffed, wrapping a shawl around her. "This is supposed to be summer?" She was afraid to see what winter was like.

Abby sighed and gave another look around the schoolhouse. She'd left so quickly that she had hardly done any research on Colorado. What would the children be like? She knew there would be a mixture of children from farmers, tradesmen, craftsmen, and miners. Tall Pine was quite the industrious little town, surrounded by fertile farms and a few ranches. It should be quite interesting, she thought, as her usual positive attitude returned. She would take whatever was thrown at her and make it good. Even if it was cold.

The sound of horses, mingled with children's laughter, snapped Abby to attention. She smoothed her skirt, fluffed her hair, and gave one last look around the classroom. Chilly and plain, but clean at least. She'd managed to sweep and dust, and of that she was proud. Already fabricating a letter to her mother about the hard work she had done, sweeping and dusting, Abby hurried to the door to greet her students.

Abby had not realized that she would be meeting more parents than students; each child was accompanied by at least a mother and father, plus a few relatives and friends. There were even couples and singles with no children at all who came up to inspect her. Everyone was eager to see the new teacher. With each family, Abby had no time to introduce herself to the child before one of the parents took her hand or merely stood in front of her demanding attention while their child rushed into the classroom.

"You look awfully young," most said.

"The other teacher lasted only a month, said Colorado was too rough."

"You not gonna last long with that many ruffles, honey."

Abby began to feel dizzy with all the comments thrown at her. She leaned against the doorpost trying to look braver and stronger than she felt when Esther walked up with a comforting voice that immediately steadied Abby.

"You are doing wonderful Abby, and my, doesn't the classroom look amazing. I have never seen it this clean, and I've witnessed three teachers," Esther complimented, looking like a rose petal in a soft pink dress.

"Really? I was up early to get it all clean." Abby clasped Esther's hand more with the need to feel calm than to actually welcome her. Somehow she knew that with Esther by her side people would like her by association.

"Well, you can tell. Doesn't the classroom look good, Michael?" Esther asked, stroking his hair. Abby about jumped out of her skin. She was a schoolteacher for crying out loud and had not even noticed Michael, who stood close to his mom with the same happy smile she had first seen him with. He wore a crisp blue shirt that made his eyes look like the Texas sky, and his arms were wrapped tightly around a beautifully bound book.

"Michael, how are you?" Abby held out her hand. Michael released the book with his right arm and shook Abby's hand like a jump rope.

"Look what I brought. It's from Chicago," he announced excitedly.

"It's an animal book," Esther told her. "Many of these children have never seen illustrated children's books. If they get rowdy, this will calm them down." Esther leaned in closer. "I have had to substitute before. I learned from trial and error," she laughed.

Abby looked up at Esther with gratitude. She had not thought of games, or what to do during recess. Esther must have truly been sent by God Himself to help her for her first day. Abby lowered the book to Michael nearly tripping on her own dress.

"Will you hold it for me Michael, until it is time to read it?" she asked. Michael nodded eagerly, snatching the book like a treasure. "It must mean a lot to you."

"I can read most of it," Michael informed her proudly. "I love animals, especially horses. My dad is going to have a big horse when he comes."

Abby frowned and looked at Esther for explanation. Hadn't Will said Esther was not engaged? Esther only smiled and caressed Michael's brow.

A petite woman came up from behind Esther and gave a little cough.

"Oh, excuse me, I am blocking the door. Come on, Michael, let's go find your seat," Esther said as she stepped out of the way.

"I want the same seat from last year," Michael told her as the two walked away, leaving Abby feeling once again vulnerable and exposed. A plain woman with intelligent eyes and a kind smile approached Abby holding the hands of two adorable curly-haired children. Abby caught her reflexes before she frowned in confusion. Surely such cute and bonny children did not belong to this mousy woman? Abby smiled at the children.

"Good morning, I am Miss Abigail, the new school teacher," she chirped sounding a bit, she realized, like the birds that had awakened her.

"Yeah, we know," the little girl giggled.

The woman urged them forward. "Go find a seat and I will be right there," she told them with a playful and gentle shove to their backs. They ran into the classroom giggling all the way. "I'm Eliza, Eliza Jensen," her voice was low and steady, but friendly and without judgment. Abby quickly decided that she was not so unattractive after all.

"I'm Miss Abigail Silver... well you already heard me introduce myself. You have lovely children, Mrs. Jensen."

"It's Miss, and please call me Eliza. Miss Jensen makes me feel like the old maid I am," she laughed, her face transforming into a jovial picture.

"Oh, I do apologize, and 'Old Maid', is there such a thing nowadays?" Abby countered, feeling more relaxed with Eliza's happy attitude.

"Out here there is. You're expected to marry young and start breeding," she laughed heartily. "And those aren't my children. Never was the type to attract a man, let alone have children." She smiled with a shrug. "Those two wild things I brought are Daisy and Billy Gable. Their momma is not feeling too well and their pa had to go to Indiana to see a dying relative. So I offered to bring them, until their momma feels better," Eliza explained. She looked Abby up and down and then with a curt nod said, "You look like a sweet girl. I reckon you will do a fine job here."

Abby smiled with gratitude. Her eyes skipped past Eliza, hoping to see the silhouette of a tall pastor.

Eliza followed her gaze. "You expecting someone? I think all the children in Tall Pine are here."

Abby felt her cheeks warm. "Pastor Will said he'd be here on my first day... to help."

Eliza nodded. "Don't think he'll make it. A small mining town a bit up the mountains had a terrible explosion. He's gone to help out for a few weeks."

Abby swallowed. She should feel less nervous, but instead she felt... sad. Sad for the town and disappointed there'd be no pastor.

Eliza gave her a friendly pat and hustled the children forward. A few more adults drifted in. Esther had been right. The last couple who came in consisted of an incredibly handsome man, pretty-like with large green eyes, pale skin, and dark hair. Beside him was a short, thin, strawberry blond woman with a swollen belly. Abby noticed with disapproval how she clung to this man like a scared child, and not like the wife that her pregnant belly and simple ring indicated she was.

"So you are the teacher, huh?" he asked her, his eyes raking up and down Abby. She shifted uncomfortably, feeling that his gaze left dirty spots on her. Maybe he was not so handsome after all. His little wife remained silent, but Abby noticed how her hands tightened around her husband's arms as her round eyes narrowed like a rattlesnake.

"Yes," Abby finally answered, pulling herself together. "My name is Abigail Silver, and you are?"

"Toby Higgins, and this here is Mary," he nodded casually to the woman at his side. Abby dared not put out her hand in greeting, for she instinctively knew that Mary wouldn't accept it, and as far as shaking hands with Toby Higgins, well Abby would sooner kiss a slimy reptile than do that.

"Pleased to meet you both," she said with a slight nod. Mary's glare deepened.

"Look here, Abigail…" Toby began.

"Miss Silver, if you please," Abby corrected coldly.

Toby grinned, clearly amused. "Look *Abigail,*" he said again slowly. "If you need anything at all, cooking, cleaning, extra help—you let Mary know and she'll come do it for you."

Abby's mouth parted slightly. Did he just volunteer his pregnant wife to come do work for her?

"Thank you, but I think I will manage." She wished this awkward and inappropriate couple would just leave.

"Well then," Toby continued, "if you get lonely being out here all by yourself, you just let me know and I'll bet I could find you some good company." He grinned with a meaningful wink. Abby was at a loss of words. Not even bothering to politely end their encounter, she just walked away.

What a despicable man! If Joseph were here, he'd have knocked him senseless.

Toby sat down in the last empty seat while Mary stood on her feet. Toby searched the crowd until he saw Esther and pressed his lips into a kissing pout. Esther's composure didn't even crack; instead, she looked at Mary with worry. The girl had no color to her skin; Esther doubted Mary was going outside or getting any circulation to her swollen ankles. With or without Toby's approval, she needed to find a way to visit Mary.

Most of the children were sitting down, with their parents standing off to the side. Abby searched for Esther. She stood by Michael looking like a queen with her hair tied back loosely and wearing little gold hoop earrings. Once again Abby suddenly felt foolish in her puffy lacy dress and puffy fancy hair. She must look like a cupcake compared to the rest of the women in the room. Standing in front of a rather large crowd it seemed as if a million butterflies were flying around madly in her stomach. She opened her dry mouth knowing she needed to say something. That very morning she had even written a speech: a perfect, simple, humble, yet impressive speech. However, nothing came out of her lips. She was frozen into silence. She did not know how long she stood like a statue. One or two nervous giggles came from the children.

"I am Miss Abigail Silver," she finally said, her voice at much too high a pitch. "I ummm…" she scanned the room. All the eyes on her seemed to be making fast assumptions and judgments; she needed to speak and quickly, but the butterflies were too strong. Her gaze fell on Esther, whose expression was filled with compassion.

"And where is it you are from Miss Silver?" Esther suddenly asked, in her smooth voice. Abby's heart-shaped lips twitched in a hint of a smile. Esther knew exactly where Abby was from. She was merely guiding her out of her stupor and fright.

"Texas." Abby exhaled. "I am from the state of Texas where I have lived all my life."

"And is this your first teaching position?" Esther asked again, stroking Michael's hair. Did she always find a way to affectionately touch her son?

"It is, yes," Abby smiled as she placed her hands behind her back and took a step forward. She remembered her own teachers doing the same routine: hands behind back, head down, step forward, and head up. They always did it when they were about to say something important and so it seemed like a good thing to emulate.

"I finished college and am trained for both elementary and secondary schools. After graduation I applied for various teaching positions. I was told that Tall Pine, Colorado had not had a school teacher for quite some time, and so, of course, I was more than eager to venture my way up here." Abby smiled brightly.

Oh, and my mother thought I was becoming shallow and men only wanted me for my father's property so my parents sent me packing, which I am still more than a little hurt about. And one more thing—I dislike the cold.

"Any questions?" Abby asked, smiling at Esther in silent thanks.

A young girl's hand shot up. She had left over breakfast in her hair, but clean clothes and a limp pink ribbon on the tip of her braid. Abby nodded at her to ask a question.

"Ya married?" she asked loudly. Abby blushed, completely caught off guard. She was slow to answer.

"No, not married."

"Why not?" another girl asked. Several of the parents chuckled, clearly amused by the show. Abby smiled and forced out a nervous laugh. She was not used to children or their blunt questions.

Generally married teachers are frowned on, she thought resentfully, but instead answered, "I'm still young."

"How long do you plan on teaching here Miss Abigail?" Eliza's pronounced voice sounded from the back.

"As long as needed," Abby replied, grateful for a genuine smile. She saw Toby wink again, the slimy snake that he was.

"Do you have any family out here?" a red bearded man asked, holding a sleeping boy in his arms.

"No," Abby replied softly. The reality of what she was doing hit her like a lightning bolt. "No, I have no one out here." She answered the next few questions confidently, though her hands trembled. Finally it was Eliza who announced that they best let the teacher get teaching. The parents and curious neighbors drifted off slowly, leaving Abby to face what seemed like a sea of restless children ready to attack.

"She seems young, doesn't she?" Esther remarked to Eliza as they walked away from the schoolhouse to Esther's red wagon with the yellow and purple flowers painted all over it like a gypsy caravan.

Eliza shrugged. "We were young once, weren't we? A girl's gotta break away from the nest at some point; better young then too late," Eliza said, and then frowned as they approached the wagon. "Esther, what were you thinking painting the wagon in such a manner?"

Esther smiled. "This little wagon Michael and I patched up together. We read about some musical gypsies in a book and Michael insisted we make our own gypsy wagon." She gave a helpless shake of her shoulders. "So we did," she added brightly.

Eliza rolled her eyes with a laugh as she grabbed hold of the wagon and pulled herself up.

"You sure you don't mind me going into town with you? I am taking the day off of work while my shop gets some repairs done and my wagon broke, and so I had to walk several miles this morning to fetch the Gable children. I am exhausted, and don't think I could walk one more step."

Esther shook her head as she untied the reins. "Of course I don't mind," she smiled teasingly. "Don't you have a horse, though? You know I would be happy to teach you how to ride."

Eliza shuddered. "Horses. I hate those beasts. One just about killed me the last time I rode, and that old thing you call my horse is only meant to pull a wagon. I rent him out to farmers and ranchers most of the time."

"You think you will ever ride again?"

Eliza shook her head. "A tornado could be chasing me and I still would not ride."

"Point taken. In any case, I'm happy to give you a ride into town. I enjoy the company. It makes going into town for molasses much more enjoyable."

"What are you making with molasses? Bread?" Eliza asked curiously; most everyone knew that Esther was an exceptional cook. Those who had a baby on a day when she made bread, or cookies, or sticky buns were considered lucky. Esther would grace the labor with a hot plate of treats for the family before delivering a baby.

"Gingerbread, actually. Uncle informed me last night he had a craving for gingerbread with lemon frosting, and since he has always been so kind to me, I try to comply with his odd cravings," Esther laughed, giving the reins a quick shake to move the horse forward.

"Gingerbread in the summer? That *is* odd, but then of course, is it ever truly summer in Tall Pine?" Eliza teased. She looked back pensively at the shrinking schoolhouse that seemed to blend in with the small meadow as they rode away.

"You think that little kitten will do alright? Miss Abigail?" Eliza asked. "She looks like the pampered sort."

"It says a lot about her that she chose to come out here, though," Esther defended. "I must say she looked very frightened. I will have to ask her to dinner soon before she gets too lonely." Her eyes softened. "It's easy for a young girl to get lonely."

Eliza made a "tsk" sound with her tongue and looked away past the dirt road. "Lonely? A girl with eyes like that will never be lonely—trust me," she said, unable to hide the tinge of bitterness in her voice. Esther glanced over at Eliza, but did not say anything. She knew what conversation was coming. It was the same one Eliza always started with her. Like a boil that constantly needed to be lanced, Eliza needed to ask one question before she could enjoy any more conversation.

"Do you ever get lonely?" Eliza finally asked. "Without a man, I mean, or is Michael enough?"

"Michael is enough," Esther said confidently. Though her lips remained in their perpetual soft smile, her eyes darkened like thunderclouds.

Eliza nodded, knowing Esther's past was locked tighter than a clamshell. The only reason she knew about it was Eliza herself had lived back East and had known Esther almost her whole life. "I think if I had a child I wouldn't be so lonely, you know?" Eliza glanced down at her hands. "I also just want the experience of having my own hands comfort a child, to stroke their little chin, and chubby cheeks, bathe them, kiss them. All those things I see other women do, and I can't." She glanced over at Esther. "You think it's wrong I want a child, even without a husband?"

"Do you for sure not want a husband?"

"Look at me, Esther. I got a hooked nose and a skinny body. A husband is never going to happen."

Esther frowned and cast Eliza a disapproving look. "I wish you wouldn't talk about yourself that way, Eliza. You become prettier every year. Some people are like flowers; they reach a youthful peak of beauty and then fade. Others are like wine; they become better with age. You are the latter."

"I don't drink wine," Eliza said flatly.

Esther smiled "Neither do I," she laughed.

Eliza sighed and stretched out her legs. "You didn't answer my question."

"I don't think it's wrong." Esther concluded, taking off her bonnet so that the breeze could play through her hair. "It's natural to want to nurture, comfort, and care. I would say your feelings are in accordance with God, Eliza."

Eliza smiled gently then sighed as she opened her basket for an apple. She offered one to Esther who shook her head.

"Do you think you will ever marry, Esther?"

Esther shook her head again emphatically.

"No, I have no desire to be with another man." She paused, biting her bottom lip. "I don't need or want a husband," she added quickly before her silence became too loud. "I have been blessed enough to have a son who is the world to me. I can ask for no more. In fact, belonging to a man is something I avoid." She laughed. "The same way you avoid horses."

Eliza nodded, knowing that it was the end of the discussion. The rest of the trip consisted of light conversation and laughter. Esther tried to appear unruffled by the conversation, but something was eating at her. She didn't like it, but it was becoming increasingly difficult to ignore.

Tall Pine had grown into a quaint, pretty town with cobbled streets, plenty of shops, and even some entertainment. There was now a bookstore, a toyshop, a bakery, little restaurants, and a small theater. It was enough to entice most of the farmers and visitors to make the trip into town often. The two women walked methodically past the windows displaying bonnets and boots. They passed the fabric store and Esther stopped to see if she could find some trimmings to go with the red silky fabric Aunt Lily had brought her.

"Now why exactly did your aunt buy you that glorious fabric?" Eliza smiled mischievously, "You know, I sell a lot of pretty dresses, some even questionable in their modesty, but I have nothing made with that quality of fabric."

Esther glanced at the perpetually busy clinic where she could see her aunt through the glass window writing down appointments and dealing with anxious patients. She was glad she was a midwife and did not work in a clinic or hospital.

"My aunt is hoping that it might attract male attention," Esther laughed with good humor. Although she had no intention of attracting a man, she was amused and touched by her aunt's efforts.

"Like you need the fabric to do that," Eliza snorted out the compliment. "Why does she want you to get married?"

Esther sighed, recalling the reasons her aunt had piled up for the past two years. "Well, she feels I should have more children and one can't do that without a man. She says it is not safe for a woman to live alone, although I can shoot as good as anyone here, and Tall Pine isn't exactly a dangerous area. I mean, poor Sheriff Ben is always looking for trouble so that he has enough work to do," she said, knowing that in reality Colorado had plenty of crime. Tall Pine, for all its beauty and neighborliness, was no exception. "She also feels that if I don't, I will die from a broken heart when Michael leaves me some day." Esther tried to sound nonchalant, but that last reason made her throat feel dry. The thought of

Michael growing up, getting married, having children… well, she wanted that for him, but it also broke her heart to think of him growing up and not being under her protection and care.

Eliza smiled weakly. "Well, I must say that I agree: You will die of a broken heart… that is to say if you ever let him go," she laughed.

Esther chose a flame-red lace that would match the poppy colored fabric, as well as some buttons for Michael's clothing. He was always managing to lose his buttons no matter how tightly she sewed them on. Under her bed she had a Christmas tin filled with buttons so that at a moment's notice she could sew one on to his shirts, coats, and trousers. But the buttons she chose today were made from bone and had carved into them a bull's head. He would ask if they looked like something his father would wear. She winced inwardly, knowing that of course she would say yes. With the buttons and lace in brown paper and placed carefully in her basket on top of the molasses, the two women walked out of the store and past the bakery.

A wave of knee-dropping aromas always circulated from the bakery. The baker, Kyle Lampton, filled the windows with artistic delicacies ranging from spun sugar shaped like white roses to hearty honey-glazed pastries overflowing with sweetened walnuts.

"My goodness, this place always smells so wonderful," Eliza remarked. The bakery door jingled as Kyle, with his massive form, walked out. Upon seeing Eliza, he smiled until his dimples were as deep as canyons.

"Well, Miss Eliza, I thank you, but I must say, my place never smells as good as you." Wiggling his eyebrows with skillful flirtation, Esther couldn't help but smile on behalf of her friend. Kyle Lampton was a respected, successful man, and he was making eyes at Eliza.

A small group of young mothers standing at the corner giggled. Eliza just stared at him blankly as if she did not understand the compliment.

"No, I think your bakery smells better," Eliza said simply with a nod. One might have been discussing the weather and if it were to rain, or not, with how blandly she said it. Kyle was not to be discouraged. He crossed his arms over his barrel chest and took a deliberate step forward. Esther noticed a small mist of flour float off of his shoulders, much how she imagined snow falling off of Saint Nicholas. Saint Nicholas! That is who Kyle Lampton reminded her of.

"Really, huh?" Kyle chuckled. He leaned in a little, inhaling a whiff of Eliza's hair. The young mothers giggled again, and Eliza frowned and leaned back looking confused.

Kyle straightened himself and sighed in delight. "Honey," he stated. "Honey is what you smell like."

"Honey doesn't have a smell," Eliza said flatly, rolling her eyes.

Again Kyle took another step forward, a rather large one, until he was no more than a few inches away from her. "Honey does have a smell and it smells like you, but one has to taste something in order to truly smell it. Wouldn't you agree?" His eyes sparkled with the innuendo.

Esther was glad Michael was not with her, or she would have had to shush poor Kyle for impropriety in front of children. Maybe he was not a good candidate for Saint Nicholas after all.

In any case, she had to admit that she was enjoying the show, although she could not decide who was more entertaining, the impudent, giant Kyle, or the clueless, tiny Eliza.

"Hmm, I never thought of that," Eliza bit her lip in thought, and Esther looked away when Kyle's eyes widened and stared at Eliza's mouth. "Well, it was nice chatting, but I must get going." Eliza spun around and continued walking, leaving Kyle to draw his thick eyebrows into a clump of confusion.

He looked at Esther as if he just now noticed that she existed. "Is she always so—" he paused, searching for a word. He decided to just nod in Eliza's direction as if that explained it all.

Esther nodded. "Keep at it, Mr. Lampton," she encouraged with an amused smile before turning around to catch up with Eliza.

"Why are those girls laughing at me?" Eliza whispered to Esther, sounding hurt. They passed the young mothers who all nodded in polite acknowledgment.

"Do you really not know?" Esther asked, looking at her friend in amazement. "I am no expert on men, and even I could tell what Kyle was doing."

Eliza frowned, slowing her pace a bit. "They are laughing at Kyle?"

"Oh, my dear friend, yes; Kyle was flirting with you... shamelessly."

"Flirting?" Eliza asked incredulously.

Esther squeezed her friend's hand. "It is not an absurd idea Eliza, and yes, he was flirting."

"Flirting," Eliza said slowly, tasting the word on her tongue. She stopped walking and looked up at Esther. "He couldn't have been flirting. It is simply not possible."

Esther sighed. She could not believe that Eliza was so oblivious. "Yes, he was, Eliza, and you treated him like some annoying bug that you brush away."

"Esther, he was not flirting," Eliza insisted, her voice rising just a little.

Esther lips parted; she hesitated before speaking, studying Eliza's face and noting traces of fear.

"Is it so hard for you to believe that a man would flirt with you? Do I really need to put a wine stamp on you to remind you that you have improved with age?"

Eliza's gaze dropped, her chin lowering in pursuit. "It is just not possible, Esther. Kyle is just a silly man who says silly things. He says them to everyone."

"No, he does not, Eliza," Esther protested, feeling both frustrated and sad for her clueless friend.

Eliza looked up, her face firm, and a resolute expression in place. "Kyle Lampton is a handsome and successful man. There is no way in heaven or hell that he was flirting with me, alright?" Eliza said stiffly.

Esther wanted to protest but held her tongue instead. The

thought of fallen hope might be too painful for Eliza, especially if she had experienced it before. Eliza probably did not want to fall for Kyle herself only to discover that he felt nothing for her. So instead, Esther nodded and the two women fell back into walking past the shops, both lost in their own thoughts.

Joseph sat solemnly, hardly aware that the Lieutenant was still talking. His mind was replaying the shot, the kill, the smell of blood, and Jesse's last breath.

"Joseph!" Lieutenant Baldwin practically shouted.

Joseph looked up and straightened himself. "Excuse me Lieutenant, I… I am having a hard time concentrating today," he apologized weakly. He didn't feel like showing the normal respect and admiration he usually felt. Right now a giant hole had settled in his chest. Jesse had been a good man, a fine Ranger. True, he had his flaws. Most Rangers did. Jesse liked his drink and liked his women, but he had a good sense of humor and a love for justice, and he was dead. No family came to his funeral. No wife. No child. Just a few Rangers who were near the area. Such a good man, and no one to witness his farewell to the world.

"Joseph," Lieutenant Baldwin repeated again gently. "I was saying that I want you to take some time off. That's an order."

Joseph scowled and leaned forward. "You blaming me for Jesse's death, Lieutenant?" he asked angrily. Why else would he be ordered to take time off? Rangers never took holidays—or time to relax.

"Joseph, you know I don't blame you for that. Don't make me gush like a woman and tell you that you are one of my finest captains, which you are." Baldwin sighed and leaned back in his chair. "You've never lost a man Joe, always took a bullet to save your partners, but there was nothing you could have done in this case."

"I could have stayed clear of the border."

Baldwin frowned. "You were ordered to go settle the border, Joe. Heavens, I've sent you into the heart of Mexico before. How were you supposed to know you were going to be ambushed?"

Joseph looked down at his calloused hands. His gut had told him to go no further; his instincts had screamed at him. His mother would call it God telling him that danger was ahead, but Joseph didn't feel a man should rely on God's whims. Instinct, however, should never be ignored. It was a mistake he wouldn't make again.

"So why exactly do you want me to take time off, Lieutenant?" he asked, clearing his throat. Might as well hear the reason.

Baldwin tilted his head side to side. "I think, Joe," he pinned Joseph with his gaze. "I think it's about time you retire from the Rangers.

Joseph shot to his feet. "You say you don't blame me and then turn around to tell me that I need to retire!" he shouted, fists clenched. "Rangers are my life, Lieutenant."

Baldwin stood up. "No one is doubting that, Captain; now sit down and breathe before you get all trigger-minded and go storming off."

Joseph narrowed his eyes and slowly sat down. "You've been talking to Jefferson?" he asked wearily, knowing his stepfather kept in contact with the Lieutenant and other captains in regard to Joseph's whereabouts.

Baldwin shook his head. "No, Joe, I haven't. Not for a while," he said as he sat down. "Jefferson is a good man and ain't the kind to coerce me into telling you to quit. I only said what I did because, well, Joseph you are a good man, too. And, I could not help but think at Jesse's funeral how I would hate to see you buried with no legacy. Joe, you are the type of man who I want to shake hands with at Christmas parties and spring festivals. I want to see you with bonny children and a pretty wife."

Joseph partly smiled. "I got no interest in marriage," he replied coldly.

Baldwin grinned. "No Ranger does. The difference, Joseph, is that those Rangers out there, good men that they are, they are parading around like tomcats and spending their free time in saloons. You on the other hand, have remained…"

Joseph raised his eyebrows with amusement as Baldwin struggled for a manly way to say pure. It was known among the Rangers that Joseph, although not very religious, lived a chaste lifestyle. He owed it to his mother's firm and good teachings. Out of respect to her, he kept the standards she taught.

"Remained a good boy?" Joseph said with small humor, despite his sorrow.

Baldwin threw his hands in the air. "You know what I mean. Anyway Joseph, I won't ever take your badge. You've earned it for life, but I think it might be time to hang it up over a dresser and not pinned to a shirt that will eventually be stained with blood."

Joseph remained silent for a bit. It was coincidence that Jeff had said practically the same thing and that his presiding officer was ordering time off. All coincidence, but still hard to ignore.

"I'll take a week off," Joe agreed.

"You'll take a few months off," Baldwin replied with a stern brow. "I don't want to see you until December. Go live the life of a normal man. Flirt with gals, attend boring church parties, live a little. Then if in December you want to stay a Ranger, I will welcome you back and never mention you leaving again. If you want to retire, I will release you with pride and honor."

Joe nodded and stood up. "Very well, Lieutenant. I won't disobey an order."

Baldwin held out his hand and gave Joseph a firm handshake. "Oh and Joe, you may want to visit your parents. I did receive a letter from your mother saying that were you not to visit her she would set fire to my office, or something along those lines."

Joseph smiled thinly and walked out of the room, shutting the door firmly behind him. A flood of emotions stirred within him—anger, sorrow, confusion. He was used to suppressing such emotions. Anger did not help him shoot straight, sorrow muddled his thoughts, and confusion just annoyed him. Maybe some time off would be good, but what was he to do with himself? He would have to stop by home, but he did not want to stay there and be bombarded with Abby's flock of friends, nor his parent's urges to take up ranching. There was Abby. She asked nothing of him, except his company. Something he hadn't been able to give her for some time. His parents couldn't scold him for leaving quickly to visit the family princess. A change of scenery should be enough to clear his mind—there was just one thing he had to do first.

Turning to the outside wall, Joseph slammed his fist, tearing the skin and leaving an indent in the wall. Pain seared through his hand and up his arm, creating an equilibrium between pain of body and pain of spirit. He felt better. Giving a casual nod to a few people staring, Joseph put on his hat and straightened his badge. Next stop, Colorado.

Four

Abby shivered as an icy wind blew through a window cracked open. She clutched the quilt around her shoulders tighter and continued to stare down at the blank sheet of paper that was to be a letter to her parents. What should she write? That it had only been a few weeks and she was ready to come home? That she couldn't control the children who drove her to tears—all except Michael who was her gem—that they seemed hardly interested in her lessons and laughed at her Texan accent?

A high whistle from the kitchen made Abby jump. She had forgotten about the teakettle. Running to the kitchen she realized that she had also forgotten about the potatoes for dinner. They were now burnt and stuck to the bottom of her only pan. The teakettle continued to scream and Abby frantically tried to turn off the stove, without realizing she had dragged a corner of her quilt onto the stove as she reached for the kettle. The smell of burnt cotton reached her before the flames could travel to her arm.

"Oh no!" Abby shrieked, dropping the kettle, shrieking louder when boiling hot water fell all over the floor and her dress. Quickly, she dropped the quilt, her only quilt, and stomped on the small flames. She managed to get them out fairly quickly, but not soon enough to save the corner. The warmest thing she had, the quilt that Will had been kind enough to supply her with, was ruined.

She would once again have no dinner, unless she wanted burnt potatoes for what seemed like the hundredth time, and she was hurt and wet from the boiling water. Abby looked around her. The kitchen was messy and smelled of smoke. She had tried to make curtains from some of her useless dresses, but instead of looking like the elegant white curtains she had imagined, they looked like wispy petticoats. When she then had tried to dye them, they came out splotchy, and now she had pink hands from the dye. She had tried to wash the floors and walls and managed to only spread the dust. All in all, the house looked terrible. It was as if the more she tried, the worse it became.

The wind blew through the cracked window again, cutting viciously into Abby's wet skin.

"Stupid, stupid, stupid!" Abby cried suddenly. Picking up the quilt, she marched into the sitting room. She didn't know what she was calling stupid—herself maybe, the situation, the house… possibly all three. All she knew was that she couldn't do this. She did not even know how to light a proper fire, although she had tried. She was starving—already her skirts were looser—and she couldn't teach. Maybe she really was only a pretty, empty-headed useless girl. She should leave and go back home to Texas where a life of ease awaited her. Will was still at the accident in the nearby mining town, but as soon as he was back he could drive her to Denver where she could start making her way back home.

Shame suddenly filled Abby. She would have to go back and face her parents, having only survived hardship for a few weeks. A few blooming weeks. The hereditary stubbornness in Abby began to rise up in her chest. She couldn't go back just yet, even if she froze and starved, she had to at least do this for a year. A year was an honorable amount of time, as her father put it. Jutting her chin with determination, Abby wrapped the now-wet-and-burnt quilt around her and walked back to her crowded writing desk. She sat down with chattering teeth. What should she write her parents? Did she lie and say everything was going well and that they had misjudged her? No, she could not lie. Abby knew she had many vices, but lying was not one of them.

"Oh for golly sakes!" Abby tapped the dry ink quill on the desk. "I can't tell them how awful it is," she moaned, "and yet, I need to tell someone." Abby sighed and folded her hands under her chin, her elbows resting on the desk. She needed help, divine help, not to mention someone in whom to confide. "Dear Lord," she began, her voice quivering with homesickness and fatigue, "I'd like to believe that it was you who sent me out here. I agreed because I believed that this was your plan for me, that you guided my parents. Is that true or was I just caught up in emotion and a need to prove my worth?"

She wiped away an escaping tear. She did have a desire to prove her worth, and she wanted to feel special. Why was that? Why did she constantly parade in the fanciest dresses and say the silliest things? Did she really need her parents' approval so much? Hadn't they always shown and expressed their love to her?

"Really Lord, I don't know what I am doing here. I can't teach, I can't clean, and no one talks to me. The women scamper away with their children as soon as school is done. I am starving…" the tears were flowing freely now from self-pity. She didn't want to feel sorry for herself, but she couldn't seem to help it. All she wanted was respect from others and maybe from herself, too, and yet she couldn't even get that. Did God respect her, or was He laughing at her like everyone else seemed to be doing?

"Please help me. I feel like I am doing everything wrong, and I don't know what to do," she pleaded, tossing down the ink quill. Before she could continue her prayerful ranting a clear voice echoed in her mind and bathed her in warmth.

I am helping you.

Abby's tears stopped and she looked around. It was not a spoken voice, just one inside her mind and heart. Again it repeated, *I am helping you.* Abby took a deep, steady breath, feeling suddenly calm and at peace. God was helping her—even if she did not quite know how. She looked to where she had tossed the ink quill. She reached over to remove it from her beloved Bible that had her name engraved on it. The pages fell open to where she had been reading last. It was about Joseph in Egypt, a young cocky boy who boasted proudly of his prophetic dreams and was confident in his father's favoritism towards him. Then in a blink all was taken from him, and his own brothers sold him as a slave. Chewing her lip, Abby wondered if Joseph felt like she did now. A life of ease suddenly replaced by a foreign and hard one. Did he know that God was simply preparing him for greater things? Happier things?

Abby stroked the beloved page. Joseph never faltered. He always remained true and positive towards God no matter what.

"Alright Lord," she said, resolution in her voice. "I promise not to whine. I promise to take whatever task you give me." She ran a hand through her loose brown curls. "However, if you find in your will to send someone my way who may help, I would not object," she laughed and concluded her prayer with an "Amen."

As she began to close the Bible, she caught Joseph's name one more time. Suddenly it hit her. Joseph! Her brother Joseph always told her that hearing her trivial problems helped keep his mind off the bad things that he saw in his work. Maybe he would even visit. She had asked him in a letter before she left if he would come see her, but Joseph was always so busy being a Ranger that she doubted he would make the journey. Perhaps another letter explaining her sorrows would encourage him to do so.

"Thank you, Lord," she whispered. "You gave me peace and reminded me that you know more than I."

The children all screamed, save a few of the boys who were immersed in chasing a large fat rat. Abby herself stood on her desk. She'd never seen a rodent so big. Her ranch back home had about a half dozen cats, so rats were scarce. Several of the children were crying, scared that the rat would bite off their toes. Michael was one of the boys chasing the rat, the classroom broom in his hand as he leaped and bounded after the speedy rodent.

"Don't you worry, Teacher, I'll fight it for you," Michael

reassured her. Even in Abby's fear, she found his choice of words sweet.

"Just chase it out of the building, Michael," she yelled. "Don't kill it!" The last thing Abby wanted was to take care of a dead rat, and she knew she could not ask one of the children to throw out a dead and possibly squashed rodent.

"Teacher, watch out!" Michael cried out as the rat scurried around her desk. Abby screeched and Michael swung at the rat, trying to reach it before the creature dodged under the desk. The children were now completely out of control. Some of the boys had used the chaos as an opportunity to create a battle of paper, pebbles, and other little things that they threw back and forth at one another. Most of the girls were now crying hysterically, and Abby felt very near to breaking down herself.

"Please, everyone calm down," Abby tried to shout, but her voice came out more as a squeak. Michael was on his belly trying to scoot out the rat with the end of the broom. "Everyone, please," Abby tried again. Little Daisy Gable had been hit on the head with a pebble and was now crying and holding her head. Abby swallowed a lump in her throat. She would have to remove herself from the desk in order to help Daisy.

"Hold on, sweetie, I am coming," Abby reassured her as she took a step timidly off the desk and then another. Just as her feet touched the ground Michael poked the rat again, forcing it to run out from under the desk and over Abby's feet. Abby squealed and involuntarily jumped. Her landing was not only ungraceful, but off balance; before she knew it, Abby was on the ground, her skirt and petticoats over her head and her bottom throbbing.

"Teacher, are you alright?" Michael cried out. Michael reached out to touch Abby who mistook his hand for the slimy rat. She screamed, hitting Michael's hand and throwing him off balance as well. Abby was ready to either scream or cry as she wrestled with her petticoats while trying to help Michael stand on his feet when a strong voice shook the schoolhouse.

"Everyone in your seats *now!*" Will roared, arms crossed over his wide chest and his longish hair combed back, making him look older and stronger than the tired unshaved boy Abby had met. "Michael, help up Miss Abigail," he ordered as the children sat down in unison. Michael helped Abby to her feet. Her petticoats fell to the ground and Abby knew her face was burning with embarrassment. Will had seen her bloomers. He'd seen her lose control of the classroom. She did not know if she would have cared as much had this been Esther or one of the other parents, but Will…that was too much to handle. She had so hoped when he returned that he would be stunned by her success, and instead he returned looking handsome and mature while she looked diminutive in her now baggy clothing and the students seemed no more advanced than when she had started a few weeks ago.

Will looked at Abby, his eyes boring into her like a hot poker. Suddenly Abby felt exposed. Will seemed to be examining her, measuring her by some unseen standard.

"Miss Abigail, are you alright?" Will asked steadily. Abby nodded; she must look like a mess, and why was he looking so sharp?

"I am fine Pastor Will. Thank you." She smoothed her skirt and folded her hands calmly in front of her as if nothing chaotic or out of the ordinary had happened. The rat now scurried past the desk and out the front door through Will's legs. Abby cleared her throat. The rat did not seem as big as it had when she had first seen it take refuge under her desk. "Is there anything I can do for you, Pastor Will?" Abby asked almost sternly. She wanted him to leave, and yet she wanted him to stay. It was so lonely living by the schoolhouse; all the parents left quickly after they fetched their young ones and Abby had gone days without having a conversation with an adult.

Will walked down the small aisle that separated the boys and girls. "I thought I would stop by and see how things are going." He now stood in front of Abby at a respectful distance, but close enough that Abby could smell the pine on his windblown skin.

"Well, I appreciate your concern, but things are under control now so please don't feel the need to stay if it is not convenient,"

Abby looked up at him, trying to hold his gaze and waiting for him to look away as a gentleman would. He didn't look away. Will took a small step closer and Abby had to clench her toes to keep herself from stepping back.

"I think I will stay," he said, his voice low, almost in a whisper. Abby's lips parted but no words came out. Will couldn't stay and listen to her teach. She still had not figured out how to keep the children's attention. Had she not had enough embarrassment for one day? Will seemed to sense her apprehensiveness because he grinned mischievously and then spun around to go sit in one of the desks dwarfed by his size.

Abby wanted to smack that smile off his face. He was not here to offer support. He wanted to validate his poor opinion of her by witnessing her stutter and fall over a lesson. Abby's jaw tightened and she turned around so that he wouldn't see her glaring. She walked to her desk and picked up the lesson plan that she had carefully written out the night before. It was now time for mathematics, a subject that Abby herself often disliked, and one that her students seemed to despise. Abby bit her lip. She had to teach differently today if she wasn't to make a fool of herself. She had to inspire these children with the desire to learn, but how could she? These were country children; their lives revolved around food, farms, and animals.

Suddenly an idea came to Abby. Why had she not thought of this before? Often her mother, in order to illustrate a point to Abby as a child, would use Abby's dolls as examples. As Abby matured, her mother would use society and social events as examples. Smiling to herself Abby turned around, looked at Will smugly, and then at the classroom.

"Mathematics," she announced and was answered with groans of boredom. Abby smiled and waited for the moans to subside. "Mathematics," Abby said again. "Why do we learn math?" she asked and was rewarded by confused expressions.

"'Cause we are supposed to," Timmy Wilson answered with an exaggerated sigh.

"And why are we supposed to?" Abby asked, walking down the aisle. Suzanne Harrison raised her hand eagerly. Abby nodded in her direction, "Yes Suzy, what do you think?"

"'Cause it makes us smarter," the young girl announced proudly with a little lisp.

"It does make us smarter, but that's not why it's so important. We learn mathematics because it can help us a lot. Let me explain," she looked at Michael for reassurance, and he flashed her one of his charming grins. "Let's say Michael here grows up and has twenty horses. Twenty beautiful thoroughbred horses that run like the wind."

Michael smiled and straightened in his seat. "Do I got a ranch, teacher?"

"You sure do—a beautiful big ranch with lots of cattle and chickens, but these horses are famous throughout the state. And one day, these bad men hear about your horses and decide to steal some." Abby paused for dramatic effect. The entire class was focused on her now. "And so Michael comes out one morning to feed and water his horses, but instead of twenty horses there are only eight."

"The bad men took the other ones?" Daisy asked, looking upset by the news.

"They did, and so Michael puts on his leather boots, straps on his belt with a big shiny buckle, and rides out to find his horses and take them back." Abby lifted her eyebrows with a smile. "Now," she said slowly, glancing briefly at Will who was still staring at her intently, "how many horses is Michael looking for?"

"You mean how many horses did the bad guys take?" Michael asked.

"That's right," Abby nodded, pleased that she had everyone's attention. "Now do the problem and the first person who has it right can come write it on the chalkboard."

The entire class quickly began scribbling. In a few seconds Henry Thompson, one of the older boys, raised his hand. Abby lifted her eyebrows in surprise; she rarely received participation from the older children.

"Henry, please come up," she said, nodding towards the chalkboard. Henry stood up proudly, his twelve-year-old body strutting like a man as he walked up and wrote out the problem.

"You see, all you got to do is minus eight horses from twenty. So Michael needs to find twelve horses," he explained clearly.

Abby thought her buttons would burst from her blouse. She was so proud that she began to applaud. "Well done! Henry that is perfect!" she cried out, although she didn't know why this meant so much to her. She fancied maybe it was because it made her look smart and capable in front of Will, but truth be told, all she could think about was how Henry would be able to tell his parents that he solved a problem in front of the entire class.

The rest of the students copied Abby in applauding Henry's answer. The boy blushed fiercely as he walked back to his desk, smiling all the way. Abby spun around to the class leaning forward, her hands on her hips.

"Alright, shall we do another problem?" she asked encouragingly. The students shouted their compliance, little Daisy raising her hand.

"Use me, Teacher, use me," she begged, nearly falling out of her seat. Abby practically giggled with excitement and pleasure, but caught herself with one swift glance at Will, whose deep auburn hair was falling into his blue eyes. If he wasn't so disrespectful, she might even think him a handsome man.

"Alright, Miss Daisy, let's pretend it is your birthday and you have to make a cake," Abby began.

"What kind of cake?" Michael asked. Abby sighed. Michael was a child who wanted to know every detail for everything.

"Well, it has ten layers with thick cream and strawberries between each one. The frosting is rose petal pink," Abby described, receiving a gasp from every young girl. She wondered if she could make such a cake. *Maybe Esther could help?* "And on the top are berries arranged like a heart. It is the most beautiful birthday cake that ever was," Abby said dramatically.

Some of the boys chuckled but not rudely.

Abby continued, "While Daisy is making the batter, she realizes that she needs three cups of flour, but she only has a measuring tin that holds a quarter of a full cup. So how many times does Daisy need to fill up that tin in order to have three cups of flour?"

Abby had to walk her students through the tricky fraction problem, all the while describing the cake and the make-believe birthday party. After that it was analogies with corn, days of rain, knights fighting dragons, and Indians hunting buffalo. She managed to teach all of her mathematics lesson while keeping the children entertained. After math was history in which she had the children act out the French Revolution. Will even raised his hand like a child to participate. Abby was a bit taken aback at his display of being a victim of the guillotine, as it was rather gruesome how he fell to the ground twitching, but the children seemed to love it.

Finally, Abby heard the arrival of parents. She was tired, sweaty, and ruffled, but she felt good. The high energy of a full day's work filled her body and soul with satisfaction. She realized she had been teaching these children like a stuffy professor would lecture college students at Harvard when in fact, these were children who breathed mountain air, worked in the soil, and had calloused hands at a young age. They needed to learn in ways that were useful and entertaining.

"Alright children, have a good weekend. I will see you on Monday," Abby announced as she dismissed the class.

"Hopefully on Sunday," Will muttered, standing beside her. Abby jumped at his deep voice, and Will chuckled. "Scared you, did I?"

"No, I just didn't notice you approach," Abby stuttered.

"Ah, didn't notice me? My, you know how to make a man feel good about himself," Will teased.

Abby looked at him with an arched eyebrow. "That is not what I meant."

"So you do notice me?" Will grinned.

Abby laughed wirily. Will was certainly not a gentleman; in

fact, she thought he actually liked making her feel uncomfortable. "What do you mean by asking if I notice you when you have not even been around these past few weeks?" she scolded. "Did my novice teaching scare you off?"

Will quirked an eyebrow. "So you have noticed that I've been gone?"

Abby rolled her eyes playfully. "Yes, though I'm sure you didn't mind being absent from me."

"My absence was unfortunately extremely necessary." He sighed and ran a hand through his hair.

Abby eyed it appreciatively. She'd never seen hair the color of deep rich cedar wood before.

"Anyway, there was an explosion in a mining town near Denver. They had no pastor and there were a lot of injuries and some deaths. So I had to spend the last few weeks arranging funerals and such."

Abby's eyebrows tilted. Poor Will! She thought teaching was stressful, or being a Texas Ranger, but Will's job was a combination of both. He dealt with the sorrow and the rough stuff of life, but where Joseph used a gun, Will had to use words.

"Oh my goodness, Pastor! I am awfully sorry; it must have been tough dealing with all that. How are you doing now? You holding up alright?"

Will shot her a puzzled expression. "Am I doing alright?" he asked, surprised by the question. Usually young women, older ones, too, wanted to tell Will their problems and get spiritual advice, which he loved—after all his calling was to bring people closer to their Maker—but he could not remember, save Esther, when the he had been asked how he was doing.

"I—I am fine," he answered slowly, still processing the schoolteacher's question.

"You sure about that? Because if I dealt with funerals I would be a wreck."

Will nodded. "Yeah, I'm fine. It is good to be back, though. Oh, speaking of being back, I will still be using the schoolhouse

Saturday nights," he grinned sheepishly, "to practice. I get nervous."

Abby bit her lip to keep down a laugh. "You practice... in the schoolhouse? That is adorable."

Will narrowed his eyes. "You are welcome to come hear my practices."

Abby's smile wilted a bit. Was he flirting? Teasing? Goodness, she wished she could tell the difference.

"A pastor who is nervous speaking in front of people and needs to practice still surprises me." Abby shook her head unbelievingly. "What is more ironic than that?" she teased.

Will shrugged. "Probably a spoiled Texas girl teaching in a Colorado mountain town," Will suggested with a smile.

Abby laughed and held up her hands in defeat. "Alright then, let's say we are even —and by the way, I am not, nor was I ever, spoiled. I just like to think I was *privileged*," Abby held up her head proudly with a small smirk on her face. She was rewarded by Will's rich laughter.

"Privileged, huh? Well Miss *Privileged* Abigail, don't be alarmed when you see someone in the schoolhouse tomorrow evening. It will just be me." He put his hands in his pockets and lifted his eyebrows at the sound of paper crinkling. "Oh, I almost forgot— Bill Thompson, Henry's father, gave this to me to hand off to you. He is our new official mailman, although he tends to delegate the passing on of letters." He handed her an abused-looking envelope that Abby took eagerly. It was from Joseph! A sudden eagerness to read the letter overcame her. It was probably a lighthearted response to her complaints, maybe some good advice even. Joseph always had good advice.

"Family?" Will asked.

Abby nodded, stroking the Texas stamp. Was it just her or did the letter smell like cattle and tortillas? Homesickness filled her with threatening tears that she quickly blinked away. "Yes, it is from my family. I do hope they are all well," she said softly, lowering her eyes so Will wouldn't see the mist in them.

Will opened his mouth to say something, but stopped as his

gaze flickered to the entrance. At his silence, Abby looked up to see him staring sheepishly at Esther, her lovely figure looking radiant, and her hair hanging loose in romantic waves down her back. Abby almost sighed out loud; she missed looking good with well fitted dresses and pink cheeks. She glanced at Will's riveted face, and a strange feeling began to sprout in her. She did not like how he looked at Esther, did not like it one bit. Her skin grew hot and she desperately wanted Will to look at her, to pay attention to her.

My goodness Abigail, she thought to herself. *You are indeed very spoiled if you don't like sharing the attention of a simple pastor boy.* Straightening her posture she walked over to Esther.

⚘

Esther saw that Abigail had lost weight, an alarming amount of weight in such a short amount of time. She also saw the dark circles settled under her eyes. Guilt seized Esther; she had been wanting to invite the little teacher for dinner or merely just check up on her. She'd thought herself too busy; busyness was man's excuse for not serving others. Esther couldn't imagine Christ looking at one of the lepers and saying that He was too busy to heal him, and yet Esther had found herself too busy to visit an obviously struggling young woman. Hadn't she herself been young and alone?

"Abby!" Esther exclaimed as the teacher approached her. "Michael was just telling me how fun your class was today."

Abby beamed. "Well, I am glad, although I must say that I don't know what I would do without Michael. He is always so helpful and happy, not to mention he helped chase out a giant rat today." Abby patted Michael's back appreciatively. He grinned and tugged on Esther's hand.

"Pastor Will cut off my head today, Mom," he suddenly announced with the excitement to tell a good story.

"What?" Esther laughed and looked inquiringly at Abby. Will had now walked over, making Abby shift self-consciously.

Why was she self-conscious?

Did she have chalk on her face?

"Miss Abigail had us act out the French Revolution," he explained. "I was Robespierre near the end of our demonstration and I'm afraid I enjoyed it a little too much," Will chuckled. Esther laughed softly, not missing Abby's keen interest in her and Will's interaction. She decided to be friendly, but not too friendly, to Will just in case Abby did have a bit of liking toward him.

"Abby, how are you doing with groceries? Town is not too far for walking, but one still needs a cart to carry groceries and such," Esther asked not only to truly inquire about Abby, but also to remind the inexperienced pastor that this girl needed some sort of transportation and payment for food. It worked because Will suddenly gasped and ran his hand through his hair.

"Ach! Miss Abigail, I nearly forgot. I got you some more food— flour, sugar, eggs, and such in my wagon. You get paid next week and maybe with that you can look into getting a horse. The school house already has a cart that I can show you how to hook up."

Abby's lips drifted in a half smile not seeming too excited about the groceries. Esther felt her forehead crinkle with concern. Something was going on with Abigail, either something private or embarrassing since she had not spoken of it. Abby had earned herself the quick reputation of being quite the talker. Parents had to practically run to keep from talking too long. Not that Abby wasn't enjoyable to talk to—everyone agreed that she was friendly and bright—but by the time mothers picked up their children they were having to hurry back home to start dinner, feed the animals, and attend to all the other chores that needed doing before nightfall. As such, she tended to speak quickly as if desperate for adult company, which is why Abigail suddenly growing quiet struck Esther as odd.

"Do you need help storing the food Abby?" Esther offered. "Michael and I could help you if—"

"No!" Abby suddenly said louder than she meant. She immediately bowed her head. "I—I mean no, thank you, I wouldn't want to inconvenience you." She turned to Will red-faced and white-knuckled from squeezing her hands together. "If you could just leave them outside my door that would be most helpful."

"Are you sure, Miss Abigail? I would be more than pleased to—"

"No!" Abby interrupted again. "I would prefer if you just left them outside the door.

Will and Esther shared a quick worried glance before Will nodded curtly and excused himself to "get right to it." Esther smiled and gently placed her hand on Abby's arm.

"How are you doing, Abigail? Truly?" Esther asked, her voice low and compassionate. Abby opened her mouth and tears threatened to roll down her cheeks.

"Daisy! Billy!" Eliza called out from outside the schoolhouse. Abby quickly dabbed her eyes and plastered on a smile, as Eliza's petite body scurried up to collect the two children.

"Their mama isn't feeling too well again, Esther," Eliza explained. "I was worried until she said that the smell of eggs makes her vomit," she laughed with a knowing wink, "and then she stood up—don't get me wrong, she has done very well hiding it—but Esther, she has got to be at least six months along, possibly more with how natural skinny she is. Her belly was swollen nice and round."

Esther's face lit up in delight. "Really? That's wonderful! Has Mrs. Gable said anything yet?"

Eliza shook her head. "No, after the two miscarriages I think she is afraid to even admit to it."

Esther saw Abby trying to follow the conversation with confusion. Poor girl had no idea what they were talking about.

"Mrs. Gable is from Florida. She and her husband moved out here so he could start his own business. He is our blacksmith and doing well, but his wife Sally Gable has suffered two miscarriages since she moved here," Esther explained to her.

"Oh, I see," Abby nodded, "and what does that have to do with eggs making her vomit?"

Esther chuckled. "Some woman get sick the first few months of pregnancy and certain smells can send them hurling outside. Some poor women, like Sally, stay sick their whole pregnancy. It was the same when I was pregnant with Michael; hardly anything stayed in my stomach and the smell of boiled potatoes made me throw up every time."

Abby smiled grimly. The smell of boiled potatoes was making her want to vomit, too, since that was all she had eaten for the past several weeks. She wanted to talk more and find out the details about Mrs. Gable, but as always, Eliza had to rush the children off, and Esther needed to get going, and so in a matter of minutes the children were gone, the parents were gone, and even Will, after leaving the groceries at her front door, had left.

Esther spread the hot glaze of sugar, butter and cream over the sweet rolls wrapped tightly around glazed walnuts, raisins, and even some coconut. Michael sat on the counter swinging his legs to and fro with an intense gaze on the rolls.

"So these aren't for us?" he asked again for the hundredth time. Esther laughed out loud and planted a smacking kiss on his head.

"How many times do I have to tell you that they are for Miss Abigail?" she said, handing him the bowl and spoon to lick. Michael shrugged and began scraping out the bowl.

"Well then, why are you making these and not cookies? You always make these for Christmas, and it is not Christmas." He looked at his mother hopefully, "Is it almost Christmas?" he asked.

Esther shook her head with a sad expression. "No; we still have all of autumn to get through," she reminded him.

Michael sighed and resumed licking the spoon. "Aunt Lily and Uncle Tim are going on a trip after Halloween. Can we go on a trip after Christmas?"

"Aunt Lily and Uncle Tim are traveling for their anniversary. That is a very special event."

"It can be our anniversary," Michael suggested.

Esther smiled and stroked his chin. "I'll think about it," she said. The truth was that Esther did not want to travel, nor did she have the funds to do so. Still, just because she liked the safety and tranquility of Tall Pine didn't mean she should rob her son of experiences. The thought of leaving, however, even for a small holiday, sent a jolt of fear through her.

Esther's forehead dented with a frown. She had left the East had she not? With a new baby and a murky past, she had jumped into the unknown. Why was the thought of travel scary? Had she become too settled and content in her habitual ways? Maybe she was getting old while still young.

As these thoughts mingled in her head, Michael suddenly jumped down and wrapped his arms around her trim waist. Warmth filled Esther's heart, chasing away her fears and replacing them with the faith found in love.

"What's that for, honey?" she asked, twirling her son's curls in her fingers.

"Because I love you." He eyed the rolls, "Do you think Miss Abigail will share?" he asked with a mischievous grin. Esther answered by tickling him in the ribs and sending him off in joyful shrieks of laughter.

It was just dusk when Esther pulled the wagon to the front of Abby's humble house. A small light burned from inside. Good, Abby was still up.

"Can I carry the rolls, please?" Michael asked, jumping from the wagon like a squirrel. Esther nodded, lowering herself down and passing the pan to Michael.

"Keep the dish towel in place so you don't burn your hands," Esther instructed, placing a hand behind his back and leading him towards the door. Michael nodded and walked slowly forward like he was in a wedding procession. Esther stopped at the door and gave it a firm knock. Within seconds the door swung open. Abby stood in her nightgown, red faced and tear streaked, clutching a letter. She startled upon seeing Esther, and a small sob escaped her lips.

"Oh, you came to see me?" she cried.

"Abby, what in heaven's name is wrong?" Esther took a step forward, but Abby stopped her by walking out and shutting the door.

"I am sorry Esther, but you can't see it… it's awful," she cried.

Esther frowned and Michael held up the rolls, their thick aroma rising up through the checkered cloth that covered them. Abby's sobs ceased and her knees buckled. Esther grabbed her elbow bracing the slight body. "Abby, are you unwell? You need to let me in," she demanded.

Abby nodded in defeat and pushed the door open. Michael whistled as the three walked in, and Abby began to cry again as Esther lowered the schoolteacher onto a rocking chair and looked around. The house was well built, with fairly new wood floors and glass windows, but the place looked as if a tornado had gone through it. There were pink splotchy clothes hanging on the windows, the floor had sticky stains and the place smelled like burnt potatoes.

A sudden realization dawned on Esther. Abby no doubt had lived a privileged life, possibly with servants and cooks. She may not know how to properly clean or cook, which would explain her weight loss and the abundance of potato peels in the kitchen. Esther continued to look around. There were no vases of flowers, no pictures in frames or books piled neatly on top of a lace doily. All in all, there was nothing that spoke of a woman living here. She turned to the ashamed Abby and walked over to her; kneeling by the chair she held back an amused smile and squeezed Abigail's hand.

"Abby, why didn't you say you were struggling?" she asked.

Abby wiped her eyes.

"Because you were busy. Everyone is always so busy here. No one has time to talk unless it is over quilting, or canning, or harvesting honey, and I don't know how to do any of those things."

Esther ached for Abby as she remembered herself being alone and friendless. How nice it had been when Eliza pulled her into social circles, or when other women invited her to soap making. Yet no one had done this for the little schoolteacher, probably because she did seem so well off in all her laces.

"I don't have a horse or cart, and I'm not used to the walking all these women can do," she sighed, steadying her breath. "I get paid much later than I expected, so there is nothing I can get in town anyway," she withheld a whimper that turned into a light cough. Michael sighed impatiently, clearly not understanding the crisis.

"Michael," Esther began, "could you go put one of those rolls on a plate for Miss Abigail and pour her a glass of milk. You may have one, too," she winked.

Michael nodded, carrying the rolls into the kitchen and placing them on the table.

"The milk is in the ice box underneath—"

She heard the icebox open and close with a thud.

"He is pretty good at finding his way around," Esther shrugged. Michael probably knew his way around this house better than Abby did, Esther thought to herself.

"Yes, of course he is," Abby said, bowing her head. "He probably knows how to cook and clean better than I do, too."

Esther gave a helpless shrug, not bothering to deny it. "Abby, have you been hungry this whole time?"

Abby cleared her throat and leaned back against the chair. "Well… yes. All I know is how to peel and boil potatoes and even that I can't do too well. I've never been one to clean much besides folding clothes, and we had the money to buy things like curtains. I didn't have to make them." She looked down at the crumpled letter in her hands.

"A while ago I wrote to my brother, telling him about coming to Tall Pine," Abby looked up to see Michael bringing a small plate with a large sweet sticky roll and a glass of milk. Esther took it from him and handed it to Abby.

"Abby, could Michael have some of your milk? I will replace it, of course," Esther asked. Abby had half the roll in her mouth; she was in absolute delight.

"Oh please, help yourself. This is delicious, by the way. I mean, I have never tasted anything like it!" Abby exclaimed, taking another bite and sighing with pleasure. Esther was silent for a moment, letting Abby enjoy her roll. "Anyway," Abby continued before taking a long drink of milk, "I wrote to him and then today I received this letter and he is coming to stay with me for a while. He said he was leaving right away and so I reckon he will be here sometime next week and…." she bit her lip. "Esther I can't have him come here—not when my place looks like a chicken coop, and all I can feed him is soggy potatoes." She took another gulp of milk and looked down at her empty plate. Esther held out her hand for the dish. Abby hadn't even left any crumbs on it.

"Do you want another?" she asked. Abby nodded and handed her the plate. Esther stood up, taking the glass as well. Michael was in the kitchen cutting himself another giant roll and licking his fingers.

"Did you need more milk, love?" Esther asked. Michael nodded and handed her his cup.

"This place is pretty messy, Momma," he whispered, taking the glass of milk. "Are you going to help her clean it?"

Esther glanced through the doorway to where Abigail was sitting quietly. "Did you bring your books like I told you to?" she asked, lowering her voice. Michael nodded.

"They are in the bag I brought, and some toys, too."

"Good boy, I am going to help, but it shouldn't take long," she said optimistically. The house was small and Esther hoped that as such it made the mess look bigger than it was.

Abby was reading the letter again when Esther came out and handed her another roll with milk.

"You are close to your brother," Esther remarked. It wasn't a question. Abby nodded and took the plate. She began eating, slower this time, although the growling in her stomach ached for her to eat more quickly.

"We have the same mother, but my father is his stepfather. Joseph's own father was killed when he was around ten years old."

"Sickness?" Esther asked. It was the most likely to assume.

Abby shook her head. "No, he was shot; he was a Texas Ranger, as is my brother."

"A dangerous occupation." Esther was surprised at hearing Abby's brother was a Texas Ranger. She imagined this Joseph to be like Abigail, thin with translucent skin and silky brown hair, hardly meeting the physical standard of a Texas Ranger.

"Very dangerous," Abby nodded, her eyes briefly clouding. "My parents are always asking him to stop. Joseph is so capable and as such gets chosen for some of the most rough and dangerous missions. He has seen many gruesome things, and I fear it is hardening him."

"Hardening?" Esther asked. She was suddenly intrigued. Her own experience had at first hardened her, making her bitter and pessimistic.

"Well, Joseph is still Joseph, easy to talk to with a good sense of humor, but his relationships with people are so distant. Even with me he has become more formal, and he hardly ever speaks flattery to any lady. Honestly, I think besides me, and of course my parents, he doesn't think much of anyone. He has seen too much bad to believe that there is good." Abby sighed, surprised that she had just shared the inner workings of her brother. "Sorry," she apologized sheepishly. "I don't mean to gossip about my own brother. It is just that it's been a while since I have really talked to another woman, and even then my conversations were..." she paused, glancing away with a look of shame, "stupid is what they were—frivolous and shallow."

Esther couldn't help but laugh. Abby was not exactly a serene woman, but Esther found her blunt humility and lack of guile very endearing.

"Abby, not every conversation needs to be full of depth and insight. Personally, I think conversation is like food. For the most part it should be healthy with good vegetables, breads, and meats," she stood up, rolling her neck as she always did when about to do a difficult task, "yet there are times when one must indulge on sweet rolls, hot chocolate, and cake." She looked around her wondering where to start.

"I feel so ashamed, Esther. I don't want Joseph to see all this."

She waved haphazardly at the room.

"He won't," Esther replied with confidence. "Abby, this needs to become your home, and a woman's home is her canvas, her outlet for creativity. So we are going to clean and organize. Then I will look at your groceries and write down some simple recipes for you, and if you want I can come over every Sunday and cook something with you until you get the knack of it." Esther looked at the windows peeking out to the darkening meadow as the sun said farewell. "This week, make a home. Go to town. I will take you and pick out some fabric that is to your liking, then I'll make you some curtains. Pick flowers and set them on your table; arrange your books prettily. Do you need some books? They offer great company."

Abby chuckled, "If there is one thing I will always have it is books. I have every Jane Austen, the complete works of the Bronte sisters, *North and South*... I love Elizabeth Gaskell."

"Shakespeare?"

Abby lifted her chin. "Of course."

"Well then, you have all the components to make a home."

"Make a home?" Abby asked with a small gleam in her eye. The way Esther spoke about housework and cooking made her suddenly excited about the two things that she dreaded most.

"Yes, a *home*."

Five

Abby looked down at her plate one more time. It was simple: boiled carrots with honey and raisins, chicken roasted to a golden brown and sliced squash that had been lightly fried. Plain as the meal was, she had made it. There had been some trial and error. When frying the slices of squash, she had stood too close to the stove and burnt the sleeves of her blouse. Half the carrots she had to throw out and then scrub the burnt pan. Still, she felt an enormous amount of pride for the little plate, and even more pride at the delicious smell and the clean kitchen behind her. Esther had instructed her to wash each dish when she was done before moving on to the next task.

"Dishes are like an avalanche," she had told Abby. "If you don't put a stop to them at one dish, they keep growing and growing."

Abby nestled herself into her chair and inhaled the steam. Then she bowed her head and gave a prayer of thanks. Thanks for Esther, thanks for the beautiful soft blue fabric that would become her curtains. Then she gave thanks that Joseph was coming. Now that her little house was clean, organized, and pretty, she felt confident that she could keep it up and impress her brother. She was excited to have his company. Joseph was gone so much that any visit seemed like Christmas, and the fact that he was traveling all the way to Tall Pine was touching.

After finishing her dinner, Abby washed her plate and cup, dried them, and put them up in their proper places. Sleep was sounding very good. Abby went to lock the front door when she thought of Will. It was Saturday night; he should be in the schoolhouse. And, he had hinted several times about her visiting him there in return for his visits to her class the past few days. But she couldn't imagine simply waltzing in. What would she say?

Hi, I think you are mighty handsome and a fine figure of a man.

No, she definitely needed an excuse or a reason before walking in.

An idea popped into her head. Esther had left some cookies for her. Will would most definitely want one, and it would be a good reason to see what he was really up to. So, wrapping up some of the cookies, Abby donned her shawl and walked the few yards to the schoolhouse.

Will was pacing back and forth, his hair disheveled and the top few buttons of his shirt were opened. Abby felt herself blush even though he had not yet noticed her. Was this a good idea? Will was obviously not interested in her. He was saving his heart for Esther, and who wouldn't? She was perfect!

Still, he had flirted with her, although Abby imagined he could just as easily have been trying to be friendly. She was obviously not Will's type. Certainly not a pastor's type. Abby took a step back. She may like Will, but she had her pride. By bringing him cookies she certainly did not want to appear as if she were trying to inveigle him into emotions he did not have. She had just about decided to leave when Will's sermon caught her attention.

"And so, if you do not repent, you shall be cast off, and that means God will withhold all His blessings from you. Remember that God is just, and does not look upon your sins as lightly as you do. Only through repentance can you escape His wrath." Will altered his voice with every other word, loud then soft, firm then gentle, testing what tone sounded better. Abby frowned as he continued on about wrath and justice. Soon she found herself walking up the steps and into the classroom. She had heard only a few of Will's sermons and they were all like this… harsh. She seldom saw people who looked like they actually enjoyed the sermons, save the young women who batted their eyelashes at Will, especially Rachel the big-bosomed blond who fanned herself suggestively.

Abby frowned. She had not been properly introduced to Rachel, but she was not sure if she exactly wanted to be.

The wood floor creaked, and Will's head shot up.

"Oh, it's you," he laughed nervously. "You scared me."

Abby shrugged guiltily. "Sorry. I heard you from the house and wanted to see if you were hungry for some cookies." She handed a cookie to him, which he took gladly.

"Well, this must be the night for exchanging gifts," he grinned, setting down the cookie for a brief moment while he disappeared behind the desk, bending down to uncover a basket.

"What do you mean?" Abby asked intrigued. She gasped with delight when Will held up a beautiful orange kitten.

"I was hoping you would still be up. I didn't want to wake you before I left." He handed her the green-eyed kitten, which Abby held up to her face as she stroked the soft fur.

"My cat back at home had three kittens. I've given two away and I thought this girl would help with the rat problem." He grinned at Abby's obvious delight.

"Will, I don't know what to say other than this is the greatest gift anyone has ever given me," she said. She did mean it. The little miracle in her arms was not just a rat hunter but a companion to remedy her loneliness and proof, like Esther's rolls, that someone had thought of her.

Will blushed and looked away. "Ahh, it's nothing really." He cleared his throat and walked back over to the cookie and bit into it. "So you heard me talking?" he asked with his mouth full.

Abby nodded, letting the cat play with the tips of her shawl and seating herself. "Do you like preaching sermons?" she asked.

Will nodded, barely swallowing before taking another bite. "I do, but sometimes the people of Tall Pine are hard to preach to."

He sighed, sitting down on Abby's desk.

"How so?" Abby asked, genuinely curious. She had noticed it was hard to get close to these people. They were nice, and polite, but reserved.

"Life in Colorado is hard, and the people are always working. They never stop to, well, contemplate God or their purpose in life. Work is good and hard work is better, but too much leaves little room for God. Then I have to deal with the drinkers, the gamblers, all who find a way to justify what they are doing."

"And you think talking about wrath and being cast off is the way to get to them?" Abby asked with the slightest lift of her eyebrow.

Will cocked his head with a frown. "That's the only way to get to them, Miss Abigail. What else is going to motivate them to stay on the right path?"

Abby shifted uneasily. She wasn't one to tell another how to do their job. On the other hand, she also was not one to keep her opinions silent.

"Well, since you asked… Why would a person want to obey a God who they don't love? I like to think that people are motivated more out of love and not fear or obligation." She smiled and started playing with her kitten. "To me, God is someone who I can turn to, someone who loves me so much that He sacrificed His only Son for me. I go to Him with all my thoughts and problems. I love Him, and because I love Him, I try to keep His commandments." Abby glanced up at Will who was looking at her with an oddly stern expression full of pensive confusion. Abby laughed lightly. "Didn't think a girl like me could be deep and religious, did you?"

The stern face cracked with a hint of a smile. "No, I didn't to be honest." He was quiet for several seconds. "You think one could really love God, like with a tender love as you would a father?" he asked in a deep murmer.

Abby opened her mouth not knowing what to reply. It was a surprising question for a pastor to ask. "I truly believe so. He loves us. Don't you think it's ungrateful not to love Him?"

"But, how can you?" Will stopped, reddening slightly. He began again slowly, "Some people might have a hard time with loving a God who they may not really know and don't know how to get to know." He ran a hand through his hair with a long sigh, "Or maybe they picture him all stern-like."

Abby stood up, nuzzling the kitten under her chin. "Well, that is one facet of God, I believe. He has to be full of justice and wrath sometimes, but He knows the perfect time and the perfect amount to be so. There is also the kind, healing, loving side to Him, and with that, there is no end." She walked over, taking the cloth in which she had wrapped the cookies. "Good night Will, I will see you tomorrow for church." Then she whisked away, leaving Will with a furrowed brow.

Will sat on the desk for several minutes, periodically glancing at his scribbled sermon. Abby's words had unsettled him with her talking about loving God and all. Will believed in God, trusted Him, wanted to serve Him, but he couldn't say if he had a tender love towards Him. Of course, what was tenderness? According to his own father, tenderness and sweetness were traits of weakness. Will couldn't ever remember when his father had placed a loving hand on his head, embraced him, or even complimented him. Not that he judged his father for that. His father was a good man. With Will, two little girls, and no wife, his father had built a home, and cared for his family with the sweat of his brow. Will would be proud to say he was a man like his father, good, even if not tender, nor loving. So was it truly necessary to love God? Wasn't it enough to just follow Him and obey?

Will stood up suddenly. Abby seemed to truly love God as one would a father. Abby… she was full of surprises. When Will had first seen her it was obvious she was from a well-to-do family, and she was beautiful…there was no doubt about that. True, she was not Esther, who he'd pined after for some time now. Abby though was infectious, her laugh, her humor, her energy—she was hard not to think about. Will had dubbed her as silly and shallow, the kind of girl who would never look at a Colorado pastor or anyone for that matter below her station. Still, he found her very lovely, which was partially why he had avoided her. Yet, seeing her teach, and then hearing her beliefs about a tender God with whom she had a relationship, he realized there was more to her than what he had imagined.

He smiled, remembering how her face had lit up when he had given her the kitten. She had truly been pleased, and Will had felt, well, pleased as well, albeit embarrassed. He had not expected such a thanks, and seeing her glance at him with her rosy cheeks and her soft hair framing her face, he hadn't known how to respond. Will looked back again at his sermon and in one swift movement crumpled it up and returned to his Bible. He had no idea what he would say tomorrow, but it would be short and simple and, hopefully, it would be tender.

The congregation of Tall Pine's churchgoers sat in silence as Pastor Will finished his sermon. Usually his sermons were like sour grapes; upon tasting them you wished you hadn't. At least that is what Esther thought most Sundays. But this Sunday was, well, edifying.

"Come all ye who labor and are heavy laden," Will quoted from St. Matthew, "and I will give you rest. Take my yoke upon you and learn of me; for I am meek and lowly of heart and ye shall find rest in your souls." He closed the Bible and looked at the congregation feeling very, very nervous. He'd never preached like this before. He always had a formula: sin, repentance, and judgment, repeat. Last night, however, he had stayed up contemplating Abby's words. Then he had prayed, wanting to know what the people needed to hear. In front of him there was no written sermon, only the Bible. He glanced up looking at Abby's encouraging smile. Odd, since he usually looked at Esther for encouragement.

"Brothers and sisters, how do we come unto Christ? How do we get to know Him as our Savior?"

The congregation all seemed to lean forward as if each one had this question in their hearts. Esther glanced at Abby who looked especially pretty in her creamy dress that hung loosely and didn't have the usual mountains of petticoats. Abby was beaming proudly at Will and occasionally glancing around as if to make sure others were noticing how good Will's sermon was.

"Well, I am not one to say that I am an expert, but from experience I have discovered that when I try to be more like Christ, when I try to be meek, humble, and to ease my brothers' and my sisters' burdens, that is when I feel closest to Christ. And, that's when I feel Him ease *my* burden—not by taking it away, but by making me stronger," Will breathed out, studying the faces of the congregation; he felt an overwhelming love for them. He suddenly realized that all this time he'd been looking for their mistakes, their sins, and so, of course, he had found them.

Trying to give a sermon that would help them and ease their struggles had opened up a new venue in his heart. These were good people, albeit imperfect. They struggled, but did not he? Had he not imposed his father's characteristics on a perfect and loving God? Had not a part of him lived in fear and bitterness toward God instead of recognizing it came from his own distant relationship with his father? He was as imperfect, if not more so, than those he preached to.

"We will now close with a congregational hymn," he suddenly announced. His gaze landed on Eliza, the only pianist in Tall Pine, who stood up and walked over to the play the schoolroom piano. *Did Kyle Lampton just wink at her?*

Everyone sang "How Firm a Foundation," and after the closing benediction a few of the women scurried out to set the long wooden tables with pies, hams, rolls, and salads. Esther whispered to Michael to go fetch Abby's curtains while she went and helped the other women.

"Should I tell her that we had a very small dinner because you were working on the curtains?" Michael grumbled. Esther lifted his chin with her hand.

"Hey, we had a great midnight snack, didn't we?" she smiled.

Michael rolled his eyes. "I did. You wouldn't eat any of it."

Michael stomped dramatically out to the wagon. Esther smiled to herself. Poor boy, he needed to get in bed early and catch up on some sleep. He was in a sour mood and had good reason to be, considering he had stayed up late the past two nights. Telling herself that she would make a good dinner for him tonight and put him to bed early, Esther walked over to the table hardly even noticing the large stallion and the rider who had stopped right by her wagon. She spared them a quick glance before moving on. One did not see new residents in Tall Pine very often; it must be a visiting relative.

Joseph looked over at what he guessed was the schoolhouse. It looked like a typical Sunday picnic going on, but with breathtaking mountains in the background instead of the lush cattle fields of Texas. He hoped his sister was among the crowd and that he wouldn't have to ask where to find her.

He slid down off of Sampson and began to tie him off right next to a brightly-colored gypsy-looking wagon when he noticed a young boy of six or seven staring up at him. Joseph blinked and the boy blinked back. Joseph smiled and the boy smiled back.

"Can I help you, boy?" Joseph asked, not knowing what to make of the blue eyes that were locked on him.

"You are really tall," the boy stated, looking at Joseph's belt buckle and then at the braided leather he had around his wrist.

"Yes, I am. You are tall, too," he returned the compliment. The boy nodded, taking a hesitant step closer. Sampson whined and Joseph placed a hand on his back to steady him.

"My dad is tall," the boy said looking at Joseph with a questioning expression. "Where did you get that buckle?" he asked.

Joseph smiled and looked down at the turquoise and silver buckle. "Texas—an old Indian made it for me for saving his life. I kept him from being hung when he was falsely accused of murder."

The boy's eyes grew wide. "What's that?" he pointed to the braided leather. Joseph looked down at his wrist and then held it out to the boy so he could touch it, which he did almost reverently.

"This I got from some Indians, too. Their reservation needed some help, and so I helped and got this in return. It is supposed to protect me," he explained.

"You know Indians?" the boy whispered with a grin bigger than his face.

Joseph laughed. "I sure do."

"My dad is from Texas, and he knows Indians." The boy was now on his toes almost bouncing with excitement. "But you already know that," Michael grinned.

Joseph frowned and scanned the crowd up ahead. He probably should take this boy back to his father. "Is your dad here, kid?" Joseph asked, stepping away from Sampson. The boy followed Joseph, keeping up with his long stride. Joseph noticed the boy had a satchel on his shoulder containing some blue fabric.

"No, I have never seen my dad," the boy explained, "but that's okay now." He smiled as if in explanation.

Joseph nodded, not sure what the boy meant. He guessed that this poor kid's dad was dead, but as to why it was okay now, he had no idea.

"What's your name, boy?" Joseph finally asked as they neared the schoolhouse.

"Michael. What's yours?"

"Joseph."

"Joseph," Michael said slowly, tasting the name on his tongue. "Okay, I like it. Joseph is a good name," he said decidedly.

Joseph laughed and instinctively tousled the kid's hair. His hand drew away quickly. This was someone's kid. He didn't have the right to do that, but Michael seemed thrilled by the action and began skipping by his side.

"Listen kid—Michael—" Joseph corrected himself. "I am looking for a young woman around here."

Michael's face fell, looking panic-stricken. "Are you married? Does your wife live here?" he asked quickly.

Joseph was taken aback and slowed his pace. "What? No, I'm not married. I'm looking for my sister. Abigail Silver is her name."

"Oh, you mean Teacher," Michael nodded, the tension in his

face relaxing.

"Yeah, the teacher—is she around here?"

Michael nodded. "She's in the schoolhouse talking to Pastor Will. I'm going there myself to give her these curtains that my mom made." Michael glanced sideways at Joseph. "My mom can do a lot you know. She can sew, clean, garden, and she is a mighty fine cook, too."

"Well then, you are a lucky boy," Joseph said half-heartedly as he walked past the crowd of people. An uncomfortable tingle began to crawl along Joseph's forearms. His mere height and bulk tended to draw attention, but not like this. Every eye was on him. Several girls giggled when he walked by. Out of politeness Joseph withheld an eye roll. He noticed and appreciated a pretty woman, but every time he saw one, he reminded himself that a Texas Ranger did well not to fall in love.

His father was full proof of that.

Michael led him four steps into the small but clean schoolhouse. His sister looked mighty thin, but seemed very animated as she talked to the broad-shouldered man before her. Joseph scowled, not sure if he liked the way Abby was looking at this man, nor how the man was looking at her.

Calm yourself Joe. Abby was a full-grown woman now and it was perfectly fine for her to talk to young men. Just because he intended to be a hermit did not mean she should.

"Hey Teacher, look what I brought!" Michael exclaimed. Joseph thought that he was referring to the satchel until he realized that Michael had grabbed hold of his forearm with one of his little hands and was pointing at him with the other. Abby looked up and squealed in delight, rushing forward. She threw her arms around his neck, her feet lifting up from the ground as he embraced her.

"Joseph, I didn't expect to see you so soon! What a wonderful surprise."

"I believe riding here on Sampson was quicker than waiting for trains and coaches," he grinned, setting her down. My, she was thin, and she looked... different. Every time he saw Abby she was so dressed up that most of the time she resembled a doll. Now, with her hair loosely pulled back and her simple blouse and skirt, she looked, well, more womanly.

"You must be exhausted poor man. Lucky for you my little house has two small beds and a water pump with a copper bath, although sometimes the pipe gets clogged and I was wondering if you could—"

"Are you already asking me for favors, little sister?" Joseph laughed, although that was one of the reasons he did decide to visit her. He figured she would need someone to fix things around the house and school.

"Well," Abby said with her hands behind her back and giving him a teasing grin, "it depends on how long you are staying."

"Two weeks… three at the most," Joseph informed her. He may have a few months break, but he wasn't going to spend it all in Colorado.

"Two weeks," Michael suddenly squeaked, dropping the bag of curtains. "But that is not enough time!" he wailed.

Abby tilted her head and brushed back a curl from Michael's face. "What do you mean, Michael?"

Michael didn't answer; instead he rushed outside without a word.

"I wonder what that was about?" Abby frowned, looking after Michael. A light cough behind her made her remember Will.

"Oh, Will," she turned and waved a hand proudly at Joseph. "This is my older brother, and Joseph this is Pastor Will."

The two men shook hands. Joseph's grip tightened a bit and Will withheld a flinch.

"Pleased to meet you, Joseph. I know it will be nice for Miss Abigail to have some family around," Will said politely. He wasn't used to being around men bigger than him, not that it mattered, especially since Joseph was a brother and not some suitor of Abby's. Not that a suitor would be bad either, Will thought with confused emotion.

"Well, it will be nice to be around and fix some things." Joseph looked around the schoolhouse. "Looks like this place could use some mending too, huh?"

Will followed his gaze, scanning the loose boards, the broken potbelly stove, and other things.

"I was going to get to those," Will told him, suddenly feeling territorial. "So you don't need to bother yourself with it. I am in charge of the schoolhouse, so I oversee the things that need to be done," Will explained firmly.

Joseph smiled. "Oh, it won't be a bother," he calmly assured Will. "I have a lot of experience when it comes to fixing things."

Abby was about to interrupt when Michael saved the situation by rushing through the entrance and practically running into Abby.

"I brought her." He looked at Joseph while catching his breath.

"Who did you bring, kid?" Joseph asked with a crooked grin. He was starting to like this boy.

"My mom, of course," Michael pointed to the entrance. Joseph looked over to see a woman walk up the steps, and he felt his blood grow warm.

Never had he seen such an exquisite woman. She was clad in an emerald green dress showing off a long neck and delicate collarbone. She was slender but strong. Rosy lips spread into an effortless smile and glossy hair was done up softly with loose curls falling down her back. She was beautiful, and more than that, she looked kind, wise, and capable and everything that Joseph never knew he always wanted.

Instinctively Joseph found himself straightening his posture.

"Esther, are these the curtains?" Abby asked, pulling out a blue calico from the fallen satchel. "I'm surprised you got them done so quickly!" she exclaimed, kissing Esther on the cheek. Joseph smiled. The woman had done something kind for his little sister, another bonus.

Michael was pulling on his mother's sleeve and pointing at Joseph. "Mom, Mom, it's him. *Look!*" Michael drew her attention to Joseph. When their eyes met, Joseph smiled gently.

"Hello," he finally said, his voice deeper than it had ever been.

His smile widened. Now it was time for this Esther to do what every single woman did upon meeting him: gape, blush, and giggle... but Esther did none of those. She didn't even bat an eyelash, nor smile shyly. Instead she nodded politely and said in an even voice, "Pleased to meet you. You must be Joseph Silver. Abigail's brother?"

"Ahh yes, yes I am, I've come to visit her. You are, well, I mean, I heard Abby call you Esther."

"Esther Callen," she announced her name articulately. "This is my son Michael who you have already met."

Joseph nodded. He was not sensing any interest from this woman other than sheer politeness. He slightly flexed his arms, hoping she'd notice, but she'd already turned to Will.

"Will, that was a wonderful sermon, one I'm sure many people needed to hear." Esther smiled genuinely. Joseph fought the urge to growl. He suddenly had an ardent dislike towards this pastor.

"Is Mr. Callen around?" Joseph blurted out.

Esther looked over at him with one shake of the head. "No, he is not," she said. Michael grinned at Joseph encouragingly.

"I don't have a father, not yet anyway; we are still waiting for him," he announced loudly. Esther turned slightly pink at this and hushed her son with a kiss on the top of his head. "We'd better go. Abby, let me know how the curtains work out and if they need to be hemmed or not." She looked briefly at Joseph." It was nice to meet you, Mr. Silver," she said before turning Michael's shoulders toward the door. Joseph gaped after her. She had called him Mr. Silver. *Mr. Silver* for crying out loud.

"Michael?" Abby interjected suddenly. "Don't forget to do your homework. Remember, you are going to tell the class why you want to grow up and be a veterinarian."

Michael looked at Joseph. "I don't want to be a veterinarian anymore. I want to be a cowboy."

Joseph gave a half smile. "I'm a Texas Ranger, kid."

Michael looked at him with wonder. "That's what I mean. I want to be a Texas Ranger."

At this Esther laughed but then picked up the boy in one sweep and settled him on her hip. Will and Joseph lifted their brows in surprise; for being such a slender thing, she had some strength.

My, she would be good on a ranch, Joseph thought, suddenly picturing her helping him deliver a baby calf or going out for an evening ride, along with other more intimate scenes. Joseph blinked hard. *What am I thinking? And on a Sunday!*

"I really do need to go. I will see you later," Esther then turned and walked down the steps carrying a protesting Michael. Joseph felt the left muscle in his jaw twitch. He was not going to let her go without knowing when he could see her again. So with no explanation to Abby he hurried out of the schoolhouse and after Esther.

"Miss Esther," he called out after her.

She turned, surprised. "Mr. Silver, what is it?"

"Please, call me Joseph. After all, you're a good friend to my sister, and that practically makes us friends." Then, without asking, he suddenly took Michael from her grip. She began to protest but Michael pulled away from her and wrapped both arms and legs around Joseph with a grin the size of the Grand Canyon. "This is a big boy; I don't want you hurting yourself." He meant to be helpful, but the slight arch in Esther's eyebrow made him wonder if he had offended her. She seemed uncomfortable with the situation and gave Joseph a stare that he'd only seen when he had played with a heifer's calf. He'd gone home bloody and bruised that day. Should he put Michael down? But, then he would not have an excuse to follow her. No, he would hold Michael. He wanted to see this woman again whether she liked it or not, and hopefully, she liked it.

"Very well," Esther said with a smile, although Joseph detected ice in her voice. The two walked side by side to her wagon.

"If I may ask, why is your wagon painted like a gypsy cart?"

"It *is* a gypsy cart!" Michael said proudly. "Mom and I painted it. Do you like it?"

"I love it." Joseph bounced Michael, making the boy laugh.

"Where I come from the people paint with bright colors. My own home has multi-colored walls stenciled with flowers and murals. I like bright colors." He gazed over at Esther who looked ahead with a periodic glance at Michael. "So, Miss Esther, do you take Michael to school every day?"

"Yes, yes I do."

"Pick him up?"

This time she looked at Joseph with her eyebrows knitted together in confusion as if he were some strange animal she had never seen before.

"Yes, I take him and I fetch him every day. I am his mother."

"Oh, well that's good." Joseph looked ahead, suppressing a smile. He would make sure he saw her every day, twice a day with some luck. He would ask Abby all about her, and maybe she could give some insight as to why this lovely woman was showing him no interest at all.

When they reached the cart, Joseph lifted Michael into the seat. Esther had begun to hitch up the horse, but Joseph walked over and placed a hand on hers to stop her. To his surprise she recoiled sharply at his touch.

"Oh, Miss, I am so sorry. I meant only to stop you so I could—"

"No, no, its fine." Esther laughed nervously, tucking a strand of loose hair behind her ear. "You merely surprised me, that's all." Esther gripped the side of her dress to keep from trembling.

"I was just going to say I will hitch the horse for you."

She nodded with an agreeable smile. "Umm, thank you, Mr.—"

He looked at her sharply.

Esther smiled and nodded an apology. "I mean Joseph. Thank you, Joseph."

When the horse was hitched, Esther walked over to the right side to pull herself up. Joseph came and stood by her and held out his hand to help her up. Esther looked at it quietly; his hand could easily crush her own. A tingle went down her spine; she did not want to take it, but she also did not want to be rude. So with a deep breath and a plastered on smile, she took his hand. To her surprise it was warm and gentle, his other hand he placed on her lower back as he supported her weight and helped her into the driver's seat. As soon as she was settled Esther pulled her hand away, hoping that her eagerness to escape his touch was not too obvious.

Esther relaxed once her body was free of his touch. "Thank you again, Joseph. It was a pleasure to meet you."

"Likewise Miss Esther," he turned his gaze to Michael. "Well Michael, I guess I will see you tomorrow."

Michael nodded eagerly, "See you tomorrow as well Mr. Joseph," he said, trying to imitate a Texan accent. Then with a farewell nod Esther snapped the reins and led the horse away from Joseph without a glance behind her.

Michael was a chatterbox the whole way home. He told her about Joseph's belt buckle, his Indian bracelet, the way he talked, walked, how tall he was. Michael even rehearsed his and Joseph's entire conversation. Esther listened not bothering to reply. Michael simply was infatuated with a man who he had deemed heroic. This was natural for children. Finally, as their home came into view Michael said, "He will be a good dad, don't you think Mom?"

"Wait…what?" Esther dropped the reins.

"I said that he will be a good dad. He is everything that you said my dad would be."

Esther bit her lip. She knew it had been a bad idea to talk about a future father who was entirely fictional. Here she had built up false hope in Michael, not thinking any harm would come of it, at least not for a while. How was she supposed to know that a Texas Ranger fitting her exact imaginative description would ride into town?

I shall never marry, Esther recited as she had countless times before.

The thought brought her comfort. Yet it had made Michael so happy to feel that God was preparing a father for him, and she hadn't had the heart to tell him that his momma was too— damaged was the wrong word—but what was the right word? Through faith and prayer she felt stronger and happier than ever, but there were too many scars, too many fears, and a distinct lack of trust and respect for men.

"Michael listen, we don't even know Joseph. He may not be your father, so you cannot go around telling people that he is, alright?'

Michael pouted but finally nodded, muttering, "I know he is, though."

Esther sighed. "How could you possibly know that?" she asked, feeling more discouraged than annoyed.

"Because when I saw him I felt warm, happy, and peaceful—and didn't you say that is how God speaks to us?"

Esther bit her lip again. It felt as if all her mothering and well-intentioned words of comfort were being used against her today.

"Sometimes it is easy to confuse emotions with what the Holy Spirit is saying to us."

Michael frowned. "I don't know what that means," he said angrily. Esther breathed out a short laugh. Michael always got mad when his young mind did not understand things.

"Listen, love, let's not worry about it tonight. Come help me with dinner and we can start a new book, then take a bath and head off to bed with some hot cocoa," she suggested.

That was enough to change Michael's mood, but Esther remained unsettled. She would have to tell Michael one day that she had no intention on marrying. Besides, what man could truly love Michael as she did?

Six

Abby was combing out her wet hair while Joseph borrowed her writing desk. He was looking more pensive than usual. "What are you writing, Joe?" she asked, walking into the kitchen to stir the soup. She prayed that it was all right. The recipe was easy to follow as was the one for the butter and flour biscuits cooking in the oven. Still, she worried. Even simple cooking seemed hard for her.

Joseph set down the ink quill and crumbled up the paper. "Nothing—well, nothing that needs to be written now."

"Oh, are we having secrets between us now?" Abby teased before testing the soup—good, not great, but good. She set about ladling a giant bowl for Joseph and then smothered a few biscuits with some honey butter that Esther had made for her. Last she poured two glasses of milk. "Joseph, I have dinner ready."

Joseph sighed, reluctant to eat Abby's cooking, but the poor girl had spent so much time over it that he felt obligated. When he sat down at the table, Abby quickly set about making herself a bowl and then sat across from him.

"I'll pray," she offered. Joseph bowed his head, the steam from the soup wetting his face. It actually smelled pretty good. When Abby closed with an "Amen" she stared excitedly at Joseph and the soup. With a brave breath Joseph lifted a full spoon to his mouth.

"Well?" Abby asked, her voice hinting of worry.

Joseph swallowed. "Not bad, Abby. Much better than those cookies you attempted last Christmas," he smiled.

Abby shuddered in remembrance. "I don't know if I would call those cookies when the dogs would not even play with them."

"Oh, they did. It was just that the cookies chipped their teeth," he teased and took a hearty bite of a biscuit. "Mmm, good spread, whatever it is."

"Its honey butter," Abby said. "Esther made me some along with the curtains."

Joseph coughed and hit his chest. "Esther, huh?"

Abby lifted an eyebrow. "Yes, Esther," she said, eyeing her brother suspiciously.

Joseph nodded. "So Abby, what do you know about Esther?" He wasn't one to gossip, but Esther had been the first woman he'd met who had shown no interest in him. And for once, it bothered him.

Abby shrugged. "Honestly, the woman is a mystery. She has been most kind to me and everyone loves her, but I wouldn't say she was close to anyone, besides maybe Eliza, who she knew from back East, but even then, I don't know how close they are."

"Do you know anything about her husband?"

Abby shook her head, "Again another mystery. Her uncle is a doctor and his wife is a nurse. They run a small clinic in town. Esther is the midwife and a right good one from what I've heard and seen. She loves it here and never talks about her life back East. As far as I know, she has no intentions of ever leaving Tall Pine. As far as a husband," Abby continued, "I assume he passed away." She began layering up a biscuit generously with honey butter. It felt so good to eat.

"Does she have, well, a suitor of some sort?" Joseph asked nonchalantly, and then regretted the question when he looked up to see Abby grinning at him wide-eyed. "Now Abby—" he began, but was cut off.

"Why Joseph Silver, I do believe you have a crush on Miss

Esther Callen! And I thought the tough, cold-hearted Texas Ranger would not be tied down by any woman," she teased.

Joseph rolled his eyes. "Calm down, Abby. I only met her once."

Once is enough. I need her; I have longed for her without knowing it.

Joseph knew Esther was the one for him, but he would die before admitting to his sister that he'd fallen in love at first sight like some silly schoolboy. And, maybe it wasn't love, but rather a divine knowledge that she belonged with him. It was as if God had placed in his heart the sure knowledge that he needed Esther.

"I always told you this would happen. I said that you would never love just any woman, but when you do fall for one, you will fall hard." She shook her head with an annoyed expression. "I don't know why people don't listen to me more."

"Listen Abby, I am not saying that I don't find her attractive—"

"Of course you find her attractive. Who wouldn't? Did you know she puts a berry juice salve on her lips and cheeks? I tried it, but it does not look as good on me as it does her. Esther is beautiful. Can you imagine what cute babies you would have? They'd be awfully tall—"

"Abby!" Joseph interrupted loudly. Abby blinked with a "what did I say" expression. "Abby," Joseph said again softly, "before you go on talking babies and weddings—"

"Wedding and then babies," she corrected with a smile.

Joseph chuckled. "Before you go on, I just want to make sure that you don't mention my *interest* to her. I don't know if she would even consider me courting her, let alone—" he was about to say marry her. *Marry her?* For goodness sake, he was actually entertaining the idea. No, not entertaining, he was planning on it. "Well, getting to know her better. She did not seem to be even aware of me today."

Abby waved her hand with a "tsk" sound. "Oh, that is just her reserved personality. All these people in Tall Pine have it, both the farmers and the miners. You have to coax them, be persistent in order to get to know them. Mind you, I haven't been here long, but still I've caught on to a few things. Back in Texas people are open and speak their minds, but here, things are different."

"Maybe," Joseph grunted before resuming to eat his soup. They were silent for a few minutes before Abby started the conversation again.

"So who were you writing, Joe?" she asked casually.

"Your father," Joseph muttered.

"Dad?" Abby asked surprised. "You were writing Dad? Careful, he may die of a heart attack from the shock of it." Abby shook her head. Joseph was full of surprises today. First he showed interest in a woman—a woman with a child. Then, he began writing his stepfather. He never, ever, ever wrote to his stepfather.

"Hmm, well don't worry, I haven't written a letter to him just yet."

Abby tapped her foot. She desperately wanted to pursue this conversation, but she had to tread carefully. She could tease Joseph about Esther because so far nothing had happened. Like he said, he'd only just met her. Her father on the other hand was a different matter. It was always awkward between them, and Joseph rarely talked about it. Jefferson was forever trying to bond, but Joseph had this fixed idea that no other man could be his father and that he did not even need another father.

"If you don't mind me asking," she began hesitantly, "what were you writing about? Maybe you just want to let him know you arrived here safely, or that I was alright?" She offered two options that he could choose from just in case he did not want to reveal what he was really writing about. To her surprise, Joseph told the truth.

"I was asking him about the ranch. Some time ago he offered to, well, to have me start taking over the cattle business. That is, if I was willing to leave the Rangers. I was merely asking him if that offer was still intact." He popped another biscuit in his mouth not making eye contact with Abby, which she was glad of, as she feared she would shriek with delight if he looked at her. Joseph taking over the ranch meant that he would be around. It meant he would live long and happy. It meant a lot of things. Did Esther have anything to do with this? If she did, how could anything happen between them if he was only going to stay two weeks?

As if reading her thoughts, Joseph cleared his throat, wiping his mouth with a napkin and settling back in his chair. "Abby, how long does the school season last?"

"Another month, maybe two; it depends on the weather, really. Once blizzards hit, school is out and then we begin again in spring. Why do you ask?"

"I was also going to let Jeff know that I will be staying longer, possibly a month."

Maybe more if it took that long.

"A month?" Abby exclaimed.

"Maybe a little longer depending how things are going... with you, I mean. I want to get the schoolhouse and this little place," he nodded at the surrounding house, "all sealed up tight before the winter hits. Colorado winters can be fierce, you know."

Abby giggled and shook her head knowingly.

Joseph frowned. "What are you laughing at?" he asked, taking a swig of milk.

"Oh, I am just thinking that if you plan on leaving in a month or two, then big brother you better move quick."

"Quick? You mean fixing the house? Abby I can have this place done in—"

"Oh, I am not talking about the house," she said with a wink. "All I'm saying Joe is that you don't have the luxury to take your time with her. You will have to forgo gentlemanly behavior and snag that woman before you leave, but you also can't scare her off."

Joseph replied with a half-smile.

Abby stood up and nodded for him to leave. "Go finish your letter, and I will clean up," she offered.

Joseph nodded and walked back to the desk again, thinking about what Abby said. After this afternoon he had decided to not be so forward with Esther, but Abby was right. He needed to be home before the winter to get his affairs in order. With only two months, he would have to make his intentions known fairly soon. On the other hand, he had not missed her flinch when he'd touched her. This was not the usual reaction that women had when he touched them.

Why had she flinched? Perhaps she was still mourning her husband?

Joseph frowned. What should be his first move? What should he say? How should he act?

After a few minutes, Joseph decided it was time for bed. When it came to chasing criminals, finding lost cattle, and dodging bullets, he could remain pretty calm. A few minutes of trying to figure out how to court a female and he was as anxious as a bronco tied down.

This should be fun, he smiled to himself before heading to bed.

Michael was not pleased. He was not pleased at all. He stood with arms folded as his mother, who usually bent to his will, sat on the wagon, reins in hand with the same stone-like stare that he was giving her.

"You always walk me up to the schoolhouse." He folded his arms and glared.

"Yes, I do, but it won't hurt you if I drop you off in the wagon. My ankle hurts. It is as simple as that," Esther said, turning slightly red as she always did when she lied.

Michael tilted his head. "It didn't hurt this morning when you were making breakfast and getting yourself ready," he noted.

Esther sighed, waving a defeated hand in the air. Sometimes Michael was too smart. "Listen Michael, I am already letting you wear that ridiculous belt buckle and that hat—"

"Ridiculous? You said I looked like a real cowboy," Michael wailed, his bottom lip trembling, "but you think I look ridiculous?"

Esther leaned her head back with motherly guilt.

She knew what Michael was doing this morning as he rummaged through the house looking for a belt buckle. He wanted to look like the Ranger, Abby's brother. *Joseph, what trouble are you going to cause me?*

Esther looked at the schoolhouse. Joseph was hammering something on the left side, probably a loose board. If she walked up with her son there would be no way to avoid him, but Michael now stood with a broken heart and little boy tears that pulled on her heart. So with a small groan she lowered herself onto the ground and went and knelt in front of her son.

"Michael, I am sorry. I am not myself today, and I am saying things I don't mean. I truly think that you look incredibly handsome, like a real cowboy. If I did not think you looked handsome I would not have let you wear this belt buckle and hat. Remember when I made you take the feathers out of your hair?"

Michael's mouth twitched. "You said I looked more like a bird than a brave Indian Chief."

"That's right, and then we made you leather moccasins instead. I am saying this so that you believe me when I say that I think you look wonderful." She stroked his cheek. She loved her son so much and fretted every day about whether or not she was raising him right. He was such a wonderful gift and the last thing she wanted was to hurt this miracle God had given her.

"I don't look ridiculous?"

"Not ridiculous in the least."

Michael scrunched his nose. "Do I look like a Texas Ranger?"

"Just like a Texas Ranger," Esther said with a sharp nod and a confident voice. "In fact, I think it is time we teach you how to ride a horse."

Michael's eyes just about popped. "You mean it?" he asked, his voice going to a high pitch. Esther smiled, loving the sparkle and joy written across his face.

"I sure do; I will have ol' Lancelot saddled and ready to go when you get home, and I will teach you how to ride him by yourself."

Michael threw his arms around Esther's neck. "Oh, Momma, that is the best news ever. I can't wait to ride Lancelot!" he exclaimed.

Esther squeezed her son and then just about tipped over with him when a deep voice startled her.

"How well trained is Lancelot?" the voice asked. Esther looked up to see Joseph Silver grinning down at them with his hands resting on his oversized belt buckle.

Typical cowboy, Esther thought, fighting to hide the annoyance. She did not like being taken by surprise, something that this Joseph was already beginning to make into a habit. Esther stood up and looked ahead: The children were entering the schoolroom and saying goodbye to their parents as Abby rang the bell. She placed a hand on Michael's back to inch him forward, but the boy wouldn't budge.

"What do you mean 'trained'?" Michael asked, imitating Joseph's stance.

"I mean, has he had multiple riders before?"

"Michael and I ride him together all the time." Esther replied, steadily grabbing Michael's hand and beginning to walk toward the schoolhouse. To her distress, Joseph fell along beside her with easy strides. Esther swallowed. He was much too close. The lace-lined sleeve of her dress brushed his arm and she could smell the scent of bacon and fresh soap emanating from his skin. She fought the tremble, but she could feel her breathing hasten.

"Well, does he only have you and Michael ride him? If so, he may be spooked easily when it is just Michael, and a spooked horse is a dangerous horse," Joseph said with an experienced air. Esther slowed her steps to a stop and looked at him square in the eye.

"Are you trying to frighten Michael into not riding? Lancelot is a good horse, and I am a decent rider." She held a smile, although her voice was firm. Joseph grinned and took a step forward. Esther gripped Michael's hand so hard the poor boy flinched. Bacon, soap, firewood, and pine swallowed her as Joseph closed the already small gap between them.

"I am sure you are a very good rider," he said slowly. Esther looked away and took a large step back.

"Thank you for your concern, but we will be fine."

"I was just going to suggest that you use my horse, Sampson.

That beast is as trained as a hunting dog. He is calm and is used to having multiple people on his back... alive or dead," Joseph tried to joke. Michael laughed, but Esther gave no reaction. "Listen, it would be safer to have him ride my horse and honestly to have me teach him. I'm tall and could grab him off the horse should anything happen."

Esther suddenly had an image of Michael being thrown off of Lancelot, who did spook easily, even if he was a gentle horse. She shifted uneasily, biting her bottom lip. Joseph smiled with a wink at Michael, knowing he had won.

"I can stay after school on Wednesday possibly. You could teach him then," she suggested.

"Oh, no need for that. Michael would be tired right after school. I will come over on Wednesday evening." He hesitated for a second before adding, "Maybe stay for dinner?"

Esther blinked several times before it registered what he had asked. He had invited himself over for dinner. Of all the nerve! Abby's cooking may not be up to par, but that was no excuse to have the rudeness to invite oneself over for dinner.

Michael was thrilled. "That is a wonderful idea! I told you my mom cooks good. We can ride together and then eat together and then you can tell me stories about Texas and then—"

"You *and Abby* may come on Wednesday," Esther said, emphasizing Abby's name.

Joseph lifted his eyebrows with an arrogant smile. "Why of course." He gave Michael another wink. "Hey Michael, you want a piggyback ride to class?"

Michael let out a whoop and ran to Joseph.

Esther held out her hand stopping Michael. "Wait," she said sternly.

Joseph bowed his chin apologetically. "I am sorry. I should have asked. Do you mind if I give your son a piggyback ride?"

Michael grabbed his mother's hand, jumping up and down. "Please Momma! It's just a little ways off."

Esther knew he was right. The schoolhouse was only a few yards away and Michael had put so much care into his dress in order to impress this Ranger. "Very well," she said. Michael hugged her and then in one swift movement, Joseph swung Michael onto his back and began striding towards the schoolhouse.

"By the way, Michael," Esther heard Joseph say, "your hat and buckle are pretty impressive—just like a Texas Ranger."

Esther watched the two disappear into the schoolhouse, Michael's laughter echoing in her ears. He certainly was infatuated with Joseph. She, however, did not like him or the situation one bit.

❧

Will was still shaking with knuckles red and clenched hands burning from impact. A part of him wished he had knocked Toby Higgins harder—unconscious even. Most of the time Will was able to control himself around abusing, drinking, womanizing men, but Toby Higgins was at the bottom of the barrel. At least that is what he thought when he saw the very pregnant Mary Higgins hiding behind limp hair. Will had stopped her, asking to see her face. She had turned away, unable to hide the black and purple swollen eye, and Will had gone straight to the saloon. When he entered, the entire bar went silent. Not many pastors entered saloons. Then, when he'd noticed red-eyed, slobbering Toby, Will had rushed forward and taken him by the shirt.

"What kind of man hits his wife—his *pregnant* wife?" Will had shouted, grimacing as the smell of whiskey and sausage leaked from Toby. The disgusting man had sneered with a snort.

"A woman ought to know her place. If she don't, then I will put her in it."

At that point Will had lost control and punched Toby in the right eye: the same eye as Mary's. He told Toby that for every bruise or cut he saw on Mary Higgins, Will would be sure to match it on Toby. Then without giving any of the staring faces a second glance, he had stormed off. Now he was a mixture of emotions as he rode his horse.

Will still felt anger, a violent anger, as well as guilt for not having done something to stop Mary from marrying Toby. Not that there was anything he could've done, but still as the pastor for Tall Pine, these people were each his responsibility, from the hard-working farmer to the drunken miner. He also felt ashamed for making a public scene. He was supposed to be a good example of someone who was gentle and forgiving.

I need to work, Will thought to himself. He needed to go to his little farm and plow and weed, cut and dig. Some hard physical labor and even harder prayer would do him good and hopefully subdue the anger coursing through him. But to his surprise, he found himself in front of the schoolhouse. He needed work, but what he wanted was laughter and humor. He wanted to see the gray-eyed schoolteacher get excited and hear her talk in her Texan accent. He wanted to tell Miss Abigail what happened and get her view on it, since she gave it so easily. But why?

Sure she was lovely and certainly not dull, but Will pictured his future companion as, well, someone fit to be a pastor's wife: solemn and not so frilly or fancy. Even though Abigail had toned down her dressing, she still wore more laces and bows than most women. Even Esther who was known for her fine dressing didn't fuss as much as Abby did with all her curls and ringlets. Just thinking about her appearance made Will smile. Before he knew what he was doing, he had lowered himself down from his saddle and was tying off his stallion.

As Will approached the schoolhouse he noticed two riding boots sticking out from underneath the steps accompanied by the echoing of a hammer. He assumed it was Abby's brother, Joseph. He sighed and ran a hand through his hair. The other day it had irked him when Joseph made the comment about the schoolhouse needing work. The school was Will's responsibility, and it did need work, but Will, although great with anything from irrigation to seed planting and plowing, was not too good with a hammer and nail, and he resented being called out on it.

"You need help?" he asked gruffly. He didn't want to be rude, but he didn't have to talk like a honeycomb.

The hammering stopped and Joseph scooted out from under the building. He gave Will a quick appraising look before shaking his head.

"No, I'm done for the day. Abby is finishing up in there." He nodded back at the schoolhouse and began wiping his hands with a rag from his pocket. "If you don't mind me asking, how old is this schoolhouse?"

Will shook his head and let out a low whistle. "Old. I believe it was built right before the war broke out back East. I honestly don't know why a new one hasn't been built. This one is a hazard."

"Ever ask the Mayor?" Joseph asked with an arched eyebrow.

Will shook his head. "You know, I'm still a new pastor—I haven't gotten to that yet," he smiled weakly.

Joseph's hard demeanor softened. The man in front of him seemed young for a pastor and he probably made a lot of mistakes, and no doubt people let him know it. Joseph didn't need to be one of those people.

"You look too young and strong for a pastor. It's Will, right? Where are your fogged-up spectacles and gray beard?"

Will shrugged. "I ordered them last month. They must be on their way," he joked. The two men gave each other a nod indicating a silent peace treaty. Then Joseph excused himself to go wash, and Will entered the schoolhouse.

Abby had her back turned pointing to a sentence in large print as the children slowly pronounced each word: "Pastor Will popped a pound of popcorn for the perfect piglets then picked poppies for Princess Poo Poo."

The children all giggled when they finished the sentence and Will could tell that Abby was laughing from the shake of her shoulders. When she turned around and saw Will her face blanched and she dropped her wooden pointer. The children's heads spun around to see Will and the laughter slowly dribbled away. Will tightened his lips to keep from smiling; instead, he narrowed his eyes, placed his hands behind his back, and walked up to the front.

"Class, I am afraid to say the reason why I am late today. Something came up that I had to do." He paused, scanning the curious faces. "You see," he continued, "I was out popping a pound of popcorn for the perfect piglets then I picked poppies for Princess Poo Poo." He no longer could hold back a laugh after finishing the sentence, and the class erupted with giggles, Abby being one of the loudest. She approached him with bright red cheeks.

"Well, Pastor Will, thank you for joining us today." She smiled brightly and then spun around to face the class, "Alright everyone, you all did so very well today that I am allowing a twenty minute surprise recess," she announced. The class cheered and stampeded out of the class like a herd of buffalo. Abby nodded for Will to follow her. "I have to watch them. Two of the older boys, Jason and Matthew Tantum, have been causing a bit of trouble," she said lightly.

Will frowned, "What kind of trouble?"

"Oh nothing drastic—they are only twelve after all. Mainly just some talk about gambling and drinking… things their father does. So they tell me."

Will shook his head. "They live with their uncle who is a good man. Their father has a bit of troubles, including some you just mentioned. He loves his boys, but knows he is not fit to raise them. Still, he tries to be involved, but I don't know if that's good or bad. A boy will want to be like his father no matter what. Trust me on that."

"Well, I'm not too worried. The other day I caught them smoking so I did a—not a very good thing." Abby's lips flickered with a smile.

Will tilted his head, now curious. "What did you do?"

"I talked to their uncle, told him of my idea first, of course. He complied and brought me two thick cigars. When I caught them smoking again, I took them behind the schoolhouse, gave them the cigars, and told them to smoke like men." She grimaced, "Of course I had to clean up the vomit and then explain why they were too young to smoke, but at least both agreed that they never wanted to smoke a cigar again."

Will blinked and then let out a rich laugh. "Oh my word, Miss Silver, you are a cunning and mischievous minx aren't you?"

Abby shrugged, "I will take that as a compliment."

Will shook his head. A few seconds of silence passed.

Abby gave him a thorough look before dusting off the small bench to sit on. "Are you like your father?" she asked.

Will shrugged. "I can't say."

"Well, was he intimidating, gruff, but also very funny?" she teased.

"Intimidating and gruff, yes, but not one humorous bone in his body," Will laughed. He hardly remembered his father smiling let alone laughing.

"You must have inherited that from your mother," Abby concluded. Did he also inherit his blue eyes from her?

"Maybe. I wouldn't know. She died when I was young," Will said, his voice void of emotion, but Abby caught the darkening of his eyes and decided to change the subject.

"Did you go into town today?" she asked and Will's face turned distraught.

"I did and truth be told, maybe I should not have gone," he mumbled, staring at his hands.

"Why not? What happened?" she asked, inching closer to him. Will sighed and leaned back, letting his hands rest on his knees.

"Do you know Toby Higgins? Mary Higgins?"

Abby scrunched up her face. "Ugh! How can I not? Odious man. I met him only once and he blatantly suggested we," she coughed lightly, indicating words too sordid to speak, "and in front of his wife. I would be quite happy to never lay eyes on that man again," she declared with a shiver. "I don't know why that poor woman is with him."

Will shrugged. "She's always wanted Toby. Did whatever she could to get that carousing devil. She swore up and down that he loved her, even when he gave her only minimum attention. I think he finally realized that she would do anything for him and take anything from him. So he married her. It would make his life easier, and with her being the kind of woman she is, he has not had to give up any of his old life style."

Abby nodded. *Poor woman? Stupid woman?* She didn't know what to think about the whole situation other than it was unfortunate and sad.

"Did you encounter them today?" she asked softly. Will nodded and began to tell her the whole story, releasing it like a festered boil.

"I was an idiot for punching him. She chose to marry him, stood up for him; what business was it of mine to interfere? Plus, I am the *pastor*. I'm not supposed to do things like that," he growled, more to himself than to Abby. He expected a kind pat or awkward silence from Abby. Instead he got a laugh. A small but definite laugh. He looked over at her to see her shaking her head.

"Really, Will? You feel bad about defending a woman's honor, putting a man in his place, and showing those godless men at the bar that a true man of God can be strong and noble?" she chuckled and patted his hand. "Feel bad about how horrible you made my first day here," she teased with a smile, "but don't feel bad when you have done something right."

Will gaped. Most women he assumed would disapprove of his outburst. Abby seemed to applaud it.

"But it was violent," he said blankly.

"No, it was proactive. Listen Will, there are certainly times to turn the other cheek, to be calm and meek, but even Christ had to cleanse the temple by driving people out and turning over the tables in order to save the temple from further shame. What you did was very similar." She stood up and smoothed her skirt. "Don't feel bad. I think you did the right thing." Then with a reassuring smile, she turned to check on the children. "Oh, by the way," she looked over her shoulder at him, the sun illuminating her silky hair, "I named the kitten Killer."

"Really? Why Killer?"

Abby chuckled. "It ran away when it saw a mouse. I am hoping that a barbarous name might instill it with a more audacious character." She turned to go but added, "Perhaps I need to change my name to Fearless Abby. It might help." She grinned.

Will smiled and continued sitting, watching Abby start a game with the children with a skill that should have taken years for her to acquire. He sat for several minutes with only the sound of birds and the muffled laughter of the children accompanying his thoughts. He felt surprisingly good—better at least. Somehow delicate, dramatic Abby had taken all the drama out of his problem and then presented it back to him in a logical and positive manner. And he believed her. She did not seem to be simply trying to make him feel better, but she genuinely thought he did the right thing. Where many women would have scorned his temper, she seemed to applaud how he'd used it. Will half smiled to himself. Abby was a surprise. In just a few months she was doing what most mountain bred teachers could not do. True, she had a rough start, but once she got the rhythm, she took to it like a fish to water.

Will stood up stretching his legs. He should go and participate in the game, but a new feeling was rising up in him. One he could not label. He felt confused about Abby, pleasantly confused but confused nonetheless. Why had he come to her when he was so upset? Why was she so easy to talk to? Somehow Will had poured out his whole story without inhibitions, knowing that there would be no judgment on her part. Despite Abby's innocent manner, she was wise. And, she seemed to know more about God and human nature than Will did—even though God and people were supposed to be his job. He found himself eager to share his next sermon with her, get her opinion, tease her about something, and watch her eyes grow wide in astonishment.

Abby's excited voice interrupted his thoughts. She was now leading the class back inside. No doubt she would be acting out some charade in order to demonstrate a lesson. He knew for sure he would not want to miss that display. Taking a moment to compose himself, Will walked in the schoolhouse to see Abby standing on her desk with a fake beard giving a speech by Abraham Lincoln.

Seven

Eliza Jensen stood in front of the bakery for a long moment, ignoring the puzzled stares of customers walking in and out. She looked in through the window; she could see Kyle Lampton shaking hands and ordering his skinny nephew around in his usual jolly manner. As she searched through the window she caught a glimpse of her face and her spirits fell: thin cheeks, hooked nose, and pale skin. She was not a beautiful woman. She admitted that she looked better than when she was younger, but still she was not a beautiful sight.

She looked back at Kyle. He was not young and handsome like the pastor, or romantically rugged like the good Sheriff Ben. Still, with his deep brown eyes, that charismatic smile, his massive body that managed to be both muscular and hearty at the same time, he was a catch for any fine woman. Especially since he was indeed successful. Rumor had it that he was doing a side business for some of the neighboring towns, baking for their weddings and parties. That was why he hired his nephew to help out while he made trips every few months. Yes, definitely a catch—handsome in his own right, hardworking, and well off. He could never be interested in her.

She pursed her lips to keep from frowning. Self-pity was not attractive, but was it bad to at least face the facts? She was still in childbearing years, but she was not young. She had a small business going, but it was nothing to brag about and certainly did not give her enough income to make her financial state appealing to any man. She might as well admit that she would die an old maid.

A thick lump materialized in Eliza's throat. She could handle the no husband part. There were plenty of women without husbands who were perfectly happy. Why there were even women like Esther who did not want a husband. Children however; a child of her own she craved with all her soul. She wanted a child to give all her love to, and to give her life to.

"You can't get that with puppies," Eliza sniffed, not bothering to halt the tear trickling down her cheek. "No matter how many you get." She forced a wry laugh.

The bakery door jingled like Santa's sleigh as it opened. Kyle Lampton walked out casting a cool shadow over Eliza.

"Why, Miss Eliza Jensen," he exclaimed as he walked towards her, "I know I told my nephew that I wanted some pretty decorations for my window, but I never imagined he would find something as pretty as you," he practically bellowed, sugar flying off his hands as he clapped them.

Eliza glared at him and put her hands on her hips. "You, Mr. Lampton are a notorious flirt who likes to play with a poor woman's emotions," she accused. The door jingled again and Sheriff Ben walked out raising his eyebrows at her insult. He walked by Kyle with a steaming bag that gave off a delicious smell.

"Kyle," the Sheriff addressed with a 'good luck' kind of nod at the baker and a slightly arched eyebrow at Eliza.

"Have a good day, Sheriff," Kyle smiled with a raised hand. Then he looked back down at Eliza with an amused smile. "Now what was that you were saying?"

Eliza felt herself go red. She'd spoken out of sadness and emotion. A silly and girlish thing to do. "It was nothing... please excuse me."

Kyle spoke before she could turn away. "A notorious flirt who plays with a poor woman's emotions. Am I correct?"

Eliza cast her gaze downward, "I am truly sorry, Mr. Lampton. I don't know what got into me just now. I… I spoke out of turn, forgive me."

Kyle chuckled and held out his arm for Eliza to take. "Lucky for you Miss Eliza, I happen to know exactly what you need." He waited, his arm held out for Eliza to take. Eliza stared at his arm, taking it hesitantly. She could not very well refuse when she had just insulted him in such a base manner.

"And what is that?" she asked slowly as he led her into the brightly-lit bakery.

"You need a slice of my triple layer chocolate cake and a cup of dark coffee," he said with a decisive nod. "Harry, mind the shop. I am taking a fifteen-minute break," Kyle called out to the overwhelmed boy who was handing out pastries and pouring coffee as quickly as he could.

"Are you sure he doesn't need help?" Eliza asked as she began to look for an empty table.

Kyle chuckled, leading her to behind the counter and back into the kitchen, ignoring the stares. "It's good for him. Besides, he's off in twenty minutes."

"What are we doing back here?" Eliza wondered if she should be back here alone with a man. What would people think? Eliza groaned, exasperated with herself. *Who cares what people think!* She was doing nothing wrong, and besides, she could not remember the last time she'd had chocolate cake—or chocolate of any sort.

"This is a private party," Kyle winked. He quickly led her to a small table marked with cuts and dusted with flour. In a blink he had it wiped down and had spread a clean cloth over it. Then he disappeared and was back before Eliza could take a breath, holding two chairs as if they were feathers. "Please sit down," he requested. Eliza sat, watching him poor a steaming cup of coffee that he gently handed to her. "Don't burn yourself," he said. Then he knelt down to one of the cool cupboards and pulled out a tall dark chocolate cake, muttering something about needing more ice.

"I was saving this as a treat for tonight, but now seems an even better time." He grinned and with a baker's skill he pulled out a small plate and cut a large piece in a perfect triangular shape before handing it to her with another one of his winks.

"Mr. Lampton, this really is not right," Eliza protested. "I made a dreadful scene out front and you are feeding me chocolate cake."

Kyle shrugged. "Take a bite for me, will you? It is a new recipe I created," he ordered, waiting gleefully for her reaction.

Eliza sighed and dug the fork into the moist dark cake. The silky frosting clung to her fork as she placed it in her mouth. A sinfully wonderful sensation filled Eliza as the chocolate made contact with her tongue. Unable to help herself she moaned in delight and swallowed slowly, savoring the delectable taste.

"Why Mr. Lampton, truth be told I have never tasted something so… well delicious and rich," she exclaimed, taking another bite with gusto.

Kyle beamed with schoolboy pride. "Why, Miss Eliza, your reaction just made my whole life worth living, and don't worry about your earlier comment. You see, I grew up as the only boy with six sisters so I have an advantage over other men when it comes to dealing with a woman's rude comments."

"An advantage?" Eliza smiled inquisitively. "You mean you calm them down with chocolate cake?"

"Well, no actually, you are the first woman I ever have allowed into my castle," he waved his hand around the kitchen, "as well as the first one to try a new recipe."

Eliza blushed. She did not want to believe him. She could not believe him. She would not entertain false hopes. "What, then, is the advantage?" she asked quietly, focusing on the pastry in front of her.

"I can read women's minds."

Eliza snorted. "Oh, please be serious."

Kyle chuckled, "Truly I can. You see, a woman often says one thing and thinks another, yet at other times she says exactly what she is thinking; most men never know which is which, but I do." He leaned forward with a wide crooked smile. "So when you call me a notorious flirt, what you are really thinking is, 'Oh, would it not be wonderful if Mr. Kyle Lampton asked me to go to the Harvest Festival with him?'"

Eliza coughed in surprise, then coughed again. She took a long drink of her coffee hardly knowing how to react. "Oh, is that it?" she sputtered. "Mr. Lampton, I am sure your confidence is deserving, but that was not what I was thinking," she denied, hoping to heaven that she was not as red as she felt.

Kyle frowned disbelievingly. "It wasn't? I could have sworn that was what you were thinking." He pulled out his pocket watch, "Well then, I got five minutes to convince you to go with me." He nodded towards the cake. "Just think of all the chocolate cakes I could make you if you were to go with me?" he teased.

Eliza rolled her eyes. She would put up a fight in agreeing to go with him, but she knew in her heart that she needed no encouragement. She wanted to go with him and had to bite her lip to keep from bursting in delight.

※

Esther was tired by the time Wednesday rolled around. Tuesday, Uncle Tim and Aunt Lily had to make a quick trip into Denver and asked her to make some medical rounds for them, checking on boils, fevers, and coughs. Her hands were raw from scrubbing after each visit. Constant worry weighed on her. Did she clean the wound correctly? Did she instruct the right treatment? Even after seven years, she much preferred midwifery to general nursing.

Today, she visited Melissa and baby Clark who was a bit on the thin side. Melissa had broken down in tears when Esther told her this.

"I'm starving my baby, aren't I?" she had wailed.

It was then that Esther noticed the disarray of the house, the rumpled appearance of Melissa, and the glossy, worried eyes of Robert. She sat down with Melissa and began to pull words from her, asking the tired mother how she was feeling. Melissa's tears and words came out like an avalanche. She was melancholy, tired, worried over her baby's health; she felt ugly and bad about herself, wanted to cry all the time, and didn't even want to go outside.

"It is normal for some mothers to feel sad after having a baby," Esther told her, rubbing Melissa's ankles as she talked.

"But I can't afford to feel sad, "Melissa sobbed. "I got wee ones at home who are getting thinner because I can't get out of bed. My Robert seems cranky all the time because I can't seem to…" Melissa blushed and looked around to make sure they were alone. "I can't perform… well, have no desire to perform wifely duties." She blushed with a trembling lip. "What I mean by that is I can't get to know him in a Biblical sense."

"I know what you mean, Melissa," Esther smiled, gently setting down Melissa's feet. She wiped her hands on a cloth and went over to pick up baby Clark who was starting to fuss. The little baby quieted when Esther picked him up and kissed the smooth cheeks. "Melissa, I want you to nurse him at least every two hours, if not more until he gains more weight."

Melissa nodded and took the baby to nurse, "Yes, but life just gets so busy, you know."

"I do know," Esther sympathized. She only had one child and even then sometimes found that she had no time. "Now Melissa back to your…" she grinned, "Biblical problem. Does it hurt?"

Melissa shook her head, "No, nothing down there hurts. There is no swelling and no bleeding, I just have no desire and I feel ugly, fat, stretched out and…" Melissa began to cry again, holding her baby tightly as she bit her trembling lip. Esther sighed and patted Melissa's back. There was no science or medicine for this feeling women had after delivering their babies. Esther would have to rely on intuition, instinct, and experience to help Melissa. Saying a prayer in her heart, she looked steadfastly at Melissa.

"Alright Melissa, there are some things I want you to do. I will also talk to Robert about certain things he can help you with."

Melissa nodded. "I will do whatever you say. It can't make me feel worse than I already do."

Esther smiled encouragingly. "I want you to bathe every day.

Try the morning. You have such a nice large tub—use it. I want you to eat more vegetables and meats. That will help with your lack of energy. You need to go outside every day, too. Go on a walk around the farm with little Clark, sing while you do, talk to God if you can, but every day I need you walking out in the fresh air."

She looked steadily at Melissa to make sure she was listening and taking in everything she said. Melissa's face was pinched in concentration, clearly soaking up every word.

"I also want you laying with your baby every day, with both of you naked, even just for a little bit."

"Naked?" Melissa asked, surprised. "Both of us?"

Esther nodded. "There is power in skin, Melissa, power in touch. Your baby's skin will calm you, nurture you, and it will do the same to him. I will visit you every week, and in turn you need to visit others. Your sister and your parents live close by, don't they? Visit them every week and go into town. We are fortunate it is not that far. Why not take advantage of it? Going to town will force you to put on a nice dress and pinch your cheeks. You will be surprised how much better that will make you feel."

Melissa nodded. "And what do I do with my husband?"

Esther smiled. "Melissa, you look beautiful, more so than when you were first married. You are just a hard-working mother who is tired and anxious. However, every day I want your husband to rub your back, massage it; that will help with your mood and it will also help... with the other problem." She winked and stood up. "Is Robert outside? I will tell him that you need daily massages—midwife's orders."

Melissa laughed and nodded. "Yes, he is outside on the farm." She looked down at her baby. "Am I being a bad mother feeling this way? Am I letting Clark down by not being happy?"

Esther walked over and placed her hand on Melissa's shoulder. "The fact that you are concerned about that shows that you are a good mother. I will see you in a few days."

After talking to Robert, Esther had gone to see Suzanne Gable, who was a basket of nerves as she expected a miscarriage any hour.

"I just know I am going to lose the baby." She fretted, unable to hide the quiver in her voice though her face was composed. "I had Daisy and Billy back to back and then all of a sudden it is like my body forgot how to stay pregnant, like it betrayed me."

"I know how nervous and scared you are Suzy, but for the sake of your baby, you must relax," Esther implored. "The baby, from what I can tell, is fine. Try to remain calm."

"Relax? Calm? What do you think I have been doing? I hardly move out of my chair for fear the poor little critter is going to die," she cried. "All I do is sit, and when I walk I feel I got to keep my legs together—or else." Suzy looked down at her hands. "Nothing good happens in Tall Pine. Back in Florida I had Daisy and Billy just fine, but Florida is warm, lots of sunshine and nice cities. If my husband had not dragged me to Colorado…"

Esther sighed. She knew that the two miscarriages Suzy had were during stressful times. The first miscarriage came when her husband broke his leg and she had two young ones to feed and a farm to plow. The second one came soon after her mother passed away—they had been very close. Esther had a feeling that Suzy's body was in strong accordance with her emotions. She dare not tell Suzy this for fear that the poor woman would blame herself and her inability to control her emotions for losing two babies.

"Suzanne listen, you are seven months along. Miscarriages usually happen long before this. I think possibly all of this sitting may drive you crazy, and we want you in healthy spirits when the baby comes. Try something—don't you like gardening?"

Suzanne raised her eyebrows in disbelief. "Why Esther, how can you ask such a question? You know my garden is the envy of all Tall Pine. Why, most women here plant vegetables and herbs, none of them have roses and tulips the way I do. You've seen my garden yourself." She frowned, suddenly leaning back with a grunt. "Although it's just about gone to ruin since I can't get out and work on it."

Esther nodded, knowing that she needed to proceed with caution. "As a midwife I feel from experience that fresh air is both very good for a mother and her unborn child. I suggest that you work in your garden every day. Bring a chair or a blanket," she added quickly, "so that when you feel the least bit tired you can stop and rest."

Suzanne gave a non-committal nod of her head. "Well, I suppose that makes some sense. My last two babies I lost fairly early in the pregnancy. Still, I worry."

"Of course you do," Esther smiled brightly, "which is why you make sure to bring out a blanket to rest when you feel fatigued. However, fresh air would be healthy."

Esther then left, hoping that Suzy would follow her advice. A woman was not made to sit, and boredom could cause as much stress as a husband with a broken leg. Esther bit her lip thinking about her past two days. The last thing she wanted to do now was to make a fancy dinner to entertain Joseph and Abby and then watch as a practical stranger taught her son how to ride. A part of her wanted to cancel, to pick up Michael, make a simple dinner, and go to bed early. Michael, however, was so excited that he had even planned the menu they would cook: roasted garlic potatoes with plenty of butter, fried beef steak, hot bread with apple sauce, green beans mixed with bacon chunks and caramelized onions, and then carrot cake for dessert. The poor boy had even gotten up early to help peel carrots.

"Go back to bed, love," she had told him. "You still have another hour before you need to get up."

"But I want Joseph to know I helped," he told her with a yawn. Esther felt the sting of tears. It saddened Esther to watch her son so desperately try to win Joseph's approval.

"Sweetheart, why don't you help me frost the cake when you get home? You are the best cake-froster around, and I will certainly need your help with that."

Michael pondered this for a few seconds. "Will you tell Joseph I made the cake?"

Esther promised she would and then sent Michael back to bed. As she began seasoning the beef, cubing the potatoes and mixing the dough to rise, her thoughts wandered to Joseph. He was a handsome man to be sure. She herself may not be interested in men, but that did not mean she was blind. His interest and kindness to Michael alarmed her. It was her experience that men who attempted to court her, even good Pastor Will, did not bother to pay attention to her son. They were polite, but wished to impress Esther more than to win the affection of Michael. So from past patterns of men, he must not be so interested in her. He probably was just one of those handsome flirts, yet he must have some reason for being so kind and attentive to Michael. Tonight if his kindness persisted she would confront him and find out what he was up to. It may be presumptuous, but for heaven's sake, she was feeding him a large and delicious dinner. She could afford to be a little forward just this once.

Eight

Abby tapped her foot impatiently. "Joseph, I don't think Esther will notice if you wear the blue shirt or the darker blue shirt," she finally called out.

Joseph glared at her. "Did I ever make comments when you spent hours in front of the mirror to go to some church event?" He shook his head choosing the light blue shirt. "Besides, you don't know what she likes a man to wear. She may be one of those picky females."

Abby looked blankly at Joseph. "I don't know if she even she cares about men, let alone is picky about them."

Joseph snapped his head towards her with a frown. "What do you mean by that?"

Abby blushed and looked down, twirling her fingers. "It's just that I was talking with some of the mothers today—" she began quietly.

Joseph raised an eyebrow. "Leave it to you to know gossip. Nothing has changed, has it Abby?" he chastened.

Abby looked up with a glare strong enough to melt iron. "I have changed, Joseph, and it is not gossip every time that women talk. That is how women bond, feel connected—we talk, all right? And never mind what I said." She opened the door. "I will wait outside for you," she snapped before shutting the door firmly.

Joseph sighed. He felt bad. There was no need to make that remark. Abby was a talker—she needed to talk. That was not wrong, and he had noticed a change in just the few days he had been with her. She was much more capable and calm with no hysterics or even tears. He felt protective over Esther, unaccountably so but that wasn't Abby's fault. Truth was that he was actually curious what she had heard about Esther, even if it was merely gossip. Whatever he could find out to help win her over would help.

The ride was silent for the first few minutes. Abby was still clearly upset. She sat with her hands clasped and her petite chin high in the air, her lips pressed tightly together. Finally, nearing the end of the ride, Joseph decided to let go of his pride and apologize.

"Abby, I am sorry I made that remark. I know women talk, and I am glad you are making friends. I should not have said that," he said, certain his apology would be enough. No more talk was needed.

Apparently, not for Abby.

"I tried so hard to impress you Joseph," she blurted. "You are the only one in the family who has ever treated me like I had brains and grit. Do you know how hard and stressful it has been trying to make a good breakfast, lunch and dinner for you, and to teach in front of you? I am not complaining. I want to do all those things, but I want you to be proud of me. It has not been easy out here. I handle it because I am not of a deposition to be melancholy. I will find happiness wherever I am, but that does not mean I have not been homesick, tired, and scared. Then you have the nerve to tell me I have not changed because I was chatting with some women who brought up Esther?" Her voice threatened tears. Joseph desperately hoped it wouldn't come to that. He did not know how to handle tears.

"Abby, I *am* sorry."

Abby sniffed, dabbing her eyes quickly. "Heavens Joseph, if I arrive to dinner red eyed and snotty, I will never forgive you," she laughed shakily.

Joseph smiled. Abby's jolly attitude and positive outlook was often confused with flightiness and shallow thinking. She had come out here alone and in a few months was handling things like a seasoned teacher and a mature woman. Just because she did not talk rough or have a solemn demeanor did not mean that she was not smart and capable.

Joseph shrugged, "What can I say Abby? Men are idiots. We'll foolishly insult a wonderful woman even though we think the world of her," he said with a brotherly shove.

Abby chuckled lightly, "Well then, at least we agree on something," she teased. Then looking ahead, she clapped her hands. "Oh, there it is. She gave good directions. And we still have some daylight left so you can teach Michael how to ride."

"Yeah, I don't think his momma is keen with the idea." Joseph bit his cheek; he did not know how to act tonight. Being forward had seemed to offend her, but he did not have a lot of time to court this woman, so he could not be timid.

"Esther is a fierce mother. Why, I heard that one of the teachers, prior to me, slapped Michael's hand with a ruler so hard it blistered."

Joseph clenched his hands on the reins; the desire to protect Esther and Michael was so fierce he could hardly breathe. His own father had never been around when he had been Michael's age. There had been many times he was hurt or wronged and there was no man to defend him.

"What did Esther do?" Joseph asked.

"Well, she went storming off to the teacher. Lucinda, Sheriff Ben's wife, said that Esther looked frightening—she was practically blazing fire. Anyway, the teacher left the next day and some of the mothers said they saw her with a swollen cheek; others say that Esther did not lay a hand on her but threatened her life. Honestly, no one really knows how, but Esther chased her away," Abby said. "Esther is my friend and I would never lay a hand on Michael or any child, but regardless, I would be afraid if I were ever to hurt Michael. Esther is a very passionate mother."

Joseph smiled to himself. He liked that Esther was protective.

Would she have that with their children?

The thought of Esther carrying his child formed in his head making his blood heat and his mind go dizzy. He pictured her round with pregnancy. How wonderful it would be to have a woman like her. A woman to call his own who would protect their children alongside him. A woman who would feed, love, nurture, and teach their sons and daughters. A woman who would be his partner and raise a family with him.

Joseph you don't know if she will even have you let alone have children with you, he reminded himself. So shaking his head and trying to rid his mind of tempting thoughts he guided the horses to the house; his stomach growled with the smell of fried beef on the air.

Michael ran out to greet Joseph and Abby before Esther could stop him. He looked awfully adorable dressed up like a full-grown cowboy. He had on an old belt buckle that Esther had decorated all fancy-like to make up for her previous comment of him looking ridiculous. His white-collared shirt was undone at the neck the way Joseph wore his, and they had combed his curls in a very manly style. Esther remained inside taking several deep breaths. People did not often make her nervous. It had been years, over seven, since she had cared what people thought. Joseph, however, unsettled her. She did not like him at all. Yet, she couldn't shake the need she felt to look especially nice tonight. Maybe it was to give herself courage at having a man in her house. His coming to her home seemed too intimate. Whatever it was, she found that she wore one of her prettiest dresses with a wide neck. Her hair was washed, brushed and styled in a flattering manner. Even now as she heard him come in laughing with Michael, a sense of both protective anger and nervous butterflies arose inside of her.

"Esther!" Abby called out, rushing forward to embrace her. Esther smiled. The schoolteacher smelled like cornbread and soup—the girl had been cooking. "Oh my, what are you making? It smells divine," Abby exclaimed before looking around the house. "Why what a lovely home. It is so—it looks like a gingerbread house or something that belongs in a fairy tale.

"Why thank you Abby; that is the finest compliment this house has received." Esther ushered her in. She was proud of her little home.

This home is proof that a wreck can be made whole, Esther thought.

"Momma, look!" Michael was practically jumping out of his skin. "Look what Joseph got me today in town."

"Oh yes, he looked everywhere for those Michael," Abby grinned.

Michael held up a pair of shiny riding boots with two silver buckles. "They are Texas Ranger boots," Michael explained. Esther's mouth dropped. She knew the cost of those little boots. She had been to town enough with Michael begging for them to know they were not inexpensive. She looked up at Joseph whose gaze was boring into her, waiting for her reaction.

"You really did not need to do this," Esther said in a tone that Joseph could not understand. It was void of any emotion. No anger but also no gratitude. Her head tilted like a cautious doe. "How did you know his size?"

Joseph suddenly felt very uncomfortable. "I asked for his shoe today at school. I measured the size before going into town."

Esther nodded taking the boots from Michael and examining them in her hands. Then with an apologetic glance at Michael she held out the boots to Joseph. "I'm sorry, but these are much too expensive for us to take. I am sure you can return them."

Michael made a lunge for the boots, and Esther caught him with catlike skill. "But he gave them to me!" he objected.

Joseph looked at the boots and then at the steady determined gaze of Esther. A peculiar feeling overcame him. It was the feeling he had when facing an outlaw, the way they stood against each other, fingers waiting over their gun, wondering which one of them was quicker. It was a feeling of competition and adrenaline that came about when two people of equal strengths faced each other in combat.

"I am not taking the boots back," Joseph said matching her determination. "I guess you are just going to have to keep them." He winked at Michael who reached for the boots again. Esther lifted them out of his reach, her face growing cold.

"Well then, I insist that I pay for them."

Joseph gave a half smile and took a step forward. Esther was by the far the most stunning standoff he'd ever had. Especially with her hair pulled back revealing such a slender neck and the deep sunset pink dress that made her cheeks rosy and eyes bright.

"They are a gift, Miss Esther," he fully grinned. "Last time I checked, you don't pay for a gift."

Esther's stoic expression cracked just a little with a smile. "Then allow me half the payment."

Another step. The smell of sugar cookies wafted off Esther making Joseph's head swim as he drew closer. "This isn't a land dispute."

No blush, no smile; she didn't even break eye contact. Instead she lifted her eyebrows imperially, tilted her head in that alluring manner, which was enough to drive Joseph crazy, and said softly, "Is it not?"

Joseph blinked. Abby frowned, obviously puzzled as to what was happening. Esther then broke eye contact and handed the boots to Michael who snatched them with a victorious whoop. Then she looked at Joseph, her face back to its normal serenity and sweetness.

The dispute resolve, Joseph extended his hand to lead Esther into the house. She stared at the open hand. She did not want to take it. Heavens, she did not, but Joseph had just bought her son a beautiful gift. She knew she couldn't be that rude. So steadily, hoping he could not see the sweat forming on her brow, she took his hand.

"Thank you, Mr. Silver," she said slowly.

"Joseph," he corrected

Esther nodded apologetically, "Joseph. That was very kind of you. I am sure Michael will wear those boots to bed." She smiled and then motioned towards the kitchen, "Shall we?"

Abby grabbed her brother's sleeve, allowing Esther to walk ahead.

"Alright what was that about?" she hissed under her breath. "I've never seen Esther go so... I don't know... cold."

Joseph shrugged. "Let's just say I won that round."

Abby shook her head. "What do you mean by that?"

Joseph did not answer. A table laden with heavenly food greeted him. There were square-cut potatoes shiny with butter and sprinkled with parsley; a bowl of creamy gravy sat next to them. There was thick warm bread, hot applesauce, large fried steaks, green beans mixed with bacon and lightly roasted vegetables. Joseph felt his stomach grumble. He was a man with a hearty appetite that was usually only partially satisfied with grits, dry biscuits, and jerky. What was laid out before him spoke to his heart. Suspending what Abby asked, and the conversation he had just had with Esther, Joseph sat down ready to eat.

Esther asked Michael to say the prayer. She did not feel comfortable asking either Abby or Joseph to give thanks, and as for her, she was terrified they would hear the shake in her voice. She had purposely touched a man, a handsome well-built man— an act she typically avoided at all costs. He had done something kind, out of place, but kind, and she had come close to offending him by refusing that kindness. As such she had compensated for her rudeness with a genuine friendly touch. The consequences were now that she couldn't calm herself. Her skin felt cold, her stomach was twisted in knots, and flashbacks of that horrible night arose in her mind. She clenched the folds of her dress underneath the table while plastering on a smile. Michael bowed his head signaling that he was about to pray.

"Dear Lord," he began, "we thank thee for sending Joseph and we thank thee for sending the boots that Joseph bought."

Esther heard a smothered chuckle from Joseph. Despite her own anxieties, she found herself smiling, too. Michael was so endearing it was hard to think dark thoughts when he was around.

Dear Lord, Esther silently prayed, *please calm my fear, and take away these memories even if just for tonight.*

Michael ended with an "Amen." Esther looked up and met Joseph's gaze. She nodded politely and he beamed. She wondered if Joseph could do anything that was not intense. There was also a protectiveness about his look; it was the kind of look one has when deciding they have the sole responsibility over something of value. This thought should have alarmed Esther further, but to her surprise, she found herself calming down. Her breathing slowed and her pulse regulated. Esther glanced away from Joseph feeling puzzled. Why was he looking at her with such… affection? What was more unsettling was the tranquility that settled over her with his inscrutable gaze.

"Please help yourselves," Esther said. "As you can see, I made enough for twenty people."

"Mom always says that she was supposed to have a dozen children with how much she cooks," Michael informed them reaching for bread. Esther looked sharply at her son mentally willing him to say nothing revealing or embarrassing about her.

"A dozen?" Abby exclaimed, "That is a lot of children. I can't hardly think about having one child right now let alone a dozen."

"Having children scares my sister," Joseph explained while heaping up a mountain of potatoes on his plate before plopping down a juicy piece of meat.

"I am just scared of the pain, even possibly death. I know it is worth it. I mean, who wouldn't want a son like Michael?" She reached over and patted Michael's arm, who was now lathering his bread with applesauce. "Still, it scares me, although I don't agree with some of my friends back home who are afraid that children will take away their freedom. I think it would be just a different kind of freedom."

"What do you think, Miss Esther? Does a child take away your freedom and cause tension in a marriage?" Joseph asked, hoping she would reveal something about her former marriage, past, anything.

Esther smiled and suddenly focused on her plate. "I can only speak from experience. Michael opened up venues of love I did not even know I had."

"But what about the pain?" Abby chirped, "I mean, each time you have a baby, there is the chance of death."

Esther leaned back, her expression glimmering with remembrance. "When I gave birth to Michael I was shocked by the pain. The pain, Abby, is beyond description, but once you hold that child in your arms, the pain is forgotten."

Joseph looked at Esther. Her face had a serene smile even though her eyes were swimming with memory.

A hard one to crack, he thought. "I have found that women are more concerned with catching a husband than they are about being good mothers. They think all their lives about wedding dresses and kisses under the moonlight and they forget that motherhood comes along with it. Then when they have a child they resent it for taking away," he glanced at Abby kindly, "their freedom." Joseph had seen this many times: a woman blaming her children for a waylaid life or lost lovers. The problem with Esther was that she did not seem to be looking for a husband, which baffled him

Esther looked him in the eye, surprised, as if she had not expected to agree with him. "I must say that in some cases that is true; however, I think most women, whether they want a child or not, are shocked at the overwhelming love that comes when a baby is placed in their arms."

"Would a woman then be content with only that child's love?" Joseph asked boldly, "or would she still need a man's love—a husband's love?"

Esther arched an eyebrow so high that Joseph thought it would fly off her face. "I would not know for certain; from merely observing others, I find that a husband limits a woman and reduces her freedom more than a child ever could." Esther smiled tightly indicating that the conversation was over.

Joseph grew silent. Esther clearly was not looking for marriage. In fact, she seemed to be against it. Feeling discouraged he glanced at Michael who was smiling at him with such open admiration that Joseph felt better, like a hero tackling a hard mission and not like a slighted suitor.

"Oh Esther, how is Mrs. Gable doing?" Abby asked, changing the subject. The two women fell into easy conversation talking about the happenings of Tall Pine. Michael in the meantime scooted his chair closer to Joseph.

"How are you doing, little man?" Joseph grinned, helping himself to more food. Michael glanced nervously at his mom, making sure she was engaged in conversation. Esther's eyes darted to Michael who smiled innocently. She must not have sensed any danger because she slowly looked away to continue talking with Abby.

"Mr. Joseph, I have a question," he asked in a whisper.

Joseph tilted his head down closer to the boy. "What is it Michael?"

Michael glanced again at his mom and then whispered even softer. "Can you marry my mom—*soon*?"

Joseph did not know whether he wanted to laugh out loud or fall off his chair. He liked this boy—his sweetness, his spiritedness, and his bluntness were endearing. Curious, Joseph lowered his voice.

"Now, why do you want me to marry your momma, Michael?"

"Because if you don't, another man may come along and marry her. I don't want another man for my dad."

"Why me?" Joseph asked, feeling a sudden rush of adrenaline with the thought of Esther marrying another man.

Over my dead body.

"Because you are everything my father should be," Michael explained. Joseph gave him a puzzled look.

"What do you mean?"

Michael looked impatient that Joseph was not understanding the urgency of the matter. "You are who momma described," Michael whispered loudly and then he grinned sheepishly. "Momma is always telling me what my dad will be like... and it is just like you. Also, Teacher says you have a ranch. Do you have horses, too?"

"Michael!" Esther suddenly said sternly. Both Joseph and Michael jumped while maintaining an earnest expression of innocence. Esther eyed both of them suspiciously, "What are you talking about?" Michael looked at Joseph pleadingly, begging for secrecy. Joseph gave him a knowing nod of assurance. "We were talking about the Harvest Festival. I overheard some of the parents discussing it today and was asking Michael about it."

Michael giggled and nodded eagerly.

Esther looked unconvinced, but then decided to shrug it off. "I am glad you brought that up," she said, turning to Abby. "You see, the Mayor's daughter is expecting—only two months along—anyway, I stopped by the other day and her mother who was visiting asked me to place these flyers in the schoolhouse so that the parents would get them. It informs them about the auction."

"Auction?" Joseph asked.

"Yes. Women put their name on a basket and then men bid for their baskets. The winner is promised a picnic with that woman."

Abby squealed and clapped her hands. "Oh, we have had those in Texas with our church. The husbands always bid on their wives and boys always bid on the girl they like."

Joseph instantly turned his attention to Esther. "Are you going to be putting your name on a basket, Miss Esther?"

She nodded. "I sure am, and then Michael will bid on it. We've already discussed it." She smiled at Michael excitedly as if they shared a secret.

"We've been practicing my bidding skills," Michael told Joseph. "Then Mom and me will go to our special place and have lunch."

"A special place?" Joseph asked.

"It's just a pretty spot by a stream," she explained with a careless wave of her hand. "Anyway, we need to inform all the women of Tall Pine. Eliza is putting up flyers in her shop window and around town. I will let people know on my visits, and I was wondering if you could let all the parents know when they drop off their children."

Abby nodded with another handclap. "Oh, yes I will! I am so excited. It has seemed like forever since there has been anything social in my life." She took a bite of her food with flushed cheeks. There was now so much to think about. What to wear? Would Will come? Would there be dancing?

Esther smiled remembering the time when dances and social events held such excitement. She still enjoyed them. She liked talking to other women, observing families and couples, but there was not the same thrill of anticipation equated with youth and being single.

Will Joseph go? The thought entered her head without her permission. She looked at him briefly. He was telling Michael a funny story and had her son crying with laughter. He was especially tall and broad for a man, handsome in a rugged sort of way. He would be a fine catch for any woman—just not her.

The rest of dinner went by smoothly. Esther was pleased by how much everyone ate. Michael always ate a lot. Abby, who was still living off simple dinners and probably not near enough what she needed, ate like a miner, and Joseph refilled his plate several times.

"Miss Esther, that was by far the best food I have ever tasted. How did you get to be such a good cook?" he asked, taking one more bite before pushing away his empty plate.

Esther laughed. "Ahh, you should have seen me when I first started to cook for myself and Michael: burnt meat, rock hard biscuits, and bland soup. It was through practice and a love of food that I learned." She walked over and took his plate, her trim waist next to him. Joseph fought the desire to wrap his arms around that waist and pull her close. Instead he stood up briskly, almost knocking into her.

"Well," he announced, "the sun is fixin' to set. Why don't I take Michael out on Sampson while we still got some light."

Esther put down the dishes with a small clatter. "All right, but I am coming with you." She turned to Abby, "Do you need a shawl Abby?" she asked, inviting her to come along.

Abby shook her head. "No, I'm fine, but I will come watch." She stood up, wiping a few crumbs from her skirt. The four of them went outside onto the porch.

Joseph turned to Esther. "I put Sampson in the barn with your Lancelot—hold on, and I will go get him." He started to walk away. Esther watched his back for just a second before turning to Abby and Michael.

"You two wait here. I will go with him. I don't want Lancelot getting spooked with it getting dark and having a stranger in the stables," she explained needlessly.

Abby nodded, saying that she and Michael would play a little game while they waited. Esther walked quickly after Joseph, running a little to catch up with his long stride.

"Mr. Silver—Joseph," she called out. Joseph stopped suddenly and then spun around with a wide grin on his face.

"You accompanying me, Miss Esther?" he asked with a slightly arrogant tilt of his chin.

Esther caught up with him. "I need to talk to you," she said simply. Joseph's grin grew even wider; he took a small step closer. "You want to go talk in the barn?" His left eye twitched as if fighting back the flirtatious instinct to wink. "It will be quiet in there."

Unable to help herself Esther sighed with a shake of the head. "It's not about us."

"Us?" Joseph asked. "You thought about us?"

Esther lifted her eyebrows and folded her arms across her chest. "Mr. Silver, there is no *us*. I want to talk about Michael."

Joseph's grin fell and he turned towards the barn. "What about Michael?" he asked, continuing ahead.

Esther fell alongside him. "I need to know your intentions," she said sternly. "It is obvious that Michael has developed some sort of crush on you, and you in turn are being very," *overbearing and inappropriate,* "generous to Michael and me. I need to know as a mother why you are being so attentive to my son, and I need to know the truth."

Joseph stopped walking. They were in front of the barn now. He turned towards, her looking down at her beautiful face and full lips. The sun had cast a golden glaze on everything, including her. She looked unworldly, seeming to belong in some portrait of mythology more than in front of a barn. How much he wanted to grab her and kiss her till her lips were bruised. He wanted to feel her arms around his neck, have the smell of sugar cookies wash over him and feel her hands tangled in his hair.

"Mr. Silver?" Esther asked again tilting her head, "I need to know your intentions, please," she added with a polite smile that failed to mask a disapproving look.

Joseph chuckled. Her politeness didn't subtract from her strength.

"Do you really not know my intentions, Miss Esther?" he asked quietly. He needed to gauge her reaction, measure it in order to know how to pursue her.

Esther looked away, the color fading from her face and her proud shoulders slightly dropping. "Mr. Silver," she began.

"Joseph."

Esther breathed out a shaky laugh. "Joseph," she paused biting her lip, "Joseph, if your intentions are toward me then I regret to inform you that you are wasting your time. I do not mean to be harsh. The truth is that you seem like a fine man; handsome, hardworking, and fun." She swallowed hard. "And it is because you are a decent man that I need to be honest with you: nothing will ever come about with you and me. So if you are being kind to my son out of hopes that it will spark some interest in me, then please stop. I don't need Michael thinking his prayers for a father have been answered only to have you leave without sparing him a backwards glance because your efforts towards me have been in vain. So please, if you want to court me, then let me tell you with conviction that it cannot happen, and with that being the case, please leave Michael alone. No more presents, no more stories, no more telling him about how wonderful Texas is." She inhaled, steadying herself. "I can't see him hurt, you understand.

I will protect him at all costs—even if it means robbing him of temporary joy so he does not have scars on his heart."

Joseph looked at Esther for a long minute. His jaw was clenched with the left cheek muscle ticking. He didn't like what she said. Maybe she was right. Maybe he should give up. What could he say to that? What should he say? The truth? Should he tell her that from the moment he saw her he knew with his heart and soul that he was meant to be with her? Should he tell her that he longed to have her, hold her, provide for her and her son? He wanted Michael as his own son. He would care for him as his own. But was she right? Was he wasting his time and hurting an innocent boy? Joseph looked away and took a long breath. He should just leave— tell her what his intentions were, apologize like a gentleman, and leave.

With a heavy heart Joseph opened his mouth to speak. Yet no apology came out. Before words were even spoken, an entire explanation of what he should say entered his head with such suddenness that Joseph's heart sprouted a small testimony of divine intervention. He felt he knew what Esther needed to hear in order to keep her from shutting the door to her heart.

"Miss Esther," he began, "I admire you for being such a good mother, and I in no way want to hurt Michael." He looked back at the distant porch to where Michael and Abby were laughing. Then he nodded towards the barn, walking in with Esther following. "You see, Miss Esther, my father died when I was around ten years of age." He smiled with a chuckle, "No doubt Abby has told you, considering that girl can barely keep a secret to save her life."

Esther gave an amused side nod, clearly calmed by his calm reaction to her blunt rebuff.

"Anyway, I was fatherless for a while. My mother, although not as attentive as you are with Michael, worked hard and was good to me, but I still felt the absence of a father. I see a boy like Michael who, despite the lack of a father, is good and happy. It is a credit to you, Miss Esther." Did she blush? "Michael reminds me much of myself. If I can, but for a brief moment, provide the feelings that come to a young boy when a respected man gives him a gift, teaches him how to ride, or how to build a campfire—well, I guess I would feel like I was doing some good in this world. Some tender good that didn't just consist of catching fugitives or shooting criminals."

Esther remained silent, looking at him with a compassion and softness that she had not shown earlier. It encouraged Joseph to go on, "So, Miss Esther, I ask that you let me befriend him. I will make it evident that I am not staying, that there will be an end to me being here. And as for you," he stopped saddling the horse and looked squarely at her, "a man would be a fool to not find you beautiful and," *alluring, desirable, bewitching and stunning,* "capable, but I only ask for your friendship. As a Texan I am loud, blunt, and obtrusive," he teased.

Esther laughed. "I did not say you were any of those," she told him with an amused shake of the head.

"No, you didn't, but those catlike eyes of yours did," he laughed, walking to remove Sampson from the stall. "So yes, I may seem flirtatious and overbearing, but I only ask and expect your friendship." *As well as a life together, your body and heart, and everything about you,* "and nothing more." He smiled with a finishing nod.

Esther squinted and tilted her head, examining him as she contemplated his words. Joseph held still, feeling very much like a man who had pleaded his case and was now awaiting the verdict. Finally Esther laughed and her face transformed. She had smiled before, even laughed, but everything about her seemed to be so guarded and tightly wound. This laughter was true, youthful, natural, and relaxed. Her eyes sparkled and her cheeks grew even rosier.

"Only friendship?" she asked.

Joseph shrugged. "Miss Esther, there have been ninety-nine-year-old grandmothers who awaited my proposal with how I talked. Please do not take offense when I come across too strong."

Esther looked down with her lips pressed together in a smile that was holding back laughter. "Well then, Joseph," she looked up with a girlish nod towards the house, "let's go teach my boy how to ride."

Joseph nodded, giving a silent thanks to whoever deserved it. No doubt Esther's walls would build back up, but for a brief moment he saw beyond them. She had room for love, his love. Perhaps with her not taking his eagerness so seriously she would be receptive to it. At least his foot was in the door—so he hoped.

Esther felt like she had swallowed rocks by the time Michael's first riding lesson was done. She kept leaping forward, afraid he would fall, biting her nails when Joseph would walk away or let him hold the reigns by himself. Her nerves were jumping around watching her young son on such a large horse. Sampson as it turned out was a fine animal, calm and obedient. Joseph was a good teacher. Esther had never seen Michael laugh so much. She was glad that Michael had this experience and she hated to admit to herself that she could not have done half the fine job Joseph did. Joseph—now he was a dark horse. She was sure that he had been interested in her; maybe he was and was simply lying in saying that his kindness had only to do with Michael. He didn't seem like the flirtatious type, and the few days she had seen him at the school he had given no attention to any of the other women. Of course, they all had husbands, but still. She needed to be careful. The last thing she wanted to do was string along a man. The thought of being close to any man, even close enough to where they thought there was a chance with her, made Esther very uncomfortable.

Michael was giggling now as Joseph pulled him off the horse and swung him over his shoulder, tickling his ribs. Esther fought back the urge to demand that he put her son down since only she was allowed to tickle him. Instead, she smiled. Although she was not fully comfortable with Joseph, his story and its relation to her son had softened her. Maybe it made her realize that he had hardships, trials, and hurts of his own that needed healing. Esther recognized that she had the weakness to erroneously picture men as impenetrable brutes who caused pain and never felt it. Yet Joseph now seemed more human, a human who was thinking of Michael's best interest. Perhaps just this once she could control her deep etched scorn of men and have one as a friend. No, even friends felt a might too intimate.

"It's cake time! It's cake time!" Michael announced, his cheeks rosy with excitement and his eyes bright with exercise.

"You made cake, too?" Abby exclaimed with delight.

Esther shook her head and nodded at Michael. "No, it was Michael who made it. He wanted carrot cake and milk for tonight."

"Carrot cake?" Joseph set Michael down, "Why that is my absolutely favorite cake in the world, and you made it?" he asked Michael.

The boy nodded with delight. "Yes I did—do you want a big piece or a little piece?"

"Boy, we Texas Rangers don't eat little pieces. I need a big slice," Joseph announced, glancing at Esther and hoping to find her looking pleased with him, but she seemed to be unaware of him as she ushered in Michael and Abby, not even looking back to see if he was coming. *Well I had a start,* Joseph thought encouragingly. Esther had just an hour ago agreed to friendship; he couldn't expect her to suddenly change into an adoring woman, could he?

Dessert went smoothly with no awkward conversations or quick glances. The cake turned out better than any Esther had ever made. She wondered if Michael's prayers that the cake would be extra delicious really had been answered. She smiled to herself. It had been her experience that God, as a loving father, was as interested in the silly things such as cake tasting good as he was in the soulful and heartfelt things.

Joseph told funny experiences such as chasing down a man who tried to hide by dressing up like a woman only to have some drunkard mistake him for a dead sister-in-law, whom he had hated, and run after him with an iron rod thinking her spirit had come to haunt him. The criminal practically ran to Joseph, begging for Joseph to save him from the drunkard. Esther actually found her sides hurting from laughing. She couldn't remember when she had laughed this hard. Even with her uncle with whom she was close, their conversations were more intellectual. This easy, simple, fun conversation was new to her and it felt good, like honey to a sore throat.

After Joseph had finished his second helping of cake, Esther stood up announcing that Michael needed to go to bed.

"Please, can I stay up?" Michael begged dramatically.

Esther ruffled his hair. "Sweetheart, I am sorry, but you turn into a little beastie when you don't get your sleep. Now, go get your pajamas on."

Michael made a scrunched up face and planted his feet. Esther responded by raising an eyebrow and mouthing the count of: "One, two…" at three Michael threw his hands up in the air.

"Fine, I'll go," he whined and then quickly stifled a yawn, "even though I'm not tired."

Abby smiled and stood up as well. "We best be going, too," she politely said. She glanced at Joseph, jerking her head for him to stand up. "Joseph, shall we go? I still have to get up early for school tomorrow. With Halloween coming up we will be doing some fun crafts, but I need time to prepare them."

"Halloween crafts?" Esther asked, clearly delighted. "Abby that is wonderful that you are having the children be creative. Many of these children do not get that chance even though it is very important."

Abby beamed, her fair skin blushing. "Why, thank you, Esther. Halloween kind of snuck up on me. It's hard to believe we're nearing the end of October." She walked towards the door, shivering as a cool breeze blew in when Joseph opened it. "When does it start snowing? I know there is no specific date as to when the fall session ends—or when the snow starts to fall," she asked. The snow was certainly not something she was looking forward to. Pretty soon she would need to decide whether to use almost all her newly-saved money and travel back home for the winter or stay through until spring.

"Usually in December," Esther said. "Here in the valley we rarely get it in November. The school is usually closed mid-December through January then opens in February. We still have snow, but it's not so intense," she explained.

"Do you like the snow?" Joseph asked. There was little snow where he planned to take her. Scorching summers and springs, but beautiful autumns and winters. If she loved the snow, she would have to learn to live without it.

"The snow is beautiful," Esther remarked with a pensive gleam in her eye. "Beautiful and wild. That I do like about it. But after a few weeks with an energetic boy who has not been outside for days, I get pretty sick of it to be honest," she laughed with a shake of her head. Esther actually did not like the snow. Snow meant cold, which meant sickness that led to sick mothers and children, coughs and fevers. No, she did not like the snow.

Joseph smiled with a nod of approval. Obviously, he would have liked her to say she abhorred the snow and longed to live in a warm sunlit place, like Texas, but what she said was good enough.

The ride back to the little house went by quickly. Abby found herself drifting off to sleep with her brother being unusually silent. Willing herself to stay awake until she reached her bed, Abby sat up and stretched before taking a good look at Joseph. His jaw was set firmly and his eyes narrowed as he looked ahead. He seemed to be in another world, lost in thought.

"You never asked me about what was being said today," Abby told him breaking his spell. "The mothers at the school... about Esther." A good part of Abby did not want to tell her brother. She loved him very much and was growing to love Esther, and she would be more than thrilled to see them marry. But she'd never seen her brother fall for a woman and she couldn't imagine what he'd do if his heart were broken.

Joseph's face relaxed just a tad. "I thought it was about scaring the abusive school teacher away," he said, smiling at the thought of Esther angry and ready for battle.

Abby shook her head. "No, that was some time ago. Today when they were speaking about the Harvest Festival and how fun it was to see blooming romances among the youth, they mentioned how Esther," she bit her cheek thinking of a delicate way to put it, "that she is just not interested in men. She treats them the same as she does women. In fact, they say she treats them below women—kind and respectful but distant. Truth is Joseph, I don't think Esther has any intention of marrying a man or even being courted by one," Abby blurted. She held still for a moment. Joseph said nothing for a while, only giving a simple nod to indicate he was listening to her. Abby wanted him to speak, to hear his thoughts, but Joseph was doing what she called "a man thing," being silent and moody. Wishing she could hear his thoughts Abby turned away, deciding that it was best not to speak further.

Joseph was thinking about what Abby said, but more so about what Esther had said, how she looked, how she had reacted to his explanation of kindness. Funnily enough, he felt no discouragement; rather, he felt encouraged. So Esther had not wanted to marry, did not want to marry? All that meant was that the right man had not come along.

Well, the right man is here now.

Nine

Will stepped cautiously onto the rickety ladder as he lowered himself down Jim Tantum's roof. Below him, young Jason and Mathew were rehearsing their horrible experience smoking cigars. "Teacher gave us chocolate the next day," Jason explained. "Said she didn't like seeing us vomit, but we had to learn our lesson."

Will chuckled. "You like your teacher?" he asked, rolling his shoulders. Six hours working on a roof was enough to give any man a stiff back.

"She's the best teacher there is," Mathew said with a forceful nod. "She makes lessons fun."

Will had to agree. Abby seemed to make everything fun.

A man with kindly eyes and thinning hair walked onto the porch. "Jason, Mathew, your aunt has dinner ready. Why don't the two of you go wash up?" Jim Tantum waited until his two nephews were inside before addressing Will. "Pastor, this is the fourth time you've repaired my house. Will you please let me pay you something?"

Will smiled and began gathering up his tools. "Jim, the fall you took was a nasty one. I don't want you risking that shoulder of yours." He stood up with his tool bag in hand. "Besides, what you and your wife are doing to help those nephews of yours... well let's just say I'll never be able to help you enough."

Jim's color heightened. "Well, we love those boys as our own. Speaking of such things, if you see Miss Esther, could you have her stop by?"

Will's face lit up. "Your wife is expecting?"

Jim tried to give a casual shrug, but the grin on his face betrayed his excitement.

Will promised he would and made his way over to his chestnut stallion. He tied his tools to the saddle, thinking he would stop by Miss Esther's house and let her know.

Will suddenly paused. Usually the very thought of seeing Esther made his nerves ring like church bells, but now… now there was only a steady heart beat and clear mind. How peculiar, he thought, that the mention of Esther brought out no passionate or even romantic emotions in him.

"Well, I'll be." Will laughed audibly as a sense of relief and jubilation ran through him. He was no longer enamored with Esther Callen, and he knew exactly why. Still smiling, Will lifted himself onto the horse and rode toward the Callen's home—all the while thinking about a pair of beautiful gray eyes.

By the time Friday rolled around, Abby was ready for school to be done for the week. Her idea of Halloween crafts had gone well, as had her lessons, but on Friday both the children and she were antsy and too full of energy and impatience to be kept indoors. For more than two months now Abby had either stayed in her little house, taught at the school, chatted with Esther, or gone on walks. There had been no social visits and definitely not enough trips to town. She tried to talk more with the parents this week but was allowed only so much time. Esther usually made more of an effort to talk to her, but she'd been monopolized by Joseph all of Thursday and Friday. It was obvious she was trying to avoid him. She would stop the wagon at different places to drop Michael off and pick him up. Still, Joseph would walk out to meet her and carry Michael on his back to and fro. When Abby excitedly dismissed the class Friday afternoon, she desperately needed a break. Michael stood up and as was now customary, rushed over to Joseph who was replacing a window.

"You ready, Michael?" Joseph asked, setting down his tools.

Michael nodded and lifted up his arms ready to be swung up. "When are you going to come over and teach me how to ride again?"

Joseph picked up Michael from under the arms and swung him around on his back. "Well, I guess we are going to have to ask your momma about that," Joseph replied.

"Ask me what?" came a velvety voice that cast a soft shadow in the schoolroom.

Joseph looked up to see Esther eyeing him with amusement.

"Momma! You came in to get me. You are back to normal!" Michael hollered.

Esther laughed, her color heightening, "I decided that I needed to spare Joseph's back." She waved for Michael to get off and come to her. With a heavy sigh, he slid down Joseph who followed him to the entrance.

"We were just talking about Michael needing another riding lesson," Joseph told her. My, she looked fine today; of course, she looked fine every day. As he approached her, he noticed she seemed a bit anxious—worried maybe? She grabbed Michael's hand and quickly kissed his head as if drawing strength from it. Instinct told him something was troubling her.

"Another riding lesson, huh?" she asked with a quick twinkle in her eye that quickly faded. She looked past Joseph and at Abby who was coming forward eagerly.

"Esther, I wanted to ask you if this Sunday you could show me how to make chili? I tried last night and it was a disaster."

Joseph grimaced upon remembrance of Abby's experiment. "Amen to that. It *was* pretty awful," he agreed. Abby glared at him and gently swatted his arm.

Esther nodded distractedly, Joseph noted. She definitely had something on her mind. He gently touched her forearm and she drew it away, giving him an apologetic smile. Joseph frowned. What was it with this woman? He'd seen her many times embrace Michael, even kiss other women on the cheek. She seemed warm and friendly despite her reserve. Yet she seemed afraid of his touch.

"Esther," he asked, his voice low, "are you alright?"

Esther gave him the same surprised look as she had the other night. It seemed unexpected to her that he would say something nice.

"Well," she began, shifting under his gaze. "I need to go visit Mary Higgins."

Abby's face fell. "Is it her time?" she asked knowingly.

Esther shook her head. "No, but anytime now. I have tried meeting with her, but she has not yet allowed me to... or better said, she does not like other women coming to her home. I have offered to take her to my house, but she won't leave unless it is running an errand for Toby."

Abby made a sound of disgust. "That man has that wife of his on an iron chain."

"A chain that she sadly wears with pride." Esther shook her head, "Anyway, I am going over there right now. She was not at home this morning so Eliza offered to go with me in order to counter Toby."

Abby frowned with a worried expression. "Are you taking Michael?"

Esther shook her head emphatically. "No, I won't let him go near that house. In fact, I wanted to ask if you could watch him. I won't be gone more than an hour or two and I have a basket of food for him that he is welcome to share with you." She looked desperate for help, yet worried to leave Michael. Joseph concluded from her apparent anxiety that she rarely left her boy.

Michael jumped up and down. "I can stay with Joseph?" he asked, now pulling with excitement on Joseph's arm.

"Of course he can stay." Abby took Esther's hand in a warm friendly gesture. "He can stay as long as you need. We will make it fun for him."

Esther smiled. "Thank you," she said sincerely and then kneeling down, she pulled Michael into a deep embrace. "You be a good boy Michael or no Harvest Festival for you." She gave him a teasing flick on the nose and looked up at Joseph. "No horseback riding while I am away, please." It was an order not a request. Joseph nodded, feeling a bit worried. He did not know who this Toby Higgins was, but it worried him that Esther was obviously unsettled and he could do nothing about it.

When Esther had left, Joseph turned to Abby. "Who are Toby and Mary Higgins?"

Abby shook her head. "A scoundrel is a polite word to call him," she said, glancing at Michael and then back again at Joseph. "I will tell you later," she mouthed.

Joseph nodded and looked down at Michael who was looking up at him like an adoring puppy. Joseph grinned, overcome with an unfamiliar feeling of tenderness towards this boy. Without thinking he picked up Michael and swung him onto his back.

"So Michael, your mom said no riding, but she didn't say anything about no fishing."

Abby watched as the figures of Joseph and Michael ambled towards a fresh mountain stream that helped nourish the valley. Joseph had discovered two random fishing rods underneath the schoolhouse, and even though he declared them ancient, he was itching to use them. Abby sighed and walked back into the schoolhouse feeling discontent and lonely. Everyone seemed to have someone. The children had their parents, the parents had each other, and so on. Even Joseph, her lone-wolf brother, seemed intent on finding someone to belong to. Everyone she knew came first to someone. It seemed a natural order.

Abby began erasing the chalkboard, her forehead tense with thought. She used to belong to her parents and she still did, but since she had come out here something had shifted. She not only wanted to be important to someone, but she wanted someone to be important to her. Maybe important was the wrong word—she wanted a binding of hearts. Being out here had put a depth into her emotions or maybe just wiped away the superficial fluff she had added over the years. Even her friendships back in Texas seemed insignificant.

Were my friends ever friends?

Girls were nice to her if she could give them a ride in her white miniature carriage or give them lace gloves for their birthday. In other words, her friends had merely been social conveniences. The men in her life had been no better than bloodhounds looking for a prize, but was she any better?

She thought of the values she had placed in her ideal man: wealth, education, a fine house… all material and socially impressive attributes. Traits like kindness, moral ethics, hardworking, gentle and noble, she had never included these. Did she even have these traits? Abby had always pictured what kind of man she wanted without thinking what kind of woman she wanted to be. What did she have to offer?

Abby tossed down the cloth and looked at the clean chalkboard. Colorado was proving to be much like the cleaning cloth, clearing her mind of false observations and thoughts. Yet even with a clear mind all she had come to realize was how undesirable she was. Her whole life had been covered with so much fluff that few really saw who she was, or even wanted what they saw. When so many men had come courting in Texas, all she'd had to do was sit, smile, laugh, and look pretty.

Abby shook her head. Why was she being so melancholy today? A soft creak from the entrance made her jump in eager delight. However, when she looked up to see no one, her expression fell. She stopped fussing with her things for a moment, pausing to contemplate why that darn pastor hadn't stopped by for a few days. Hadn't they begun to build a friendship of some sorts? Had they not laughed and teased? So why did he suddenly disappear out of the blue? Was it because he saw how Joseph looked at Esther and it angered him? Did Will still have feelings for Esther? The thought made Abby shift uncomfortably. She did not want Will to have feelings for Esther. She wanted him to have feelings for her.

Abby's eyes went wide. "By golly," she whispered as self-realization washed over her. She liked Will! Really, really liked him. In fact, from the first day she met him, she had fallen for him. She realized how often she looked up at the entrance hoping to see the blue-eyed pastor. She loved the way he teased her, made her mad, spoke sincerely, and didn't hide his flaws. Had she indeed in such a short time lost her heart to this young auburn-haired man of God?

"A pastor's girl—a pastors *wife*?" she whispered, testing out the titles. Could she and Will have a life in Tall Pine? Could she be away from Texas? Was that what she wanted? To start anew in a place where people did not know her as the spoiled rich girl? She had come to like Tall Pine, maybe even love it. She liked the feeling of fatigue after a hard day's work. She liked to see mountains surrounding her, and she had yet to explore the town that she heard was growing rapidly. Yes, she could make it here. She wanted to make it here, and she wanted to make it with Will. The former scary thought of having children suddenly vanished and was replaced with images of chubby babies, Christmas visits to Texas, summer picnics, and holding hands on the porch.

Abby felt elevated. She wanted Will! How delightfully unexpected this was. A sudden sense of worry made her frown. She wanted Will, but did Will want her? Esther had one time told her that Will was the biggest catch to all the single ladies of Tall Pine; even some in Denver had their eye on him. What if Will did not want her? Out here in Colorado, her father's ranch did her no good. All she had to offer was herself—and was that enough?

She was certainly not like Esther: queen-like, stunning, composed, and wise. Maybe Will wanted a more refined woman, or at least a capable woman who could sew, cook, and handle a farm single-handedly. Abby could learn those things, couldn't she? She wanted to learn those things. The life of parties and coach rides along the river now seemed as boring as the men who'd once offered them to her.

Abby turned away from the chalkboard and quickly gathered

her things. With so much to think about she left the schoolhouse to start dinner, chubby babies still bouncing in her mind.

Esther bit her lip, a feeling of trepidation gnawing at her gut. She looked over to see Eliza twirling her fingers; she was nervous as well. "Thank you for coming, Eliza," Esther said warmly. "I know this is not the excuse you wanted to close up your shop for the day."

"Oh come now, Esther. Do you think I was going to let you visit that odious man alone? Besides, Toby Higgins does not frighten me, and the fact that many women find him attractive is beyond me. I mean he has a pretty enough face, but something about it is, well, disturbing," Eliza scowled.

Esther nodded. "I think as one gets older it is impossible to hide one's character. It eventually shows through even the most handsome faces."

Eliza nodded. "Let's just hope the opposite is true. Maybe if I get a real good character my face will start looking nice, huh?" Eliza teased. Esther gave her a "we're not having this discussion" look, before pulling the horses to a stop as they arrived at Toby Higgins' home.

"Well," Esther said quietly, "let's get to this."

Eliza gaped. "Esther, are you sure this is the right house? I thought this place was abandoned. I'd wondered why no one had claimed it and fixed it up."

Esther nodded. "This is the place." She looked over the slatternly home with chipped paint and broken windows as ghost-like curtains swung lightly in the breeze. There was no garden, no flowers, only a few scrawny chickens pecking hungrily at the garbage-littered ground. Mustering her courage, Esther climbed down to tie off the horse. Eliza followed muttering something about dirt, filth, and pigsty. Ignoring her comments, Esther walked to the front door and knocked soundly.

"It's primitive," Eliza whispered one last comment.

In only a few seconds the door swung open. Toby stood in front of them, his shirt opened. He grinned widely, his lips spreading thickly over his straight teeth.

"Well, well, Miss Esther," he smacked her name on his tongue, not bothering to acknowledge Eliza. "I didn't know that all I had to do was impregnate some woman in order to get you inside my home." He winked suggestively and looked her up and down.

Esther swallowed, feeling exposed. Toby had a way of undressing a woman with his eyes that made her feel dirty. He barely stepped aside as Esther moved past him, forcing her to brush against him. By some power greater than herself she was able to stand strong. Eliza followed her, escaping the crude gaze of Toby. Esther gripped the sides of her skirt. There had been a time when she had purposely forgone vanity. No shiny hair done up, no beautiful clothing or even a dab of rouge. It wasn't until Michael was three months old that she realized she needed to look good for him. People tended to treat him better, talk of him better, if Esther was well dressed and done up. After that she made a special effort to appear beautiful even though for quite a while she was afraid to walk in public looking nice. Soon, however, it became habit and then it became something she enjoyed. Not, however, with Toby licking his lips at her. She longed for a cloak of invisibility.

"Where is Mary?" Esther asked with firmness and more strength than she felt.

Toby nodded in the direction of a closed door. "She's lying in there like some swollen pig. Says everything hurts." He suddenly stepped in front of Esther, his hot breath covering her like a suffocating blanket. "She can't do what a wife is supposed to for a husband, if you get my meaning."

Esther braced herself for the wave of anxiety, but instead she lifted an eyebrow as a thought crashed through her fears. *Joseph would strangle you if he knew what you were saying to me.* Esther felt her mouth twitch with a hint of a smile. For some reason the thought gave her courage and drowned her usual fears. Why would the thought of Joseph comfort her? she wondered. *He's not my knight in shining armor, and I do not need him or any other man to fight my battles.* Yet, she couldn't deny the calm that had come with the thought of Joseph.

"Step aside Toby," she said calmly, "and let me do my job."

Toby smirked and stepped aside. Not knowing what to expect, Esther opened the door and walked into the dark room. Eliza gasped behind her, covering her mouth.

"Lord have mercy," Eliza whispered through her hand. Esther glanced swiftly around, not wanting to embarrass Mary who lay on a small bed covered in gray blankets and dirty sheets. Empty whiskey bottles littered the floor as well as limp clothing. The walls were covered with nailed-up pictures of obscene women in compromising positions. With her lips parting slightly Esther put on her midwife smile and walked over to Mary.

"Good afternoon, Mary; I appreciate you letting me come," she said gently as if talking to a wounded animal.

Mary barely returned the smile. It was more of a grimace mixed with a small moan. "Toby don't like people coming in and out. I try not to need a lot—don't want Toby thinking I take too much work," she explained with a grunt as she tried to lift up her body.

"I see," Esther said, helping Mary sit up a little higher. "Well, I will just examine you and make sure the baby is in the right position and that both you and your baby are healthy." She nodded towards the sheets, "May I?"

Mary hesitated then finally nodded. Esther began to remove the scratchy blanket. Eliza sucked in a breath as Esther took off the cover and pulled up Mary's skirt. Huge blue veins in oddly twisted shapes bulged through the white skin. There was no shape between the knee and foot, only swelling flesh. The smell that escaped made bile rise in Esther's throat. She clenched her muscles forcing it to stay down. She heard Eliza gulp and quickly glanced in her direction. Eliza was looking away, her fingers pressing lightly on her lips also trying to keep down the urge to vomit.

"I used to have me such pretty legs," Mary moaned, tears springing to her eyes. "Nice long legs, slender and white. Toby liked them."

Esther nodded and began to take some cooling lotion and rubbed it lightly on the legs and then massaged her ankles. Mary sighed with pleasure.

"Your legs will go back as they were before, Mary. This is rather common, especially when women are in their last month as you are," Esther said, trying to smile brightly.

Mary guffawed bitterly. "Toby don't like me being pregnant… wish I wasn't. This baby has ruined everything. I can't be giving Toby what he wants because of it, and I ain't pretty because of it. Honestly, I don't want this here baby," Mary scowled and crossed her arms like a child.

Esther made no reply, merely pressing her lips together and biting her tongue. Eliza on the other hand let out a gasp, her own eyes brimming with tears, "How can you say that Mary Higgins?" she hissed. Esther snapped a look at Eliza trying to silence her. Eliza ignored her. "A child is a blessing and a privilege."

Mary snorted. "You don't know. You don't have no children. It ain't a blessing and it ain't no privilege."

Eliza gaped at Mary, shaking her head; she looked away and held up her hands in surrender. "I… I'm sorry Esther I can't," she turned and ran towards the door. "I just can't." Esther heard the front door slam. Her own heart ached for Eliza, as well as Mary. To Mary, Toby was the world, and without him, she was nothing. All in all Mary, was a baby and was not ready to have a baby herself.

"Silly woman," Mary muttered, referring to Eliza. "That's why she ain't married—don't know how to take care of a man."

Esther gave a non-committal smile and raised Mary's blouse. Shiny stretch marks danced across the taunt belly like shooting starts testifying to a miracle. Esther grinned, tracing them with her finger before moving her skilled hands around the belly.

"Your baby is in the right position, Mary. Hopefully you will have a fairly easy labor," she said optimistically with a smile that she hoped hid her clouded eyes. She finished her inspection and then pulled out a bottle of rose water and muslin squares.

"You gonna wash me?" Mary asked excitedly. Esther nodded and began bathing down Mary, determined that the unborn child would have a clean mother. "I'm gonna be smelling real pretty after, huh?" She leaned back grinning and wiggled her puffy toes. "I ever tell you about the time when Toby proposed to me?" she asked, lighting up.

Esther shook her head. "No, but I would love to hear it," she said before holding her breath to clean Mary.

After some time, Esther pulled out a clean blanket from her basket. She had felt to take it without knowing why, but through the years she'd learned to follow promptings from the heart. Now she was glad as she laid the soft blanket on Mary who stroked the "pretty thing" like a kitten. Esther bit her lip. She did not know what orders to give to Mary. The intense swelling in her legs was not good. She needed rest and lots of water. On the other hand, some movement might help get the blood moving and usher in the labor.

"Mary, I need you to drink lots of water," she finally said, "and I will be visiting you every morning." Esther decided that was best. In this way she could gauge how Mary was doing on a daily basis.

"I don't know if that be a good idea," Mary said, a line of worry wrinkling her forehead. "Like I said, Toby don't like it when people be coming over."

A shadow fell across the room sending an involuntary shiver down Esther's spine.

"Well, it depends on who is coming," Toby laughed and again licked his lips at Esther.

Disgusting! Why can't this man keep his slug-like tongue in his mouth?

Mary's countenance fell; she held the blanket close as if it would protect her from dark thoughts and fears.

Esther stood up and felt something she had not felt for a long time: Rage. Feeling fearless, she picked up her basket and strode over to Toby. "Mr. Higgins, a word please," she demanded, walking past him.

Joseph really would strangle him, a fragmented part of her brain brought up again. Esther bit her cheek with annoyance. Why was she thinking about Joseph? But again, courage and calm welled up inside of her.

"You want a word, Miss Esther?" Toby smiled and stepped close to her. *Too close.* "I can give you a lot more than a word," he winked.

Esther fought the urge to step back, instinct told her Toby would translate it as fear and fear would excite him, possibly encourage him.

Sick man.

Esther lifted her chin and pinned Toby with a gaze so sharp that his smile fell. "Mr. Higgins, as soon as Mary shows signs of labor, no matter how early, I am taking her to my home where she will deliver the baby. Understood?" Her voice was full of resolve. Toby scowled in confusion. He wasn't used to being told what to do.

"I say what goes on here," he finally snapped through slurred speech. "That's my woman and I say what she does, where she goes, and how she does it. You understand *me?*"

Esther stared down the insipid man. With a sigh of disgust she pulled out a bag jingling with coins. She watched as Toby's greedy face lit up. "That there sounds like a lot," he commented with sickening glee.

"It is, and it is yours if and when you allow me to take Mary to my home," she bargained. Bribery may not be godly, but a baby's life was at stake and God loved babies more than anything. That she knew for sure.

Toby huffed, knowing he was defeated. "Fine. You can take my pregnant pig to your house. Honestly, I didn't want no baby junk on my bed." He scowled as Esther put the coins away.

"Well then, we have a deal. Good day, Mr. Higgins," Esther spun around and left the musty house. She shut the door behind her and took a deep breath of the fresh air. It felt like pure deliverance. She had seen many rough things; Tall Pine in general was a good town with well-meaning people, but like everywhere it had its dark corners and troublemakers. Men like Toby Higgins though were just plain ol' wicked. He delighted in evil and Esther knew that no innocent baby under her watch would be born in that home.

Eliza was waiting in the cart, her elbows on her knees and her chin resting on her hands. "I'm sorry," she blurted out before Esther could pull herself up. "I don't know what came over me." Her eyes were still glistening with tears.

Esther shook her head. "Don't apologize. You have nothing to be sorry for," Esther assured her, flicking the reigns. She wanted to drop Eliza off and get to Michael as soon as possible.

Eliza was silent for only a minute before a sob escaped her lips. "It's just so damn unfair, Esther," she cried out and immediately lowered her eyes. "Excuse the language."

Esther smiled. "I took no offense Eliza," she said with a twinkle in her eye.

Eliza sighed and wiped the tears away. "Why are you so strong, Esther? Tell me how you live your life without bitterness, because I can't do it. I used to ask God for a child, but now I know it is too late." She hesitated, "Even if I were to marry," she continued not wanting to think of Kyle Lampton but unable to help herself, "I am no longer young."

"You're not old," Esther objected.

"Yes, but I am not young," Eliza cried. "Who knows if I will ever be able to have a child? Now I ask God why. Why when I have tried my whole life to be a good Christian, to follow God's will, tried to be Christ-like and serve others, why am I denied the one thing I want more than anything in the world? While scum like the Higgins are expecting a child that they don't even want?" Her voice was broken in between sobs as tears soaked her skirt.

Esther was silent for a moment listening to Eliza's heartbreaking words. Words that she understood all too well. She herself had been angry at God, had cursed His name and had shaken her fist at heaven. How could He have abandoned her when she had been faithful to Him? What kind of Heavenly Father allowed a daughter to experience such grief? She'd had to fight demons in order to see that He had kept angels around her. She'd had to experience hell in order to have heaven. Growing up, her life had been one of encouraged naivety. But now she was strong and had compassion, which opened her up to more understanding and joy. Above all, she had Michael. She would go through any pain and suffering again to have Michael. He was proof of God's eternal and incomprehensible love.

"Eliza," she said softly, "I wish I could give you the answer, but God's plan for everyone and His relationship with them is so individual that answers only come when you are willing to bruise your knees with prayer and weary yourself with faith. You will have the answer one day. It may not be at the time you want, but it will be in the Lord's time, which is always best." She paused, studying Eliza's face to make sure that she was not hurting a wound. Eliza nodded and looked at her hopefully, encouraging Esther to continue. "God loves you more than you can imagine. He does not always stop bad things from happening to us, and I don't know why. But I do know every hardship we have, when we remain faithful, God sanctifies and turns into a blessing. I like to think of our trials as stinging nettle, and beside every stinging nettle there is a horsetail plant that has a liquid to sooth the rash. God does not keep us from getting stung, but He always gives us our own horsetail. Look at Michael—he is my world. What happened to me was horrible, but what God gave me was wonderful... perfect even. Besides, my sorrow and anger forced me to turn to God where I have found peace and true happiness." She smiled softly, "As humans we have a tendency to turn to God only when dark clouds are in our life." Esther bit her lip, she didn't want to preach to Eliza, merely comfort her, but she also knew that God's love and ways could not be described, only felt and experienced.

Eliza smiled. "Michael is a miracle isn't he?"

Esther nodded. "A living, breathing miracle."

"Well, Esther, I thank you. Truly, from the bottom of my heart, I thank you." Eliza leaned over as Esther pulled to a stop and embraced her. "Now, I will go inside and have some chocolate cake that was left at my shop by some stranger," she laughed shakily. Esther smiled in delight, knowing full well who left the cake even though Eliza found it difficult to speak of Kyle Lampton, as if speaking of him would bring bad luck. She watched the slight figure of Eliza walk away then turned the horse towards the direction of the schoolhouse. She was now hungry, very hungry, and missing her son. No doubt Michael was thrilled beyond measure as he played with Joseph.

Without thinking Esther smiled. "Joseph," she muttered softly before shaking her head and singing a song to keep her mind clear.

Ten

Michael's face hovered an inch above a pile of fish bones and eyes, fascinated with the gore.

"Take a bite Michael; I am sure it is delicious," Joseph prodded teasingly. Michael scrunched up his face and shook his head as he made a "yuck" sound. Joseph laughed, casting a warm smile at the boy. Michael was at the age where he found everything amazing; his wonder was contagious and Joseph saw himself seeing things through Michael's eyes: the fishing was amazing, the fish guts were awe-inspiring, the freezing cold stream was hilarious. All in all, Joseph couldn't remember the last time he'd had such fun.

A memory flashed back at him when he himself was sixteen; his stepfather had nervously asked to take him fishing, then hunting, riding, many things. Each time Joseph refused. Jefferson had treated him awkwardly for the first few years of being a stepfather. Joseph had interpreted that awkwardness as a lack of caring; after all, how could Jefferson care for a boy who was not his own? Now here he was feeling tenderness toward Michael and even a protectiveness, jumping any time Michael slipped in the stream or walked out of his sight. He wondered if Jefferson had cared for him. Maybe it took a while to know what to do with a young boy still mourning for his father. Joseph had not been like Michael, quick to love and accept a man who was not his father. No, Joseph had been reserved and standoffish. Perhaps Jefferson was being delicate with him, not wanting to rush Joseph or scare him. Perhaps that was why it had taken a few years before Jefferson tried active bonding, but by then, Joseph had already formed a strong opinion about their relationship and would not let it change.

I must write to Jeff, Joseph told himself as these thoughts paraded through his mind. He had been putting it off, unsure of what to say. Still, he needed to ask about the ranch and maybe express some sort of gratitude… not a lot. Joseph was a grown man after all. Even so, Jefferson deserved some form of thanks for what he had done.

"Are we going to cook these?" Michael asked, wandering over to Joseph's side. "I hardly ever have fish," he said with a contemplative flex in his voice as if the fact just occurred to him.

"Your momma doesn't cook fish often?" Joseph asked. Maybe she didn't like it.

"No, she prefers beef I think."

Joseph smiled; he knew he liked the woman. "Beef, huh, but no fish?"

"She tried to take me fishing one time, but it didn't work out so well."

Joseph cut open the last trout. "What happened?"

"I didn't listen to my momma and went too far out in the water. Momma had to swim out and get me before I drowned."

"She saved you?" Joseph was now much more interested in the story.

Michael nodded. "I told her I would never go near the water again, so the next day she took me back and taught me how to swim. She took me every day until I could swim as well as her," Michael said with pride. "Now I am no longer afraid of the water."

Joseph smiled: Esther was a good mother. He imagined her in the water, laughing and letting down her long hair, wet and carefree. Joseph suddenly shifted, feeling mighty warm. He quickly stood and nodded to the basket of fish.

"You want to carry the rods or the fish?" he asked Michael.

Michael took the fish and fell in step with Joseph who was wondering if Esther would be back soon. Not that he minded spending time with Michael; in fact, he realized he loved spending time with Michael. As if reading his thoughts, Joseph suddenly felt a warm little hand slide into his own. He looked down to see Michael's smile beaming up at him. A lump formed in Joseph's throat. He smiled back and squeezed Michael's hand gently.

"Hey, that is what my mom does," Michael laughed, swinging their arms together in rhythm with their steps. "Joseph," he said quietly and with a hesitation that made the man slow his steps and look at the young boy.

"What is it, kid?"

Michael took a deep breath, "I love you," he exhaled.

Joseph's lips parted as he stared at the eager blue eyes hungry for attention and love from a father. Joseph's own heart seemed to melt like a pool of butter. It was obvious in Michael's face that he wanted those words said in return, but should Esther refuse him, how could he lead Michael to believe he loved him and then return to Texas? How could Michael love him after such a short time? But wasn't that hypocritical when Joseph himself knew that he was in love with Esther from the moment he saw her?

At Joseph's silence Michael's eyes brimmed with tears. "I said I love you," he repeated with a catch in his voice.

All walls and inhibitions dropped. Joseph blinked back his emotion and grinned at Michael. "Love you too, kid," he said, his heart flip-flopping at Michael's jubilant smile. The two fell back into an easy pace. Joseph held tightly to Michael's hand. He didn't care what he had to do—there was no way in heaven or hell he would be leaving Tall Pine without Esther or Michael.

❧

Esther had to be the most frustrating and alluring woman who ever walked the earth. She returned looking tired, stressed, and so dang good. A goddess in cotton who would not even acknowledge Joseph; in fact, she seemed keen on ignoring him. When she returned she inquired how Michael was, and then abruptly began to take him home. Joseph had looked pleadingly at Abby who skillfully insisted that they stay for dinner.

"Oh, thank you, but you have helped me enough for today."

"Please Esther, it's nothing special—just rice and beans and the fish Michael and Joseph caught—but it would be awfully nice to cook with another woman, and I am making an apple pie from that recipe you gave me," Abby pleaded. Michael, who had discovered Abby's orange kitten Killer, was now gleefully paying with him as the ball of fluff pounced all over the giggling boy. Esther finally consented, not sparing Joseph a moment's glance as she brushed past him. Brooding over her obvious aloofness, Joseph sat outside the kitchen pretending to read a book, although he found himself reading the same sentence over and over as his ears strained to hear the conversation of the two women.

"You put butter in your rice?" Abby asked, tilting her head in awe. Everything about cooking now amazed her: the way bread rose, the crackling noise of meat fried in oil.

"Only a little. Just remember everything tastes better with a little butter," smiled Esther.

"How is Mary Higgins doing?" Abby asked. She was a specimen of worried gossip among the church-going women of Tall Pine, all worried about her while also being disgusted and fed up with her stubborn adoration towards a no-good husband.

"There is a lot of swelling," Esther said, her voice grave. "Too much swelling often means complications for the mother."

"Meaning death?" Abby asked, lowering her voice to a whisper.

Esther nodded, "Possibly. It is as if the body poisons itself, which can kill the mother unless she has the baby early, and at that point, it is a question of either getting the mother to move in order to speed up labor or have her rest because the body is doing an okay job fighting the poison. The body is left with no energy to fight, and there can be bleeding, long labors, and so forth."

Esther didn't speak like other doctors or nurses that Abby had met; good people who seemed to look upon their patients with a more scientific and detached perspective. Esther's whole face looked worn from the weight she seemed to carry as if it was completely her responsibility to assure the safety of whomever she helped.

"I'm sure you're doing all you can," Abby said, touching her arm. Esther paused and gave Abby a thoughtful look that turned into an embrace of gratitude.

"Thank you, Abby," Esther said as she pulled away. "I do all I can, but sometimes I fear it is not enough. I begin to understand my uncle's frenzy for new research, his obsession for medical advances. There is so much we don't know, and, God willing, I hope the knowledge to save more lives comes soon."

Abby nodded as a strange feeling of helplessness settled over her. Back in Texas she had known there was sufferings, sickness, and hardship in the world, but the desire to fix it never overcame her as it did now. She suddenly felt so small, so inadequate to help, and yet she had a great desire to do something.

"My mother always says that a good woman feels constantly guilty for not being able to do more," Abby muttered, feeling a buried gratitude for her mother. Now she understood—her mother had saved her from being one of those silly women who speak of their youthful glory days for years to come. "I suppose though I would rather feel guilt and pain and have substance to my soul than to live a life of superficial ease and have nothing to me... no soul as it were."

Again Esther gave Abby a pensive look. The little schoolteacher had come to Tall Pine as a child, a young girl stuffed with giggles and lace. Frivolity now seemed to have been replaced by wisdom. "I wholeheartedly agree," Esther said, feeling the heaviness lift.

"How was Toby with you? I can't stand the man." Abby shivered and began seasoning the beans.

"Well, I had to bribe him in order to have Mary come to my house when she goes into labor," she began before telling the story, although she left out Eliza. There was no need to share her friend's battles. When she retold Toby's suggestive comments, which she modified, she heard a thud from the living room as Joseph threw down his book and rushed into the kitchen.

"That low-life bastard said what to you?" he roared.

Both Esther and Abby blinked in surprise. "Joseph Silver, watch your language. And, more to the point—were you eavesdropping?" Abby asked. Her mouth twisted in a mixture of surprise and amusement.

"I was sitting in the living room, Abby! That could hardly be classified as eavesdropping," he bellowed before pinning Esther with his gaze. The magnitude of his concern was vivid in his piercing eyes and clenched jaw. So vivid that Esther found herself getting... warm? Not afraid, nor anxious, nor smothered? She tried to look away but found she couldn't. Had she not already belittled herself when she discovered that the thought of Joseph had comforted her in Toby's presence? She did not want a man. She did not trust them. She would not allow a handsome face or even kindness to her child to seduce her away from her resolve. Yet, if this were true, then why couldn't she look away? Why did her cheeks feel flushed?

"You are not to go to that man's house again," Joseph demanded, his chest heaving.

In an instant Esther's emotions fired into resentment. "I beg your pardon, Mr. Silver," she said with a pronounced arch of her brow.

"It's Joseph—and I said you are not to go to that man's house again. Not when he is speaking to you in such intimate terms," Joseph growled.

Esther tilted her head with a half-smile. "Intimate is hardly the word I would use... inappropriate, yes. Intimacy implies two parties whereas with Mr. Higgins, the suggestive nature was from him and not me."

"Still, you should not, will not—"

"I will go and do as I please," Esther said kindly with her tone rising only slightly. "I appreciate your concern, but maybe you did not hear that there is a pregnant woman who is completely incapable of caring for herself, let alone her unborn child. I would not deserve to call myself a midwife if I did nothing."

Joseph glowered; he didn't know how to answer. "And helping means you going there *every* morning?"

Esther lifted her chin and folded her arms, "Yes. It does," she said firmly.

Joseph looked away. He had not met this Toby Higgins, but anger and aggression swelled within him. He had seen many terrible things in his time as a Ranger, and he'd learned to develop a sort of numbness to them. Meeting Esther and Michael had stirred emotions long buried. Abby whispered something to him about calming down, but he did not hear it. He needed to go do something before he spoke out in anger. Outside. He needed to go out and cool off. Firewood! *Surely more firewood needs to be chopped.* Storming off without a word, Joseph walked fiercely into the cool evening air.

He took several deep breaths before walking to the back of the house where the firewood was kept. How he wished he could meet this Toby Higgins and punch him in the face. Had not Abby said that the young pastor did something similar? Perhaps Will was a better man than what Joseph had given him credit for. Grabbing a large log Joseph set it in front of him, picked up the ax, and swung it clean through the log. He did another and another; he didn't know how many logs he'd chopped, but he swung until his muscles burned and sweat dripped from his brow.

How much of his life had been spent as a Ranger when he could have been preparing a home, a place for him and Esther? Would that have even mattered? Would Esther ever give him a chance, or would she refuse him and send him off with shattered hopes and a broken heart? How he longed to grab her, press his body against hers, and call her his. Yet, just when his hopes started to rise, Esther would shut them down. Joseph had always believed that if he was relentless in his pursuit, he could obtain whatever he wanted. Esther was filling him with doubt.

He placed another log in front of him and swung. He thought of Michael's hopeful face when he had told Joseph that he loved him.

He thought of Esther's beautiful and methodical ways, making the most mundane chore seem more like an elegant dance. He could not abandon his quest to win her over, but he now doubted he would ever be successful.

Pray. His mother's words echoed in his mind. Joseph blew a lock of hair out of his eyes. He never prayed—did not need to. He was perfectly fine on his own.

Pray. The word repeated itself again. A smile hinted on Joseph's lips. He could never escape his mother's words: pray, be strong but gentle, save yourself for the one woman who will matter; be kind but not weak; when in doubt, when in need, always pray.

Joseph swung the ax again, and again.

"Dear Lord," he said with a gruff voice. He swung again, "I don't know exactly what to say," another swing. What should he say—that he had no idea what to do with Esther? Why would God even care about that?

"Joseph?" A gentle voice surprised him. Lowering the ax he turned to see Esther.

Well I'll be. Lord, that was quick. "Yes, Miss Esther?" he asked. He felt both confused and elated that she had come to see him.

She nodded toward the house, "Supper is just about ready," she said, taking a step forward. Joseph stared at Esther quizzically. He liked how she carried herself with ease, no need to chatter or move abruptly. Her natural serenity in expression, voice, and movement showed a strong assurance in herself. Yet, right now she looked different. After the long day, her hair was falling from its done-up form, allowing soft tendrils to fall along her neck and making her look more youthful. Her cheeks seemed flushed, her gaze, usually steady, glanced away every few seconds. As she approached he noticed that a small constellation of freckles danced over the bridge of her nose. Esther was always stunning, but there was a barrier that surrounded her, making her seem untouchable. Only in his mind could he embrace her, kiss her. In this moment, as she continued walking towards him, she seemed more girlish, more approachable. What was different now?

Esther felt bad as soon as Joseph left. His sudden explosion and impudence in telling her what she could and could not do had flared her anger. No man would control her, even if he meant well. Yet when Joseph had stormed off, she could not help but feel a bit flattered that he cared so much. Still, she did not need a protector; for so long she had looked after herself. Her uncle had come to her aid, but even then it was she who had cleaned up the old house, chased off wolves, looked after the property, stayed up with Michael during feverish nights, taught herself how to shoot and shoot well. Not only could she take care of herself, but she was capable of taking care of others.

Joseph seemed bent on helping her, and the thought made her feel, well, soft and almost elated. She had a sudden urge to giggle. Shaking her shoulders to clear her mind, Esther had tried to focus on the rice and beans. Men were naturally beasts, save a few, such as her uncle. She would not allow herself to let go of her distrust and anger. It was those feelings that would protect her, and more importantly they were feelings that would protect Michael from getting stuck with an unloving stepfather. Esther would not bereft herself of the lessons she had learned seven years ago.

Try as she might, she could not focus on the meal at hand or on the comforting chatter of Abby. The thought gnawed at her that she had possibly offended Joseph when he was merely showing concern for her. The feeling that she should make amends pecked at her brain until finally she put down her wooden spoon and dismissed herself to go check on Joseph.

Esther expected to find Joseph brooding. When she heard the wood cracking she hurried to the back and then froze when she saw him. His thin shirt was damp with perspiration and clung to his swelled and taunt muscles. The dark brown hair hung loosely over blazing eyes. He looked powerful, manly, and so very handsome. Esther almost turned to go back inside. What was wrong with her? Was she really admiring the raw form of a particularly fine man? She was stronger than this, had more will power than this. She should go, continue to ignore him, ignore this mixture of emotions between fear and admiration. Esther tried to turn, but she could not; she stood transfixed watching him work. It was no secret that there was little about men she admired, but as she watched the tall broad figure work with such strength, it was like watching a wild mustang run in the fields or a wild cat stalk its prey; it was natural, wild, and in some primeval way, beautiful.

Recognizing that it would be awkward should he look up and see her staring at him, Esther called out his name. When he looked at her, she felt her cheeks flush. Reminding herself of her indifference towards him, she walked forward. She told him that dinner was about ready knowing that it appeared as a weak excuse to come see him.

"Actually, Joseph," she said with a slight quiver in her voice, "I came to—to apologize. I recognize that you were simply being an honorable man who would defend and watch out for any woman. I thank you for your concern and hope that I didn't come across as ungrateful." Her lips twitched and her hand brushed back a loose strand of hair falling across her face.

"Any woman, huh?" Joseph dropped the ax and walked forward until he was only inches away from her. The woman was so darn composed, an attribute that he both admired and one that also drove him mad. How he wanted to touch her, although from experience he wondered if she would pull away. The impulse to touch was overwhelming. To gently touch her fingers, entwine them with his. His glance moved to her hand, long-fingered, elegant despite the hard work she obviously did. He could hold her hand, stroke it, kiss it, hold it to his chest, and then pull her in for a dizzying kiss.

What would she do?

Smack him?

Fight him? Or melt into his body with an equal fervor to the passion he was feeling.

Esther withdrew her hand from her side, crossing her arms. She was used to men leering at her body or simply admiring her face.

The way Joseph was staring at her hand made her skin prickle with a feeling that she couldn't name. It was if her skin were hungering for something, but she did not know what. He was close—too close. She felt uncomfortable, but not fearful. It was more like an anticipation. She cleared her throat and lifted her chin to meet his gaze. It was a mistake. His eyes captured her in an instant, holding her like a vice, demanding silently that she stay put.

"You think," Joseph said, his voice husky, "that I would get so riled up over *any* woman?"

Esther shifted her weight. An icy autumn breeze raked down her arms, so why did she feel so hot? "Yes, any woman, or any woman at least whom you considered a *friend*."

Joseph laughed more out of frustration than humor. "A friend?" he asked. "You think I would want to beat a man senseless for being suggestive to a friend?"

Esther raised her eyebrows, as her lips parted, "Yes, Joseph, after all that is what you said we are—friends."

Joseph felt the angry twitch in his jaw. He knew very well Esther was not reminding him of his words so much as she was telling him what they were—*friends*. He looked away for a moment wishing to kiss her, yell at her, drop to his knees and ask, no, demand her to be his bride. But he knew he would just frighten her away, which continually begged the question as to why she was frightened. Why would a woman of intelligence and faith be so afraid of a man? She was not intimidated or spooked like some wide-eyed horse. No, she was more like a female wolf guarding her young, her territory. Joseph looked back at Esther realizing his mistake. He had seen Esther, wanted her, known she was for him, and gone after her without proper investigation. Most women were keen on telling their life story, naming off a list of lovers, offenders, hopes and dreams. Esther was different—she was sealed tight and full of mystery. Esther's eyes were too wise, and she had too much confidence to have had a life of ease and clarity. It was evident to him now that she had a story, a story that was prohibiting her from letting down the wall around her heart.

"Of course, Miss Esther," he finally exhaled. "We are just friends."

Esther didn't trust the look on Joseph's face. His eyes were filled with an unsettling understanding, as if he had realized a secret. She also knew by his tone of voice that he thought the title of friendship was ridiculous when it came to them. Esther eyed him warily for a second before taking a step back.

"Are you coming?" she asked, her voice a bit too high pitched.

Joseph nodded her to go on. "You all start without me. I'll need to wash up first."

Esther's shoulders began to turn, but then she stopped. Cocking her head to the side she smiled shyly. "When I came out were—were you praying?"

Joseph felt his windblown cheeks warm up.

Am I blushing? The thought horrified him.

"No, well, I began to but… you know, I am just not the praying type."

Another tilt of the head to the left. "Hmm, you know, Joseph, when Samuel Colt invented the majestic pistol he did so with prayer. The design came to him in a dream after praying."

Joseph's lips parted. The woman knew who Samuel Colt was? He truly was hopelessly in love. "Is that really true?" he asked, cocking a brow.

Esther laughed. "I have no idea, but wouldn't it be wonderful if it was?"

Joseph chuckled, having no reply to give.

Esther gave him one last curious glance before turning away. Somehow there had been a change just now, she towards Joseph and he towards her. She realized that Joseph was the first single man who did not repulse her or scare her. She still felt uncomfortable with him, but this time when she had seen him she felt—attraction? The word stung Esther. She was not supposed to be attracted to a man. Esther clenched her jaw. She was not attracted to him. She was tired, confused, and worn out. Glancing behind her, Esther expected Joseph to be gathering the chopped wood, yet as fate would have it, he stood straight staring directly at her. When they made eye contact Esther quickly looked away, but not before seeing the victorious smile of Joseph.

She had looked back! Heaven be praised, she had looked back. Abby always told him that if a woman was interested, she looked back upon departure, and Esther had just done that, with her piercing eyes and flushed cheeks. She had looked back. He would find out her story and would court her even if it killed him. He would win her heart.

Abby was surprised at how good the rice and beans were, especially with the fresh fish fried to perfection. Esther hardly ate, although she assured Abby it was because of fatigue and not because the food was not good. Michael ate with as much gusto as usual, and when Joseph finally arrived, hair wet from bathing, he too helped himself generously.

"I was just telling Esther that I am determined to learn how to knit. In fact, I wanted to know if you could take me into town tomorrow so I could buy some yarn," Abby said to Joseph.

"My little sister is cooking and now knitting. What will be next?" he teased, taking a large bite of rice.

"Hopefully, a garden in the spring. Will is supposed to be a great gardener—maybe he can help me," Abby said, blushing slightly.

Esther suppressed a smile. Abby and Will definitely had a spark between them. What a wonderful couple they would be. "Will is a great gardener Abby; he knows when to plant and what to plant. I would definitely ask him for his advice," she encouraged.

Joseph wanted to growl. What did he have to do to receive a compliment from Esther? He was as good as this pastor. "Miss Esther, just curious to know, are you from these parts? Born and bred in Colorado?" he asked, turning his attention towards her. The question must have surprised Esther because she almost dropped her spoon.

"Uhh, no, I am not."

Joseph knew he would have to dig for details. "Where are you from?"

"Back East," she said. She focused on her plate though she merely twirled the beans without taking bites. Noticing Joseph's inquiring look she sighed and looked up while pushing away her plate. "Boston to be exact," she said, glancing at Michael who was feeding Killer tidbits from his plate.

"A city girl!" Abby exclaimed. "I never imagined you were a city girl. You handle the roughness of Tall Pine so well."

Esther laughed nervously. "To me the city is rougher than the country. At least that was my experience."

Joseph was not satisfied, "And your parents, they still live in Boston?

Again Esther glanced at Michael whose little ears had perked up. "Yes—yes, they do."

Abby now looked interested and confused. She had never seen Esther look so uncomfortable. She shot Joseph a warning look to stop talking, but he ignored her.

"Do your parents ever visit?" he asked.

Before Esther could reply, Michael spoke up: "Momma's father came a year ago. I was five almost six, but he was not nice and he told me—"

"Michael!" Esther stood up, jerking the table an inch forward. Her face was red and her hands shook slightly, Joseph would not have noticed had he not been sitting close to her. She looked at Abby and Joseph apologetically. "I am so sorry; we must go."

Michael looked heart stricken. "But what about the apple pie?" he wailed.

Esther shook her head and held out her hand to him. "Michael, I am serious. We need to go, now!"

Abby now was on her feet. Joseph followed. "Esther is everything alright?" Abby asked full of concern.

"Yes I—I am not feeling well," she said too quickly as Michael began to protest with angry tears. Abby attempted to comfort him by wrapping up a slice of pie to send home with him.

Joseph walked Esther out. "Let me hitch up the horse," he offered.

She shook her head walking quickly, "No, thank you Joseph, please go finish your meal. I am quite capable."

She reached out her hand for the horse's reins, but was stopped when Joseph placed his hand on hers. He expected her to pull away, but instead she froze, staring at their touching hands. Joseph felt her pulse quicken, her skin sprout tingly bumps. She swallowed, still not moving. Joseph closed his fingers around her hand, slowly lowering it away from the reigns and down to her side.

"Esther," he said gently, "let me help you."

Esther nodded, stepping away and slowly pulling her hand from his.

Joseph did not push the physical contact any more. He turned and began assembling the cart and horse with experienced skill. After a few seconds of silence with only the faint talking of Abby and Michael in the distance, Esther came beside him.

"Listen Joseph, a year ago my father came to visit. He met Michael and me in Denver. I can't give you details, but I can say that is was a heartbreaking experience for us. I beg you to not bring it up with him; for that matter, please do not ask any questions about my parents or my past," she pleaded. "Please Joseph—please no questions."

Joseph nodded as Michael walked out holding a covered plate of pie; his cheeks were tear streaked and his nose red. Joseph looked at Abby who mouthed helplessly, "I tried."

"You ready to go, sweetheart?" Esther asked her son sweetly. When she reached out for him, Michael jerked away from her, glowering. Esther politely ignored his attitude and allowed Joseph to lift the upset boy into the cart.

"Michael, I got something to tell you," Joseph whispered as Esther said good-bye to Abby.

Michael looked up curiously. "What is it?" he asked in a quivering voice.

Joseph leaned in closer, "I need to go into town tomorrow, so I was thinking how about I pick you up a present and give it to you on Sunday?"

Michael's lips parted into a cherub-like smile. "Really? You'll get me a present?"

Joseph nodded. "A good present, I promise."

"Promise what?" Esther asked, taking up the reigns.

"I promise that I will see you and Michael on Sunday," Joseph replied with a knowing half wink to Michael. Esther gave him a "sure you did smile" before making a clicking sound and leading the horse away.

Abby and Joseph stood watching the fading cart until it disappeared. When it did, Abby spun around to Joseph. "Alright Mr. Inquisitor, why were you relentless in asking Esther about her parents? It was obvious she did not want to talk about it, and yet you persisted." She shook her head with a sigh, "And, I thought you wished to win her over."

"I do," Joseph said firmly. "But that woman has a past, a hidden one from what I can tell, and there is no way I will reach her unless I know what I am dealing with," he said and began to walk back to the house. "Luckily, I know a detective back East with whom I corresponded for a time over a case. I am going to write to him and have him find out what happened with Esther Callen."

Abby blinked incredulously before catching up with Joseph. "Wait—wait!" she called out, grabbing his arm in haste. "Did I hear you right? You are going to hire a detective to find out about a past which she is desperately trying to keep hidden?"

"Desperate times call for desperate measures, Abby, and time is one thing I don't have right now."

"But Joseph, do you not see how wrong that it? Esther is an intelligent woman, and if she is not speaking of her past, then there is a good reason why. Besides, things have a way of revealing themselves without anybody's help. If you force it…" she bit her lip thinking of an analogy. "Well, remember you told me that no Ranger was able to catch that crazed killer, Cut-Throat Nick? You said it was because he'd barricade himself in until it caused the Rangers to force their way to him… they all ended up dead or injured. You caught him by waiting three days until he came out.

Now Esther is certainly no Cut-Throat Nick, but the same concept applies. I promise you, Joseph that if you go behind Esther's back and pry into her past, nothing good will come of it and you will never win her."

Joseph sighed, rolling back his neck and looking at the star-filled sky. "Goodness Abby, you should have been a lawyer. You do make a good case."

"That's because I am right. Just let Esther be for tonight and come have some pie; otherwise, I will eat the whole thing myself," she said, nudging him playfully.

Joseph nodded, glancing over his shoulder one last time. What did Esther have to hide? Would she ever tell him? Did it have to do with Michael? Joseph felt sorry for the disappointed kid. He would make sure that tomorrow he found Michael the finest cowboy hat there was—and maybe a slingshot, too.

Michael was silent during the ride home. Esther tried talking to him, but each time she spoke, he huffed and would look away. Once they were home Michael began running to his room, but Esther caught his shoulder.

"Hang on mister, we need to talk."

Michael pulled away. "Why did we have to leave? We were going to have pie and play," he cried.

"Michael, you can't spend all your time with Joseph, and besides, you know why we left. You were about to tell our secret."

Michael's eyes swelled with tears, "You mean that my dad was a bad and evil man like your dad told me."

Esther, too, felt the sting of tears pooling. She sat down holding out her arms to Michael, but he did not come. "Michael, the man who got me pregnant is not your dad. A father is someone who loves and protects you and the man who hurt me was bad, but then God sent me you to make it all better. You are special… you are my miracle," she practically pleaded with him, wanting to take away his pain and disappointment.

"But you promised me a father, remember? And you told me what he would be like—that he would be like Joseph." Michael's tears streamed down his face. "Why can't you marry Joseph, Momma? Then we can be a family."

"We *are* a family," Esther cried. "You and I are enough. We don't need a man."

"But why? Why can't I have Joseph as a father?"

"Because men are terrible, Michael," Esther blurted out. "They are cruel and bad."

Michael went very still, his face written with devastation. "But Momma... *I* am a man."

Esther felt a stab in her heart as the realization hit her. She had wounded her son, damaged his hope and self-worth. "Michael, I didn't mean you. You are still a boy, my sweet boy. You are different."

"But I will grow up to be a man. Does that mean I will be terrible, cruel, and bad?" His lips trembled.

Esther stood up reaching out to him. "Michael, listen—" she began.

"No!" Michael shouted and ran from her. "I *hate* you!" he sobbed before slamming the door to his room.

Esther sank down onto a chair, her head falling into her hands as she allowed pent-up tears to fall freely. What a horrible thing she had done. Her own fears were scaring her son, denying him a father, and making him feel bad about himself. Was she being selfish holding onto her fears thinking that they would keep her safe, justifying them by telling herself she was keeping Michael safe? What kind of woman was she if she could not let her past go for the sake of her son?

"Dear Father in heaven," she pleaded through sobs, "I know I have wearied you with my prayers and surely seem ungrateful when I ask for help after all that you have given me, but Lord I know the sacred nature of parenthood, and I know you hold it close to your heart, so I beg of you—help me, heal me from my past that cripples me like a disease. I have thought I was enough. I believed that I was sufficient to take care of all Michael's needs, and yet I see a void in him needing to be filled with the love of a father. But, dear God and perfect Father, I hate men. I distrust them and fear them. Please heal me of this prejudice and dislike. I do not want to be filled with hatred when my son needs so much love. Please help me." Her words were muffled in sobs and her shoulders sagged as her body shook. After several minutes Esther sat up and took a long steadying breath to calm herself.

"Dress," she told herself. She needed to finish the red dress for the barn dance. She needed to do something, for although she felt calmer after praying, she was still shaking and seized with guilt. She walked to her room and began hemming the bottom of the flame-red dress. As her hands fell into a pattern, her mind cleared. She worked for a solid hour before feeling the effects of a long day. Just before she finished the hem and was ready to cut the string, a staggering image filled her mind and it almost made her cry out. The image was of Joseph carrying her laughing son on his back, his face lit up in genuine delight as he played with her son. The image faded into another. This time of Will dripping with sweat as he plowed a sick man's crops for a whole season and then used his own money to buy shoes for the children. Then a scene of Sheriff Ben organizing a charity donation for a widow whose husband had been killed, husbands praying on their knees that their wives would live through labor, and fathers rushing sick children to Uncle Tim as they pleaded with tear-soaked faces for their child's life. The baker who handed out free samples to the poor, the bookstore owner who saved picture books for Michael, her own uncle who had welcomed her into his home when she had nowhere to go. Memory after memory of good, honest, and hardworking men filled her mind until she had seen almost a lifetime in but a few moments. The images faded, leaving her feeling warm and peaceful. She felt the familiar sting of tears, but not of sorrow; this time they were from a joyful realization that God had spoken to her, answered her prayers. After seven years of hate and anxiety, He seemed to have healed her in a matter of minutes by showing the good that existed among men. There was still the fear of touch, the fear of being controlled, but the crippling hate was gone.

Esther set down the dress and stood tall. *Esther,* she told herself, *there are good women out there and bad women. There are bad men, but there are also many good men. You are wrong to hate them. You are wrong to mistrust them. It is time to grow up and move on. You may not want to marry or need to marry, but it is wrong of you to hate any of God's children, including men.* She bowed her head reverently. "Thank you Father—thank you so much," Esther whispered, her heart filled with a newfound peace. She then washed her face, braided her hair, and tiptoed into Michael's room. The perfect little body lay deep in sleep on his narrow bed tucked under the thick quilt she had made him. Esther went and sat on the bed, stroking the angelic face that she loved so much. Michael stirred and opened his eyes.

"Momma?" he croaked.

Esther leaned over and kissed his forehead. "I'm here love," she whispered, kissing him again.

"Do you still love me?" he asked in a whimper.

Esther lay down next to her son and pulled him close, "Michael, I love you so much and will always love you. There is nothing you can do to stop me loving you."

"But I said I hate you... I didn't mean it."

Esther smiled and nuzzled her face into his hair. "I said some things I did not mean as well. How about we both start over?"

Michael nodded. "I think that is a good idea," he said before relaxing fully into her arms. His breathing slowly turned into a light snore and Esther scooted herself fully onto the bed and fell asleep.

Eleven

Will walked agitatedly past the bookstore, the butcher shop, and then the post office. He wasn't quite sure what more he needed. He had bought garden tools, seeds, and socks. All was packed away in his wagon, and yet he continued to walk. Maybe it was because his mind was muddled with confusion; he had no idea what to write for tomorrow's sermon. He admitted that he wanted Abby's advice. His best sermons had been guided by her insight, but he had avoided her the past week. Will knew why. It was simple: he'd fallen in love with her. Somehow it had snuck up on him. The little schoolteacher with her giggles and big gray eyes, she was the complete opposite of the composed stately woman he had pictured himself with.

Now he was unsure. She was what he wanted, but was he what she wanted? After all, she was a gorgeous woman with a father who owned a large and lucrative ranch—what would she want with a pastor who only had a small farm and an old Bible to offer? He could say love was enough, but every father with a beloved daughter would scoff at that. He could give up being a pastor and move to Texas, but he knew nothing about raising cattle. Besides, a pastor was what he had been called to be. During the whole course of his life his father had engraved it in him to make money, no matter what it took—being a man of God was pointless. Will still had studied to be a pastor. It had felt right, and that was how Abby's presence felt—right.

Will inhaled deeply; the smell of autumn was crisp and refreshing and calmed his nerves. He had to realize that just because he never earned his father's good opinion did not mean he could not earn Abby's, although Abby seemed to have a good opinion of everybody. How could he distinguish himself from everybody else?

Will was so immersed in his thoughts that he bumped shoulders with a man as tall as he.

"Excuse me, I was not watching where I was going," Will politely said, not wanting to offend—a trait he was trying to work on. The man glanced over and Will saw it was Joseph, Abby's brother.

Was Abby with him?

"Pastor Will, you look like a man with a lot on his mind." Joseph slapped him on the shoulder as if he were a kid. Will didn't know if he should be offended or not. He chose to ignore the slap.

"I do, as a matter of fact. What are you doing in town?"

Joseph looked around squinting, "Looking for a hat for a young boy."

"Michael?" Will guessed. He, like everyone else, had seen the way Joseph looked at Esther. Though everyone smiled and gossiped, no one had the heart to tell him it was futile trying to court her.

"Yes, Michael! I know the shoe shop and I see places for dresses, fabric, books, and groceries but no hats."

Will pointed across the way. "You see that supply store? It has plows, shovels, whips, and hats. That is, I am assuming you are looking for a rancher's hat, and not one with lace and flowers," Will teased.

Joseph grinned. "No, I don't think Michael would appreciate lace and flowers."

They were about to part ways with a nod when Sheriff Ben joined them on the corner. "Good day, gentlemen," he greeted, nodding at Will and turning to Joseph. "I don't think we have had the pleasure of officially meeting. I've seen you at the Sunday picnics and my wife Lucinda has mentioned seeing you when she takes the children to school."

Joseph stuck out his hand and the two men shook firmly, "Joseph Silver, older brother to Abigail."

"Ahh yes, our fine school teacher. She is doing wonders. You and your parents should be proud."

"That we are, Sheriff," Joseph said, glancing at the bakery. Will followed his gaze to see Abby emerging next to Eliza. Abby was talking gaily, as usual, and looked especially radiant and fairy-like. Her hair hung in ringlets down her back and her frock was soft, allowing him to make out the form of a lithe and feminine form. He barely heard what Sheriff Ben and Joseph were talking about, something about Rangers and Sheriffs, crime in Texas versus crime in Colorado. A fragment of his brain kept him nodding and making sounds of agreement, but his main attention was on the ethereal girl holding a pastry bigger than her hands. She seemed to be examining it as a scientist would examine a rare species. Eliza was laughing at her. Eliza herself was looking finer and finer by the day. Odd how that could happen to a person.

"Pastor," Sheriff said loudly, snapping Will out of his Abby-induced trance.

"Hmm, sorry, I have a lot on my mind," Will said weakly.

The Sheriff glanced across the street at Abby with a superior smirk. "Ahh, I see. You do have a lot on your mind."

Joseph smothered a laugh with a cough and Will thought he ought to crack both men's heads together.

"Pastor," Joseph addressed him still grinning, "please tell my sister that I will meet her in the book shop and not the dress shop."

Before Will could say yes or no, Joseph excused himself. The Sheriff gave one last chuckle at Will before shaking his head amusingly and walking away.

❧

"This is amazing!" Abby stared at the wondrous flaky pastry that was stuffed with a sweetened creamy cheese and apricots. "How does he make it so stuffed without breaking the light shell?"

Eliza shrugged, still feeling flustered as she always did when she was around Kyle Lampton. "I couldn't say. However, I do need to get back to my shop. Lunch time is over," Eliza said, thinking about all her beautiful dresses. Kyle had asked her what she would be wearing to the dance with him, and she had not been able to reply. Eliza had never worn an especially pretty dress or done up her hair in a fancy way other than a simple bun. With her looks she felt it would seem ridiculous and desperate if she tried too hard.

"Oh, your dress shop is so lovely. Such a variety of beautiful and yet wearable clothing," Abby complimented.

Eliza gave a slight nod of shy gratitude. "That's what I try to keep. It's hard finding a balance between constrictive fashion and wearable clothing. Women out here work hard, but they also want to look pretty."

Abby thought of this for a moment. To her, clothes had either been practical or pretty. The two never meshed, but Eliza was right: women out here couldn't be wearing stiff-necked, thick-laced things, yet most of the women looked lovely and put together, if not fancy.

"Eliza, would you say most of my clothing is a little, well, suffocating?"

Eliza snorted. "Miss Abigail, you have some very fine dresses. But most of them do over-shine you. I tell ladies when they come in that *they* want to be the focus, not the dress. The dress is to emphasize them. I will say though, that you are dressing more and more becomingly."

"It's not like I had much of a choice. All my blouses and dresses are burned or stained due to my failed cooking attempts," she laughed at herself. "Still, I would like something that made me look especially nice." She paused thinking of Will, "—for the barn dance, to be precise. Some of my nicest things I have given away to some of the mining mothers who have to travel a bit longer to reach town. Of course, they simplify them."

Eliza huffed a laugh, "I've noticed some of them looking

especially nice. It is amazing how a nice dress can persuade one to do their hair and powder their nose, isn't it?" Eliza looked at Abby with the same concentrated eye she used for her customers, examining her color, body, features, and general look. Most were surprised that Eliza had an eye for what looked good on a woman, but once they took her advice they fully admitted that she had a gift. "I think I know what I would dress you in. You have time to come by?"

"Oh yes, I would love your help. I don't want to go looking like a peacock, which is sometimes my downfall. So yes, I will come by."

"All right, Miss Abigail," Eliza chuckled. "I will be seeing you soon then."

Abby nodded, "Oh yes, but in a few minutes most likely. I just don't want to carry this among all those fine clothes."

Eliza laughed, "I appreciate that." She gave a polite bow of the head and wandered off. Abby decided to find a nice bench and enjoy her pastry; Joseph would need a few things and so she had plenty of time. She was just about to walk over to a nice sunny spot when, to her amazement, she saw Will walking towards her. Her pulse quickened as she frantically tried to compose something witty and amusing to say.

"Good afternoon, Miss Abigail," Will took off his hat, thank goodness. She loved his reddish brown, sun-kissed hair, and his taunt muscles didn't hurt either.

"Hello, Will," was all she could manage to say.

"Your brother told me to tell you that he would meet you in the book shop and not the dress shop." He eyed the pastry, "Are you going to eat all that?" he asked incredulously.

Yes, every bite.

"No!" she answered quickly with a scoff as if the idea was ludicrous…"Only half."

Will's lips curled, seeing right through her blundering lie. "Only half?"

Abby blushed. "Fine, I was going to eat all of it, but I will have you know that I have not had breakfast and with Joseph, the food flies by. I hardly eat at all these days."

Will laughed and motioned for her to walk with him over to a quaint little bench under a small tree. "Abby, I will find it impressive if you can eat all that."

"You know I can't now, because first I will be self-conscious eating it all in front of you, and now I must share so I don't look like a dominant puppy growling over my share of food," she said as seriously as she could.

Will threw his head back with one of his deep rumbling laughs. How Abby loved that laugh, even if it had mocked her so many times. It was rich and full of life and was infectious and now it made her skin tingle. "Abby, my goodness you make me laugh," he leaned back still chuckling.

Abby frowned. She made him laugh? Was that a good thing? Was she special because of it, or did he mean that she made him laugh the way a child might amuse him? Shrugging to herself she gently tore the delectable pastry in half and handed it to him. "You have to eat some so that I can eat my share comfortably."

Will shrugged and bit into the pastry. "Well, if it's to make you more comfortable," he said with his mouth full.

She nodded, her nose in the air to emphasize she was right. The pastry was rich and creamy. Kyle Lampton was a downright wizard when it came to baked goods. Abby glanced over at Will, his smooth lips moving gently as he chewed. What would it be like to have those lips on hers? Would it be awkward? Wonderful? Had he kissed many girls before? She herself had shared only a few little kisses in the moonlight, but nothing to gossip about. Will did not seem like the type of man who would do a soft peck. With his temper she imagined his kiss would be like fire, wild and passionate—like in the books she read. Her hopelessly romantic mind pictured herself in a Renaissance dress standing on a cliff looking over the ocean with Will riding up in an open white shirt, a sword at his side and—

"Abby?" Will asked, noticing a sort of dazed expression on her face.

Abby flinched. "Oh, I was just thinking about—" she paused, *you and me kissing.*

"About what?" he asked curious.

"Uhh, Thanksgiving," she blurted, grasping for any previous thought she'd had.

"Thanksgiving?" Will tilted his head and took another generous bite.

"Yes. You see, I have been trying to figure out a way to encourage more friendships among the children from the mining community and the children of both the farmers and tradesmen. I thought, considering school will most likely end in December, that we should have a Thanksgiving play." Abby had actually just fabricated the idea while talking to Will. Now, as the words fell from her mouth, her eyes grew wide: it was actually a great idea. In truth, she had wanted to do something to build better relationships between the children, but nothing had come to mind. Will's prying into her thoughts was truly heaven sent. She would be putting on a Thanksgiving play.

"A play?" Will asked with an amused twitch in his lips. "You mean with Pilgrims and Indians?"

"Pilgrims, Indians, costumes. Esther has been promising to teach me how to sew, and I have so much useless clothing that it would not cost a thing. I could talk to Eliza about playing the piano, Esther could help direct it, and Kyle Lampton could bake pies and cakes." She began naming various people who could help out in order to make it a great event. She was getting excited. She'd always been one who liked social events but had never thought about organizing one for a good cause.

A waste of talent, Abby thought to herself. She was going to use the talent she had and put on the perfect Thanksgiving play. The children would love it.

"I think a Thanksgiving play is a great idea!" Will nodded. "In fact, I'll help you with it," he found himself offering even though he had told himself that he should distance himself from Abby until he was sure of her feelings.

"Really?" Abby clapped her hands. "That would be *wonderful!* We can practice every day and have the children write their own script as part of their writing curriculum."

"Talking about how our country was settled could cover history," Will offered, starting to share Abby's excitement.

"And we could use the number of turkeys and guests for math," Abby's voice was several pitches higher and her cheeks glowed with enthusiasm. She stuck out her hand with a grin, "Partners?"

Will chuckled and took the smooth hand, enveloping it in his own. "Partners."

Abby's skin heated up. Oh, she liked the sound of that. Liked how he said it with a twinkle in his eyes, and loved how his strong hand wrapped around hers like a glove that was too big, but somehow fit just right.

Please don't let go, she silently pleaded.

For a moment Will simply stared at her with an unreadable expression. His lips parted and his gaze dropped to their hands as if he might say something important. A current sparked between them.

Was he going to kiss her?

"Why, Pastor Will—is that you?" came a high-pitched voice. Will's expression fell in disappointment as he looked past Abby to an approaching figure. A curvy young woman with an expensive looking dress and a hat that took up half the street walked towards them. As she approached Abby saw that it was Rachel Nelson, the banker's daughter. Something told her that this blond showing an abundance of unnecessary bosom, inappropriate *and not the fashion*, Abby noted, was not a simple acquaintance of Will. She had seen Rachel throw herself at Will every Sunday.

"Why, Pastor Will! I have been hoping to run into you," she said with a wide smile that revealed a whole set of straight teeth.

Will politely stood up. "Good day, Miss Rachel," he glanced at Abby who also stood up and plastered on a polite smile. "You know the school teacher, Miss Abigail Silver? Miss Abigail this here is Miss Rachel Nelson, the banker's daughter." He introduced them with a low voice, not making eye contact with either woman.

"Oh, the little schoolteacher," Rachel exclaimed superiorly. "It is a great pleasure to meet you. I see you every Sunday but have never officially been introduced to you."

You've made no effort to meet me. In fact you've avoided it. Abby nodded, "Likewise."

"Will often talks about you. He says that you are just too *amusing* to watch," she said.

"Amusing?" Abby looked at Will, her eyebrows knitted together. She felt hurt. It was not unknown to her that she could be bubbly and talkative, but did Will really think of her as an amusing girl and not a woman? Not a woman who was smart and good, who might even make a fine pastor's wife?

Will blushed. "I merely said that the first week you were here that is was obvious you had never taught," he gulped, "but you caught on so quickly."

"He did say 'amusing' though. Said it was so funny to watch you, and I can see why. You are just so cute, like a little doll." Rachel giggled.

Abby was too hurt to be angered by Rachel. She looked down at her pastry. Maybe she was merely viewed as a silly girl and not a woman. She would never be like Esther, maybe not even like her own mother. She would always be the chatty, flighty girl from Texas' social elite.

"Anyway, Will, I just wanted to remind you of what time to pick me up for the barn dance next week," she told him while casting a snake-eyed look at Abby who now felt like a fool.

"Oh," Will stammered, "you are still able to go?" he asked, hoping that it would sound as if he had asked her some time back.

"Well of course, silly. You only just asked me the other day."

Abby didn't want to hear another word. "Excuse me. Miss Rachel it was a pleasure, but I promised Eliza I would be stopping by." Rachel began to say something, but Abby walked off as quickly as she could, biting her lower lip.

Don't you dare cry Abigail Silver. You are stronger than that.

Michael bounded out of the house when the little white carriage pulled up.

"Uncle Tim and Aunt Lily are here!" he shouted back at Esther who was pulling pork chops and apples from the oven.

"Tell them to come in, sweetheart." She stood up and stretched her back. Aunt Lily and Uncle Tim would be leaving after the Harvest Festival to New Orleans. Esther would be taking over a few patients who needed home visits as well as feeding their beloved cats.

"Esther, what are you cooking?" Uncle Tim walked briskly into the kitchen, his face lighting up at the sight of apples and pork. "You know I didn't ask for dinner when I told you we would be stopping by?"

Esther winked. "Did you already eat dinner?"

Uncle Tim scoffed, "Of course not...not when I knew there would be a chance you'd be cooking."

Esther shook a wooden spoon at him. "You are a cunning one, Uncle."

Aunt Lily joined them, her eyes brightening as supper's aroma washed over her. "Mmm, what a wonderful smell. Too bad they can't turn pork into a perfume," she chuckled.

Michael bounded in and tugged on his uncle's sleeve. "Do you want to come see my new book?" he asked. Uncle Tim said he would and the two left the kitchen after Uncle Tim sampled a bite.

Esther shook her head with amusement. Another week had passed. Joseph supposedly had ordered a present for Michael from Denver. The shopkeeper said he would be picking up merchandise in the city and would bring Joseph what he needed, but for a higher cost. Joseph had agreed and then had bought a little picture book for Michael until the better present came. Joseph continued to inquire about Toby. Esther, having learned her lesson, kept the details of Mary and Toby minimal. Michael had received another riding lesson in which Esther found out a little more about Joseph, his likes, dislikes, fun stories about his work, and so on. The poor Ranger had still tried relentlessly to ask Esther about herself, but after the last incident she was very careful to not reveal anything too intimate.

"What are you thinking, my dear?" Aunt Lily asked as she pulled out the plates to set the table.

Esther looked up with a small shake of the head. "Oh, just about, um, Michael."

Aunt Lily gave her a hard look. "You are a good mother, Esther. I hope you know that."

Esther tossed Aunt Lily a grateful look, "I hope so. So often I feel that I fall short."

"I have noticed that handsome Ranger being awfully kind to Michael on Sundays. I've also noticed he seems mighty attentive to you. Doesn't even give any of the other sighing females a glance."

Esther began vigorously stirring a sauce to drizzle over the pork and apples. "I worry that Joseph thinks there may be a chance for him and me," she sighed feeling a little sad suddenly, and yet again she found her lips smiling despite herself. When Joseph had showed up for Michael's riding lesson, he had brought a bouquet of flowers for Esther and she had loved it while also being highly embarrassed and flustered.

"And does he have a chance?" Aunt Lily asked unabashedly.

Esther looked up with surprise. How could Aunt Lily even ask that question? She knew what Esther had gone through. "No, of course not—I—you know I can't marry!"

"Can't?" Aunt Lily asked.

"Yes, I *can't*. There are too many complications and too many changes that would have to happen."

"Change is not always bad, Esther," Aunt Lily paused setting the table and turned to face her niece.

"It is if you have worked hard to make a life—a happy life."

Aunt Lily bit her lip, pondering the conversation for a few seconds. "You know Esther, your mother and I did not have the most, well, *supportive* of mothers. She allowed our father to be harsh with us in both word and in body. I still remember going to school trying to cover the bruises on my arms and occasionally my face. Your mother learned to be quiet. She learned to be submissive so as to not anger our father and mother. Her outcome was marrying a man exactly like our parents. I, on the other hand, became aggressive—wild in word and morals." Aunt Lily's usually bright eyes clouded over. "My body was no longer my own. I am not saying my experience was as awful as yours, but at least you have the dignity to know that your values were intact. Mine, on the other hand, were handed out with my consent. It created a horrible self-loathing."

Esther froze, shocked by her aunt's revelation.

"Finally, I found God. I got my life cleaned up, took a job as a waitress, and paid my way through school to become a nurse. I never looked back. I kept going and eventually met your uncle."

Esther had had no idea about her aunt's past. Her own mother had said Aunt Lily was wild, but Esther had assumed that she was simply referring to Aunt Lily's wild ideas of women voting, having equal rights, working outside the home, and such, not that Aunt Lily had lived a wild life.

"Aunt Lily, my goodness, I had no idea. You are such a godly and good woman."

Aunt Lily shrugged nonchalantly, "That is because the past is the past. I figured if God could forgive it then I should, too. We are taught to forgive others and that includes ourselves. I tell you this Esther because had I held on to my past, my mistakes, my bitterness and fears, I would not have had the full life that I've experienced. One thing I have learned as a nurse is that every human being has a past—they have scars and traumatic experiences. Those who can move on become happy and those who don't eventually become empty like."

Esther nodded. "Do you not think though, that some things are just too hard to move past?"

Aunt Lily began setting the table again. "I think some wounds take longer to heal than others. And it is not our job to tell God when to heal them or how."

Esther poured the sauce over the pork. "Wise words from a wise woman."

Aunt Lily laughed and shook her head. "No, experienced words from an experienced woman."

Joseph had no idea what was wrong with his sister. She'd changed her outfit six times yesterday, redone her hair three times this morning, burnt rolls and dropped a pan of buttery pancakes for breakfast.

"Stupid pancakes! I should just cancel dinner with Esther. I'll only make a fool out of myself."

Now it was getting serious. "You can't cancel with Esther. Michael will be so disappointed," he argued, walking into the kitchen to help her.

"Well, Michael has a good mother so he will be fine. A good mother who everybody likes and respects and a mother who even my own brother wants to marry," Abby blurted out and tossed down the wet rag, putting her hand over her face with a shaky sigh.

Joseph sighed and sat down on the kitchen floor with her. "This isn't about the pancakes is it?" he asked. He did not know a whole lot of women, but he did know that they were a confusing species.

"No," Abby whimpered.

"Do you want to talk about it?" he asked hesitantly.

"No!" Abby cried.

Joseph nodded, relieved, and began to help her silently.

"You don't want to know *why?*" Abby asked as if he had done something wrong.

Joseph looked down. "Alright Abby, what is wrong?" He sat down again. "I want to hear."

"Will asked another girl to the barn dance and," she bit her lip, "I like him—*really* like him—possibly love him."

Joseph blinked. His socialite sister had fallen for the poor pastor? Life was indeed grand. "Have you told him that?"

Abby looked shocked. "Of course not! How can I tell him I love him if I don't even know how he feels about me?"

Joseph shrugged, "Abby, he either does not know you are interested and so is pursuing other women, or he's just not interested in you." Joseph said, pleased that he could help.

Abby's bottom lip quivered. "I knew it! He doesn't like me. He thinks me a foolish, silly girl—no, worse, he thinks me *amusing*."

Joseph stood up abruptly. "Abby, stop please. I think you should talk to Esther. I am sure she will know what to say."

Abby made a frustrating growl, "I love Esther, but why is she so right all the time and so desirable."

Joseph smiled. Esther was indeed desirable. "Because, Esther knows exactly who Esther is," he said, thinking of her gracious movements, her constant smile, and her almond-shaped eyes. "And as far as I know, Esther does not whine. Remember this, little sister, men every now and then like a damsel in distress, but they don't want an insecure girl. There is a big difference."

Abby rolled her eyes as Joseph left to go fetch the beautiful cowboy hat with the snakeskin band, which matched his own, for Michael. He found himself looking forward to Michael's reaction and wondering if Esther would approve. Curiosity had him in a tight grip when it came to Esther and her past. He had promised Abby not to write to the detective in New York, and he promised Esther he would not pry and ask either her or Michael, and yet he doubted Esther would ever tell him voluntarily. Abby said things would take care of themselves and to have faith.

Joseph sighed. Faith was such an ambiguous term. Besides, he was an action-oriented man. Simply waiting and hoping was something he had never been able to do well.

"Joseph, you ready?" Abby's voice halted his thoughts.

He shook his head and ran a hand through his thick hair. "Yes, I am ready."

Ready for Esther to shun me and Michael to embrace me.

Esther was having a hard time concentrating on the Sunday sermon. Her mind was filled with concern for the people she'd personally taken under her care. Her eyes drifted to new mothers, and mothers to be. Melissa had attended with her gurgling baby who already looked a bit plumper. She seemed better, more rosy and bright-eyed with her husband's arm around her. Suzanne Gable was there, sitting very tightly cross-legged. Esther had to smile knowing that she was trying to keep the baby in. Still, her skin was sun kissed and glowing. She had taken Esther's advice and had been tending to her garden. Not losing the baby had given her courage to move about and come to church.

Esther then glanced at the three non-pregnant people giving her concern: Will, Abby, and Joseph. Will's sermons had improved dramatically in the past few weeks. His actions had always been kind and serving, but his sermons had been rough and harsh. After the arrival of Abby, his Sunday message had grown softer, portraying God as a loving father. Today, however, his words were slightly jumbled and unfocused. He kept glancing at the smiling Rachel and then at the grim-faced Abby who looked like a woman slighted. Then Esther glanced under lowered eyelashes at Joseph. His jaw was set tightly and his lips pressed into a thin line. She could not tell if he was focused on the sermon or upset about something.

Michael fidgeted next to Uncle Tim and Aunt Lily. "This is a long sermon," Michael whispered impatiently.

Esther gave a single nod. "I'm sure it's almost over. You are being very patient." She glanced over at Joseph who looked extremely pensive... no, more agitated than pensive. The right side of his jaw twitched repeatedly and his eyes narrowed. Despite looking like a frustrated bull he was very handsome. *Especially handsome.* Esther looked away. She could appreciate a fine face and figure, but that did not mean she should linger on it.

Michael sighed loudly. He was no longer patient. "Can I go sit with Joseph?" he begged.

Joseph caught Esther's attention while she tried to keep her fidgeting son from rocking the bench back and forth. Goodness, he liked that woman. Who was he kidding? He loved her. Much to his delight Esther gave him a friendly little wave with her fingers. When he motioned silently for Michael to come over to him, Esther nodded her head. She bent over and whispered to Michael, instructing him to walk quietly. Michael gleefully stood up and tiptoed through the congregation over to Joseph.

"Did you bring me the present you ordered?" he whispered. Several heads turned to stare Michael into silence. When they met Joseph's challenging look, they decided it was better to ignore the boy's chatter.

Joseph picked up Michael. "I sure did," he said softly. "I'll give it to you when the sermon is over."

Michael sighed, covering the side of his mouth to whisper into Joseph's ear. "Are you going to the barn dance?"

"Sure am," he replied in a whisper. "Are you?"

Michael nodded. "Will you be asking my mom to dance?"

Joseph smiled. "I will ask her, but I just don't know if she'll say yes."

Michael furrowed his eyebrows trying to look like a hard thinking man. "She never dances with men. At least, I've never seen her dance with one." Looking back at his mom, Michael held up his hand again and leaned toward Joseph's ear. "She was hurt by a man you know." Then as if worried what Joseph would think he added, "but all men aren't bad."

Joseph glanced at Esther while putting the pieces of Michael's words together. Esther had been hurt? Physically? Emotionally? The thought of a man hurting her body made Joseph angry. Yet the thought of her loving a man and him abandoning her with a child also enraged him. Had she loved another? Had he left? Did she still love him?

Will finally closed the sermon with a relieved sigh. He had not practiced. He had not even written a sermon. Yesterday's events had him in a conundrum. He had been a fool to ask Rachel to the barn dance, but it was too late to take back the invitation. When he realized he'd fallen for Abby, he of course convinced himself that she would not be interested in him, and then acting on impulse, he asked Rachel to accompany him. She was always after him and would be a boost to his self-shattered ego. Yet Abby's obvious disappointment when she found out that Will would be taking Rachel made him re-think the possibility of courting her. Yet she had done nothing to indicate her interest in him. Maybe he'd only imagined her disappointment yesterday. Either way, the whole event had ruined his sermon—all in all, he was in a sour mood. Rachel's batting eyelashes and Abby's ignoring him was doing nothing to help it. Abby was still polite to him, but there had been no announcement of the Thanksgiving play as Abby explained that there were several tests the children had to complete, and so the announcement was to be postponed. But Will wondered if she simply did not want him around. Whatever she was feeling, he needed to talk to her.

Abby thought her fingers would spring out claws when Rachel practically draped herself on Will. Had the girl no shame? Relentlessly showing off her bosom and trailing her finger along the hem of the neckline? The scene made Abby want to gag. Will seemed to be heading toward her now, but she avoided him. She would not be his little pet, his little *amusement*. Instead, she threw herself into a frantic conversation with Sheriff Ben and his wife Lucinda.

Joseph grinned as Esther approached. He liked how her eyes smiled as much as her mouth.

"Your sister seems bent on avoiding our starry-eyed pastor it seems," she noted with a laugh.

Joseph shrugged. "Yep. She said something about him being confusing, or was it her being confusing. Frankly, Miss Esther, I have no idea what she was talking about."

Esther laughed, "And that is why women need women."

"I am in full agreement there," he chuckled. "So Michael was telling me your aunt and uncle are leaving for an anniversary trip, correct?"

"Yes, they leave after the Harvest Festival. I'm happy for them. They could use a real holiday."

Joseph nodded. "Have you traveled outside of Tall Pine?"

Esther shook her head, "No, I am afraid not. I've been feeling a little itch for—not necessarily a change, but maybe doing something adventurous. I've been thinking of taking Michael somewhere for Christmas, but I don't know where."

I don't know where because I am feeling that something needs to change in my life, but I don't want change. I don't trust change. Esther cast her eyes downward. What a confusing mess she was.

Michael tugged on Esther's arm. "Joseph brought the present," he told her. He turned to Joseph, "Can I have it now?"

Joseph looked at Esther for permission. There was a difference in her today, not just towards him, but in general. Her eyes seemed brighter, less weighed down, and she moved with a spring added to her usual grace.

Was it because of him?

Or was the change due to someone else?

He didn't like that thought at all. Joseph grunted, quietly crossing his arms.

"We are staying for dinner after the church picnic to help Abby cook. You can have the present then."

Michael looked as if Esther was asking him to wait an eternity. He began to protest when Joseph surprised him by swinging him up and behind his back. Michael squealed in delight, giggling loudly. Joseph nodded towards the entrance.

"You want to accompany me and my deputy here for some

pie?" he asked.

Esther looked at the two incredulously. "Michael is your deputy now is he?"

Joseph caught a mix of conflicting emotions on Esther's face between disapproving of his closeness to Michael while also being pleased with it. He decided to ignore the disapproval. "He sure is. Every man needs his own deputy to help him out," Joseph grinned. He did in fact feel that he needed Michael. At first, he wanted Esther and felt the need to help Michael. Now he loved the kid, and he needed the boy in his life as much as he desired and needed Esther. Joseph offered his arm; Esther seemed not to notice.

She simply turned away and began walking before turning back. "Well then, let's go get some pie. I would be glad to dish up a piece for you two boys," she said cheerfully."

Joseph bounded after her. Had she ignored his arm or had she just not noticed? What was it with this woman and his touch? Would she not like his touch were he to kiss her, caress her, make love to her? The thought worried Joseph. He was willing to work through anything, but how could he if he didn't even know what the problem was.

Abby would not look at Will, and he couldn't shake off Rachel without being hurtful to her. During the course of the picnic he tried to maneuver over to Abby, but every time he did, Rachel either started a new conversation, or someone stopped him to say they needed help with a fence, branding cows, harvesting, repairing the roof, and so on. When he finally reached the spot Abby had been, he would find that she had evaded him. The picnic ended and Abby, who was always the last one to say goodbye, was the first to leave, practically running to her little home. Will grunted. He'd have to talk to her tomorrow at school where she could not escape.

Twelve

Esther listened patiently to Abby's woes as she related her story about Will and his asking Rachel to the Harvest Festival. Then Abby railed about how she was nothing more than amusement to him. "Will clearly doesn't like me, and I am a fool to have even entertained the thought," Abby huffed.

Esther caught Joseph's eye and he winked as if the two shared a funny secret. Esther found herself smiling at the sight of him playing cards with her son.

"Abby, I personally think that Will does like you very much. It is just that Will is considered quite the catch here in Tall Pine. He is handsome, strong, hardworking, and kind."

Joseph made a disgusted grunt from the corner. Esther's lips twitched; his annoyance was tangible. Did she like his jealousy?

No, of course she didn't. Then why was she fighting a smile?

"Anyway, with him being so sought after," Esther continued, "he has never had to pursue a woman. They all chase him like flies to honey."

"He pursued you. He courted you, and quite strongly for a season if what I have heard is true," Abby pointed out with a pout.

"Well maybe, but—"

Abby shook her head interrupting Esther, "And why not? You have every man after you, and I can't even get Will to look at me seriously. Maybe I do need to be more quiet and composed. I am awfully talkative—that's probably irritating. If I'm to get any husband, especially Will," she looked down at her hands, "I will have to learn to be more mature."

Esther let a few seconds of silence pass, making sure that Abby had finished. "What I was going to say is that men, in my experience, like women who joyfully live and not simply pine. No matter what Will does, go and dance, eat, meet new people. You can't force Will to do anything, but you can learn to have a good time independent of men."

Abby nodded. "You're right, but what if I go and no one asks me to dance?" She bit her lip. "I may not have any other men interested in me."

"Oh, you have plenty," Esther corrected. "You get more smiles and sighs at church than all the single girls put together. You've just only had eyes for Will since you arrived here so you haven't noticed. Your entire focus is on a rather handsome pastor."

"You find him handsome?" Abby asked.

"Objectively handsome—as would any woman. Am I interested? Absolutely not!" Esther said with a reassuring smile.

Abby blushed. "Sorry, I don't know why I feel so jealous."

Esther checked the chicken potpie, golden and baked to perfection. "It is only natural that you feel jealous Abby, and I'm surprised you have not acted on it. That shows a great deal of fortitude and maturity."

"Oh, I've wanted to show it—especially when Rachel is all over him."

"She's always all over him, isn't she?"

"Yes, but her attentions have increased and I never worried because he hardly seemed interested until he asked her to the festival, and then all of a sudden I start remembering different things between them. Him laughing at her crude jokes, or letting her stand close to him with her—" Abby did a type of messy wave with her hands in front of her chest. "You know, her overabundance of —" again she waved.

"Breasts?" Esther asked, her lips curling in good humor.

"Yes!" Abby exclaimed. "I believe in looking feminine, but does she really have to show so much all the time?"

Esther laughed. "You know in all truth my heart goes out to Rachel. I have a feeling that if we were to go into her heart and mind we would find a very insecure young woman. Despite her beauty, considerable wealth, and status, she doesn't seem to have any sincere relationships."

"Except with Will," Abby said sadly.

"You don't know that yet. Listen Abby, my advice if you truly like Will or even *love* Will," Esther began to set the table, "then you need to let the matter go. Let Will be a man and pursue you naturally... without any drama."

Joseph had now walked into the kitchen alongside Michael. "Do women always put this much thought into snagging men?" he teased with a grin.

Abby spun around to face him. "We either do that or sit on our velvet cushions waiting for you to make up your mind and come after us women."

Esther began to laugh and stopped when Joseph's gaze locked with hers. "I always know exactly what I want, and I go after it," he said.

Esther feigned indifference, although her heart quickened when Joseph refused to lift his eyes from her. She tried focusing on Abby's words, something to do with men's ignorance and women's desperation, but she found herself melting under his gaze. Finally feeling like a foolish schoolgirl she set down the plates, stood straight, and looked up, her own flashing eyes clashing with his. She would not be intimidated by any man, nor coerced by his attractiveness.

Joseph was surprised by Esther's sudden boldness. Her eyes pinned him with a challenging expression. He suddenly felt awkward, like she had caught him in a forbidden act. Esther usually acted standoffish, irritated, or even frightened by his abrupt nature. This time her face clearly read that she was challenging him to stare at her in a "what are you going to do about it," sort of way. He almost looked away when the corner of her mouth twitched and her head tilted in that foxlike way that drove him crazy. She was playing with what he gave her—straightforward temerity.

Joseph grinned, lifting his hands in surrender. "I thought I was too old for stare offs," he laughed.

"A stare off, was it?" Esther said under lowered eyelashes.

Joseph frowned, not knowing what she meant by her words. Heavens this woman drove him crazy.

"Dinner is ready," Esther announced suddenly, sitting herself down and motioning for Michael to come sit by her.

Joseph motioned for everyone to wait. "Hold on, I think now is a good time for Michael's gift." He left the kitchen, and Abby clapped with excitement.

"Oh, it's wonderful," she squealed. "We went into town yesterday to pick it up."

"Pick up what?" Esther asked her in a whisper. Abby merely winked.

Joseph returned holding something under a woven cloth. "Here it is Michael—ordered especially for you and Texas Ranger worthy."

Joseph swung off the cloth like a magician to reveal a beautiful cowboy hat with a snakeskin band and an elaborate silver piece. Michael whooped and jumped out of his chair. Esther expected him to grab the hat, but instead he flung himself at Joseph, knocking the grown man back a few feet. Esther felt a lump solidify in her throat. Shamefully, she silently acknowledged her jealousy. She had tried with all her might to be a good mother. She had loved her son beyond description. Everything she did was with him in mind. Yet, it had been so easy for Joseph to waltz in, fitting the image of the perfect father that she herself had described, a man Michael chose as his ideal father, and suddenly her son's love was split between her and Joseph. Joseph, who had never been there during Michael's hard times. Joseph, who no matter what, could not love Michael as she did and could not love him as a real son. How Michael's heart would break when Joseph left! Her son would have to learn at some point that she would not marry, but what a hard way to learn. She dreaded the moment.

"Momma, look! Look!" Michael tried on the hat, which fit a little on the big side but fit nonetheless. He jumped up and down in front of her like an excited jackrabbit.

Esther took him by the shoulders, holding him still and then turned him around to examine the hat. It looked like a Joseph-type hat: masculine, strong, intimidating, and certainly not understated or plain. To her surprise, she loved it.

"Well, sugar cake, I don't think I have ever seen a finer hat. You look just like a Texas Ranger," she said with pride, pulling her son in for a tight embrace.

"So what you mean is that he looks handsome, strong, rugged, and unforgettable?" Joseph said with a smile.

Esther calmly nodded while secretly wanting to throw her plate at Joseph to knock the confident smirk off his face. Winning the affection of her son did not mean winning her, and for all his talk of friendship, he certainly was not acting like *just* friends. Not with the way he kept scrutinizing her. Such audacity! His forwardness made Esther angry while at the same time making her sit a little taller and feel a little better.

When Michael had settled down, the four sat down and enjoyed dinner. Afterwards Abby stood up to go fetch dessert, which she said was a surprise. Tossing Joseph a knowing glance she asked Michael if he would come with her to the icebox. He agreed, sporting his hat with a bounce to his step. When they were a small distance away Joseph scooted his chair closer to Esther.

"Have you been visiting Mary this week?"

Esther nodded her head. "Yes, I have. I only visit her during school hours so that I do not need to leave Michael."

Joseph nodded, his brows furrowing, which Esther had learned was an indication of him debating what to say. "So I have been thinking this week on what I could do about the situation, and I have an offer." He laughed softly at himself, "You see there is no way in heaven or hell I want you near that man."

Esther opened her mouth to protest, but Joseph raised his hand. "Wait," he quickly added, "I understand you have a duty to his wife, and honestly I admire that, but I want to go with you. I'll drive you to the door and stay outside the room until you have finished."

Esther shook her head. "You don't understand. Toby will not allow another man in his home. If you come, I might not be able to examine Mary, which means there may be complications, which means she can lose the baby or her own life," Esther said firmly; the light quiver in her voice was the only hint of the deep desperation she was feeling.

"Toby won't have a choice. I am a Texas Ranger, a servant of the law."

"In Texas." Esther reminded him dryly.

"In Texas, yes, but also of the United States of America. Sheriff Ben himself said he could use my help, and in Colorado that means I am practically a certified deputy," he said lightly. "Listen Esther, I will go with you no matter what, even if Sampson and I follow behind you and track you down."

Esther shook her head with a laugh that turned more into a sigh. "Do you always take away people's choices?"

"I try not to, but with those I care about, I will do anything to protect them," he said, his face turning serious and his voice deepening.

"It's easy to confuse caring and controlling," Esther said, her voice tinged with ice. "It has been my experience that often caring is used to mask the selfish need to control."

Joseph nodded in full agreement. "You're right. I know I can be a little too…" he grinned sheepishly, "alpha wolf. But as I said, it is only because I have a strong desire to protect and care for those I love—not control them."

Esther studied him for a good moment before her lips curled into an amused smile. "An alpha wolf?"

Joseph threw back his shoulders in jest.

"Joseph the Alpha Wolf sounds pretty nice I must say," Esther laughed with a slight shrug and glanced around for Michael out of habit, but he was still gone with Abby. "You know, a study in Europe was done recently concerning wolves. Michael has a weakness for animals, and so we often buy books about them. This study found that, as you have confirmed, each wolf pack has an alpha but it is not always a male. A female can lead her own pack without the help of a male. She can hunt, provide, protect, and lead as good as any male wolf." Esther cocked her head with an "I win" flick of a smile. "Interesting, is it not?"

Joseph laughed. "I know the study as well. It also described how the wolves mate for life." He leaned forward, the veins in his forearms tensing. "For life," he repeated slowly. "The male courts the females by laying his kill at her feet."

"Out of submission," Esther concluded.

"Out of respect and admiration. I believe that the reason wolves mate for life is because the male and female are equal. The male knows he needs the female, her intelligence and speed. Her ability to stalk, hunt, and kill matches his own. He admires this and as such considers it an honor to care for her—" he leaned even closer, "to mate with her."

Esther wanted to look away; her skin was warm and her pulse throbbed in her neck, but Joseph chained her attention to his words, willing her to listen to him with his husky voice. "Respect and admiration?" Esther asked, her voice catching.

"He is not trying to subdue her nor does he think her incapable of caring for herself. He merely admires and respects her as an equal and wishes to be a part of her world. A man who truly loves a woman and thinks her strong and virtuous will want to take care of her, for she is the blessing that he must value."

"A man?" Esther asked, unable to help the smile that crept onto her lips.

Joseph grinned boyishly. "I'm sorry, did I say man? My mistake. I meant wolf."

"What are you saying about wolves?" Abby asked, carrying out a cake with white frosting and sweet berries.

"Good heavens, Abby! Did you make that?" Esther exclaimed.

Abby beamed. "Yes, I did. I worked all morning to make this."

"She finally got it after three tries. Wonder why we had so many birds today? They were all pecking at burnt or doughy cake crumbs," Joseph revealed.

Abby ignored him and set down the cake with pride, her hands on her hips. "What do you think Esther?"

"It is beautiful Abby—and it looks delicious."

Michael was an inch away from the cake, biting his tongue with impatience. "We should try it!"

Joseph laughed. "I agree with Michael. What is the point of it looking pretty if it does not taste good?"

Abby giggled, "It does taste good, and I can guarantee it." She began to slice her creation with a type of careful reverence. "So what were you saying about wolves?" she asked again.

Esther glanced at her hands. Her knuckles were white from how tightly she'd been gripping her skirt. "Oh, just about a study in Europe," she shot a glance at Joseph then back at Abby. "You know, Abby, I was thinking if after the festival Will is still not pursuing you with a vengeance," she smiled at Joseph, "then maybe you should move on and find yourself an alpha male."

Thirteen

Michael sat patiently watching his mother trying to hold her temper as she tampered with the wheel that had broken on their way to school.

"I should have just ridden Lancelot," Esther scolded herself, "but I needed to take so many things to Mary and Melissa and then Suzy and then—" her voice faded as she began playing with the wheel. Each time she made an exclamation of success it was followed by a disappointed sigh and an insult to the wheel.

"You know, I don't have to go to school, Momma. We could go for a walk, maybe go to town, make me a shirt to match Joseph for the festival and—"

Esther spun her head to look at her son. "Match Joseph? Sweet heart, I am sorry but with your hat and belt and boots, I think you match him enough." She turned back to the wheel, "Besides, there is enough talk going around."

Michael frowned. "What do you mean?"

Esther shook her head. She was about to burn the whole wagon. "Nothing sweetheart, nothing at all."

"You mean the talk that you think you are too good for the men in this town so you will marry Joseph because he is from a big ranch?"

Esther dropped the useless tools. She turned to face Michael again. "What did you say? Who is saying this?"

Michael shrugged; apparently the gossip did not offend him. "Some of the parents and the kids at school."

Esther bit her lip. It was not a good morning. "Joseph is a Ranger, not a rancher."

Again Michael shrugged and focused on the cloudy sky. "His father has a ranch. A really, really big ranch. His father wants to give Joseph a ranch because he is getting old."

Esther blinked at her six-year-old son. "How is it you know all this and no one tells me anything?"

Michael smiled. "I don't know," he said honestly. "I just listen."

Esther tried to shake off her irritation, but with each failed attempt at the wheel her irritation grew. How could people say she thought herself better? She had tried so hard to be kind, to serve, and this was what they thought of her? Not that she cared a great deal of what they thought of her, and maybe that was the problem—but still.

Esther was just about to unload her things and begin a walk back to the house when Michael jumped to his feet and began running down the road.

Esther instinctively flew to her feet. "Michael stop! Where are you going?"

She began to run after him when she heard Michael shout, "Joseph! Joseph!"

Esther squinted ahead. Sure enough, the tall broad figure of Joseph with his outrageous belt buckle shining in front of him was walking toward their wagon. Esther turned away, putting her hand to her forehead. After she had spoken about women being able to handle themselves, here she was the next day stranded with a stupid wagon that she could not fix.

"I thought something was wrong," Joseph laughed. "I had a premonition."

Esther took a calming breath before turning to face him. "A premonition?"

Joseph shrugged. "Plain ol' instinct." He nodded towards the wheel, "Need help? When you two were late I figured you were either sick or something had happened on the road. In both cases I wanted to make sure you were alright."

Esther bit her lip. She needed help, needed it badly, but she in no way wanted it, especially from Joseph. "Thank you, Mr. Silver, but we are managing fine."

Joseph cocked an eyebrow so fiercely that it actually made Esther look away. "Mr. Silver, is it? You know, Miss Esther, I've figured out that when you call me Mr. Silver, it means you are uncomfortable, which means that right now you are lying to me." He grinned triumphantly. "You need help with the wheel 'cause you can't fix it."

Esther's lips parted in a frown. He sounded happy about her distress. "Really, I can figure it out, Joseph. I have done fine learning how to fix things and taking care of things myself," she said. True, she knew how to fix things: a leaky roof, rusty pumps, and simple carpentry, but for whatever reason this wheel had a vendetta against her.

"Esther, let me fix your wagon," Joseph said, his voice turning gentle.

Esther felt flustered. "No really I—"

"Esther," Joseph said her name with tenderness and took her hand. She began to pull away but stopped. His touch was not demanding, nor hard. He really was trying to calm her, comfort her. "Please, Esther," he stepped in closer, "consider this my kill I am laying at your feet."

Esther blinked, his words sinking in as he moved her aside and began fixing the wheel. Michael jumped into action, sitting by Joseph and handing him tools. The mountains in their goodness sent an icy breeze to cool Esther's moist forehead. Her hands shook, and her eyes were misty. She walked some paces away from her son and Joseph. Part of her felt silly. She had behaved like a little girl trying to prove her independence. She needed help and should have accepted it graciously. Then Joseph had said—she'd known that he had strong intentions towards her, but had hoped it was nothing more than an infatuation, something that would burn off when he left for Texas. He, however, was not merely infatuated. He wanted something more. He wanted a relationship. No, not just a relationship but a mate—a *wife*. It would not only be Michael's heart that would be breaking when Joseph left, but Joseph's heart as well. Esther wrung her hands. She would not deny that a part of her heart would break, too. She did not love Joseph. She may not hate all men anymore, but that did not mean she was capable of romantically loving one. Still, he had grown on her. She liked his intensity, his strut, his humor, and his kindness to her son. Joseph, she knew, deserved a woman who could passionately love him, a woman whom he could hold in his arms, kiss her lips till they were raw, and caress her skin without her shaking from horrific memories. Esther was not what he needed, nor deserved.

Michael bounded into the classroom announcing his excuse and pointing to Joseph to validate it. "The wheel broke but Joseph fixed the wheel. He fixed it really fast."

Abby smiled and motioned for Michael to take a seat. She gave a quick wave to Esther before continuing with her lesson.

Esther turned to Joseph, choosing to ignore, at least for now, his previous comment. "Thank you again, Joseph; I truly appreciate it. Sorry if I seemed ungrateful. Today was not my finest moment," she laughed nervously.

Joseph chuckled. "Why Miss Esther, I did not think it possible for you to have any moments other than fine. It makes me glad to know that you might be human after all."

Esther laughed with a small shake of her head. "Oh, believe me when I say that I have my flaws." She gave him a good-bye nod and then began to walk back to her newly-mended wagon.

Joseph followed. "What are you doing?" Esther asked him with a frown. "You do not need to walk me to my wagon."

"You're going to the Higgins, correct?"

"Well, yes, but I have other appointments also so you need not spend the day with me," she said, frantically thinking of how to convince him not to come without being rude.

"I am looking forward to it. I would love to hear about midwifery."

Esther suddenly laughed, her head falling back, her eyes twinkling. Joseph looked with surprise, loving how her freckles caught the light of the sun and strands of her hair fell around her face.

"What is so funny?"

Esther looked at him still laughing. "Interested in *midwifery*? Come Joseph, you can do better than that. No man is interested in midwifery."

Joseph gave a defeated shrug and chuckled, "Very well, maybe I don't want to know all the intimate details, but I do want to know about you and what you do."

"And if I choose not to tell anything about me?" she asked with an arched brow.

Joseph stopped walking and turned to face her straight on. "Esther, you name one man who wouldn't enjoy a silent ride next to a beautiful woman. If you want to talk, I would love to talk. If you want to remain silent, well I do well with silence."

Esther was unable to keep a straight face and laughed again. "Very well. Come along, although I am tempted to scare you away by telling you all the details. Trust me, the intimacies of midwifery have sent men hurling their dinners."

Joseph shook his head. "Oh, Miss Esther, when are you to understand that nothing will scare me away."

❧

"He can't come in! Get out of here!" Toby shouted while shrinking beneath Joseph's gaze.

"Mr. Higgins, Mary is in a critical condition. I need to see her for her safety as well as your child's," Esther pleaded.

Toby scoffed. "Who knows if that bastard of a child is even mine."

Before Esther could reply, he was flung back as Joseph drove through the door and into Toby.

"Trespassing!" Toby shouted. Esther hurried in; the stench was worse than before. Toby's drinking was escalating, and she guessed Mary was too miserable and depressed to do any cleaning such as empty the waste or wash the dishes. Joseph seemed unaltered as he picked Toby off the ground, holding him by the shirt.

"Now you listen here, you scum; if you don't allow Miss Esther to do her job and that woman or child in there dies, then it will be known that you allowed that, and you will be responsible for their deaths." He dropped Toby. "Men who are imprisoned for killing their wife and child don't last long. They are usually murdered before a rope can even touch their necks; they die in ways that leave them begging to be hanged, understand?"

Esther stared wide-eyed at Joseph. This was no false bravado or temper. He was calm with a face of steel, rather impressive in a frightening way.

Toby scrambled up. "I'm going for a drink. You'll find me out for a drink every morning when you come by," he spat at Esther.

Joseph nodded. "Wise man," he said quietly before Toby practically ran out, cursing under his breath. Joseph nodded for Esther to go on. "I will be outside if you need me."

Esther gave him a weak smile and began to turn away when she stopped. "Joseph," she called out to him. "I know you just fixed my wagon and took care of Toby, but as long as you're here you might as well be useful. Would you fill up some buckets of water for me? They are in the wagon."

Joseph nodded. "This place has a pump?" he asked.

Esther shook her head. "No, but there is a well in the back. Can you leave the buckets outside this door?" She motioned towards Mary's room. Joseph agreed, and Esther could not help but feel grateful that he'd come with her.

Mary was in a bad state. "Why did you chase away Toby? Suppose he don't come back?" she wailed, her limp hair damp with sweat.

"He will come back," Esther reassured her. "With such a pretty and loving wife, he has to come back, yes?" she smiled and pressed down on the baby. The child was lower, very low. The heartbeat was steady and the size seemed to be normal from what she could tell. When Esther removed Mary's blanket a thick and fishy stench tainted the air so strongly that Esther's eyes stung.

"It's been itchy down there," Mary groaned. "Itchy and swollen like.

Esther nodded. She was worried that infection would come soon with the lack of bathing and hygiene.

Please dear Lord, protect this child from any negligence, she prayed.

Mary would have to be bathed thoroughly every day. Thank goodness for Joseph who had filled every bucket with water to the brim. It would have taken her too much time to do it alone.

After bathing Mary, applying ointments, and hearing the proposal story one more time, Esther began massaging her legs and ankles.

"Oh, it feels so good," Mary sighed with delight. "I ain't never been touched gentle like this."

Esther looked over the swollen legs. Touch was powerful; it could heal, bring comfort, show love, or it could hurt, scar, and ruin.

"What do you mean you've never been touched gently Mary?" she asked. Perhaps if she could understand this lost soul, she could know how to help her.

"Was always being hit on you see. Ma was angry at me. Said I ruined her life. Da—well I never saw Da. He had other children with other women he liked better." Her face lit up. "Men liked to touch me once I got me a figure and some pretty eyes," she said proudly, "but it was never gentle like this."

Esther nodded, imagining a poor and uneducated girl doing whatever she could for love and acceptance. Perhaps this baby would fulfill that need. She prayed that it would. She also prayed Toby would soon be out of Mary's life since no baby should have to suffer a father like him.

Abigail about tripped on her own feet when Will ran into the schoolhouse breathless. He clumsily found a seat making several students laugh at his awkward arrival.

"Pastor Will, how nice of you to join us," Abby said calmly. She was determined not to show that he had upset her.

Will nodded, studying her face. "Have you told them about the..." he mouthed the word "play"?

Abby shook her head. "No, but they know at the end of school today I have a special announcement, right class?" she asked. The children shouted in different ways that they were ready to hear the announcement now. Abby grinned, admitting to herself that she had purposely held off telling them about the play just in case Will showed up. She wanted him to be there and see the children's faces.

Will suddenly stood up. "Well, I think now is as good a time as any." He stood next to Abby, their arms grazing one another's. Abby felt a stream of sparks shoot through her at his touch. She wanted his touch, wanted to see if he felt as giddy as she did.

"All right every one, Miss Abigail has come up with a brilliant idea," Will announced, smacking his hands together in a large casual clap. "She has decided that we will be doing a Thanksgiving play for Tall Pine."

A few exclamations bubbled up.

"That means I will be here *every day* to help out," Will said, looking straight ahead other than a fleeting glance at Abby whose lips were pressed tightly together in a teacher-type smile. Little did he know that inside she was smiling broadly. He would be here every day! "I also have talked to some of your parents, and Miss Abigail has been making inquiries, and after the play, we are to have a Thanksgiving feast!" Will practically shouted his last announcement, which catalyzed cheers and yells as well as jumping and spinning from the children.

Abby laughed joyously. She loved seeing other people happy, especially children. Her heart did a little thump. What would it be like to see her own children smile and get excited? Would it bring her as much joy—more?

"Well I'd say that had the desired effect," Will chuckled. He looked over at Abby who was calming the children and beginning to explain how the practicing would work.

Will sat back down, watching Abby talk with her bright eyes and active hand gestures. She talked as much with her hands as her mouth, and he loved it. He loved everything about her. After wrestling his emotions for a whole week, convincing himself that Abby was not his type, he had come to realize that she was exactly his type. He had confused her strength and her happy character with what he had thought was a shallow personality when in fact, she had more depth than he did. Every woman he had courted, save Esther who never gave him the chance, used him and his position as a caring pastor to solve their problems, but not one had ever asked him about himself. Not one had asked him about his faith, or why he became a pastor, or what did he like to do. No one besides Abby had asked him such things, and come to think about it, he had done a horrible job asking her about herself. He just wasn't used to it. Most girls were eager to tell him about themselves. Abby talked a lot—she analyzed, pondered, and philosophized about many things out loud—but hardly about herself. She was wonderful, the perfect pastor's wife—selfless and gentle—but more importantly, the perfect woman for Will. She was full of life and good humor. Most of the time Will uplifted others, but Abby, without even trying, uplifted him.

"Will. Will?" Abby asked.

The class laughed when Will jerked his head high, "What?"

Abby smiled. "I have the start of a script. Will you help me cast it? We can start with volunteers."

Will nodded. He wished to heaven that he could take Abby to the barn dance, but she would understand once he explained why he had to take Rachel. Especially when Rachel told him that young men hardly asked her to go with them anywhere. What was he supposed to say after that? He had to invite her. Still, he had decided not to worry too much about the Harvest Festival. Abby was indeed understanding, and to his knowledge, there were no other young men who she was interested in.

Esther was surprised how much she enjoyed the rest of her visits. Melissa was doing better; she still felt a trifle sad at times, but then would go for a walk, read a book, or do something that made her feel better. Suzy was still nervous, but growing more confident especially since her baby had begun to move more and more. After each visit Joseph would ask about the patient and she found it easy to talk to him. He genuinely seemed interested, asking questions and even trying to relate them to life on the ranch—the closest he'd been to pregnancy.

"I doubt heifers get feelings of sadness after having a baby," Esther laughed.

Joseph did not look convinced. "You never know. A heifer has a heart and soul, cares for her calf. Perhaps I ought to start giving my female cows massages and nap times."

Esther narrowed her eyes at him playfully. "This is why men aren't midwives."

Joseph gave a nod of agreement. "Maybe. What made you become a midwife?"

Esther bit her lip trying to think of a way to explain without revealing too much. "I studied nursing back East, and when I moved here with my uncle, he took over my training. The people here trust me and know I am good at what I do. Back East I was still uncertain if I wanted to be a midwife. I loved the joy that babies brought and wanted to be a part of it, but the worry of having a life in my hands made me feel so terribly responsible, but when I came out here I had no choice. I needed a way to pay for my keep, even with my uncle's generosity." Esther twirled her fingers. She had said enough. It was time to change the subject. "Michael tells me you have a ranch?"

Joseph nodded. "It's my stepfather's. It's the third largest in Texas—beautiful ranch, green and fresh."

"Green? Texas is green?" Esther asked with an unbelieving smile.

"Texas has its green parts. It is not like Massachusetts mind you, but it is green. We have hot summers, but also cool winters with good rain. When you get closer to Mexico, then it becomes dry and dusty."

"Have you ever been to Mexico?" Esther asked, her interest piquing.

Joseph's eyes clouded over, the left muscle in his jaw ticking. "Several times; it's a favorite hiding place for criminals. I've had to track them down there."

Esther wanted to ask more, but she gathered from his expression that it was a sore subject. She tried to remain silent, but curiosity got the better of her.

"Do you mind if I ask about what criminals you were chasing?" she asked quietly and pulled her shawl tighter around her shoulders.

Joseph stared into the distance; his jaw ticked again. "The last man I chased down in Mexico had murdered a bartender just because he was angry. The bartender's eldest son was there working as well and he tried to avenge his father and," Joseph shifted his shoulders, "well, you can guess what happened. That was just the beginning of the tragedy. This bartender had three other sons, each of whom tried to avenge the deaths of their father and elder brothers. Finally, a heart-stricken widow who had lost all her sons and husband came to us begging for justice after it was clear that the local Sheriff could do nothing."

Esther felt sick. She thought something terrible had happened to her, but it was not to be compared to this poor widow. Esther couldn't imagine losing her son. The mere thought shook her very soul.

"I tracked him down to Mexico," Joseph continued. "Had to do some serious investigating before I found him. The man was smart and one hell of a shooter. When I found him, I tried to bring him back for a trial, but he would not have it. Killing four men had given him arrogance in his gun-slinging skills. He fired at me and took off like a coward." Joseph pulled down his shirt at the neck to show a twisted scar along his collarbone. "He thought he had killed me, but I had moved in time. I knew if he got any further in Mexico I would lose him for good, so, hurting and bleeding, I went after him."

"Did you kill him?" Esther asked with no judgment in her tone.

Joseph gave a one-jerk nod. "Didn't have a choice. I tried wounding him, but when he shot me in the arm I had to take him down." Josephs grimaced with the memory. "Didn't trust anyone to stitch me up down there, so holding a leather strip between my teeth I dug out the bullet and stitched up my own skin." He grinned at her, "So yes, I have been to Mexico,but I can't say that I enjoyed it."

"I'm surprised you used leather and not a strong drink to help you dig out the bullet. That must have been very painful."

Joseph nodded. "It was, but I've never been one for what you call strong drink. My old man was always downing whiskey, wine, anything he could get with alcohol. It helped him become numb to the things he saw. Eventually, he preferred drinking over everything—even his own son and wife. He did some ugly things when drunk, and it made me swear that I would never go near the stuff."

Esther blinked at Joseph. She was seeing him in a new light. She knew he was a good-natured man, a kind and strong man, but the fact that he had seen and experienced terrible things without becoming coarse said something remarkable about his inner fortitude and heart. He, like her, had drunken out of the bitter cup without becoming bitter, something she herself had struggled with.

Suddenly wanting to know more about Joseph she asked, "If your father took to drinking, what did you do to numb the pain? Turn to God?"

Joseph sighed and rolled his neck. "That was my mother's advice and my stepfather's, but I could never bring myself to believe God truly cared. I believed in His existence, but I saw too many horrors to believe that He worried about others and answered their prayers. I just had to turn off my emotions, control my feelings. Abby says that is why I have never succeeded in a relationship," he laughed.

"You don't allow yourself to feel?" she asked curiously.

Joseph's face softened. He looked over at her tenderly. "Until now," he said softly.

Esther's heart leapt. Whether out of fear or joy she didn't know. Breaking eye contact, she looked ahead. The clouds had darkened with a promise of rain and the trees covered the mountains in shades of gold and red. She loved autumn, especially in Tall Pine. Soon there would be Christmas trees, nativity sets in the windows, and the smell of mothers baking sugar cookies with their children. She loved this beautiful place.

As if reading her thoughts Joseph asked, "Would you ever leave Colorado?"

Esther shrugged. "No, I don't think I could. I love it here." *Except for the winter* she added silently. "It's beautiful, the people are good, and it's become home."

"You know, Texas is beautiful, too," Joseph said with a nervous twitch to his lips. "My stepfather wants me to take over half the ranch, eventually all of it. You can ride your horse for miles both to the east and west and still be on the ranch, and you're not far from town which has a huge bookstore." Joseph grinned at her. "It even has books about wolves."

Esther laughed and twirled a loose strand of her hair. "Texas, huh?" she said.

Joseph swallowed. Was now the time? Should he tell her that she could come to Texas, live in Texas as his wife? His parents would love her. He loved her and he would do everything he could to make his home hers.

Was it too soon?

If he chose to take the ranch, and that choice depended on Esther, his mother would be thrilled if he returned with a wife and son. Jefferson would be proud. The ranch, a family…it seemed almost too good to hope for, but it was a dream that would be worthless without the woman he adored. Joseph glanced at Esther who was enjoying the scenery around them. He did love her passionately and fully. The more he saw her, heard her, and talked to her, the more his love grew. Despite his sudden urge to propose and seal it with a kiss, a hand in her hair, their bodies pressed together, he decided to wait. If he acted too soon, he could chase her away.

"There's the schoolhouse. I'm surprised we made it back in time," she laughed, arching her back slightly like a cat. She turned to Joseph, "Thank you. I know I was reluctant, but I do appreciate you coming with me."

Joseph nodded. "My pleasure, Miss Esther, and don't forget I will be coming with you every morning," *and I will love you always.*

Fourteen

Esther stared at the red dress. It was by far the best sewing she had ever done, and the fabric still took her breath away. Still, should she wear it tonight to the dance in front of everyone—in front of Joseph? Tonight, she felt unusually self-conscious about how she would look in front of others, but mostly how she would look in front of Joseph. The thought of him being pleased with her appearance made her blush and also scared her. She didn't want him to fall for her any more than he had done. Maybe she was enjoying his attention, but she did not want to toy with him. She didn't want to be cruel.

Biting her bottom lip with conflicted intensity, Esther finally flung off her calico dress and put on the red one. After all, she had promised her aunt, and it would not hurt to see how it looked on her with her hair done up and her lips and cheeks rosy. She would wear the ruby-drop earrings her uncle had given her for a birthday. The shimmery satin fabric slid over her slender body like poppy petals. She buttoned the back, put on her shoes and earrings and looked in the mirror. Her own appearance surprised her. True, she usually made an effort to look pretty, but now she looked—

"Wow!" Michael exclaimed as he walked into her room. "Momma, you look beautiful. You're like a princess from a story book."

Esther grinned lovingly at her son. "Thank you, handsome, but I think I may change. This dress is a bit too fancy."

Michael looked at her like she was crazy. "But you have to wear it. You look beautiful!!" he exclaimed.

Esther looked back in the mirror. She took two of the small red roses from a vase on her vanity and placed them gently in her hair, which she had done up in soft silky curls. Maybe she would wear it. What harm would it do?

Nodding to herself with courage, she turned to face Michael. The boy stood proudly in his shiny boots, his crisp white shirt tucked into his leather belt with his worn, gaudy belt buckle and his new hat that barely covered the rebellious curls sneaking out from underneath. He looked both handsome and adorable. Esther held out her arm.

"Would you be so kind, sir, as to accompany me to the dance?" she asked in a mock proper voice.

The two laughed and Michael rushed over taking her arm, "I love you, Momma."

Esther pulled him close. "I love you, too."

❦

Abby could hardly contain her excitement as she and Joseph pulled up to the dance. There was an abundance of pumpkins, painted squashes, strings of autumn leaves, brightly-colored lanterns, and jars holding candles. It looked like a fairy dance, beautiful and festive. She was already in a good mood and felt especially lovely.

After Joseph had settled down his horse and tied him to the hitching post, he and Abby walked together into the dance. Joseph felt the eyes of a dozen women flicker at him. Abby noticed it, too, and she gave Joseph a small nudge. "Well, big brother, if Esther doesn't work out, there are plenty of other women who I believe would be more than happy to take her place," she giggled, and then stopped short when she saw Will with Rachel. Goodness he looked handsome, and Rachel, much to Abby's despair, looked rather pretty.

You don't need him to enjoy yourself, Abby reminded herself. *You're an independent woman.*

"Speaking of Esther, do you see her or Michael? I see her uncle and his wife talking to Sheriff Ben, but I don't see Esther."

"She's probably coming along with Michael. I'm sure she will be here any minute," Abby reasoned, scanning the dance for young men to talk to. Her eyes fell on Harry, Kyle Lampton's nephew; he was a nice boy, handsome and shy. "Excuse me, Joseph," Abby fluffed up her hair and pinched her cheeks.

The Mayor suddenly stood up on a stack of hay bales, ringing a bell for attention. He was a little man with thick glasses and a kind, intelligent face. By him stood his short, plump wife who looked up at him with pride.

"Alright folks, we welcome you tonight for our annual barn dance hosted by our very own Sean Pennsworth." He nodded to a ruddy-looking rancher who blushed when everyone cheered. "Now, we have dancing and then in an hour we will break for our picnic auction and some dinner generously put together by the good women of Tall Pine." Another cheer. "And then we will resume our dancing until Sheriff Ben is ready to arrest us all." The Mayor rang the bell again and everybody laughed.

Joseph chuckled as Sheriff Ben held up handcuffs to the crowd threateningly. A fiddle and guitar began to play in unison and people lined up to dance. Joseph sighed, wondering if Esther was even going to come. He started to make his way toward Ben when he saw several heads turn in one direction. Joseph followed the spectators' gaze, and his jaw dropped.

Esther had arrived wearing an intoxicating red dress that emphasized her slender, curvaceous figure. Her proud shoulders were bare of any shawl, and her eyes sparkled. Joseph rushed forward. Esther would be his tonight, and he pitied any man who thought otherwise.

❧

Abby gave a whoop along with all the other women dancing. She usually did not do vigorous dancing such as this, but goodness it was fun. Her skin was hot, refreshing after the chilly days of late, and she loved the sense of camaraderie she was now feeling among the people of Tall Pine. Harry, as it turned out, was a good dancer, and stronger than his thin body looked. He easily spun her, lifted her, and all in all was an excellent partner. After Harry she talked to Spencer who asked her for a dance; he was not as good as Harry, but Abby was surprised how good-looking he was. He had such a nice smile. How come she had not noticed before? So enthralled with her enjoyment, Abby hardly noticed Will who, despite being kind to Rachel, was glowering at Abby. She certainly seemed to be enjoying herself and Will felt like a boiling teakettle about to explode. Men's gazes were lingering on her lithe form, talking about the lovely schoolteacher. She did look especially nice in the silvery-gray dress that highlighted her eyes and fairy-like features. And, she seemed especially popular with the young men, which enraged Will.

Rachel finally huffed and folded her arms, "If you are gonna stare at *her* all night then I best be leaving, huh?" she asked with a scrunched-up nose.

Will shook his head. First and foremost he was a pastor, and a pastor was supposed to be kind. He held out his arm to Rachel, "Shall we dance the next one?" he asked with a smile, knowing full well from the musical introduction that the next dance would be one of switching partners.

Abby stiffened when she saw Will come onto the dance floor with Rachel. Were pastors even supposed to dance? It didn't matter. She was enjoying herself, and though she loved Will, he had not asked her to the dance, and she need not sit on the bench and wait pityingly for him.

The dance began and Abby tried to keep her focus on the music, smiling gaily with Spencer when he spun her around, but this was a complicated dance where one switched partners every few seconds. Soon Abby was spun around to another man and then another.

She knew she was coming closer to Will. When she finally reached him, his arms clasped around hers like a vice making her wince.

"What are you doing?" Will hissed at her.

Of all the nerve. "Excuse me, Pastor? What in heaven's name do you mean?"

The two linked arms and skipped in a circle before Will pulled her to him, closer than the dance allowed. Firecrackers went off through Abby's chest as her torso was pressed against Will's.

"Dancing with all these different *boys.*"

"Young men," Abby corrected, "and why can't I dance with different men? I'm not tied to anyone," she said with a mischievous smile before being whisked off to the next partner.

Will practically tripped over the older woman in front of him, as he was still looking at Abby. He apologized to Lucinda Hampton, Sheriff Ben's wife.

"I'd be stuttering, too, if I were a young man," she laughed with a knowing glance at Abby. "She's an awfully lovely woman."

Will smiled politely. Abby was not merely lovely. She was bewitching, enchanting. How could he not have fallen for her the moment he saw her? Why had he been so stubborn? What if he was too late?

Rachel returned to him as his partner. He noticed her eyeing Spencer with Abby, and she looked perturbed. Will clenched his fists when he saw Spencer kiss Abigail's hand and heard her giggled response. He may not have taken Abigail to the dance, but he sure wanted to be the one driving her home.

Esther had barely sat down, letting Michael run off to where several games for children were being hosted, before a shadow fell over her. She looked up to see Joseph. He was especially handsome tonight with his longish hair combed back and his face clean-shaven.

"Is that another gift from an Indian?" she asked, motioning to his bolo tie with a miniature carved cattle skull.

Joseph looked down at it and grinned. "Would you believe me if I said it was?"

Esther laughed and shook her head. "Probably not."

Joseph shrugged, defeated. "The bracelet and buckle are all I have from them besides a few close friendships. Sadly, even the friendships don't always last since they're being moved around," he said grimly.

"Our country doesn't treat them as we should, do we?" she agreed.

Joseph gave a curt nod, his hand stretched and then tightened. "Miss Esther, would you give me one of your disapproving stares if I told you that you look incredibly beautiful tonight?"

Esther smiled, meeting his gaze unabashedly. "Even if I disapproved, that doesn't mean I wouldn't enjoy the compliment."

"And would you refuse me if I were to ask you for a dance?"

Esther blanched and looked away. The dancers looked like a rainbow of colors, and the air held an intoxicating smell of pumpkin pies and pork roasting on the spit. All in all, the atmosphere should have induced her to dance, but dance meant touch, close touch. She didn't think she could do it.

"I'm sorry Joseph, but I don't dance. However, there are many young ladies here who I know would love to dance with you."

"There are other ladies here?" he asked, blinking as if he had not noticed.

Esther's cheeks flamed. The man was incredibly charming.

"Sorry, I can't dance."

"Can't? Or won't?" Joseph asked persistently.

Esther's smiled faded. "Does it make a difference?" She really didn't want him to ask any more.

Joseph sighed and sat down on the bench. "Well, Esther," he was past using Miss, "you leave me no choice."

Esther frowned. "To do what?"

"I have formulated a list in my head as to why you have to dance with me. Let's just say I came prepared." He cleared his throat. "I bought your son boots, and a hat; I taught him how to ride without breaking his neck. I have accompanied you for a whole week on your calls. I fixed your wagon, and I plan on doing whatever it takes to get you on the dance floor."

So eager was Joseph's mischievous grin that Esther could only shake her head with a laugh. "You're blackmailing me! Goodness, and I thought your intentions were pure," she teased.

Joseph stood up and held out his hand. "They were and are, but let's just say that I don't let important opportunities pass me by." He held out his hand, again.

Esther stared at the hand for several seconds. It was large, calloused, and had experience written all over it. She could see where the skin was roughened by the long days of riding. He was right. He had been very kind to her and Michael. Surely she could swallow her fears and her anxieties for one dance.

Lord, give me strength. She placed her hand in his, feelings his fingers hungrily clasp around hers.

Joseph smiled gently, his eyes filling with triumph as he led her out. Esther could feel every one gaping at her and Joseph, whispering to each other. It was common knowledge that Esther danced with no one, and here she was holding hands with a Texan.

Why did I have to wear red? she moaned to herself.

The music began and Joseph twirled Esther in front of him. She laughed nervously, feeling awkward. It had been so long since she had done anything like this. Thankfully, this was not a slow dance but a lively one. She need not touch him often. In a heartbeat, Esther was clapping and stomping along with the other women. The men followed and then joined hands forming a bridge for couples to dance under. The laughter and music had a magical quality. Esther found herself feeling energized and having fun. Some of the couples tripped or did funny things as they paraded under the human bridge. When Joseph took her hand, he lifted her by the waist, sending an unexpected jolt through her as he spun her in the air before setting her down so they could skip to the end.

She knew he was trying to make eye contact, to see if she were mad, upset, or pleased. Esther would not look at him, focusing on the following couples. Truth was, when he had held her waist she felt something strong: it could have easily been anxiety, and yet she was not shaking.

The dance ended and everyone applauded. Esther gave Joseph a grateful nod.

"Thank you, I enjoyed that. It has been so long since I've danced." She did an awkward curtsy and began to walk away. Joseph grabbed her wrist as a slow dance began to play.

"One more?" he asked.

Esther swallowed. Not a slow dance! Before she could shake her head Joseph had stepped close to her, taking her right hand in his left, and placing his right hand on her lower back. Hesitantly, Esther placed her left hand on his broad shoulder, feeling the involuntary flex of his muscle. She exhaled slowly, unable to look at him as she concentrated on keeping her breath steady.

They began to move in unison, slowly for a minute before Joseph gently pulled her closer. The satin of her dress rustled against his crisp shirt, his head above hers was close enough to feel his breath. Her ears pounded with her own heartbeat, and she began to tremble, but not out of fear. No, she felt far from fearful. Her skin began to prickle, tiny bumps running over her smooth arms. Her whole body, starved of physical affection, yearned to be closer to him. It needed more, more of being held by this strong man, more caresses, more skin, more everything. Esther wanted to break away. She was not used to these feelings; she had never had them, or if she had, she could not remember. It worried her and yet elated her. Hardly knowing if she were responding to the feeling in her soul or her touch-starved body, Esther allowed herself to be pulled closer, her chin brushing his arm, her lips close to his scarred collar bone.

Joseph's hand on her back tensed, pressing deeper into her skin, his breathing quickened, and he clasped her own hand tighter, placing it on his chest. He wanted to speak, but he was afraid if he did it would shatter the moment. He wanted to hold her forever. He wanted her to want him as much as he wanted her. He needed her to need him.

The music stopped and for one more breath Joseph held Esther before she pulled away. Her cheeks were flushed, her lips parted in confusion.

"I—" she stuttered, "I need to go check on Michael," she said before turning like a frightened doe and disappearing into the crowd.

❦

Will left Rachel chatting with some of her friends; he had pulled Spencer aside when he was left alone after Abigail had been asked to dance by another cursed young man. Through careful manipulation that Will was not proud of, he had convinced Spencer to take Rachel home at the end of the dance, explaining that he needed to do a pastoral visit to someone after the dance. Spencer had agreed and actually looked excited about it. Rachel herself did not seem too disappointed and began asking her friends what they knew about the handsome cobbler.

Will found Abby talking with Eliza who looked unusually lovely. Her hair was done up, and she wore a pink dress that brought color to her face. Next to her was the giant Kyle Lampton who seemed unable to go a moment without touching her hands, wrist, fingers—anything that he could properly touch in public.

"So you would not mind playing the piano? I thought it would be so much fun to have lots of music interspersed in the play," Abby said, her eyes bright.

"I think it's a great idea. Let me go through some of my music to see what songs would work with a Thanksgiving theme."

Abby clapped her hands. "Oh, that would be wonderful, and Mr. Lampton, you don't mind making pies and cookies, do you? Yours are the best and I don't want to tax the mothers too much with Thanksgiving and Christmas coming up and all."

Kyle chuckled in his Saint Nicolas way. "I'd be offended if you didn't ask me. Besides, I'll take any excuse to work with this lovely lady here." He nodded at Eliza who gave him a "you are crazy" look. "Count me in."

Abigail was about to reply when Will somewhat rudely stepped, in placing his hand on her back. "Miss Eliza, Kyle," he nodded curtly, "would you excuse Miss Abigail for a moment? I need to speak with her."

Abby smiled apologetically and allowed herself to be led away.

"I was discussing the play," she explained with annoyance. "You could have waited for me to finish."

Will said nothing, leading her out behind the wagons where they were out of sight and hearing.

"Why are you taking me back here?"

Will spun her to face him. "I just want to know why you are behaving in such a ridiculous manner. I am the pastor of Tall Pine and it is my job to oversee the school, and to make sure the teacher is acting proper."

"Proper?!" Abby exclaimed, her face turning red with anger. "You dare suggest that I am not behaving properly when you allow 'Ravishing Rachel' to drape herself all over you? When you rudely interrupt a conversation to lead me away secretly behind the wagons? Proper my foot! Pastor or no Pastor, what right do you have to tell me how to behave? I don't need *your* permission or approval."

Will's eyes narrowed and he stepped closer, his large frame towering over Abby. "Do whatever you wish, huh? Not if it means flirting outrageously with other men."

Abby laughed sarcastically. "You mean being kind? If you want to see me flirt then let's go back and I will show just how outrageous I can be," Abby snapped. She was so mad she could punch Will. What right did he have telling her what to do?

Will's jaw clenched.

"So help me, I will not allow you to flirt with any man," he growled.

This time Abby stepped forward. "And just what are you going to do about it?" she challenged him. Will made a guttural sound, a mix between a groan and a growl. Then with a speed Abby didn't know was possible, Will grabbed her by the shoulders and pressed his lips to hers.

Abby's feet were lifted off the ground as Will's kiss deepened, his smooth lips moving against her own trembling ones. She should pull away. Yes, she should, but she couldn't. She found herself responding. Abby wrapped her arms around his neck, pressing her body against his. His kiss was deep and hungry. She'd never been kissed like this before. He was all consuming.

The sound of a bell calling for a gathering brought Abby back to her senses.

She pushed against Will who, with a reluctant moan, set her down. As soon as she was stable she looked at the cocky smirk on his face and then slapped him smartly across the cheek.

"Of all the arrogant and conceited nerve!" she hissed. "Calling me improper and then stealing a passionate kiss. What were you trying to do? Brand me like cattle?"

Will grinned. Her slap had barely left a mark on his strong jaw. "Spoken like a rancher's daughter," he chuckled. "Branding you, huh? I like the sound of that."

Abby gasped and raised her hand to slap him again, but Will caught her wrist. "Now, Miss Abby, if I really did offend you, then I will never kiss you again, but it seemed to me that you rather enjoyed it."

Abby glared. "Why did you kiss me? Did you just want to make me feel like a fool?"

Will frowned, confused that she still did not know. "I kissed you because I am in love you with."

Abby blinked once and then twice. The bell sounded again as the Mayor called for the picnic basket auction, but Abby did not hear him. All she could hear was the beating of her own heart. Will loved her!

He loves me as I love him.

Will felt a surge of panic as Abby's face stared at him blankly. Had he spoken too soon? He was desperate and had responded to instinct. What if she did not love him or even care for him? Had he just made a fool of himself?

"Listen, Abby, I am sorry. I did not mean to offend you or—" his words were cut off as Abby attacked him with a kiss of her own, knocking him back against a wagon. The auction would have to wait.

Esther sat next to several women doing her best to keep from glancing at Joseph and Michael who stood laughing with one another. She needed to stay away from Joseph—far away. Luckily tomorrow was Saturday and she would not be seeing him. Sunday she would find a way to evade him, and when she dropped Michael off at school, she would need to do it fast before Joseph could reach her. Abby had said that he would leave after Thanksgiving. That was only a few weeks away. Then he would be gone, and she could go back to normal—just her and Michael, happy and content. She was content, right? She didn't want anything more than what she had, and yet why after one dance did she feel such a hunger inside her?

The Mayor stood up on one of the hay bales. "Folks, it is time for the auction, which will be led by our very own Lucinda Hampton."

Lucinda walked to the front, her cheeks flushing as everyone applauded. Esther smiled. Lucinda was a good woman. And Esther suddenly realized there were many like her in Tall Pine, people full of good works and pure intentions. The town would do fine if she ever left. Family and neighbors would continue to help each other, and Esther could go find a new life, new people to help, new people to encourage. This place no longer needed her, and she did not even know what she needed.

"Good evening folks! Is everyone having a swell time?" Lucinda's voice was strong as she took hold of everyone's attention.

Whoops and hoorays lit up like fireworks over the crowd.

"Wonderful, wonderful—well, we will go back to eating and more dancing, but first we are raising money for a bigger clinic. After, of course, the new chapel is built." She looked over at the Mayor. "Right, Mayor?" Laughter arose as the Mayor bowed submissively to Lucinda.

"This spring we start the construction!" he shouted.

Lucinda nodded with approval. "Very well folks, let us begin the auction." One of the Sheriff's daughters handed the first basket to her mother.

"Alright, here we have Miss Rachel Baker's basket, and you all know how Miss Rachel cooks. So sinfully delicious."

Esther looked around for Will. He was the one who brought Rachel. She scanned through the thicket of people. No Will. No Abby either now that she noticed. Esther wondered where they were. Suddenly it dawned on her. Two young, beautiful people were missing. Esther smiled smugly. She did not doubt Will or Abby in their virtue, but she also did not doubt that those two were enjoying each other's company very much at the moment.

"Ten cents? Ten cents folks—that can't be too much."

Spencer stepped forward, "I'll give you ten cents," he announced proudly.

Rachel, standing among her friends, burst into giggles.

"Ten cents, well now, someone set the stakes high." Lucinda laughed, obviously enjoying the role of auctioneer. "Do I hear fifteen cents?"

Rachel's father stepped up beside Spencer placing his hand on the young man's shoulder playfully. "I'll give you fifteen cents for my daughter's basket." He raised his eyebrows at Spencer, daring him with good humor.

"Twenty cents!" Spencer called out before turning to Mr. Baker, "With respect Sir, all I brought was twenty cents; I didn't expect to bid at all," he said loudly.

Mr. Baker laughed as well as a few others. "Alright Mrs. Hampton, I think this boy deserves that basket."

Lucinda grinned. "Twenty cents going once, twice, and sold."

Rachel was as red as a rose. She rushed over to Spencer and linked arms with him as he took her basket. Esther guessed that she would no longer be going after Will.

Basket after basket was auctioned off. Periodically Esther tried to catch Michael's eye. She wanted him to come sit by her, but he and Joseph seemed to be conspiring some plan as they whispered and laughed under their breath. Part of her wondered if she should go stand by them, but rumors had been spread enough, and she didn't wanted to add to them, and she certainly did not want to be standing by Joseph.

"And now we have Miss Esther's basket—you all know what kind of food she makes." Sheryl held up the beautiful basket decorated with a large velvet ribbon. Everyone began whispering to each other. They knew that at any kind of auction they had for raising money, it was Michael who bid for his mother. Any dance, festival, wedding, it was only Michael who accompanied Esther. Tonight, however, people wondered if it would be the Texas Ranger who would be taking her on a picnic.

"Do I hear fifteen cents?"

One man raised his hand. "I'll do twenty cents."

Esther looked at Michael who gave her an innocent smile but said nothing.

"Twenty-five?" asked Lucinda.

The bookkeeper raised his hand, "Twenty-five cents."

Esther looked at Michael again, narrowing her gaze. She had given him ample money to bid for her. Still he just smiled and stood next to—

Esther looked around. Where was Joseph? From the corner of her eye she saw Will and Abby appear looking a bit ruffled, but where was Joseph? She did not have to look long. The now familiar deep voice rose up over the sea of whispers.

"Forty cents," he announced.

Esther's heart did a somersault.

"Fifty cents?"

The bookkeeper again raised his hand. "Fifty cents."

Lucinda smiled like the cat who'd just ate the cream. "Fifty-five?"

"Sixty cents." Joseph crossed his arms, eyeing the small bookkeeper with a determined set in his jaw. The bookkeeper raised his hands in surrender and took a step back in the crowd.

Michael now skipped ahead and stood next to Joseph. He looked up adoringly at the tall man. "Sixty-five," Michael said.

The crowd laughed. It was obvious the two had planned the auction battle between them. Esther felt herself calming down. No doubt Joseph had agreed to go against him in order to put on a good show.

"Seventy!"

"Eighty."

"One dollar."

Esther felt her pulse quicken. Two dollars was all Michael had. She hadn't thought anyone would go over one dollar out of sheer politeness. Surely Joseph would not go over one dollar unless—

Esther gulped down the warm air. Maybe they were putting on a good show and Michael was allowing Joseph to win, wanting him to win.

"One and fifty!" Joseph shouted.

Lucinda looked hesitantly. She glanced at Esther who stared back dumbfounded. "One and seventy-five?" she asked hesitantly.

"Two dollars!" Michael exclaimed in a high squeak from the excitement of having everyone's attention.

Esther put her head in her hands. What a night! What was Joseph thinking? Two dollars was a lot of money for a basket, although she knew it was not the basket. Tradition said you were expected to go on a picnic with the man who won the basket. She would not go out with Joseph. She simply would not.

"Two dollars and fifty cents?" Lucinda asked, wide-eyed.

Joseph raised his hand, "Two and fifty."

Michael grinned and shook his head. "I give up!" he giggled. A ripple of laughter softly went through the crowd, although Esther missed it for the buzzing in her ears. She felt—pleased? Angry? Desired? Worried? She had no idea what she was feeling.

Lucinda pounded the pulpit. "Two dollars and fifty cents going once, twice, and sold to Joseph Silver, our guest in Tall Pine." Lucinda began to applaud and was joined by everyone else.

Esther wanted to flee. She wanted to grab Michael, hitch up

their little wagon and go, but that would be much too obvious. If there was one thing Esther never did, it was parading her emotions. So putting on a good show, she smiled and stood up to go find Joseph and Michael.

"Wasn't that great, Mom?" Michael was filling up his plate with sweet pork, beans, and a buttered role. "Did you like how I bid?"

"I loved it, Michael. You were amazing!" She pulled him in tight against her. "You were the best bidder I have ever seen."

Joseph offered her a plate, but she shook her head. Her stomach felt like a million butterflies were trapped inside, and she doubted pork with beans would be a good fix.

"So I guess that means you will be going on a picnic with me, huh?" Joseph winked.

Michael lifted himself on his tiptoes as he always did when asking a question. "Can I come, too?"

"Of course!" Esther exclaimed. She definitely wanted Michael to be there. She did not want to be alone.

"When would be a good day?" Joseph asked.

Esther shrugged. It was useless trying to put off Joseph. He was relentless. All she could do was wait until he left. "Thursday? I am hoping that Mary has her baby in the next few days. Before Thursday with a little luck."

"Thursday it is," Joseph nodded. "You are seeing Mary tomorrow, right?"

Esther nodded. "Yes, but please do not feel that you need to go with me. You accompanied me all last week. I can handle this week alone. And, there are a few more women I need to visit, even up in the mining community."

Joseph looked at her as if she had said something ridiculous. "Of course I am coming with you. I'm enjoying the time with you. Besides, you need to be safe."

Esther knew she should not feel offended, but she did. Just because this man could fix a wagon and throw Toby out the door did not mean she needed his help or protection.

"Joseph, really, I know these parts and these people better than you. I carry a pistol with me that I know how to shoot, and I know what places to avoid. As you can see, I have managed to keep myself and my son safe."

Joseph's face went still. He looked steadily at her. "You think you don't need a man to protect you?"

Esther stared equally back. "I know that I don't."

Joseph nodded, looking away for a few seconds at the lanterns. "You know Esther, my mother used to say it was arrogant of a man to assume he did not need a wife. A woman completes a man. She gives him purpose and direction. He has a reason to be a good man because of her. She feeds him, creates a home for him, gives him a family. Men are idiots if they don't want that." He stepped closer. "My mother is a fine woman. She did not need to re-marry in order to give me a good life, but she knew that with a good man at her side, she could give me a better life and a safer life. She proved that to me one night when our home caught fire. My mother was able to get Abby out, but we would have lost everything had my stepfather not saved the animals, the corn, grain, and everything else so we didn't starve. He still has burn scars on his hands from that night, but it wasn't from saving the cattle or the barns that he got those burns. They came from him carrying me out so my mother could carry my newborn sister. Things would have been different had it just been my mom."

Esther did not respond. Joseph gave her a polite nod and took his plate to go talk to Will and Sheriff Ben.

"Can I go with Joseph, Momma?" Michael asked.

"Not right now," Esther sighed, feeling a headache forming.

Abby could not believe it—Will was driving her home. Never mind that they had swapped kisses, several of which had left her breathless and wanting more. It was finally Will who pulled away. "Abigail," he had said, "if I steal one more kiss I won't be able to call myself a good pastor."

Now, he was silent, pensive, and stern looking. Not the

romantic ride home she had thought it would be. No doubt he was worrying that she would now want a marriage proposal and public acknowledgement of his affection for her.

Unable to endure the silence any longer, Abby sighed: "Will, what's the matter? Are you upset thinking that I am planning my wedding dress and thinking of my bridesmaids already? Let me assure you, I am not." Abby laughed wryly, hoping to relieve the stress that she was sure he felt.

Truth was, Abby had spent weeks thinking of wedding dresses, bridesmaids, cake, decorations, and whether the wedding should be in Tall Pine or Texas. However, there was absolutely no way she would scare off Will. She did not want to coerce him into marriage. She wanted him to want it.

Will laughed nervously. Abby had responded to his kiss, and favorably too. After smacking him of course. Did she truly like him or did she simply like kissing him? Abby did not seem that type. He had wondered if he should propose to her right then and there, but he had no ring and no great savings. He still had to expand his farm. How could he propose with nothing to offer? And now she had said she was not even thinking about marriage. Was she trying to hint to him that she did not want to marry him? Maybe she simply wanted a fun romance with nothing serious, or maybe she was playing some female game that pretty girls were so good at. Yet, Abby didn't seem like that type either.

She knew he liked her, loved her, but did she reciprocate those feelings? Will frowned as realization dawned on him: Abigail had not said that she loved him. She'd merely returned his kisses without expressing a thing.

※

After the festivities, Esther allowed Joseph to follow her and Michael home. Uncle Tim and Aunt Lily had gone home earlier and Joseph wanted to make sure Esther and Michael arrived safely. When they reached their home, Esther sent Michael in to get ready for bed while she and Joseph unhitched the horse and put him in the barn.

"Thank you, Joseph. I really am grateful for all that you've done." She looked away from his smoldering eyes. "For the kindness you have shown."

Joseph grunted. Esther sighed. She had hurt him: when she had not shown enthusiasm for him winning her lunch, when she had told him that she did not need his protection, and when she had also insisted he no longer come with her on her midwifery rounds. Now that she replayed the evening, she realized she had been a right shrew. Unkindness was never justified no matter what issues it revolved around. She saw his hand calming Lancelot. A strong hand that seemed capable of such gentleness. He had touched her hands many times. She had held it dancing—surely she could take it now.

Joseph was surprised when Esther took his hand. He looked at her face. Her expression was sincere and smiling, and she was so alluring in that red dress. He had struggled all night not to kiss her, but now as they stood in a dark barn, with the smell of fresh hay around them and the autumn moonlight peeking through the rafters, the urge to hold her was overwhelming. He looked away, fighting the temptation. Esther must have thought this as a rejection of her touch because she stepped closer, taking his other hand in hers.

"Joseph, please, I am truly sorry about how I behaved tonight. It has just been so long since I've danced with a man, let alone go on a picnic with him, or even ride in a wagon with him as I have done this past week. I fear my actions have been very awkward."

Joseph looked down at her. The smell of sugar cookies overtook him. Her lips were rosy and moist with berry stain. Would they taste like berries? He longed to try, but something told him not to. Instinct? The Spirit? He did not know what. Surprised at his own will power Joseph smiled and pulled away from her hands. Her face fell, and for a moment he wondered if she was going to cry, but she didn't. Was Esther capable of crying?

"They have been confusing." He put on his hat, motioning for them to walk outside. He needed to get out of the barn. "I simply hope that you tell me what you feel before I leave."

Esther looked at him sadly. "Joseph I made it clear from the beginning that I cannot offer more than friendship and that I am not interested in—"

"Stop it, Esther," Joseph growled, taking off his hat and running his hand through his hair. "You can't lie to me like that. I know you have feelings for me. I see your eyes light up. I see you blush. You fight it—I will give you that—but you're losing the battle." He stepped forward, holding her by the arms.

Esther cringed out of habit but not fear.

"When I danced with you tonight," Joseph said, his voice low, "I could feel your heart beating fast. I could sense the desire in your body. You are a strong woman Esther, but certain things even you can't hide." He loosed his grip, trailing his hands down her arms before releasing her. Esther let out the breath she had been holding. No words came to her mind. As always with Joseph, she felt the tornado of emotions swirling about inside her.

Luckily, Joseph did not press her to speak. He put his hat on for the second time and walked away.

He was about three yards off when he turned around. "Oh, and Esther, Sheriff Ben told me that Toby has given some threats and received some as well. Last time he made a threat the man disappeared."

"They looked into him but he had an alibi—well, Mary was his alibi. I remember that incident," Esther said grimly.

"Then I don't need to explain why I will be going with you to see Mary. Toby is dangerous, and Michael needs his mother."

Esther nodded, wishing she had something to say, not that it would have done any good. Joseph was already gone.

Esther stayed outside for a few more minutes, hoping that the cold air would clear her mind. She had come to peace with her past, accepted her fears and the consequences. She did not want or need a husband and had thought it was God's will that she be single. Now, however, everything seemed so muddled and confusing.

Surely God would not send Joseph to her when she felt damaged beyond repair? Surely He would not think to give Michael a father who could not love him as his own? Why then did the thought of Joseph leaving fill her with both relief and heartache?

"Dear God, I am sure I weary you with my prayers," Esther sat on the swing tied to a large oak tree. "What do I feel toward Joseph? What is his purpose in my life and Michael's life? What would you have me do?" Esther waited in silence. No insight came, only the soft hoot of a barn owl. Sighing and reminding herself that answers came in the Lord's time, Esther walked inside, but not before looking back, hoping to see Joseph behind her—but the road was empty.

Fifteen

Uncle Tim and Aunt Lily set off for New Orleans early Monday morning before Esther took Michael to school. Sunday had been a blur. Joseph had hardly spoken to her. Abby was preoccupied. And Esther needed to get home as soon as the service was done to help her uncle and aunt pack. She was somewhat relieved when they left. She needed time alone to think and sort herself out.

Too many feelings were swirling inside of her, and if she were self-consumed she could not help others in their struggles. As a mother and midwife, that was what she needed to do—think of others, right? Why was it so hard this morning? Why did she keep doing her hair over and over, change her dress three or four times? Why was she looking at her figure in the mirror?

"Mom what is for breakfast?" Michael shouted from the kitchen.

"Goodness, Esther, take hold of yourself," she scolded herself before rushing to the kitchen. This was exactly why she could not have a man in her life. Romance made a woman less of a mother. Esther rolled her eyes: That was not true and she knew it. She need not make up truths in order to justify her choices.

"How about some toast and eggs, Michael?"

Michael nodded. "Joseph told me last night that one time he ate crickets. Can you believe it—crickets?" Michael scrunched up his face in disgusted delight. "What do you think they taste like?"

Esther raised an eyebrow at him. "If you are thinking about eating some crickets, may I advise you to dip them in chocolate first."

Michael laughed. "Mmm, maybe for Christmas."

"You want chocolate crickets instead of gingerbread cookies and hot chocolate?"

"No!" Michael shook his head, "Let's do cookies."

"Excellent choice," Esther winked, whipping up a plate of eggs and toast.

Michael's face suddenly grew serious. "Momma, do you think come Christmas Joseph will be with us?"

Esther sucked in a breath. "What do you mean, Michael?"

"I mean would you have married him by then, and will he live here or will we be in Texas? He said he'd buy me a pony in Texas," Michael told her hopefully.

Esther sighed and sat down at the table. "You never know Michael." *No, it will never happen.* "You never know."

Abby had already stopped two arguments of who would be the Indian and who would be the Pilgrim in between measuring the girls' heads to make some simple headdresses for them. Will had come early with an awkward smile and hello. Luckily they had a project to distract them, so soon they fell into their easy laughter and conversation.

"I don't think you can slaughter an actual turkey in the school house," Will told her during lunchtime.

Abby teased, "If you don't have the stomach for it, then you are welcome to turn your head at the time."

"What? I've slaughtered more turkeys than you've eaten," he defended himself. "I am just saying that there would be a lot of feathers and blood to clean up. Not to mention you may terrify some of the kids."

"Yes, but think of how *dramatic* it would be," she laughed with a playful shove. "Oh, and I stayed up late making invitations to give to the parents when they pick up their children. They are rather charming, if I say so myself."

Will looked at her, his eyes softening. "I am sure they are more than charming."

Abby smiled, biting her tongue to keep from talking. She wanted to talk; oh, she wanted to talk so badly. She wanted to ask what he felt about her. Why was he sending mixed messages? Why did he say he loved her and then on Sunday ignore her? Did he really love her? Why had he not kissed her again? Had he not enjoyed it?

Abby said none of these things. She did not want to scare Will away. She needed to talk to Esther; Esther knew everything. She would know why Will was behaving oddly.

"So Pastor Will, I did want to point out that yesterday when you were talking about Ephesians chapter five and the verse twenty-four where it says: "Let the wives be to their own husbands in everything—"

"Yes?" Will asked eagerly. Perhaps Abby would tell him she was ready to be his wife. That would make things so much easier for him.

Abby giggled. "Well, what *you* said was: "Wives be *on* their husbands *on* everything."

Will turned so red that Abby had to laugh out loud. "Did I really say that? Is that why everyone kept chuckling?"

"Yes," Abby hiccuped with laughter. "The whole time men kept making eyes at their wives, and then after they were all saying, "Now remember what the pastor said, my love. You got to be on me on everything." I wouldn't be surprised if there are a lot of babies nine months from now."

Will burst into laughter. "It was probably one of my better sermons then?"

"Oh, most definitely," Abby agreed, wiping her eyes before picking up her bell. "Well on that note, shall we continue our endeavor?" she asked, beginning to ring the bell.

Will smiled. He would continue with her in whatever she wanted.

"Mary, you need to move, walk, stand, anything. This baby needs to be born soon. It is not healthy for you or your child to be pregnant this long."

"But it hurts to move, and besides, I can't have Toby seeing me like this. He don't notice as much when I am covered and laying down," Mary argued stubbornly.

Esther hung her head, thinking of what to say. She had compassion for Mary, well, was trying to have compassion at least, but right now she wanted to strangle the idle woman. "Mary, listen to me. If you don't move, your labor will be long and strenuous and the baby could die."

"I don't care!" Mary shouted, hitting the bed. "I never wanted a baby. I never wanted to ruin my figure. Toby don't want a baby either."

Esther bit her lip. She could not take this woman anymore. Picking up her basket, she began to walk out.

"Wait!" Mary called out, "Ain't you gonna wash me and put that rose water on my skin. I like to smell nice for Toby."

Esther stopped at the door. Joseph had filled up the buckets without her asking. Washing would do Mary a little good, but Esther was not sure if she wanted good for Mary at this point. The woman was incapable of thinking past Toby and her own comfort. The higher self of Esther told her to not judge and that washing Mary might relax her, get blood moving, and help the baby come. So gritting her teeth, Esther opened the door, carried in a bucket, and began to wash Mary.

Joseph had heard Mary and Esther speaking when he had finished placing the buckets outside the door. Esther had grit, compassion, and strength molded into the fine woman that she was. Yes, he had found her ravishing the other night with her curls and red dress, but even now with her simple hair and dress caring for a woman who didn't deserve it, working with patience and kindness, she was intoxicating. It made him furious. He was beginning to lose patience. Not with her, but with the whole situation. He loved her, showed it, had done all he could, and still she seemed skittish. Yesterday at church he had been normal with Michael. He loved that kid, but had tried to avoid Esther, afraid that he might spontaneously propose or be too blunt in his affections. He had pushed the limit at the dance and now had to wait, and Joseph did not like to wait. He thought of his mother often scolding him to be patient. What would she tell him? What advice would she give? To pray? That was her answer to everything: pray.

Joseph's thoughts were suspended as Esther walked out carrying the empty buckets. He rushed over to help her.

"Thank you," she said, her voice strained.

"Everything alright?" Joseph asked, knowing full well it was not.

Esther shook her head, getting into the wagon quickly without his help. She was eager to leave this place. "The baby needs to come out now. It is overdue—much overdue—and I don't know how well Mary has eaten. She may not be supplying the proper nutrition for that baby."

Joseph gave a small snap to the reigns and Lancelot began his slow trot. "Is there anything I can do to help?" Joseph asked. *Like marry you? Give you a new life and a husband who adores you?*

Esther smiled and shook her head. "No, you already do plenty."

Joseph didn't reply, instead he reached over and took Esther's hand, wrapping his fingers around her palm. At first Esther's hand stiffened and then slowly, she, too, clasped his hand, but only for a few moments before she gently pulled it away.

Michael was bouncing like a Mexican jumping bean. "A picnic! A picnic! We're going on a picnic!" he sang in a funny tune.

Esther laughed and looked out the window as she packed a

basket full of rolls, jam, cold beef, chicken salad, apples, and pie. It had rained straight for the past few days. Today, although cloudy with a slight breeze, the sky looked like it would be giving Tall Pine a break. Joseph had offered to come by and fetch them, but he was closer to the stream that Michael wanted to fish, so Esther had insisted that they go to him. Esther had offered that Abby could come, but she was going to town to meet up with Eliza and Will.

"Michael, make sure you wear a warm coat and your boots," Esther reminded him. She had already packed an extra coat, and shoes, and trousers because no doubt Michael would find a way of getting wet and dirty.

"Do you think Joseph is excited about our picnic?" Michael asked.

"How could he not be?" Esther grinned at him. "He gets to spend time with the most amazing boy ever."

"Should I wear my hat?"

Esther chuckled. Michael would wear the hat anyway, but it warmed her heart that he wanted her approval. "Oh, I would definitely wear the hat. You look so handsome in it."

Pleased, Michael bounded off leaving Esther to finish the basket. She was in a good mood for really no reason at all. She'd woken up with a sense of peace, a tranquility that everything was going to work out fine. Maybe Joseph would be done with his infatuation or whatever it was and would leave without a broken heart. Maybe Esther would finally have insight to her own feelings and be able to communicate them. Whatever happened, she was determined to have a good day with her son and Joseph.

Michael knocked loudly on the door, clicking his little cowboy boots with excitement.

The door opened after four knocks. "Well, who is this handsome guy, huh?" Joseph grinned. Michael hugged Joseph's strong legs, making Joseph grin wider. "You ready for some fishing today?"

"Yes I am, and we brought food—lots of food!"

Joseph looked up at Esther with a wink. "Lots of food? Well, then it will definitely be a good time." He put on his hat, shut the door, and walked over to the wagon. "The stream isn't far, walking distance, but let's go ahead and take the wagon since we have stuff to carry. I imagine Lancelot will enjoy some time in the woods."

Esther nodded and scooted over to make room for her son and Joseph's large frame. Joseph took the basket and peaked inside.

He whistled. "Mmm, let me tell you how excited I was for this. Abby's cooking is getting better, but it isn't yet up to Miss Esther's cooking."

"Oh, she'll get there. You should have seen my cooking when I started living on my own. Granted, it was only me I cooked for— Michael was still nursing—but still it was pretty bad."

Joseph told himself to laugh and he did, but his thoughts were focused on what Esther had said about it being just her and Michael. There had been no man around? No husband, possibly? Had Esther become pregnant out of wedlock? For some reason he had assumed she'd been married, and her husband had died. He frowned. Not that he judged her, but for Esther to become involved with a man out of wedlock meant that she must have wanted him so badly that she suspended all her values. The thought disturbed him. He was quiet the rest of the way.

"You two go find a good fishing spot while I set up the picnic, all right?" Esther told Michael and Joseph. They agreed and began hiking up the stream to look for an even better spot than the one they had last time.

"We won't be gone long. Just scouting," Joseph called back.

"Yeah, just scouting," Michael mimicked, taking Joseph's hand.

The two of them hiked for about five minutes when Joseph couldn't hold his promise any longer. "Michael, do you remember your father?"

Michael shook his head. "No. Mom says he is no father. He just got her pregnant with me. You see, he did something bad to her and God sent me to make it better." Michael smiled like a child remembering a good part of a book.

"What did he do bad to her?" Joseph asked, wondering how much Michael knew.

"Well, when my mom's dad came to visit me, he said I did not have a good father, and that my father was a bad man, but mom had to tell him that the bad man was not really a father," Michael grinned again.

Joseph smiled patiently thinking it odd that Michael did not use the term "grandpa." "Did your mom's father say what this bad man did to your mom?"

Michael nodded. "He said that he…he," Michael furrowed his eyebrows, trying to remember the word, "he racked her… no rapped her, no…"

Joseph grew still, and his heart skipped a beat. He knew what word Michael was trying to say. "Raped?"

"Yeah, that's it. I asked mom what that was and she said it meant he hurt her very bad and then she got pregnant, but like I said, I was sent to make things better."

Joseph nodded. He wanted to hurt, no kill, the man who had dared to do such a thing to Esther. Every instinct he had screamed at him to take action. Who was this man? Was he dead? Alive? What had happened? No wonder Esther flinched at his touch, or was hesitant with him, and avoided all men. In his line of work, Joseph had met more than his share of rape victims. Some became very loose in their ways, feeling so worthless that they let themselves be handed out. Others became conservative and cloistered. But none that he had met had a child.

Joseph then realized that Esther's father had told this to Michael, sweet, innocent Michael. What was he thinking? More fury filled Joseph.

"Joseph?" Michael asked, tugging on his hand.

Joseph shook his head. "Sorry Michael, I got distracted." He looked around, "Well, this spot looks good. We'll check it out after our picnic. Why don't we go back and eat?"

Michael nodded and the two started back with Joseph taking deep breaths to calm himself.

Joseph tried to act normal, but it was hard. Every time he looked at Esther, saw her grace, her gentle smile, he wanted to kill the monster who had done such a thing to her. His usually large appetite was hindered by his rage. Esther must have noticed he was out of sorts because after a while she suggested that Michael go look for frogs in the stream.

"Don't run off though, sweetheart. Stay where I can keep an eye on you, alright?"

"Alright," Michael chirped, happy that he had permission to look for frogs.

Esther watched him walk off for a moment. "He used to stuff frogs in his pocket as presents for me," she laughed with soft eyes.

Joseph smiled grimly. Esther had raised him alone with no man in their lives besides an uncle who was very busy with his own life.

"Joseph, what is wrong?" She glanced at Michael, her voice tense. "Did my son say something to you?"

Joseph glanced at her and saw the worry in her eyes. "He told me that you were raped and that your father told him," Joseph said bluntly.

Esther's face paled and her shoulders sagged. She looked away and seemed to be holding her breath. "I knew he would tell you eventually. Bribing him with books and treats was probably getting old." She tried to smile but failed.

"What happened, Esther?" Joseph asked, cautiously reminding himself that talking about this would be like approaching a badger caught in a trap.

"Well, what Michael told you: I was raped."

"Esther," he said his voice low, "it might be good for you to talk about it. Do I need to take care of the man who did it?"

This time Esther did smile. She shook her head. "No, I don't even know where he is," she sighed and straightened her back, assuming her capable pose, but Joseph did not miss the shaking hands that clenched her dress. "I suppose you will not let this matter go, so I'll tell you." She cleared her throat and looked down briefly as if gathering courage and then calmly looked him in the eye.

"His name was or is James Clement. He was a law student and very, very wealthy. The kind of wealth that makes one believe they should have anything and anyone they want. James was the talk of the city, handsome, intelligent, and rich. He could have any woman, but he wanted me. Everyone told me what a catch he was and what a fine husband he would make. My father and mother were thrilled beyond measure." Esther bit her lip glancing away for only a second to steady her voice. "But he repulsed me. Every time he smiled or touched me my skin would crawl. I never trusted him. One night, his family had a fancy dinner party at their mansion. I did not want to go, but my parents insisted. They were furious that I would not accept James and hoped that the more I saw him the more I would be inclined to change my mind. After the dinner, dancing commenced and James came and told me that one of the servants had been struck down sick. The doctor was coming, but would I mind attending her in the mean time? Being naïve, I agreed and followed him to his room, far enough away where no one could hear me scream. He shut the door, made an—" she grimaced, her hands gripping her dress tighter till the knuckles were white, "offer, and when I refused, he forced himself. I fought, of course, but he was a big man who'd had too much to drink at dinner."

Joseph's jaw was clenched so tightly he thought his teeth might shatter from the pressure. He would have given anything to be there to save her.

"Did you tell your parents?" Joseph asked through clenched teeth.

Esther actually laughed. "Oh, yes. I did. They were so, well, uncomfortable with facing James Clement and his family that they refused to believe me. When I showed them the bruises and threatened to make it public, my father went to James Clement." She smiled wryly. "James told him it was consensual, and that our passion got out of hand on both sides. My father returned angry at me for trying to blame James, but also thrilled because James had told him that he would marry me anyway, even though I had let my morals slip," Esther said sarcastically. "Even though I was now tainted, James would still marry me. Then, I discovered I was pregnant, and I fled. I wrote to my parents letting them know I was safe. They implored me to come home until I wrote I was with child. After that they sent some money, and that was all. My uncle managed to get a hold of me and offered me a job as a midwife. I hadn't finished nursing school, but he said he would train me. So I moved out here to Tall Pine."

Joseph nodded, encouraging her to go on.

"It changed the course of my life," Esther continued. "It changed how I thought and how I felt. The whole time I was pregnant, I cried every day for hours at a time. I hated God, hated my life, but when I had Michael things got better. It is amazing how loving someone so much can heal you. Still, there was more than a little bitterness and fear. It was not until I turned to God, that bitterness turned to gratitude, and fear turned to strength." She looked down, twirling the lace on her sleeves. "Some things, however, go too deep. The fear of a man's control or his touch surfaces memories that I have long since buried." She swallowed. "It would not be fair to marry a man to whom I could not be a good wife."

Joseph reached out and took her hand, "Even a man you love?"

Esther blinked, a small crease marking her forehead. Was Joseph asking if she loved him? Even after what she had just told him about her scars running as deep and long as the Grand Canyon? Who would want to deal with that?

Michael was now running back yelling at Joseph that he saw a fish jump.

"That's my cue to go fishing." Joseph released Esther's hand and stood up. "Listen Esther, you have every right to distrust men, to worry about intimacy, emotionally and physically, but as a Ranger I have seen horrible things happen to people, and one thing I know for sure is that everyone eventually heals—if they allow themselves to." He gave her a gentle smile before picking up the fishing rods and walking over to Michael.

Esther's heart was in cartwheels. That was the first time, besides to her aunt and Eliza, that she had told anyone about her experience. Telling Joseph had been hard. It was like lancing a large boil; it hurt but once the infection had been cleaned away, there was a relief—a feeling of cleansing and clarity. Joseph had asked if she loved him. Did she? Despite all that had happened, did she love Joseph?

Esther looked ahead, her son, her precious and treasured son was laughing as he always did with Joseph. The muscular Texas Ranger was gently guiding Michael with loving hands teaching him how to properly cast the fishing line. Joseph had seen her and loved her from the beginning. He had not been faint at heart, but rather he had persisted even with all her mixed messages and often-cold demeanor. He was kind, handsome, strong, and good-hearted.

Esther gasped. She loved him! With her full heart, she loved Joseph. Heat rose to her skin, washing away the chill. Hot chocolate seemed to coarse through her veins. So this was what it felt like—pure warmth and joy. Joseph looked back at her and Esther's skin broke into a million goose bumps. She wanted this man, wanted him badly.

A chill wind kissed Esther's face. She felt cleansed, but now her heart ached with each beat. She would have to let Joseph go. She loved him too much, and although Joseph said all wounds healed, she would not bind him to a lifetime of celibacy waiting for those wounds to heal. Yes, he would have to go. Was that not the plan from the beginning? No, the plan had been to not fall in love with him, to keep her distance, to protect her son's feelings, her feelings, and Joseph's feelings. She had failed at protecting all three.

Michael would be devastated, his dreams of the perfect father, the father that Esther herself had described and was physically manifested in Joseph, all of that would be lost and gone for good. She who had worked so hard to get on her feet and had bloodied her knees with prayers would have to move on one more time. Joseph? Surely Joseph with his looks, good nature, and charm would find another woman.

The thought made Esther uncomfortable. She did not want him with another woman, although she knew that was selfish. Still, the mere thought made her cringe. "Be strong Esther," she told herself quietly. She knew she had issues, but she knew God loved and cherished her and that she did her best to be a good woman. She was a good enough woman for Joseph, but she could not be a good wife, not in the way a man like him would want.

Esther was silent when Joseph and Michael returned with only three fish. He did not push her to speak. Joseph imagined it had been hard enough to describe her past, and he himself was still rigid with anger. Luckily, Michael's presence soothed him. God bless that kid. He indeed was a miracle and so lucky to have the mother he did.

⁂

Eliza couldn't focus. After Abby had left her shop and the two had discussed songs during her lunch break, Eliza had an odd feeling, a restlessness as if her instinct or intuition were telling her something, but she could not make it out. She accidentally ignored customers, knocked down dresses, and kept looking at the time, feeling that she was late for something.

"Dear Lord," she half prayed, half talked to herself, "what in daylight's name is wrong with me?

It was not until Will burst through the door shouting her name that her mind cleared.

"Eliza—Eliza where is Abby?"

Will's face was white with worry and he was breathing rapidly.

"She left some time ago, Will. She had her brother's big stallion so she should be home by now. Why, what's wrong?"

Will shook his head. "Joseph. We need Joseph. I need to check on Abby." He began to go, talking to himself. Eliza ran after him trying to grab his sleeve to halt him. She didn't need to, because before reaching him, Will spun around just about knocking her over.

He didn't apologize, just grabbed her shoulders. "I need you to go fetch Esther and take her to Mary Higgins."

Mary? The pregnant woman who did not deserve her child? "Will, what is going on? Tell me this instant." Eliza steadied herself and spoke sternly.

"Toby has killed two men. Shot them in the chest. Sheriff Ben went by his home and Mary is in labor wailing about her Toby."

"Where is Toby?" Eliza asked, already reaching for her shawl.

"He fled. We are sending out a search party before he gets too far. We need Joseph's help, and I need to make sure Abby got home safely." He turned running out the door. "Go get Esther!" he shouted.

Eliza's heart was pounding. Something greater than herself told her that Mary's baby was in trouble and it needed her. But she had no carriage. It was still broken and it was too far to walk to get to Esther in time. Kyle? No Kyle was coming home today from Denver, but she had recently stopped by his bakery, and he was still gone.

Eliza's breath quickened. She'd have to ride. She hated riding a horse—those big beasts spooked to easily. In fact, she could not ride. There had to be another way. Besides, her horse was only used to pulling her little cart.

A sharp and clear image of a wet, crying newborn filled Eliza's mind. A strong sense of familiarity to this unborn child overwhelmed her. She had to help. Tossing aside all fears, Eliza rushed out of the shop.

Sixteen

A bby handed Joseph a cup of coffee, her face solemn.

"I probably should not have told you, Abby. I just needed to say something." Joseph rubbed his temple, a habit when he was stressed.

Abby smiled sitting herself down. "No, you were right to. I love Esther dearly and this just makes me admire her more. I just feel bad for all those things said about her that she thought she was better than men—it all makes sense now."

"I just don't know what to do. I understand now why she is skittish and why I could never read her. She must hate men."

Abby shook her head. "I don't think Esther can hate anyone. I would imagine she just does not trust them. Her father controlled her and the one man whom she had any social interaction with hurt her. What man has helped her? Been in her corner? Of course, logically she may know you are different, but emotionally, she may not be able to overcome the barriers that she constructed to survive."

Joseph nodded. "I see your point, but Abby, I would do anything for her. How can I help her? I only got two weeks before I need to head back in order to get my final pay for being a Ranger, beat the snow, and begin overseeing the ranch." He looked down. "Even if I came back in spring, my gut tells me she will be gone. So what do I do?"

Abby looked down into her cup of tea gently swirling the chamomile liquid. "You don't help her Joseph. You can't."

Joseph narrowed his eyes. "Abby, I don't think Esther is beyond help or—"

Abby held up her hand. "Wait, wait! I have not finished yet. Esther one time told me something very wise. She said that women are always looking for a man to help them, heal them, and fix them. When in fact the only one who can fix them is God. There is no other way."

"So what am I supposed to do? Just let her go?"

"No, you love her and wait for God to heal her. He will heal her, and it probably won't be with angelic music or anything grand. He'll provide circumstances, situations, all which will lead Esther to where she needs to be."

"She needs to be with me," Joseph growled.

"Joseph, you have always been needed. For heavens sake's the state of Texas needs you, but you can't force someone to need you. Let Esther take her time in—"

"I don't have time, Abby," Joseph slammed the table, shaking the teacups.

Abby sighed and began to reply but was interrupted by a loud knocking on the door.

Joseph shot Abby a puzzled look before answering the persistent knock.

"Will?" Joseph opened the door with surprise. "Is everything all right?"

Will looked past Joseph to see Abby, his face softening with relief. "Toby's murdered two men. Killed them right outside town. Tried to hide the bodies, too, but a woman witnessed it all. Toby took a shot at her and missed, barely singed her shoulder. Sheriff wants any armed man to search for him."

Joseph nodded. He always kept a revolver at his hip and left to get another one as well as his rifle.

Will looked at Abby: "Abby—lock the door and don't let anyone in unless it is Joseph or me, understand?"

Abby nodded, picking up Killer, scratching his ears. "Both of you be safe, alright?" Abby instructed softly.

Joseph's face suddenly paled. "What about Esther? I need to—"

"Esther will be fine." Will said, walking out. "Mary needs her, and I sent Eliza to fetch her."

"Fine against a murderer?" Joseph exclaimed. "I am glad that you worry about my sister, but Esther—"

"Esther carries a gun in that gypsy wagon all the time. She keeps a pistol strapped to her leg most times as well. Not to mention, she is a better shot than most men around here." He stopped and turned to Joseph who shut the door behind him.

"The best thing we can do for the safety of these women is to find Toby, Ranger."

Joseph tensed. "Don't need to be told what to do, Pastor."

The two men gave each other a nod signaling they would speak no more and set off.

Esther squinted at the figure approaching, small, delicate and riding on a giant horse. She had heard her name being called as she pulled up to her home.

"Esther!" The strained voice shouted again. Esther stood up in the cart; it could not be Eliza! Eliza hated riding horses. The figure came closer and sure enough, Eliza was riding at a fast trot towards her. Fear sized Esther. Something drastic must have happened.

"Eliza, what is wrong?" she quickly helped Michael down.

Eliza rode up out of breath and cheeks flushed. "It's Mary. She's in labor and Toby—he's run off. He killed two men and has the whole town looking for him."

Esther's eyes darkened. With Toby gone, Mary would be going into hysterics and a hysterical woman did not lead to a safe labor. She quickly kissed Michael on the head.

"Sweetheart, I need to go. Can you stay here with Eliza?"

"We will play games!" Eliza said breathlessly, sliding off the horse.

Michael looked worried. "Did Joseph go after Toby?"

Esther smiled. "Joseph is a Texas Ranger...no one can hurt him." She smiled, but in her heart she said a quick prayer for all the men looking for Toby, especially Joseph. She motioned Eliza closer and placed her head close to her friend's ear, whispering softly: "I keep the rifle under the bed. When I arrive back here with Mary, Michael and you will need to go to the barn. I doubt this will be a smooth and pleasant labor. If Toby by chance comes—"

"I will place a hole in him the size of Texas, Esther," Eliza said firmly, her eyes turning to steel. Esther gripped Eliza's hand knowing she would do just that. Then, with another kiss from Michael, this time for her comfort, she climbed in her cart and snapped Lancelot into a run.

"My Toby's left, he's left me. I gotta go to him!" Mary yelled as she fell on her knees with a contraction. "Damn baby is keeping me from Toby. I hate it!" Her hands dug into Esther's back as she supported Mary's weight. Esther held her, counting through the contraction.

"Mary you are about six minutes apart; we need to get you to my house. Hurry!" She wrapped Mary's arm around her neck and hobbled to her cart.

"Sheriff said Toby killed two men, but he wouldn't leave me. He would at least take me with him," she sobbed, tears and sweat dripped down to her pale cotton blouse. "I want Toby. I can't live without him."

Esther used all her strength to haul Mary into the wagon. Mary was now trying to fling herself out. "Mary, what are you doing?" Esther cried out. A muscle in her hip tore as she braced Mary to keep her from falling out of the wagon. Esther cringed in pain.

"What if Toby comes back? I need to be here," she wailed.

"Toby would not *come* back here if the Sheriff is looking for him. I promise you that I will help you find Toby when the baby is safe."

If Toby is not gone for good by then.

Mary stopped struggling and began to wail as another contraction hit. As if with wings, Esther flew into the wagon and headed home.

Eliza, bless her, had covered the bed with blankets before taking Michael to the barn when Mary came crying into the house.

"I hate you! I hate you!" She struck out at Esther who now was either dodging the blows or taking them. "You're taking me away from Toby."

Esther replied with soothing words, her thoughts far from the half-mad screams of Mary. The baby would be large this overdue, and there would be tearing unless she could calm Mary and instruct her pushing.

"Mary, I need you to lie down, alright? I need to check you."

Mary sobbed as Esther laid her on her back. The contractions were closer now—less than a minute apart. Mary must have labored alone for quite a while before Esther came. Hiking up Mary's skirts, Esther kneeled on the bed, reaching in her fingers to feel the baby.

"The baby is almost here. We need to breathe through these contractions. You only have a few more till you will feel the need to push."

Mary shook her head, "But I don't want a baby. I w-want Toby."

Esther ignored her sobs and went to place pillows underneath Mary's back and neck. She needed her more upright so Mary could breath. Then Esther grabbed a jar of oil from her basket to help make way for the baby.

Mary screamed, "I'm dying! I'm dying!"

Esther checked the baby. The head was right there. "Mary, tell me when you feel pressure. Right now, I want you to take a deep breath: In nice and easy and out. In and slowly out."

Mary inhaled and exhaled with a loud moan. "Oh pressure! I feel like a cannon ball is coming out!"

Esther nodded. Mary's legs were shaking and so weak she could not keep them up. Ignoring the screaming muscle in her hip, Esther placed Mary's legs on her shoulders. "All right Mary, I need you to push—one big push."

Mary grunted and pushed, yelling out as she did.

"Stop!" Esther commanded and then quickly rubbed oil around the opening, massaging and moving it with her fingers to prevent tearing. "Good girl, small push now... good... now stop and pant," more massaging.

"I can't do this!" Mary cried, her body shaking.

"Mary you are doing great. Now deep breath and another big push."

Mary groaned and exhaled into a push that melded into a scream. Esther tensed; there was a lot of blood. Something was wrong.

"Alright Mary. Pant... pant." The crown of wet blonde hair spattered with blood was rubbed with more oil.

"I gotta push now!" Mary screamed.

"Wait Mary, hold it, hold it or you'll tear... a few more pants."

"I hate you!" Mary screamed and began to push.

"Mary!" Esther cried, but there was nothing she could do as flesh tore, allowing more blood to flow. Wrapping her hands gently around the head, Esther guided the newborn head out into the air. "One more push, Mary, good... good."

A perfect slippery body slid gently into Esther's arms, and Esther held the newborn close to her with one hand while skillfully cutting the umbilical cord with the other. The baby's lungs flaunted their strength with a perfect cry. The color was rosy, the head a little cone shaped but not too bad. Esther wrapped the piece of heaven in a warm blanket. She walked over to Mary who looked away.

"I don't want it," Mary snapped, her face was pale—much too pale.

Esther kissed the baby and placed it in the cradle she still had from Michael's newborn days. The baby cried and instinct told Esther it needed to nurse, but Mary would not take the poor golden-haired girl. She walked over to Mary in concern.

Too much blood. She had to stop the bleeding.

"I need to go find Toby... before he leaves without me." Mary was trying to stand on her feet.

"No, Mary. I need to stitch you up. You are not well yet, and your baby needs feeding."

Mary pushed her, hard. Esther, already weak from the pain in her hip, fell to the ground. Mary was shaking her head, her eyes wild like an animal: "Toby, I need Toby." She stood and rushed through the bedroom door.

Esther scrambled onto her feet running after her. The sound of feet sloshing through puddles of blood freely spilling from Mary and the cries of a hungry newborn made her desperate to keep Mary still. "Mary, stop! Please!" she cried, grabbing the crazed woman's arm.

Mary spun around and slapped Esther across the face. "Leave me alone. I hate you! Toby could've come back for me and he's now gone."

Esther stood her ground in the doorway, blocking Mary's escape. "Mary, think of your child, please! That little girl in there needs you. She needs to eat."

Mary grabbed Esther's hair, trying to yank her out of the way. "Toby, I'm coming—I'm coming."

Esther pulled Mary off, taking hold of her wrists. The woman, normally unstable, was now delirious with fatigue, blood loss, and pain. "Mary!" she shouted, "Listen to me, please. Your baby needs you, and you're bleeding—you're bleeding too much. You can't abandon your daughter to—"

Mary spit at Esther. "I have no daughter. Toby did not want a baby, especially no worthless girl. I promised him I'd kill it if it were a girl."

Mary's skin was dropping color by the second, but Esther let go of her wrists with a face like stone; loathing and disgust flashed across her face. Silently she moved out of the way and let Mary go.

Eliza ran onto the porch, Michael behind her, as Mary's ghostly pale body disappeared into the fields. "Esther! Esther, what—"

Eliza halted in the doorway.

Esther was now rocking the baby, her face a reflection of frustrated pain and sorrow. She looked relieved to see Eliza.

Eliza looked at the bundle. *She's yours*, an eternal inner voice told her. "Was that Mary I saw?"

"Eliza, listen carefully: I need for you to go get Melissa. She is not far and I need her now!"

"But—"

"I need Melissa *now!*" she almost shouted. Esther hardly ever raised her voice. Loathe to leave the baby, but frantic to help, Eliza twirled around—it was time to ride.

"Michael, my love," Esther said gently to her wide-eyed son. "Can you be a big boy and go fetch me some goat's milk and one of my little leather baby bags?"

"The kind they suck out of?"

Esther nodded. "Exactly. Goat's milk and a baby bag... hurry."

Dusk darkened the light when Melissa at last handed her gurgling son to Eliza and took Mary's newborn to her breasts. The infant latched on with no encouragement, and all three women sighed with relief.

"Did she take any of the goat's milk?" Melissa asked.

Esther nodded, feeling her face begin to bruise. She placed a tray of tea and sandwiches for Eliza, Melissa, and Michael, who had delved into one of his picture books.

"It took a few tries, but she is a determined eater," Esther said calmly although her mind and soul were running around in chaos. She had let Mary go... bleeding, weak, crazed... Could she have done anything? Could she have helped her? Was that even in Esther's power?

Melissa unlatched, handing the infant back to Eliza to burp. "What will happen to her? I can take her if—"

"No!" Eliza broke in, her eyes moist. "Please, I want her. I will take her." She turned to Esther. "Everyone knows how I have longed for a child, and I doubt anyone would object."

Esther smiled. "No one would Eliza, but—"

"I know it will take a lot of work, but just tell me what to do. I can sell the shop, or hire some girls to work there if I need to. I'll do whatever it takes to care for her."

Melissa grinned at the cooing baby. "Lucky little princess. You just struck gold for a momma."

Esther smiled tenderly. Of course Eliza should have the baby: How right that felt. "You will need to feed her canned milk with a little sugar, but that will not be enough for her to grow and be healthy. I know all the nursing mothers… you will need to make rounds at least for the first month to those willing to give you breast milk."

"They will all be willing," Melissa said with a click of her tongue. "Everyone will just be so glad this little beauty escaped Toby and Mary that they'll do anything to help."

"Your whole day will be feeding her, Eliza, between taking her to homes to get breast milk and then the canned supplement milk.

Eliza nodded, tears streaming down her cheeks. "I don't care if I don't sleep or eat for ten years. I'll do anything to keep her."

"Now, legal documents—"

"Oh legality," Eliza waved her hand with a tearful laugh. "I'll take care of that mess. Besides, who in Denver, after I sign her birth certificate, is to know that she's not mine? As far as I am concerned she is my daughter… a gift from God."

Esther smiled, glancing at Michael whose eyes were growing heavy with sleep. "A gift from God," she agreed.

Will was sent to inspect and search the south side of the valley with all the small ranches. He found no trace of Toby, and none of the ranchers had seen him. Joseph had inspected a good number of the farms, and Sheriff Ben had been up to the mining community, but they found nothing. Joseph decided to check west of town before checking in on Esther to see how things with Mary had gone, although Joseph doubted Toby would venture back for his wife. Will himself was about to check out a few more farms when uneasiness settled over him. Abby was probably fine; he told her to lock the doors and not answer to anyone. After all, why would Toby go by there?

Will froze, remembering suddenly Toby's reaction to her. Abby had, in her beautiful descriptive manner, told him of Toby's offer to her and his comments about her being alone. Toby would know she was alone. The man was a coward; he had used Mary as an alibi for his first murder—why not use another female as a way out, as a hostage. Fear seized Will as he kicked his horse in the flank and rode at a full gallop toward the schoolhouse.

Joseph's mouth dropped when Esther opened the door. Her hair was completely undone, the left side of her face was swollen and beginning to turn purple, and her dress was smeared with blood. She smiled weakly, her eyes dark with sorrow. Behind her he could see Eliza cooing at a baby in her arms and another woman with her.

"What? Where is Mary?"

Esther took a step outside, shutting the door behind her. "Joseph, I was wondering if you could do me a favor. Eliza said Kyle Lampton was due to arrive this evening. Would you please ask him to come to my home? Melissa will need to be escorted home as well as Eliza who will be adopting Mary's baby," Esther said as calmly as if she'd been describing the weather.

Joseph held up his hands. "Wait, why is Eliza—"

"Mary left," Esther said with a small catch in her voice. "She left to go find Toby. So Eliza is taking her baby."

"Do you think she knows where Toby is?"

Esther shrugged. "It doesn't matter—she is already dead at this point."

Will stopped his horse in front of the teacher's small home. A weak light shone through the curtains. He jumped off his horse, not bothering to tie it up, and pounded on the door. "Abby, its

Will. You all right?" he shouted through the door.

No answer.

He pounded harder. "Abby! Can you hear me?"

Still silent.

"Abby, if you don't answer, I am breaking down the door!" he shouted.

He heard a rustle.

"I'm—I'm fine, Will. I am just bathing so I can't get the door," she called haltingly.

Will felt his blood go cold. Abby would have laughed, teased him even, not spoken with a tremor in her voice. He pulled out his gun, cocking it gently so as not to make a noise.

"Abby, are you sure you're fine?"

Silence and another rustle. Was it a whisper?

"Yes, Will," she said without a tremor, but her voice was vacant of emotion. She said slowly and steadily. "I... am... perfectly... fine."

Will stepped back. He would break down the door; one kick should do it. It was an older lock. "Okay Abby, I guess then I will see you tomorrow."

One, two, three, and NOW.

Will kicked open the door, stepping through with his gun cocked and aimed at Toby who had his arm around Abby's neck and a gun to her head.

"Drop the gun, Pastor," Toby snarled.

Will glanced at Abby. Her hair was wet and it was obvious she wore nothing underneath her thin robe.

"Toby, release her or it won't be my fist knocking you to the ground this time—it'll be a bullet," Will said more confidently then he felt. He could shoot Toby, but what if Toby moved? The bullet would hit Abby. Fear, anger, and a frantic prayer pounded through Will's head. Abby could die. By Toby's hand or his own unskilled marksmanship, she could die.

Will swallowed hard. The thought of losing her was unbearable.

Dear God, keep her safe.

"A pastor wouldn't kill a man," Toby laughed. "And, this pretty little teacher is gonna be my girl for a long while. If any one comes after me I'm gonna put a bullet through this lovely head of hers, and that would be an awful loss."

"It is all right Abby," Will told her calmly.

Abby's face twisted. "How is it alright?"

Toby chuckled. "She's got spirit. I am gonna have fun with her."

Will took a step forward and Toby pressed the gun harder to her head.

"Don't do anything stupid, Pastor." He jerked his head toward Will's gun. "Now drop your gun before you hurt someone."

Will hesitated and Toby squeezed Abby's neck tighter. She whimpered.

"All right!" Will shouted, slowly lowering his gun to the ground.

"Now, kick it over," Toby snarled.

Will couldn't look at Abby. How could he save her without putting her life in more danger? If he let her go, she would die. If he shot, she could die by *his* own hand.

Please, Father in heaven, send me a miracle. I beg thee, Will pleaded silently.

"Toby, take me as your hostage. I will cooperate if it means letting Abigail go."

Toby snorted. "Why Pastor, I can't do with you what I plan on doing with this filly. Now, kick over the gun or I shoot her and then you."

Will looked down at his dropped gun. He could pick it up, shoot and pray that he hit his target, but aiming was not one of his best skills. Yet kicking the gun to Toby sealed Abby's death—or worse.

"Pastor, you got three seconds. Three, two,"

The pop of a gun sent a bullet whizzing through the curtains and straight through Toby's head. Abby cried out and flew out of the dead man's falling arms. Will rushed forward, catching her and pulling her trembling body to his chest. Like an avenging angel, Joseph walked in, his face calm with the composure of a trained killer.

"I had a feeling I needed to stop by before going to town." He walked past the embracing couple and checked Toby. "Dead."

Abby pulled away from Will and threw her arms around her brother sobbing, "Oh Joseph, what would I do without you!"

Joseph put an arm around her and kissed her on the top of her head. Then his gaze found Will.

"Pastor," he said sternly, "you were right to worry about my sister."

Will smiled grimly. "I worried, but I was not the one to save her."

At his words Joseph gently moved Abby aside and strode toward Will. In a movement that shocked Will so much he about choked, Joseph grabbed his shoulders and pulled him into a strong hug.

"Will, I heard just about everything you said. Saw it, too, through the window. Had you fired, you would have hit Abby. You didn't have a clean shot. I couldn't have made that shot." He gripped Will's shoulders like a father lecturing a son. "You made the right call, and you gave me time to take aim. Abby owes you her life." He looked back at his sister. "Abby, don't let this one go," he winked. "And get some clothes on."

Abby's body was shaking, but she mustered a weak laugh. "Always so sensitive."

Joseph smiled and walked over to give her another kiss. "We Texans are tough. You prove that every day." He ruffled her hair. "Now, if you excuse me, I got to go fetch a baker. Will, you can take care of this body?" Joseph asked casually.

Will arched an eyebrow, his own body was still shaking. It was obvious this was a scene Joseph was used to.

"Yeah, I got the body."

Joseph gave him a smile and headed toward the door.

"Wait, Joseph," Will called out.

Joseph turned looking at him inquiringly.

"Was—would you really have missed the shot if you'd been in my place?"

Joseph grinned. "Will, I can shoot a coin out of a flying crow's mouth. Of course I could have made that shot, but you couldn't have, and that is why I thank you."

Will nodded, watching Joseph go before turning back to Abby. She hadn't moved, but the fear was slowly fading from her silver eyes. Saying nothing, Will walked toward her and pulled her to him, pressing his lips to hers. Tears flowed freely down his cheeks and he did not bother to hold them back. He'd almost lost her.

"I love you, Abby. I love you so much," he gently whispered into her hair.

She said nothing for a while, but Will did not care. He didn't care if she ever said it. All that mattered was that she was alive.

Abby felt her body began to relax against Will's fast heartbeat. His arms squeezed the breath from her, and she could smell the autumn air on his skin. Oh, she loved him. She had been afraid to say so, afraid to scare him away. What foolishness! Life was fragile, and death came unexpected. Who cared if she seemed desperate? She *was* desperate—desperate for his love, for his presence, for a life with him.

She pulled away from him just long enough to speak, "And I love you Will—with all my heart."

No sooner had she said the words then Will took her by the arms and held her away, his eyes boring into hers. "What did you say?" he asked, breathless.

"I—I love you."

"You mean it?" he asked incredulously.

"Of course, I mean it. How can you doubt it? I have loved you, I think, from the day I met you."

Will laughed his face lighting up, "But when I declared myself to you at the Harvest Festival, you said nothing."

Abby blushed. "I was afraid to scare you off. I didn't want to pressure you or make you feel like I was trapping you into—"she shut her mouth, looking away.

"Trap me into what?" Will asked, a wickedly handsome grin creeping onto his lips.

"Nothing. I just did not want you to feel trapped. I mean, pressured."

Will chuckled and took Abby's hand to lead her outside. Then with a brave sigh he knelt down on one knee.

Abby's mouth gaped.

"I had planned to do this in front of a waterfall or underneath a full moon and stars, but you never know what tomorrow will bring," he chuckled, kissing her hands gently. "Abigail Silver, would you do me the great honor of being my wife?"

Abigail wondered what power was keeping her feet from leaving the ground. Joy surged through her and into the tears that rolled down her cheeks.

"Yes!" she cried, falling to her knees and placing her head on top of their hands. "Again and again, yes," she looked up at the face she loved so dearly. Will squeezed her hands and kissed them again.

"I have no ranch. I don't even have a ring, but I promise to work every day of my life, proving myself worthy of you."

Unable to speak of the joy and love she felt, Abby leaned forward pouring all her happiness into a kiss she hoped could last forever.

※

It was morning by the time Melissa was accompanied home and Eliza and Kyle left, cooing over the baby girl they had named Bless, short for Blessing. A bit unusual, but Eliza did not care. The baby girl was a blessing and should be known as such to all who met her.

Joseph stayed until he and Esther stood in the doorway alone. Michael was sound asleep, and Esther had cleaned her bed, deciding to burn the blankets Mary had used.

"It has been quite a night," Joseph sighed. "And I thought Texas was wild."

Esther gave a half smile, her eyes still clouded. "Well, I can use a cup of tea. How about you?"

Joseph nodded. The scarlet sun was barely peaking over the mountains, offering a small stream of sunlight that flickered on the porch and teased the potted flowers. It was beautiful. Joseph often marveled at the beauty of nature; it was the closest he came to believing God cared. Maybe God did not stop bad things, but he softened them with good things; good women like Esther, sweet words from children, and a beautiful sunrise.

He heard Esther moving about in the kitchen. He should go in. It was cold, but his heart was still racing from Abby's close encounter. He had remained calm, mainly because another man was around and because he knew if he was calm, Abby would be as well. Still, he had almost lost a beloved sister; he needed the cool air.

Esther returned with a steaming cup of tea topped off with cream and sugar.

Joseph took it, his fingers brushing against hers. Her skin felt cold, but she seemed to need the fresh air as much as he did.

"I think you ought to know—Mary's body was found. She died the same night as her husband. Maybe the two really were destined to be together." Joseph took a drink. He usually wasn't a big tea drinker, but he had come to realize that anything made by Esther tasted good. He took another long drink emptying the whole cup. When he lowered it, Esther's face was tense and her lips pressed tightly together in an attempt to keep them from trembling.

"Esther?" Joseph asked softly. She did not look at him, instead, keeping her gaze straight ahead. "Esther, what is wrong?"

Esther took a sharp breath. "It's my fault," she exhaled, not bothering to hide the quiver in her voice. "I let Mary die. When she slapped me, spit at me, pushed me, I still tried to stop her. I knew that if she left she would bleed out, but when she said she would kill her… would kill her own daughter I…" Esther looked down into her cup, tears streamed down her face mixing with the tea.

"A part of you wanted her to die?" Joseph asked.

Esther closed her eyes. "I don't know. I don't think I wanted her to die, but I no longer wanted to help her. It's like I didn't care what happened to her." She pressed a hand to her forehead, keeping her eyes closed for several seconds. "I always knew Mary did not deserve a child, but she was still a human being who was entitled to help from me, both as a woman and a midwife."

"Help, but not control," Joseph corrected.

Esther looked at him with confusion. "What do you mean?"

"Esther, you can help people, but in the end they make their own choices. We can't control them, even if we want the best for them. Mary did not want you to help her. She wanted to go after Toby, and there was no way you were going to keep her from it if she did not want to be kept."

Esther stared at him, her face written in an unreadable expression. Finally, she looked away and rolled her neck: "You know, I have been feeling it might be time to leave Tall Pine. I thought perhaps of sending inquiries to other towns needing a midwife, but I don't know if I can still be a midwife anymore. Every child I deliver I feel that their life is my responsibility and if they were to die, it would be on my hands, and if they are sick, I feel that maybe I could have prevented it. So often there is joy with the birth of a baby, but also sometimes grief and guilt. It is not fair to Michael to have a mother constantly battling with emotions that I have a hard time controlling. I need to find employment as a seamstress or a cook, anything without the guilt and anxiety."

"How about a rancher's wife?" Joseph meant to say it clearly, but it came out as a mumble.

Esther looked up sharply. "What did you say?"

Joseph took a step toward her, setting down the cup on the porch table. "I said, how about being a rancher's wife? Although, Michael prefers the term cowboy," he chuckled shyly.

Esther blinked. "Joseph are you suggesting—asking that—" she stopped abruptly, unable to finish the thought.

"I am asking you to be my wife, Esther, to come back to Texas with me. You can have your own home. It will be beautiful with a pond that Michael can swim in and plenty of space to run. We can be a family. I can take care of you. For once in your life, you can be the one to be looked after." Joseph closed the gap between them, taking her face in his hands. "Please Esther, say that you'll have me."

Esther swallowed, her hands lifted to Joseph's wrists and lowered them. She loved him, she did, but what he was asking, she could not do it. There were too many nightmares haunting her and too many barriers that would come between them.

"Joseph, I care for you, I really do, but I can't. I was not lying when I said there are certain things I cannot overcome. You need a woman who can be a woman to you in every way."

"I'll be patient, Esther," he promised gripping her hands so tightly they hurt. "Please just give me a chance. Give *us* a chance. If it takes years for you to open up to me, I will wait. As long as I can call you my wife." His eyes were desperate, so loving and willing that Esther, despite her efforts, could not hold back the tears.

"Joseph, I will not trap you into a marriage you do not deserve. My feelings forbid me to be in any union with a man, emotionally or physically. My mind tells me you would be fair, and my heart tells me I care for you, but I cannot change." She stepped back looking away from his crestfallen face. "I'm sorry Joseph, but no. I can't be your wife.

The silence that followed was deafening. When Joseph finally walked away, the angry stomp of his boots was a stab to her heart. He yanked Sampson's reins with aggression and flew onto the saddle.

"Esther!" he called out to her a few paces from the porch, "I leave after Thanksgiving. If your answer has changed, you will make me the happiest and luckiest man in the world, but if it hasn't then I will leave. But Esther," he put on his hat, "for both our sakes, I will not come back." Then he stormed off like a wounded wolf into the early morning light.

Esther stood still, feeling numb; she had come to accept how she was. Gratitude filled her heart every day for the blessings God had given her. Her trials had made her strong—wasn't that what she told herself every day. Then why did she feel so empty and incomplete as Joseph rode away?

"Dear God," she spoke out loud, "you cured me of my sorrow when you gave me Michael. You cured me of my hate after years of bitterness. Why can't you cure my distrust, my fear of letting another man close to me? You are enough for me. Michael is enough, and I recognize that," she paused, brushing a loose strand of hair out of her face, "but is it wrong to want more in my life?"

"Who are you taking to?" Michael asked sleepily from the doorway.

Esther jumped, knocking over her tea. "Oh, sweetheart, you scared me. What are you doing up so early?"

"I wanted to see if Joseph was still here." Michael yawned and came to lean his head against her ribs.

Esther wrapped her arm around him rubbing his back.

"Who were you talking to, Momma?" Michael asked again.

"God," Esther replied softly. Her eyes felt heavy. She needed sleep.

"Did He answer back?"

Esther smiled. "God always answers, but not alway in the time we want, or the way we want."

Seventeen

The next week dragged by for Joseph. It was hell. He'd stayed away from Esther; he couldn't take watching her flashing eyes, full lips, and slender body knowing that she would never be his. His parents would be disappointed he had not brought home the beautiful woman and child of whom he had written much about. Texas would be the same place, but no longer bright without Esther. Without her and Michael to build a life with, life on the ranch held no appeal to him. He would go back to being a Ranger; he would die a Ranger. That was how things worked. That was how things were meant to be. No waking up to a wife by his side, no fat babies, no making Michael Christmas presents, just himself and a badge.

Will and Abby were no help to Joseph. The happy couple announced their engagement with the wedding planned for the spring. Abby would return to Texas sometime in the winter to say a final farewell to her home, her parents would come for the wedding, and then she and Will would visit that coming summer. As Joseph heard their plans, their ambitions, it wrenched him apart. He found himself working non-stop on the schoolhouse, even though he had already repaired everything.

Esther seemed to be ignoring him as well. Any time he saw her, she looked away, as if already breaking ties. On Sunday, Esther stayed by Eliza who was also sickeningly happy with a new baby who had become the princess of Tall Pine. Kyle Lampton had proposed to Eliza, and the two had decided to marry right away. Supposedly he had asked Eliza five times before she realized he wasn't joking. The two were gooey over their daughter who was dressed in the softest and silkiest gowns. People seemed to be blossoming with good cheer and festivities all around Joseph, and yet his own world was growing darker and smaller.

The day before the Thanksgiving play, Joseph was outside working on some sets that Abby had requested he make.

"This is going to be wonderful," she giggled. She did that a lot now. "A play to kick off Thanksgiving!" Her face fell when Joseph did not respond.

"Joseph, why don't you talk to her? Heavens, you only have three more days to win her over."

Joseph clenched his jaw, threw down the hammer, and stood to his full height. "What would you have me do, Abby? I have already begged, pleaded, made my intentions fully known. You yourself said I could not help her."

"I said you couldn't change her, Joseph, not that you could not win her. Just try again."

"No!" he said firmly. "She made it clear, and I am afraid that if I ask her again then I will...I don't know. I know I won't be able to take it." He knelt back down over the wooden scenery. "Esther will not allow herself to forget the past, Abby; she holds onto her distrust like a protective shield over her and Michael, and there is nothing I can do."

Abby took a step closer and softened her voice, "You can always pray, Joseph."

Joseph snorted. "Ha, ha, you sound like Mom!"

Abby's face turned red, "And is that a bad thing?" she practically shouted, placing her hands on her hips angrily.

Joseph raised his eyebrows. "Calm down, Abby," he said patronizingly.

"No! Don't you tell me to calm down, Joseph. You think you

have always been so independent and that you have never needed anyone, not even God. You blame it on Him, saying that He does not care. Well, that is as dumb as an ox's rear end." Abby's eyes flamed, her Texan accent thickening. "Our mother has always shown you great love, my father—*your* father—has always been desperate for your approval, your love, and yet you won't give it because of your pride. And that is what this comes down to—your pride. Your pride of asking another for help, meaning God." She flung her hands in the air. "Heavens Joseph, you have as many issues about your own sex as Esther does. You could not rely on your own father for love and help and so you won't ask for it or accept it from any other father figure whether it be a stepfather or God. Grow up, Joseph! You may lose the one thing you want more than anything because of your blasted pride. *Grow up*," she added before storming off.

Michael was running out as she was coming in.

"Michael, what are you doing?" she asked, still fuming.

"I need to talk to Joseph! Momma says he leaves after Thanksgiving, Teacher. I need to talk to him now." Michael looked desperate. "I finished all my work. That's why I have been so quiet so I could get out early."

Abby sighed and looked back over her shoulder. It might do Joseph good to talk to Michael after her intense lecture. "Very well, Michael, but don't talk long. We need to rehearse the play for tomorrow."

Michael nodded and quickly bounded off.

"Joseph!" Michael called out.

Joseph looked up to see Michael's curls bouncing among the swirling golden leaves. "What's up, kiddo?" he asked grimly, faking a weak smile.

"You leave soon."

"Three days." Joseph informed him, not wanting to look at the pleading blue eyes.

Michael was silent for a long moment. Joseph finally looked up and wished he hadn't. The boy's eyes were filled with fat tears that rolled down his rosy cheeks.

"My momma says we're not going with you," he cried. "I want to go with you. I want you to be my dad. I love you." His nose was now runny and his voice broken with hiccups.

Joseph tossed down the nails and pulled the boy into a hug. "I love you too, Michael, and I want you to know I gave it my best shot. I love your mom and I want you to come back with me so badly it hurts, but there is nothing more I can do."

Michael clung to Joseph soaking his shoulder with tears. "Are you going to find another family? Another little boy?"

Joseph swallowed hard. He would not cry. He never cried. "Of course not! You are my Deputy Ranger remember? No boy could ever replace you."

Michael allowed himself to be held as he sobbed. Joseph hesitantly put his hand on Michael's head and stroked his hair gently as he had seen Esther do. The action seemed to calm the boy, and his sobs lessened and eventually turned into shaky breaths.

"Will you ask her again?" Michael sniffed, pulling away and rubbing his nose.

Joseph smiled and ruffled Michael's hair. "I don't think it will do any good."

"Please ask her again. She'll say yes if I tell her again that I want to go. My mom loves me more than anything, so she would do that for me."

"Of course she loves you, Michael. You are a fine young man, but I just don't know if your mother can love me."

Michael looked thoughtful, contemplating Joseph's words. "But she has to love you. You are the dad she told me about before she even met you. The one she made up in her head."

Joseph sighed and took the young boy's hands in his own. "Listen, I will think about asking her again, but right now you need to go back to class before Abby gets mad and turns into a bear."

Michael laughed shakily and nodded with a final sniff before heading back toward the classroom. Joseph watched him leave and waited until he was in the schoolhouse before he turned his head up to the cloudy sky.

"Uhh, Lord… God? I'm not one to pray much and, well, I am sorry about that. Maybe my sister is right and I have *issues*. It pretty much seems everyone has issues so I hope you can give me some allowance." He swallowed. This was foolish. He felt like an idiot, and yet he continued, "So, I really love Esther, and I really love Michael, and I would like to think you sent me here for a purpose; so if you could help me out that would be appreciated." He chuckled softly at himself. "Thank you. Oh, and, amen," he concluded awkwardly.

An icy wind danced through the small meadow running a shiver through Joseph. It would be getting colder soon, and he needed to finish as much as he could today and do the rest in the morning. The hammer was by his feet. Joseph snatched it up and then reached for the box of nails. He frowned, shaking the sparse sounding box. There had been more nails, had there not? He could have sworn there were more nails, more than two.

Joseph let out a growl of frustration. He was now fully committed to these stupid wooden props, and if he was building them, then they'd better be good, and they could not be good if they were falling apart without nails. He flung down the hammer. He'd have to paint now before the wind picked up any more, and then he would need to ride to town before the shops closed so he could buy some more nails.

"There goes my day," Joseph muttered. The last thing he wanted was to make a trivial trip to town, but what else could he do?

Sheriff Ben sat outside his office feeling conflicted. He liked to be friendly to visitors and strangers. This last one, despite his rich and professional appearance, had given him a bad feeling. Then, when the handsome stranger began inquiring about one of Tall Pine's local residents, Ben's instincts went on high alert, but he couldn't very well cuff the man on account of his dark demeanor.

Now, he wrestled with the choice as to whether or not he should check on this resident or stay put in town. Evening was always when things got a bit rough, especially around the saloons. Besides, he and his deputy were still trying to rat out some of Toby's gambling buddies.

A tall, familiar figure caught Ben's eyes. It was that Ranger Joseph Silver, the one who had taken out Toby with a clean kill shot. Too bad he was leaving. Tall Pine could use a man like him. Everyone had suspected he would be marrying Miss Esther, but so far nothing had been announced.

It suddenly hit Ben that Joseph was the answer to his dilemma. He put his hand on the side of his mouth and called out across the cobblestone street.

"Joseph! Joseph Silver!"

The Ranger looked up in Ben's direction and lifted a hand in greeting. Ben waved him over. "Hey there, Sheriff, how are things?" Joseph asked, his face looking stern and angry.

"Hello Joseph, sorry to interrupt your trip into town. I was just wondering if you've talked to Miss Esther Callen today, meaning recently, as in in the past hour?"

Joseph's eyebrows scrunched together. "No. No, I have not. Why do you ask?"

Ben shook his head, "A stranger came by asking for her. Well, asking for an Esther Callen. I told him she was indeed in Tall Pine, and he then asked where she lived and if she lived with her son. He seemed awfully curious about the boy."

Joseph's eyes were narrowed, his face pale with concern. "Did you tell him where she lived?"

Ben shook his head. "No, absolutely not. I regretted saying she lived around here at all, but I did not know if he was a relative. Once he realized I would not be telling where she lived, he took off. But a handsome, rich-looking man will get told pretty quickly where she lives. I was just hoping you knew who he was."

Joseph grabbed Ben shoulders. "A name, did you get a name?"

"Uhh, something Clement," Ben stuttered in surprise.

Joseph released him so fast it knocked the Sheriff off balance, but Joseph didn't even notice. Fury and fear gripped him as he jumped on Sampson and sped off toward Esther's home.

The road to Esther's house never seemed so long, and Sampson never seemed so slow. *Is it the same Clement? James Clement.*

Why would he give his real name?

Because he planned on leaving—it would not make a difference. Most likely he did it out of habit. Maybe he was a relative of James Clement. Come for forgiveness or to give compensation. Joseph could only hope, but his gut told him otherwise.

Joseph pulled Sampson in front of Esther's home.

"Esther?" he shouted. "Esther? Michael?" He jumped off his horse slamming himself through the front door. Nothing in the front room, all tidy except… his heart skipped a beat as he noticed a knocked over chair near the kitchen. Esther would not leave a chair knocked over.

Joseph ran into the kitchen, and his blood turned cold. Esther was laying limp, blood matted through her hair from being struck. Her hands were tied to the stove and her feet bound.

"Esther!' Joseph ran, sliding on his knees by her side. He pulled out his knife and cut her loose. "Esther, speak to me!" He checked her pulse, alive and breathing. "Esther!" He pulled her into his arms, shaking her slightly.

Esther groaned, rolling her head. "Michael," she muttered.

Joseph looked around. Michael. Where was Michael?

Esther fluttered her eyes open. "Michael?" she said again. Her eyes opened fully. "Michael!" she said louder, trying to sit up. She looked at Joseph who was steadying her. "Do you have Michael?" she asked, her voice breaking into a cry.

"No. Esther what happened?"

Esther's eyes went wide, and she leapt to her feet staggering into the counter as she did. "He took him. He took Michael. I need to go," she cried, running crookedly out of the kitchen.

Joseph raced after her, swinging her to face him. "Esther, what happened?"

Esther's face crumpled in pain and fear. "James Clement came," she sobbed. "Michael was playing on the porch, and suddenly James walks in with a gun; he told me to tie myself up or he would shoot Michael, and then he knocked me unconscious." She yanked away from him. "What have I done? He has my boy—my baby," she ran out the door.

Joseph had never had such a desire to kill, a desire to hurt and hunt another man. This man had come and taken Michael, his Michael, his boy, his deputy, his *son*. He would find this bastard and kill him. He would track him to hell and back if that's what it took to get the boy back. Placing his hand on his holster he walked out as Esther was bringing out Lancelot.

"Esther, stay here," Joseph snapped. "I'm going to find him."

"I'm coming, too," Esther snapped back, hauling herself onto the saddle.

"No, you are not!" Joseph ordered. "I can't be rescuing Michael while having to protect you. You are staying put."

Esther's tears ceased for a second, "And if James shoots you? Joseph, I need to come. Please, if it comes to saving me or Michael, save Michael."

Joseph looked at her sternly and then gave a short nod before turning toward his horse.

Esther nearly shouted at Joseph when he stood still. She expected him to fly onto his saddle, but for a brief moment he froze with his head bowed. She opened her mouth to say something until she noticed his eyes were closed and his mouth moved silently. He was praying. The lines in his face were etched with fear, worry, and heartache. Everything she felt was manifested in his tortured expression as he prayed.

When Joseph's eyes opened they were dark. His jaw was set. Esther knew what the transformation was. He was no longer the kind, humorous Joseph Silver. He was the Texas Ranger, a deadly shot, and an inescapable tracker.

Joseph lifted himself onto his horse in one fluid movement. He glanced at the ground, calculating. "They went east by the looks of it."

Esther began to speak, but Joseph held up his hand. "Esther, I know you are scared, but I need you to be silent while I do this, all right?" His voice was serious and powerful, and yet it did not jar Esther. In fact, he calmed her. She was suddenly grateful for his strength, his assurance, and the aggression that she hoped would save her son.

Esther followed Joseph quietly. Watching him as he studied the ground, getting off his horse to check the tracks when they left the main road. Every now and then he spoke out loud. "The man was smart getting off the road. He is probably going to ride out of state to be safe from Colorado's jurisdiction and then head back east on a different route. He won't be taking any main roads," he said, but again, not to Esther. It was as if he was counseling with himself.

After an hour, Esther and Joseph were deep in the forest. The sky was turning dark. This worried her. Michael would be cold. He had no coat. Just thinking of her little boy cold and afraid made her want to cry out. She looked at Joseph who every now and then would close his eyes and silently pray. This was usually followed by a curse and muttered threat to James Clement.

Esther held on to Joseph's strength. For some reason every time he swore to himself to wring James' neck, it made her feel better. Every time his lips twitched with satisfaction when he re-found the tracks, she felt better. The traits in a man that for so long had frightened her: aggression, a strong temper, a desire to take control, were now soothing. Joseph was an ointment to her fear.

Esther tightened her grip on Lancelot's reins. She wanted this man. She had wanted Joseph as a person, but now she wanted him as a man, a strong, masculine man. She wanted to be his companion. She wanted to be one with him in heart, body, and soul. Being with him would not be captivity, it would be freedom. Marriage to Joseph would empower her, not subdue her.

Joseph looked up to see Esther's pale face watching him with an intensity that he had never seen in her before. He looked away, his mind was focused on one thing and one thing only: Michael. He was on his feet now as he walked through thick brush. It was getting dark and cold. Esther muttered that she was worried about that, but to Joseph, the dark and cold were his allies. Dark would force the scoundrel to stop, and the cold would force him to build a fire. Joseph walked through the thicket following the stomped brush where a grown man and child had walked.

The gleam of moisture caught his eye. Joseph knelt down; it was too cold and late for dew. He looked closer—blood. Michael was bleeding. The bastard had made his boy bleed!

Joseph sprung up. "Dear God, help me find this animal," he whispered through clenched teeth.

A small sound caught Joseph's attention. He stopped breathing. He heard it again. What was it? A voice?

He looked back at Esther, motioning for her to get off her horse and silently follow him. Esther did as instructed, hiking up her skirts so they would not cause any noise through the brush. Joseph followed the trail. He could hear the noise. A cry? Was it crying? As he followed deeper, the smell of smoke and fire reached his nostrils. He held up his hand for Esther to stop. Up ahead, he could see the flicker of a fire and make out two figures amidst the dark trunks of the trees. Taking one inhale before holding his breath again Joseph walked forward, rolling his feet with the stealth of a cat stalking a bird.

When he and Esther were closer to the clearing, he stopped her. "You stay here," he whispered close to her ear. "You got a gun?"

Esther shook her head. She had removed it back at home and in her frantic run to find Michael, she had left it. Joseph nodded and handed her one of his. Then he walked forward. He planned on shooting James clear through the heart with no negotiations, no prison. A man who raped a woman and kidnapped a child did not need a trial, especially when that child was one Joseph loved as his own.

Reaching the clearing, he frowned. Michael sat tear streaked by the fire, his hands tied behind his back. James was nowhere.

He must have left in search of firewood. Joseph drew out his gun, waiting a breath before hurrying to the boy. His priority was getting Michael, not killing this man. The gun clicked as he cocked it back, and he froze... nothing. The man was gone, hopefully long enough for him to get Michael to safety.

Michael jumped as Joseph stepped into the clearing. Joseph quickly held up a finger to his lips. Michaels' face lit up into a trusting smile.

"I knew you would come for me," Michael whispered, his voice hoarse from crying. "The man said that I was his son, but I told him I already had a dad, and that it was you."

Joseph patted Michael on the shoulder as he quickly untied him. "That's right Michael. Your mom is back in the woods. We need to go now."

A twig snapped. Joseph jumped up, instinctively shoving Michael behind him, with his gun pointed at the intruder.

"Well, well, well," a broad athletic looking man with jet-black hair and smooth, tan skin stepped forward with a gun raised. "This must be the famous Joseph I've heard about." He laughed. "The great Texas Ranger here to save the boy of the woman he loves."

Joseph glared, itching to shoot. This man couldn't be a faster shot than him, but his finger was on the trigger; he needed to gauge a little longer.

"Oh yes, Ranger, word gets around in a close-knit town like Tall Pine. The beautiful reclusive Esther and the handsome Ranger." He stepped forward but stopped when Joseph aimed his gun at his head. "Too bad the story ends with you dead and the woman alone."

"How about the story ends with me walking away with the kid, and then maybe I will leave you alive. Or, at least, give you a less painful death," Joseph said dryly.

James shook his head. "Points for bravery, Ranger, but I take what belongs to me, and that boy is mine."

Kill now, Joseph thought. No, he still had to wait. If James shot him, it could go clean through him and hit Michael.

"I'm giving you one more chance," Joseph warned through gritted teeth. "Put the gun down and I walk out of here with you alive."

James glowered. "Maybe I did not make myself clear. I take what is mine. Just like I took Esther." He smiled wickedly. "Tell me, Ranger, have you had a taste of her yet? She's good, isn't she? Though, she doesn't seem to be quite the kitten that she was when I played with her."

The shot came so fast that Joseph's instinct reacted before his mind could. James fired his gun before his words were finished. Joseph flung Michael aside and to the ground, twisting as the bullet grazed his right shoulder.

Not waiting for the second bullet, Joseph flung himself at James and pushed the gun upward. The impact knocked James' grip loose. The gun flew, and both men struggled to reach it. Joseph grabbed James by the neck and slapped his head to the ground. The man was barely stunned; alert enough to punch Joseph in the face.

Stars blurred his vision, and blood poured from his nose. Somewhere from the corner of his eyes he saw Esther picking up Michael and running into the woods. Good, they were safe. James must have seen them, too, because he staggered to his feet running for the gun. Joseph grabbed the man's legs pulling him to the ground and pinning him as he knelt over him, punching him in the face one, two, three times.

Strong pain in Joseph's ribs sent him toppling off James, who had grabbed a sharp rock and driven it into Joseph's side. Joseph attacked again, wrapping his arms around James' neck, bringing both men back to the ground. James grabbed Joseph's arm with one hand and reached for a knife strapped to his belt with the other. He drove his right hand backward, intent on sinking the knife into Joseph's heart.

Joseph saw the glint of the blade and released James' neck, catching the hilt of the knife in time. James spun around trying to drive the knife downward. Joseph was stronger. He began to lift the knife further away from his face. James suddenly kneed hard between Joseph's legs, dropping him. He plunged the knife down and Joseph managed to steer it away from his face, but it still sunk into his right arm.

Joseph cried out, punching James with his left arm. James pressed down on the knife, forcing Joseph to his knees.

"You know, I've never liked guns. Knives always were my favorite toy," he laughed breathlessly, raising the knife to slit Joseph's throat.

Joseph braced himself to throw his body at James when a gunshot sounded and James staggered back. He looked down at his chest; blood seeped through his shirt. The two men looked up to see Esther holding a gun cocked and smoking.

"Esther, you—" James coughed.

Esther fired another shot into his chest. James fell backward with one final breath before lying still—lifeless and bloody.

Joseph staggered to his feet, clutching his wounded arm. "Michael? Where is Michael?"

Michael rushed out from the trees. "I'm here, Joseph!" he cried.

Esther stumbled back as Joseph brushed past her, dropping to his knees and griping Michael close to his body.

"Thank God! Thank God," he cried. His voice shook with sobs as he buried his face into Michael's neck. "Thank God, you are alright Michael."

Esther stood stunned. Her body was not shaking. Her mind was at peace and her soul calm. She had her son and she had... Joseph. She had her family. Watching this grown man cry over her son, having seen him track and pray, how could she doubt that Joseph did not belong to her and her to him? He was her equal in every way, and she was his.

Michael placed his head on Joseph's shoulder as the grown man continued to sob.

"Joseph," Michael said, "are you crying because you love me?"

Joseph laughed and pulled Michael away, cupping the little boy's face in his hands and kissing the freckled cheeks.

"Yes, Michael, I am. I love you so much." He kissed Michael's face again. "You are my joy Michael, and you always will be." He looked back at Esther. "The first shot would have killed him, you know."

Esther's lips fluttered with a quick smile. She arched an eyebrow. "Oh, I know. The first shot was for taking my son—the second was for seven years ago."

⚜

Joseph did not know how long he stayed by Michael's bed. Esther had put the boy to bed, not leaving his side until she heard Joseph's stomach rumble. Reluctantly, she covered her boy in soft kisses and allowed Joseph to take her place.

Joseph took the limp hand, running his own thumb over the soft skin. His own love for the child surprised him, the protective instinct he had was a strength he had never felt before. "Dear Lord, thank you," he wept, placing his head on the bed. "Thank you for keeping the boy safe. I give my life to you. Take it, it's yours."

"Joseph," Esther called softly, "I have supper for you."

Joseph gave one last kiss to the hand before standing up. The poor boy had not wanted to go back home unless Joseph came, and so all three had to ride into town to explain what had happened to Sheriff Ben before returning home. Michael had fallen asleep before he even touched his bed.

"I don't want him to have nightmares," Joseph whispered.

Esther smiled. "He won't, knowing you are here."

A bowl of hearty stew with chicken made Joseph realize how hungry he was. He sat down, devouring it in a few mouthfuls. He would miss Esther's food.

The thought made him drop his spoon and rub his temple. Two more days, and he would leave. Two more days.

"What is it, Joseph?" Esther asked, pinning him with her eyes.

Joseph stood up shaking his head. "I need to go, Esther. I am sorry." He headed for the door.

Esther stood up, touching his bandaged arm. "Joseph, wait—please don't go. Stay here tonight."

Joseph spun around to face Esther; he took hold of her shoulders, boring his gaze into hers. "Esther, do you not understand how painful it is to be around you? To be around that boy in there? In two days I will be gone, and I will never see either of you again. That boy whom I would give my life for, will be out of my life, and you—" he lowered his gaze before pulling her closer. "And you who I've wanted from the day I met you, the woman who I loved before I even knew what love was, you will never stop weighing on my heart. You will never again be by my side, though you'll never leave my thoughts." He released her. "I am sorry, but I can't take the torment."

"Joseph!" Esther clasped his face, pressing her body into his. Warmth filled her while need consumed her. "Then don't leave me," she whispered, moving her lips closer to his.

"Esther what are you—what do you mean?"

"I want to be with you, Joseph. I want to be your wife. I long and ache to be your wife, in every way."

Joseph's hands wrapped around her waist; cautiously he pulled her into a kiss. Esther felt a lovely dizziness come over her as his mouth teased her own, pressing gently, his hands digging into her skin as he tried to control himself. Suddenly, a sensation unlike anything she had ever felt consumed her. She was a woman who had been thirsty all her life and was finally drinking water. Lifting her hands from his face Esther tangled her fingers in his thick hair, pressing into him, needing to feel his warmth, deepening the kiss.

Joseph groaned in disbelief and pleasure as he wrapped his arms completely around her torso kissing her with such firmness and desire that her lips felt raw, and it was wonderful.

Esther's soul soared as she allowed herself to love this man. Her love seemed to grow with each passing second, or maybe it had always been there and was now being released. All her love seemed to be springing forth with newfound vigor.

When Joseph finally pulled away, he stroked her bottom lip, trailing his thumb along her jaw and down her neck, staring into her eyes with wonderment.

"Esther," he said softly. "Do you need me?"

Esther smiled. "No, but I want you."

Joseph grinned in his cocky Ranger way Esther loved so much. "Even better," he said before taking her breath away once again.

Epilogue

Texas, Silver Ranch

Joseph wrapped the rope around the two hooves peeking out. He looked up at Michael who was petting the moaning heifer's face and speaking soothingly to her.

"You're doing great Michael… keep her calm." Joseph grinned. What would he do without Michael? The kid had a gift with animals that was uncanny. No doubt he would be the finest veterinarian in Texas.

"How is it looking, Dad?" he asked

Joseph tugged. "A few more seconds," he groaned, tugging again. A wet, slippery, and perfectly formed calf slid out and onto the straw.

"Oh golly, he is a beauty!" Michael exclaimed. "A big one, too. No wonder the poor girl was having a hard time."

Joseph laughed and moved aside. The heifer stood up and immediately positioned herself so her new calf could eat.

Joseph and Michael stood, looking pleased.

"I'm proud of you, son," Joseph said, putting his arm around Michael's forever-growing shoulders, his smile melting Joseph's heart as usual. "I couldn't handle this ranch without you."

Michael shrugged teasingly. "I guess I'm all right."

The sound of footsteps and giggles broke the serenity. Joseph spun around to see his youngest son, Caleb, coming towards them. "Momma says dinner is almost ready, and she's made apple pie."

Joseph whistled, swinging the sturdy boy into the air. "Your pretty momma sure knows how to take care of her men."

"And girl," Caleb corrected when he was set on his feet again. "Momma is nursing baby Eliza right now." He looked back at the heifer, "Like the cow. Momma is like the cow."

Michael and Joseph exchanged glances before bursting into laughter.

"Caleb," Michael looked down at his little brother, "I don't think I would be calling momma a cow."

"Sound wisdom," Joseph agreed.

※

Esther gently laid her little girl in the crib Joseph had first built for Caleb; it was now adorned with pink and lavender blankets. Such a beautiful baby girl who had managed to get Esther's features with her father's thick dark hair and hazel eyes.

"How are my two favorite girls doing?" a husky voice asked from the doorway.

Esther turned around to see Joseph freshly washed and shaven after delivering the calf. He strode in and leaned over Eliza, kissing her little chin and cheeks.

"I just can't seem to get enough of her," he sighed, stroking her head as she cooed in happiness.

"You have a good effect on females," Esther teased, looking around the room. It was beautiful. She remembered fondly when she'd first seen it, only halfway built with miles and miles of green stretching out on all sides. The first month while the house was being finished, they had lived with Joseph's parents who had quickly become like the parents Esther had always wished for. Soon enough, their own home was completed with large windows looking over the lush ranch and gardens.

"What are you thinking?" Joseph asked, giving Eliza one more kiss.

Esther shrugged. "About Will and Abby arriving with their young ones. There can't be happiness anywhere beneath the heavens greater than here."

Joseph grinned mischievously. He moved closer, placing his hands on her waist and pulling her close.

"You know what I was thinking? I was thinking about how unfair it is to the world of women that you look this good after three children, better even than when I met you—and I thought that was impossible."

Esther laughed and wrapped her hands around his neck. "It's called happiness, handsome. It does wonders for one's complexion."

Joseph leaned in nibbling her ear and then her neck. "Is that right?"

Esther closed her eyes as his kisses danced across her skin. "Joseph, dinner will be late," she whispered without conviction.

"Dinner can wait," he whispered.

Esther smiled. Dinner often waited.

Acknowledgments

Special thanks to my family for all your love and support. Mom, I can never thank you enough for all the 11:00 pm calls to get your advice on a chapter, a character, mothering, being a wife, emotional and spiritual council, and so much more. My hope is that one day I can one be half the woman you are.

Dad, what more can I say than that you are the best father a girl could ask for. I thank my Father in heaven every day for having a man like you in my life. Thank you for always believing in me.

Thank you to my sisters for letting me talk your ears off with my ideas. Also, thank you to my brothers for helping me laugh at myself.

To my agent Rebecca Anderson. You rock, girl! I can literally say that I would not have been able to do this without you. Thank you for demonstrating your faith in me and guiding me in this journey. Your wisdom and knowledge never cease to amaze me.

Special thanks to all those at Light Messages Publishing who made this book possible. To my editor, Elizabeth, your gifts are beyond compare. Thank you for all the time and effort you put into this. You are a true artist, one from whom I have learned much. Thank you for your patience, your kindness, and your belief in this book.

A huge hug to Kit who shared her midwife and doula experiences with me so that I could share them with others. What you do is miraculous, and I admire you so much. Thank you for not only what you have done for me, but for all the babies you have helped bring into this world and for the mothers you have supported and loved in their time of need.

An eternal amount of kisses to my children. I don't think that I every fully understood God's love towards his children until I held each of you in my arms. My life is full of light and joy because of you and I will treasure you forever. You are the inspiration for all that I do, and the force that keeps me going. I love you!

About the Author

L indsey Barlow has a Bachelor of Arts in Humanities and Religious Studies from California Sacramento State University. She has traveled throughout Eastern Europe as a missionary teaching English and serving those in need. She has worked in the Saint Petersburg Hermitage Museum and has visited the Mayan ruins in Mexico. When Lindsey is not writing, she enjoys discovering new bookstores, going on hikes with her children, and pretending she knows how to sew. Lindsey resides in northern California with her husband and children in a house with too many books.

If you liked this book...

Check out these other inspirational fiction titles from Light Messages Publishing:

Tea and Crumples *by Summer Kinard*
Welcome to Tea and Crumples where the click of chess pieces, susurrus of fine papers, and grace of friendship accompany Sienna when every bit of her has been poured out. They keep vigil when all that's left is faith, tea, and love.

A Sinner in Paradise
Deborah Hining
The prequel to *A Saint in Graceland* and winner of the *IndieFab Book of the Year Bronze Medal* in Romance and the *Benjamin Franklin Award Silver Medal*. Readers will quickly fall for Geneva in this exquisitely written, uproarious affair with love in all its forms, set in the stunning landscape of the West Virginia mountains.

A Saint in Graceland
Deborah Hining
Grieving her mother's death and yearning to see more of the world beyond her mountain home, Sally Beth sets out on a journey that leads her across the American Southwest and ultimately to a remote mission station in Tanzania, where she finds a new kind of freedom in the African plains and the people who dwell there. But when war comes to the mission gates, its horrors shatter her world. She must find a way to rebuild her life and choose whether or not to serve the people she's grown to love—a choice that will shake the simple faith of her childhood and ignite her passion for a wounded man.